THE SALEM SYNDROME

Robert H. Bartlett

D1602620

First Page Publications
12103 Merriman • Livonia • MI • 48150
1-800-343-3034 • Fax 734-525-4420
www.firstpagepublications.com

To those who share the responsibility,
the joy, and the anguish that comes
with caring for sick children.

Library of Congress Control Number: 2004117396

First Page Publications
12103 Merriman • Livonia • MI • 48150
1-800-343-3034 • Fax 734-525-4420
www.firstpagepublications.com

PROLOGUE

The double doors from the ambulance entrance banged open, admitting a pair of nervous ambulance attendants steering their stretcher which held a young man in the process of dying. There was a little snow in the frigid wave of outside air that rolled in with them, circling the room, blowing aside the papers of a half-finished workup, and settling near the floor of the nursing station. The charge nurse was talking on the telephone, but turned to the ambulance entrance when she felt the cold air around her ankles. Seeing the look on the face of the usually blasé ambulance attendant, she covered the telephone mouthpiece with one hand and asked, "What is it?"

"Trauma. Gunshot wound."

"Trauma bay two," she said, pointing to a space near the door where dangling black and red wires attached to unblinking electronic monitors and plastic tendrils leading to bottles clear fluid hung in sinister anticipation, as a spider web awaits a fly. A surgical intern and two staff nurses had felt the cold air also, and now lurched into frantic activity, cutting off clothes and attaching wires before the stretcher had stopped rolling.

The charge nurse returned to her telephone conversation with the chief surgical resident. "Tom, you'd better come down here now. The ankle and the belly pain are back from X-ray, there's a kid with a head injury, and they just rolled in a gunshot wound." She paused, twisting to observe the activity in trauma two as she listened. "Sure the intern's here. He's putting a cutdown in the gunshot wound, but he's eight charts behind and you need to see the ankle and the belly pain anyway. Thanks. Bye."

Up on the fifth floor, the chief surgical resident was in the recovery room writing post-op orders on the bowel obstruction he had just finished. He hung up the phone, signed his name to the order sheet, and handed the chart to the nurse. He had reserved a late supper, and had spent the last twenty minutes of the operation imagining that his day-long hunger would soon be satisfied. He would have stopped by the cafeteria long enough to bolt down the creamed chicken on rice that had his name on it, cooling slowly under a stainless steel lid, but the intern was new and ten minutes of his time might make a difference. Not for the belly pain or the ankle or the other bumps and bruises, but it might make a big difference to the patient with the gunshot wound. So, since descending five flights was more expedient than waiting for the elevator, he took the stairs, passing the door to the first floor, which would have led him to the cafeteria, and arrived at B1 just outside the emergency room.

He passed through the walk-in clinic–unusually busy for a Thursday night–without looking directly at any one of the dozen patients sitting on the wooden benches, lest one might stop him to plead a special case. (Doctor, would you help me please? I've been bleeding for hours and I haven't been seen yet.)

After five years at Detroit Presbyterian Hospital, Tom had a special affection for the emergency room. Initially the ER was intimidating, and his heart would jump to his throat every time he was paged for 666. Now it was his turf. Here he had, by necessity, learned to sew up lacerations, examine a belly while half awake, and differentiate between dots of red dye stain and the elusive gonococcus under the microscope. There were ten cubicles divided by curtains around the sides of the big room. Each one held a dozen recent memories of being squirted with blood, vomit, or pus, the feeling of broken noses, broken ribs, broken femurs. Memories of making diagnoses that made him famous for a week, like ectopic pregnancy, pneumothorax, and SBE. And missing diagnoses that haunted him for months, like ruptured appendicitis and hangman's fracture. The nurses and the clerks and the techs, once his mentors, were now his assistants and they looked to him with confidence that he would take charge and solve their problems. This year, when he walked into the emergency room, he felt like a conductor mounting the podium before a full symphony orchestra. No longer was he just another second violin.

There was an entry wound on the left chest just above the nipple, and an exit wound in the back, still bleeding slowly, with bits of scapula sticking through the jagged hole. The intern had placed a cutdown–a large plastic tube–directly into the vein at the right elbow and the second liter of Ringers was running wide open. Tom was pleased that his lesson to this intern had been remembered. No neck lines, no wimpy IVs. Big cutdowns for trauma patients.

The young man was as pale and cold as a cadaver, but alert, scared, and saying that he couldn't breathe. In a few seconds Tom determined that his pulse was detectable but thready, his belly was soft, and the sounds of lung inflation could be heard on the right side but not the left. The intern was earnestly dabbing brown disinfectant on the man's flaccid penis with gloved hands. He was planning to insert a catheter, but Tom recognized this as the procrastination of insecurity.

"What the hell are you doing?"

"I'm putting in a Foley to measure his urine output. He's in shock."

"Really? Maybe we should order a cardiac output and send off some blood gases too." The intern looked up, recognizing the sarcasm, and realized that he was screwing up. Priorities out of line. "Come on Henry. What's next? You get one chance."

"Intubate him?"

"Lost your chance, Henry. He needs a chest tube. Now watch because you're going to do this the next time." The nurse had a chest tube tray ready, and held the patient's arm above his head while Tom pulled on a pair of gloves and poured some iodine on the chest wall. Feeling ribs with his left hand, he injected the liquid contents of a syringe with his right. "If the patient is conscious, it's worth half a minute to get some anesthesia. This should be a painless procedure." With a scalpel, he made an incision about an inch long through the blanched skin which seemed to be, indeed, painless. Through the incision he pushed a huge hemostat, feeling the ribs as he went.

"I'm in the mid-axillary line and I'm aiming for the fifth interspace. It's right about . . . here." He pushed on the hemostat with both hands and it popped between the ribs with a sound that could be heard across the room, followed by a gush of black blood which doused his scrub pants even though he tried to jump out of the way. The patient screamed and tried to pull away from the nurse. "Guess I didn't get much local into the pleura. Is the blood on the way?" This rhetorical question, referring to blood from the blood bank, was so obvious that it did not require an answer. Now Tom pushed the index finger of his left hand beside the hemostat, then withdrew the instrument, leaving his finger to mark the space and to feel the inner lining of the chest. He grabbed the tip of a large plastic tube with the hemostat and forced it through the hole, trading the tube for his finger. The popping sound was heard again, the patient screamed, and more blood, now made foamy with a rush of air under pressure, poured from the end of the tube. Soon the tube was connected to a collection bottle and attached to the skin with a heavy suture. The whole procedure took about two minutes.

The intern was impressed, but dismayed at his own reticence. "I thought we needed a chest X-ray first. I ordered a chest X-ray."

"Very good, Henry. By the time they get here we can use it to check the position of this tube." A quart and a half of blood collected in the drainage bottle, accompanied by gushes of air bubbling through the water, which served as a valve. The young man was pale and sweaty but breathing much more slowly and easily. By the time the second unit of blood was hanging, the bleeding had stopped and the bubbling occurred only when the patient coughed or shouted in pain. For Tom, the management of penetrating injury had become a complex sort of game. Once the moves were mastered, it was just that, playing the game. He played it well, and although there were still moves to make for this young patient, the game was essentially over and he—and the patient—had won again. He left the intern to insert the Foley and check the chest X-ray. He thought about his supper still slightly warm in the cafeteria, but the charge nurse handed him three charts.

"Thanks, Tom. We needed you." A grin and a pat on the shoulder.

"You guys were great. I didn't have to ask for anything." A return grin. The emergency room equivalent of shared high fives.

"These are waiting for you. The ankle's in six with his films. They're negative. There's a kid with a head injury they want you to see in walk-in. The belly pain is in eight."

"Is she sick?" He focused on the one patient that might keep him from his dinner, and his question to the charge nurse really meant, 'Does she need an operation tonight?'

"GYN thinks she has PID, but she's vomited twice since she has been here. I'm betting on an appy."

"Damn. My supper's getting cold."

"You'll make it," she said, looking up at the clock and pushing the charts into his hands. "If you don't, come back down after midnight. We're having a potluck tonight."

The ankle was sprained. Bad enough to justify a cast but already very swollen. Tom settled for an Ace bandage and crutches.

The young woman with acute abdominal pain had been in the emergency room for four hours and had been examined by a student, an intern, and a GYN resident. The thought of yet another doctor was frightening if not disgusting, and she let him know it. While listening to her tirade ("Don't you mash me no more, hear?"), he pushed gently on her abdomen with two fingers. Soft. Soft. Soft. Soft. Soft. Bingo.

"Lordy that hurts. Don't mash me no more."

"Now Miss Green, I'm sorry but I just have to examine you down below again."

"Oh Lordy, not again. Why don't you axst that other doctor? He just did it."

"Now, this will just take a minute." Standing at her side, he guided her knees up, and then apart, then felt for landmarks and orifices beginning at her coccyx. "Bear down a little." With one gloved finger in her vagina and another in her rectum, he nudged her cervix from side to side. She cried and grimaced but didn't reach for the chandelier. Pushing higher, she was boggy and tender on the left but had a hard mass the size of an orange on the right. When he pushed it, she grabbed his leg and screamed. That was it. Doesn't matter what the GYN resident thinks. Ticket to the OR tonight.

He knew there were two rooms running and he wouldn't be able to operate for an hour or two. Just a quick check with the pediatric resident in walk-in and time for supper! He walked through the triage room to the pediatric ER.

The senior resident in pediatrics was a young woman who had once been on his service as a junior medical student. Then she was meek and lethargic, now she was pompous and abrasive.

"I want to admit this kid for observation but my staff–who is at home and hasn't seen him–insists that surgery see him first. There's no neurosurgeon in the house, so we thought you might check him out. I mean, it's just to satisfy my staff."

Tom wanted to tell her to stuff it, but swallowed this impulse and tried to look calm. "What's the story?"

"This little boy is one and a half years old. He was playing in the

5

kitchen when his mother went down to the basement. She left the door open and the kid fell all the way down the stairs. That was yesterday. Tonight the grandmother is babysitting and she thinks he's acting sleepy."

"Not surprising. It's the middle of the night."

"Sure, I know. But the kid has ecchymoses and hematomas all over. He took quite a spill."

"Skull films?"

"Negative. Long bones are negative too."

"Neurologic signs?"

"Nothing, really."

"Then why do you want to admit him?"

"I don't know. The story doesn't sound quite right. The grandmother's worried. And it's just easier than trying to organize a big follow-up in the outpatient clinic."

Tom was not impressed. He went into the room and picked up the child who whimpered and whined as he touched the bruises. He was alert and his pupils reacted well. He couldn't hold him still enough to look into his fundi, although he tried. "Looks like a bad fall," he commented to the grandmother, who sat grimly opposite the exam table. "Why did you bring him in tonight?"

"I just seen him tonight, that's why. All these bruises. This child always has bruises. I don't think he fell down the stairs. I think Roger gave him those bruises."

Assigning blame to settle domestic arguments was commonplace. The girl with appendicitis that he had just examined had blamed her boyfriend for bringing home a bad disease. The kid who had nearly died from pneumothorax had been shot by "a friend." "Who's Roger?"

"Roger is my daughter's boyfriend. He's no good, that Roger. He's mean. He's mean to my daughter."

"Is he the baby's father?" he asked, continuing his examination and finding no signs of neurologic injury.

Grandmother sat silently, picking at the frayed edges of her quilted overcoat.

"I said, is he the baby's father?"

"I heard you. I . . . I don't know. You'd have to ask my daughter that. He's there all the time, though. They sort of live together."

6

"Where's your daughter now?"

"Out. I don't know. She just went out. Called me down to babysit and out they went. Both of them. That's when I saw all these bruises. They told me the child fell down the stairs but I ain't never seen a black eye like that. Never."

"I'll talk to the pediatrician," he said, and left the room. "The baby looks okay to me," he said when he found the pediatric resident. "He has a few bruises but I didn't find anything else."

The charge nurse came in from the emergency room looking anxious. "Could you come back to the ER a minute, Tom? The gunshot wound just put out another eight hundred ccs and his pressure is down to fifty. And the girl you admitted to the OR wants to sign out AMA."

"Well, give him some more blood. Can't Henry handle it?"

"Come on, Tom, help me out. I'll feed you later."

The pediatric resident handed him the chart and her own pen, as he had none in his scrub suit. "I can see you're busy. If you'll just write 'okay to admit' on the chart, I'll take care of the rest of it."

"Don't tell me what to write on the chart. This kid looks fine to me. If you want a neurosurgeon to see him, call a neurosurgeon." He wrote 'okay for discharge' on the chart and signed his name. She turned red, grabbed the pen and the chart, and stomped away. Tom returned to trauma bay two in the ER.

* * * *

By the next morning, the hot appendix was out and the young man with the chest tube was asking for breakfast. By noon, Tom had finished a thyroid and gotten two hours of sleep.

At 6 PM, the little boy who had been sent home the night before was brought back. This time by paramedics. This time dead on arrival with bilateral skull fractures. Both the mother and the boyfriend were taken into custody and later convicted of manslaughter.

When the interview with the grandmother was published in the *Free Press*, the hospital, in fact the city, was in an uproar. Editorials called for decent pediatric emergency care. The hospital administrator offered a public apology and promised to suspend the responsible physician until an investigation could be completed. The chairman of pediatrics was furious, and actually pounded on the desk of the chairman of surgery, demanding that the resident who cleared this patient for discharge should be fired. Any medical student, any school-teacher could plainly recognize an abused child who should have been protected from a hostile environment. Criminal charges against Tom were discussed in the district attorney's office.

No one mentioned the sprained ankle that had healed nicely, the girl with appendicitis who was discharged after a week, or the young man with the gunshot wound who went back to work at the liquor store.

Tom wasn't fired. There was an official reprimand, but no measure of formal punishment could equal his personal remorse. He went into practice somewhere in the South carrying his own baggage of victo-ries, defeats, and guilt.

The resident's name was Thomas Salem and the year was 1967. In teaching hospitals, technical and judgmental errors are often named after the residents who committed them. Months, years, even a decade later, the chairman of pediatrics and everyone else in Presbyterian Hospital labeled the failure to recognize child abuse as the Salem Syndrome.

CHAPTER 1

Hospital cafeterias all smell the same. Astringent and antiseptic clinical vapors pervade the greasy aroma of grilling cheese-burgers and the musty odor of steaming vegetables. The Detroit Presbyterian Hospital cafeteria had been refurbished to appear less institutional in the summer of 1976, but now, only two months later, it smelled like any hospital cafeteria. The smell was neither good nor bad, but was made unpleasant by association with concerns and uncertainty. Peter Blake was not consciously aware of the smell as he settled his plastic tray on the just-wiped tabletop, but he felt vaguely unpleasant. Pulling the chrome and fiberboard chair up to the table, he unbuttoned his coat, smoothed the folded edge of his French cuff, and adjusted his gold watchband, the unconscious mannerisms of more elegant surroundings. He spread the flimsy paper napkin over his lap and straightened the flatware with outstretched fingers, lining up the base of the spoon and knife with his right thumb.

Although it never crossed his mind, he appeared quite out of place in his very dark blue three piece-suit and silver tie. But then, in an hour, he would deliver the closing argument in the case of *Davis v. First National Bank*. He was defending the bank in a dispute over property, and would have reviewed his notes in the back booth at Gallagher's across from the courthouse if Peter, his youngest son, were not in the hospital. "Petey" was thirty months old, all dimples and giggles and enthusiasm. A broken arm caused his current incarceration in the pediatric division of Presbyterian Hospital.

"It's only a crack—a green stick fracture—but it can cause neurovascular complications in that particular area, so we'd better keep him a few days," Ed Browne had explained. Browne was not only the family pediatrician, but also a neighbor in Hunting Valley and chief of pediatrics at Presbyterian. His advice was always followed, so Petey remained in the hospital, although he had looked as healthy and active as ever, cruising around his crib with a cast on his left arm. "Couldn't afford a complication in a lawyer's kid," Browne had said, smiling. So today Blake had brought Petey one of those soft sponge rubber baseballs and had talked his way past the head nurse, even though visiting hours didn't start until two.

His thoughts alternated between images of Petey reaching through the crib bars and *Davis v. First National Bank,* and he was halfway through the cole slaw and creamed chicken before he paused to sip his coffee and look around. A nurse four tables away was staring at him. She looked away, embarrassed that he had noticed. She was an extremely pretty nurse, slender with dark hair and large dark eyes. He thought it interesting, how an ordinary girl can become so attractive in a white uniform and a starched cap. She glanced back, then turned to resume conversation with her companions. He made a mental note to complete his impression when she stood up.

Laughter erupted from a group of nurse's aides. Three black and two white girls were eating lunch from paper bags, all wearing ill-fitting raucous yellow dresses. The laughter exposed a missing front tooth in one of the girls. The noisy glee contrasted sharply with the forced composure of the family at the next table. There, a rough-edged man with a baseball cap bearing the logo CAT pushed back on his head sat silently beside a somber woman whose hanging clothes, sunken cheeks, and sparse wispy hair bespoke severe chronic illness—cancer perhaps. They seemed annoyed at the laughter; they were consumed with thoughts of death and life.

In the cafeteria line, two young men were engaged in a good-natured argument over a collegiate football game. The short white coats identified them as medical students. "Volare" was coming through the invisible Muzak speakers in the ceiling. Blake had always hated "Volare" for some reason that he had never understood. It seemed particularly offensive today.

Dr. Arnold Feinberg, Cardiology—so defined by the plastic name plate pinned to his long white coat—had left the cashier's stand and was proceeding to the doctors' dining room when he noticed Blake. He smiled in recognition across the room and mouthed the word "Hi," raising his bushy eyebrows—a gesture that would have been accompanied by a little wave of the hand had he not been carrying the tray. He walked on without stopping. If he stopped he would have to remember Blake's name, and he was drawing a blank.

Blake's attention returned to the cole slaw and canned peas. He smiled slightly. It was obvious that Feinberg had been unable to quite recall his name. Five years ago Blake might have been offended, ten years ago he would have been insecure. Now he was accustomed to being semi-recognized as a semi-prominent community figure. Feinberg–Cardiology–couldn't place him out of context. If he had been at the country club, or the Rotary, or at his usual table at L'Auberge he would have been quickly recognized. Blake imagined that by now the good doctor was sitting down with his colleagues saying, "I think I just saw Peter Blake in the cafeteria. It was Peter Blake."

Frederick Peter Blake II had worked hard for his success. He didn't flaunt it, but he had come to expect recognition, even deference. When he drove the old Ford wagon to Valley Building and Supply on weekends he was greeted with "Good morning, Mr. Blake" by the yard hands who loaded him up with Scott's Turf Builder or rock salt for the water softener. He sat on the splintery, peeling stands at the Little League games and put up his own storm windows and raked his own leaves, although he allowed himself the luxury of a monthly car wash for the BMW.

He had been a senior partner in Briggs, Briggs, and Harrington for seven years. He had a reputation of thoroughness, precision, and calm-under-fire with the local and state legal community. With the partnership had come a little more time and a lot more money–a combination that led to the summer house on Nantucket, vacations in the Bahamas, and the annual family trip to Vail. The frequently renewed suntan emphasized the growing lines around his eyes and cheeks, improving his appearance as he passed fifty.

Valerie had commented on that and the absence of gray hair, as she camouflaged her own. Since they were married in his law school days, she had been particularly proud of her hair–blonde and soft and always attractive, whether carefully prepared for an evening out or tousled over a pillow in the early morning. She had weathered his affair with a legal secretary and feigned ignorance of another. They considered their family more secure than that of their friends.

Blake deliberately readjusted the plates on his tray to allow better access to the pasty cherry pie. He looked up to see if the dark-eyed nurse was preparing to leave. She was looking his way, but past him at the black fellow at the next table. Blake followed her gaze.

* * * *

Kevin Washington was scared. His hands and feet felt cold. His pulse was rapid. He took a deep breath every minute or so. He sat on the edge of the chair, forearms on the table, occasionally moving the coffee cup from the saucer to his lips with a combination of wrist and neck motion–the table habits of a person who often eats alone. As he bent over to the cup, his eyelids raised and he peered ahead as if trying to keep his eyes on a television. The cup clattered in the saucer when his shaky hand touched it, and the warm coffee did not improve the cold knot deep in his chest.

He had come directly from work at Metro Buick. His khaki army shirt was clean because of the coveralls, but the grease under his fingernails and on his steel-toed shoes gave him the general aroma of an auto shop. This was his second trip to the hospital, and he was afraid of what it would bring. He and his wife had spent most of last night here, following the paramedic van carrying their daughters to the emergency room. Then came the terrified waiting as impersonal professionals hurried in and out, rarely bringing bulletins, occasionally asking questions, always responding, "We don't know yet," to the question, "Will they be all right?"

He had tried to see the girls, but the ward clerk in the pediatric ICU pointed to the sign on the door and lectured him. "Two o'clock, two o'clock. Honestly!" she had muttered, returning to the clutter of loose paper before her. She seemed unusually bitter, but, as a black man in Detroit, he was used to it. He did get a look through the wired glass window to see the nursing station and the cribs beyond, surrounded by young women in gray-green dresses. Near the bottom of the blackboard above the ward clerk's desk was written: "#8 Washington, Rebecca, Drs. Browne and Redford. #9 Washington, Susan, Drs. Browne and Redford."

A notice was taped to the glass above the patient ID card rack. Written in red felt tip pen and surrounded by asterisks, it proclaimed, "Note: Two Washingtons." "That's strange, of course there are two," he had thought, as he found his way to the cafeteria to wait. To him those little girls were the only patients in the hospital. He didn't understand the need for the reminder to identify lab slips, X-ray reports, and drug doses. He didn't feel the constant sense of uneasiness that occurs in nurses and ward clerks when two patients with the same name are in the ICU.

The waiting, the bitterness, the serious condition implied by the need for the ICU contributed to his fear. He had never talked to Dr. Browne or Dr. Redford, but the idea of calling one of them never occurred to him. He had grown up on clinic care. His mother didn't have a doctor. When he was sick, she had taken him to the clinic and surrendered him up to whomever claimed authority. She had never asked questions or waited for the young doctor (or more often the clinic nurse) to explain the treatment. No questions.

He found the last cigarette in his crumpled pack of Camels, put it in his mouth, and fumbled through his pockets for a matchbook.

* * * *

Blake studied the black man with a morbid fascination, as one might watch an unfamiliar driver turning the wrong way into a one-way street. He pieced together the evidence. Grease, the stiff khaki shirt, the scar through the upper lip, the shiny wedding band, the medical center parking ticket sticking up from the shirt pocket. He was young, twenty-four or twenty-five. He was hard and muscular, and probably over six feet tall–his hunched position made it difficult to tell. He was obviously nervous, even apprehensive. Blake concluded that his wife was having a baby–probably their first–and going through a long labor. Blake watched Washington's difficulty finding the last cigarette and how he put the empty pack back into his pocket automatically. "Probably been up all night," Blake thought, elaborating upon his hypothesis.

The gelatin cherry filling was palatable, but the crust was like cardboard. He pushed it to the back of the plate, arranged his fork carefully, and placed the paper napkin on the tray. When he looked again, the expectant father was still searching for a match, feeling pockets for the fourth time, the bent Camel dangling from his lips. Partly out of curiosity, partly out of his compulsive condescension for the common man, Blake slipped the silver plated Calibri lighter from the pocket of his coat and leaned across the aisle. "Need a light?" Blake smiled to indicate potential good will.

"Huh?" Washington looked startled, as if in his preoccupation he'd even forgotten the cigarette. "Oh, yeah, thanks."

The Calibri was a butane pipe lighter. When Blake thumbed the wheel, a two-inch flame shot out sideways with a sound like a small blowtorch. Washington jumped back. He was shaking so badly that it took several seconds to light the cigarette. Blake held the lighter calmly. Washington avoided eye contact; he seemed embarrassed at his reaction, but unable to stop shaking.

"Your first baby?" Blake asked, putting the lighter back in his pocket.

"Huh?" Washington looked bewildered.

"Is your wife having a baby?" Blake questioned, sensing the guess was incorrect.

"No, no." Washington paused. "She's home," he added unnecessarily.

An uneasy silence followed, and Washington glanced quickly at the questioner. Blake was watching him. Washington smiled briefly, barely a twitch of his facial muscles. "You seemed a little nervous and I thought your wife might be in maternity," explained Blake.

"Oh." Washington nodded acknowledgment.

"My son's in pediatrics. He has a broken arm." Blake surprised himself. He wasn't inherently gregarious, but having started the conversation, he felt obliged to make another comment.

"That's too bad." The shaking had stopped. "My little girls—" Tears welled in his eyes. He coughed and took a deep breath. "My girls are real sick. Makes me—you know—nervous."

"I'm so sorry," Blake said sincerely. His incorrect deduction had caused him to intrude into Washington's private thoughts. He intended to turn away, but Washington continued. "They don't tell ya nothin'. You can't get in 'til two. Y'know they only let ya in there certain hours."

"Right," affirmed Blake, hoping to end the conversation.

Washington seemed more relaxed, as if talking drained the tension. "I sure hope they—"

"Dr. McDowell, stat ICU, Dr. McDowell, stat ICU." The voice of the paging operator interrupted the Muzak. The announcement seemed to come across at twice the volume. "Dr. Mc-Dow-ell-stat ICU." She pronounced each syllable equally with that flat nasal tone heard only in hospital hallways. Muzak came back on immediately, a muted trombone playing "Laura" over a string background. Conversation and table noise in the cafeteria resumed immediately also, having frozen during those four seconds as if stop-framed on a movie projector.

Washington's eyes widened. He sat upright and looked to both sides, watching for a response. He started to rise, then sat back uneasily.

"My girls are in the ICU," he explained urgently, and looked around again. The obvious lack of concern around the big room seemed to reassure him slightly.

"Oh man, oh man," he sighed, addressing himself.

"Code blue ICU, code blue ICU." the operator's voice had the same dispassionate quality, but activity followed the first "blue." By the time the fourth "code blue ICU" was over, two respiratory therapists were through the door, followed by an intern. A resident in a long white coat stood, stooped, and slurped the last of his coffee before starting quickly to the back door. Two nurses, older, less casual, one wearing a blue sweater over a stiff knee-length dress stood abruptly and followed the resident, slowly but deliberately. Blake recognized one as the day supervisor. Three young women wearing green scrub dresses under white coats with "ICU" embroidered above the pocket bussed their unfinished trays and hurried across the room. "Dr. McDowell, stat, code blue ICU. Please do not use elevators four through six, elevators four through six for emergencies only."

Washington was standing. Blake sat him down gently with a hand on his shoulder. "Don't worry, Dr. McDowell is a neurosurgeon. It's not your children." Washington didn't look relieved. "ICU means adult intensive care. If they meant pediatrics they'd say ped ICU. Don't worry."

Blake had a mental image of the ICU. During his father's terminal illness two years ago he had witnessed many "code blues." One of the monotonous beep-beeps suddenly becomes a single tone; a nurse with a stethoscope hanging from her ears interrupts the usual hush with a terse, "A little help please. Hit the code button, please." The ominous cart is wheeled over, the curtains are hastily drawn, and the arrest board is taken down from its hanging place. The board is just that—a big varnished board, an anachronism in the stainless and plastic setting. Fifteen seconds later, the door opens and the crowd begins to collect. "A Chinese fire drill," one resident described it.

Blake had learned to judge both the efficiency and the severity of the emergency by the amount of time he and the other visitors had to spend in the little waiting room. Short meant false alarm, or hopelessly gone. Long usually meant technically successful, although when the visitors were permitted to return, a breathing machine had been added to the bedside paraphernalia, and the patient was now supine, mostly uncovered, immobile.

"Oh man," said Washington, as if in continuing pain.

"Don't worry. It's not your children," Blake repeated.

"Yeah, thanks." Washington slumped again. "How do you know that stuff? You a doctor?"

"No, I've just spent some time here. And Dr. McDowell is a friend of mine." Washington sighed and looked relieved. "Who's your doctor?" Blake asked, hoping to reinforce his reassurance.

"They didn't tell me yet."

Blake had no concept of clinic care and it never occurred to him that Washington's medical experience was profoundly different than his own. He thought he had misunderstood. "Surely you have a doctor, someone in charge of the case."

"It said Dr. Browne on the board. Dr. Browne and somebody else," said Washington.

"Dr. Browne? Edward Browne, the chief of pediatrics? He's my Petey's doctor too. He's very good. I'm sure your girls will be just fine."

Washington appreciated this unsolicited companionship. His initial impression of a nosey, patronizing, rich white man had given way to gratitude. Their common problem gave Washington a feeling of camaraderie for his newfound friend. With unjustified familiarity he moved with his coffee cup to the other table, across from Blake.

"My girls, y'know, got burned. They got burned with hot water in the bathtub. That's not too bad, is it? Bath water, y'know?" Blake shrugged without speaking, taken aback more by the young man's sudden intensity than the question.

"The nurse in emergency said they were critical. She said they were burned real bad. I didn't think . . . Oh man, they hurt so bad."

16

"I'm sure they'll be fine," Blake said, not wanting to hear more.

Washington continued, feeling better as he recounted the story. "Sally—my wife Sally—was off at work. She's a waitress, y'know. I always give the kids a bath before bed. I let 'em play, y'know, the girls. Well, I just put them in the tub and started the water when the phone rings, y'know, four or five times. So I go answer it. It's my brother, my kid brother. He's in San Francisco, says he needs money and I'm tellin' him I don't have no money when Becky starts screaming, awful screaming." He trembled and covered one ear, remembering. Blake was silent.

"So I run in and the water is going full hot—steaming y'know—and little Susie's crawled under the faucet. All that hot water running right on those kids, hittin' Becky and runnin' on Susie's back. Becky's standing up and screaming, just standing right there in front of the faucet and screaming—it's like they're frozen there—oh man." He shuddered again and tears filled his eyes.

Blake waited, horrified but strangely fascinated. Washington was shaking again. "What did you do? Turn the water off?" asked Blake.

"No, I just grabbed 'em out. I got Becky out easy. I picked up Susie out of the water—it didn't burn me none." He looked at the backs of his hands and rubbed them, once again finding no damage. "But Susie, when I picked her up, her skin . . . " He shook violently and looked at Blake—terrorized, pleading, Blake thought. "Her skin just came off in my hands. I dropped her on the edge of the tub and she fell back in. Her skin was in my hands—so thin it was like wet paper. I grabbed her out again and put her in a towel. She was pale, oh man, I thought she was dead. Her face was cut where I dropped her. Little Susie . . ." He covered his face. "Oh man." He was sobbing. Forgetting about Blake, he sobbed uncontrollably. It was the first time since the accident. Blake shuddered too, squeezing his elbows into his chest. He had a mental image of the little bathroom with water pouring into the tub, Washington on his knees frantically wrapping the little black girl in a towel—an old green one, he imagined—with the other girl standing, screaming, her hands and fingers outstretched, her little belly protruding—dripping and steaming. A feeling of nausea came and went.

Washington was crying loudly now, his head buried in his forearms on the table. A feeling of empathy gave way to self-consciousness as

Blake noticed the attention of the others in the cafeteria. He reached over to Washington's arm. "It's okay, okay. What happened then?" he asked, hoping that a return to conversation would have a calming effect. Washington rubbed his face on his sleeve and sighed.

"I wrapped up Becky and she stopped crying. Susie was breathing real fast. I tried to make her drink but she wouldn't take none. I called the place where Sally works. Sally said to rub baby oil on 'em and she would come home. I tried but I couldn't do it. The towel was all stuck to 'em. When Sally got home she said we should take Susie to the hospital. She called the fire department, y'know, the paramedics. They came right away. They brought a fire truck. Maybe they thought there was a fire. All those firemen in hats and boots, y'know, in our apartment. They took Susie and Becky too, sirens and all. I ain't seen 'em since then." Washington looked up at Blake for the first time in two minutes. "Hey man, I'm sorry—I'm scared, y'know man?" Washington reached over and clutched Blake's wrist. He felt much relieved, very close to Blake. It was a closeness that was not returned, Washington noticed suddenly. Blake was sitting stiffly, glancing at Washington's hand as if he wanted to push it away. The lawyer was looking around the room, then at Washington. He smiled uncomfortably.

Washington drew back slowly, realizing he had overstepped both emotional and social bounds. "Anyway, I'll see 'em at two o'clock."

"They'll be all right," Blake repeated, smiling warmly—aware that his brief intolerance had been detected. He really liked this fellow, he thought. He blamed his embarrassment on watching a man cry, not class distinction. He smiled again but Washington's affect had cooled to its original reticence.

The dark-eyed nurse had watched this exchange openly, and wondered what the emotional discussion was about. She had seen Washington on the pediatric floor and had noticed his trembling hands and his acquiescent nod. She stood, smoothed her dress, and picked up her tray. Washington had his back to her. Blake was smiling at him, but looked at her as she turned and stacked her tray with the others on the rack. "They'll be all right," Blake was saying again. He was thinking that she was a little taller than he had guessed. Poised, and rather elegant.

CHAPTER 2

One large dot of black paint became the nose, another became an eye, and the figure of a clumsy dancing bear appeared within the penciled boundary. An oafish, happy bear it was, with a sagging belt line, enjoying an unnamed reverie with half-closed eyes. Details appeared in almost magical succession–a few whiskers, a single tooth, now two teeth, a frumpy orange tie. The artist–a plumpish, graying woman whose general shape and attitude bore more than a slight resemblance to her subject–added details at the gleeful suggestions of her little audience.

"He needs a hat, give him a red hat."

"Put polka dots on his tie."

"He doesn't have any feet."

"Wait, wait, wait," said the artist, rolling her eyes in mock despair. "One at a time! What next? Lisa?"

Lisa was the quietest of the four, not by choice, but because of weakness. She sat very still in the wagon wheel chair so as not to dislodge the IV in her right hand. It was the last good vein, and she had saved it for Dr. Crane to use that morning. Even though the chemotherapy burned, she hadn't moved and it was still running. "A hat," she said in a very soft, high voice.

"A hat it is!" An orange pork pie, tilted carelessly over one eye, materialized with six strokes of the brush.

"But he doesn't have any shoes!"

"He doesn't even have any feet!" Uncontrolled giggling resulted from this repartee between five year olds. Both Billy and Todd had appendectomies on Saturday afternoon, three days ago. After the first miserable day they had amused each other with toy cars and ribald noises. They were going home tomorrow. "Give him feet and shoes," directed Billy, loudly, rocking back and forth on a little tricycle.

"Feet it is!" agreed the artist, groaning down onto one knee and taking up the wide black brush.

Each year the halls in pediatrics were repainted–the same pale, uninteresting yellow–covering the dents, scuffs, and scratches under a thick plastery coat. Each year someone from "Teddy's Friends" came in a pink smock and created a veritable parade of cartoon animals. All happy, all musical, all connected by a ribbon of notes and little birds leading down the hall around the corner to the elevator. Teddy himself–a round, juvenile looking bear–was on the elevator door. He seemed to hide behind the wall when the door retracted.

It was like a rite of spring to Steve Crane. A juvenescence which occurred each October. The old ward became instantaneously clean and the cast of characters was reborn, a little different to be sure, but ever young. It had happened during each of his three years at Presbyterian, and now, as before, he marveled at the conversion from pale yellow flatness to cavorting celebrants with the touch of a brush. He sat between Lisa and the boys, perched on a kindergarten-sized chair turned backward. As a senior resident he was "allowed" to wear dark trousers and a long coat, but he preferred the hospital-issue white pants. (The laundry was free.) He did agree to wear a tie, which was always pulled loose at the neck, and a blue oxford cloth shirt with buttoned down collars, with the cuffs rolled up twice. As he had progressed from intern to junior resident to senior resident, the packet of three-by-five cards in his front pocket had gotten smaller. He was now down to two cards–one with names and numbers and the other a combination of personal memos–haircut!–and scut.

"Your turn, Dr. Crane," said the artist, now on both knees.

"I think we should paint shoes on . . . Todd!" Steve said, grabbing a bare five-year-old ankle.

"Why, he does need some shoes!" concurred the artist, getting a dab of black paint on one toe before Todd wriggled away, both boys collapsing in laughter, each holding the lower right side of his abdomen. He saw Lisa smile–just a little–as she pulled her right arm closer with her left to protect the precarious needle. He rose with the chair in one hand, cupping her pale cheek in the other for an instant. She smiled a little more. "Well, back to work," he announced. "Thanks. It's even better than last year's bear."

"Thank you, Dr. Crane. Come now, Lisa, we have to make a big mouse." The painter wheeled Lisa ten feet down the bare hall.

Steve pulled a three-by-five card from his pocket as he replaced the chair in the playroom. "Appys–disch. Lisa–IV, T+X, M+M cases, call Sue re. Saturday, check burns, Blake–ortho." It was a habit from internship that most doctors never lose. He kept it up, not so much as an aide to memory, but as a scorecard in the game of mind over matter, the individual over the system. Each task completed (and during internship there were two cards full every evening) was crossed off with a bold stroke of the pen–a point for the underdog. He paged Jim Bishop, and when Bishop answered the phone, Steve crossed off "Blake–ortho".

"Hi Jim, this is Steve Crane. Listen, on this kid named Blake with the fractured humerus. Browne says we can send him home if it's okay with you guys."

By "you guys" he was referring to the orthopedic service of which Bishop was the chief resident. Walter Henry, chief of the orthopedic service, had examined Petey Blake on admission and stopped in daily, but Jim Bishop helped the intern put the hanging cast on, and Crane wrote the daily orders.

"Fine with me," said Bishop. "Tell the parents to make an appointment with Henry next week."

"Okay. Hey, are you off this weekend?"

"Sunday."

"How about a little football?"

"You got it–if you don't mind playing with surgeons." Steve could visualize Bishop grinning, twisting his neck and shoulders to adjust imaginary shoulder pads. Bishop always did that while talking about football. He had been a second string tackle at Wisconsin.

"I can play with pain," Steve retorted. "See ya then."

It was unusual for pediatric and medical residents to socialize with their surgical counterparts. It wasn't the difference in age, although the surgery residents were two to three years older. It was the difference in attitude–in approach to life. Surgeons, in their own eyes, were aggressive, able, and confident. They moved at a different pace. As seen by others, the surgeons were indeed aggressive, but also arrogant, overly confident, given to hasty decisions, and not to be trusted with the delicate care of children. The latter generalization–attributed to pediatrician Ed Browne–was the background for the policy which required every child under fourteen to be admitted to the pediatric service, regardless of the medical problem. Some of the best surgical specialists in Detroit refused to come to Presbyterian for this reason, and it was rumored that the motivation was mostly financial (Browne's Law of the Blue Cross it was called), but the policy had been in effect so long that it was impossible to change. For the residents it was tolerable, since all of them spent equal time at Children's Hospital downtown, where each service had its own separate floor. While at Presbyterian, the surgical residents had a full adult service to look after, and they were glad to have the "pedy" types doing the legwork. The pediatric residents liked the arrangement because it was their only opportunity to see trauma, hernias, clubfeet, hydrocephalus, and the other surgical disorders of childhood. But socializing was very rare. Steven Crane was the exception.

Steven Crane got along with everyone. He had run the low hurdles at Stanford. That almost qualified him as an honorary orthopod. Bill Redford, the other pediatric chief resident, liked him because he always got his work done. Also because Steven volunteered to cover for the married residents on Thanksgiving and Christmas. The nurses liked him most of all because he cared about patients—nurses can always tell. Even Edna, the radiology file clerk, (who was known to refuse X-rays to Dr. Browne himself unless he had the file number), was known to find special films for Steven.

The yellow Nerf ball landed at Steve's feet as he walked through the door. He picked it up and tossed it over the bars into Petey's crib, and then glanced back through the hall window to see if the supervisor was watching. There was a new supervisor who insisted that anything that fell on the floor had to be sterilized before returning it to a baby. She had gone from a degree nursing school to a nursing instructorship in a junior college for six years, then straight to supervisor. Fortunately, she rarely came out into the wards. Petey's cast was loose at the top, a little-finger sized gap. But the purpose of the cast was to provide traction by its weight. That's why it violated the usual principle of immobilizing the joint above and below the fracture—or so said the ortho residents. Steve examined the Webril padding, the cleanly cut edges, and the big eye made of plaster through which the stockinette sling was passed. There was always something satisfying about plaster, he thought. It's possible to make it exactly right. Petey was sidestepping from bar to bar, banging the crib sides with the cast.

He was certainly a more active baby now, compared to his passive withdrawal at admission four days ago. When Steve started to retreat Petey shouted, "Ball!" and threw the Nerf ball over the side. "Ball, ball," Steve put it under the sheet. He knew the toss and fetch game as well as any mother. He noted that the ball hadn't been here yesterday. It must have come with the visit of Mr. F. Peter Blake, Esquire, who popped in at noon. Steve had not met Petey's father but had heard about him from the head nurse. "Distinguished, business-like, a friend of Dr. Browne," she had said.

* * * *

By two-thirty everything was back in its proper place. Keeping an orderly bedside was always difficult, and in an isolation room, almost impossible. Some nurses contributed to the disarray. Most left it as they found it, cluttered but manageable. Only a few nurses put every-thing in order. Not just the linen or the vital sign sheet or the suction catheters, but everything. A box of Pampers, the electronic ther-mometer, and a rolled blood pressure cuff were placed–just so–on a towel spread over the counter by the window. The overbed table was pushed into the corner, empty, still glistening from Cidex. The little bedside table was covered with a Chux to protect it from the plastic carafe, the A&D cream, the gauze dressings, and the hospital version of Kleenex. Beth had left it that way, but during her forty-five minute lunch break, every horizontal surface had mysteriously filled with debris: an oxygen mask, two irregular piles of diapers, IV bottles (one full and one spent), and a wet washcloth wadded onto the edge of the sink. Jason Hartman, the little patient, had become similarly cluttered with EKG leads and misplaced bandages. Now order was restored.

Jason had varicella–chicken pox. At least that was the working diagnosis. If it was varicella, it was the worst case Beth had ever seen. He was peppered with crusty, round, red nodules all right, some draining serum and some bleeding where he had scratched. But under his arms and in his groin the crusty spots grew together. All the surrounding skin was bright red, firm, warm to touch, and swollen. Yellow-white pus oozed from the nodules, drying to an adherent paste where it pooled on the bed. His white blood count was very low, espe-cially the lymphocytes, and some sophisticated tests were being done to determine if this abnormality was due to the viral infection itself or a primary disease which made Jason unusually susceptible to this, his first major childhood illness. In any case, he was in isolation to prevent spreading his chicken pox and to protect him from the flora in residence at Presbyterian Hospital.

For most nurses, isolation is the worst of all assignments. First the warm and clumsy garb, then the patient—usually miserable and barely communicative, but always frightened and alone. Then the smell, and finally, the boredom. Eight hours—give or take a half-hour break—in a ten-by-ten room alone with a sick patient. Feeding, cleaning, wiping, rolling, measuring, feeding, all in those flimsy polyethylene one-size-fits-all gloves that stick to sweaty skin. Beth didn't mind it, though. She preferred isolation. She could work at her own pace, deliberate without a wasted movement. She could organize the room, clean and soothe the patient, and focus on the challenge of bedside nursing without interruption, comment, or direction. Best of all she could talk to the patient or think to herself. Either was better than the insipid conversation of the smoky nurses' lounge, the nonstop TV game shows in the four-bed rooms, or the constant bantering at the desk. Every hour or two the charge nurse stuck her head in the door, holding a mask over her nose with one hand. "How's it going in here, need a break?"

"No, Jason and I are very busy," she would say lightly, contented. "Thanks, Joannie."

The pediatric nurses had quickly accepted Beth, though she had been at Presbyterian for only a month. She was reserved, somewhat distant, professional but always friendly and a reliable worker. "A damn good nurse" was Dr. Browne's description, based on a few minutes' observation.

Now, having prepared everything for the change of shift, she decided to work on the infected skin.

* * * *

Fifteen months old, Jason was normally more alert. Today, his eyelids swollen, his lips cracked with pox and fever, his brain dulled by Benadryl and sleep deprivation, he lay still, moving only his eyes. His pudgy right hand opened and closed slowly and regularly, grabbing aimlessly at the Chux under him. He pouted and whimpered as Beth filled a big plastic basin at the sink. That type of activity was a preface to pain. The whimper became a weak cry. Beth tried to divert his attention as she put four cloth diapers into the hot water. "Look at the card your brother made. He sure is a special brother!" Taped inside the foot of the crib was a piece of manila-colored construction paper bearing a second grade version of a person, a dog, and a tree–all the same general size–standing on the horizon, which sloped down from right to left. "Jason I love you Tim" was written in purple crayon across the top. Jason gave no acknowledgment. He was watching her wring out a diaper and clutching faster at the Chux.

"This is going to feel so good," she said. "You'll see. . ." She placed a hot wet diaper in each groin. He screamed initially, then stopped and returned to whimpering. She dripped more water from the basin on the compresses until they overflowed between his legs and around the sides. Seeing that the crusty scab was softening, she carried the basin back to the sink and squirted in a shot of liquid soap by stepping on the rubber bulb. Gently, with dexterity that only comes from experience, she washed and cleaned his lower abdomen and legs, talking, soothing, shielding her debridement from his vision. In a few minutes the crusts were gone, the diapers were yellow with pus, and clear serum dotted the surface between rivulets of blood where the crusts had been. "This looks better now. Doesn't that feel better? Now when the bleeding stops . . ." She talked to him and herself simultaneously. She pressed a diaper onto the bleeding surface, picked it up, pressed again, then again; soon the bleeding stopped. From the drawer of the bedside table she took a large blue jar, scooped the white creamy content onto her gloved fingers, and spread it over the raw surface. Although it looked painful, the application was obviously pleasurable to Jason who continued pouting but became silent, watching her move between the jar and his belly. "There." She sighed and discarded the gooey gloves. "Now for your arms. They look so sore."

* * * *

While Steven dictated the discharge summaries into the telephone, he consumed six selected chocolates from the big box at the nursing station. The card said, "Thanks, from the Blakes," so he reasoned that he was included. Having found the last thin chocolate chip, he rattled off, "X-ray showed acceptable position, neurovascular status remained normal, patient was discharged on the fifth day to be followed by Dr. Browne and Dr. Henry, Dr. Crane dictating, thank you," all in one breath. He wrote, "D/C sum dict. SRC" after the final progress note. Opting for one more white-coated almond, he started down the hall, headed for the pediatric ICU.

He glanced through the hall window into isolation number one by habit, then stopped abruptly. He watched until he was sure of what he saw, and then pushed the door halfway open. "Excuse me, just what the hell are you doing?" The only thing that made Steven Crane angry was mismanagement of patients. Beth looked up and stopped washing. If she was startled she didn't show it.

"I'm cleaning up this cellulitis," she said, and went back to soaking the skin under Jason's arm.

"Since when do we treat chicken pox with Silvadene? Miss–Miss–?" Crane entered the room and came to the other side of the crib. Jason started crying.

Beth felt her face flush. She recognized Crane from a few brief meetings; she was surprised at this approach. For a moment she considered ordering him back to the hall for gown, gloves, hat, and mask. Instead she said, "Miss Bonnell, Dr. Crane," in her softest and most vulnerable voice, carefully erasing any bitterness.

Crane was slightly disarmed. "Miss Bonnell, there is an old axiom regarding viral xanthems which states, 'If it's dry, wet it; if it's wet, dry it.' This child has an oozing, pussing, smelly, wet. . ." he paused, realizing that he had just made the case for debridement and antibiotic dressings ". . .wet, wound."

She was tempted to say, "Old axioms die hard," but instead she said, "Dr. Greenfield suggested that we try to clean it up." Dr. Greenfield was the staff pediatrician on Jason's case. In reality she had asked him if she could clean Jason a little and Greenfield had said okay but she felt she did not need to explain the details of the conversation to another inexperienced resident. She returned to the basin.

"Well, Greenfield didn't tell me." He was noticing how gently she cleaned the tender skin. "Jason does seem to approve," he admitted.

She smiled with her eyes, and he responded. She was pleased at her own self-control in avoiding a confrontation. He was recognizing the senior resident pomposity in himself, a trait he detested in his predecessors. She applied Silvadene to the last raw area.

"I should be–"

"Do you think–"

They broke the silence at the same instant. Each waited two seconds and started again, then they both laughed, each having been discovered at trying to break more-friendly ice.

"If Miss Whitely sees you in here without a mask I'm going to be in trouble," she said, citing the new supervisor.

"Oh, Miss Whitely." He imitated fear and furtively moved to the door, retrieving a paper gown from the small stack. He slipped the gown over his jacket and donned a cap. The caps were light blue paper bouffant affairs that looked like old shower caps. They made men look foolish and he drooped it to one side like a tam. "And will Miss Whitely approve of my hat?" He offered a profile after the manner of Barrymore.

"It's charming." She rendered a matching curtsey, holding a paper mask in her outstretched hand. He took the mask, then the outstretched hand, bending over it, playing out the role. "Now Miss Bonnell, regarding the Silvadene." There was a loud rap on the hall window. Steven looked startled and dropped her hand. Beth, who could see it was only the social worker, waved and walked back to the crib.

She rapped again, even though Steven was looking directly at her. She didn't acknowledge Beth, but pointed at Steven, then at the door. "It's not soundproof, Sue," said Steven, regaining his composure. "Bye Jason." He smiled again at Beth and went into the hall, dropping gown and hat into the red hamper inside the door.

He hadn't been caught in a compromising position, but Sue could make him feel a hand-in-the-cookie-jar self-consciousness at will.

"Steven." It was clear that she wasn't going to say anything about Jason or the nurse–the ultimate disdain. "Steven, I need to talk to you." She nodded down the hall–an unspoken marching order to which he reacted quickly.

Suzanne Hathaway could be strikingly beautiful. Her long Anglican features were emphasized when her hair was pulled back tightly, as it usually was. Her eyes were basically green with hints of blue. Her eyebrows were precise–partly make-up. She wore round, gold, dangling earrings for every occasion, emphasizing a long graceful neck. In her highest heels she was as tall as Steven. Today she was wearing knee length boots with three-inch heels, a Pendelton skirt, and a tweed jacket with suede patches on the elbows. She almost always wore a man-style shirt, as she did today, and a bright scarf–the only dash of color. She considered it a trademark. She was slender, with only a hint of her figure revealed by the manner of her dress.

"Sue, I was going to call you. Saturday night . . . ."

"Later, Steven, later." When she had her head down and walked quickly like that, conversation was useless. They were heading for her office. Past the elevator, past the ICU (pediatrics on one side, neonatal on the other), past the residents' room, the student conference room and library, until they came to the made-over solarium that served as offices for nursing supervisors, social service, the dietitian, and respiratory therapy.

Steven had been dating Suzanne for two years–exclusively since last Christmas. On their first date, while opening a door, he had said, "Let us go, then, you and I."

And she had responded, "When the evening is spread out against the sky like a patient etherized upon a table." He had never met anyone, before or since, who could quote from T. S. Eliot without hesitation. He had been awestruck. She knew about Miles van der Roe, Bix Beiderbecke, and the world record times for the mile and the 440, facts that were unknown to most of the women he met. As a birthday present he "gave" her the third movement of Mahler's Fourth Symphony. For his birthday, she had found the old recording of *La Boheme* in which Maestro Toscanini could be heard singing along with Jan Peerce. Over a three-day weekend in late September of that year they took their first trip together–a drive through the gold and scarlet forests of northern Michigan, seeking out the landmarks of Hemingway's early stories. The first night of that trip had been spent at an inn overlooking Little Traverse Bay. They had returned there just two weeks ago to celebrate the anniversary of that sensual memory.

But this afternoon she was all business. When they reached her office he closed the door, waiting for the uplifted chin and shake of the head that meant serious business. It came.

"Steven, tell me about Dr. Redford."

CHAPTER 3

The rasp of the telephone cut through the still air like a sharp ax splitting dry wood. For an hour she had heard only a stifling silence. There were sounds—the elderly refrigerator was humming, the steam radiator in the living room hissed softly and occasionally sputtered, the constant traffic on the freeway a block away droned, and the faint high-pitched buzz which sometimes occurred when she breathed in through the left side of her nose wheezed. These sounds blended with the air molecules beating on her eardrums to produce a roar which she interpreted as silence. With audio awareness set to this high level of sensitivity, the loudness of a sudden, unexpected, full volume, ringing telephone was enough to elicit pain, particularly when she feared bad news. The unease which had kept her from sleeping was injected with terror by the shrill ringing. Sally stared at the telephone, expecting it to move, the sound was so intense. The ringing ceased as abruptly as it had started. Although she knew the second ring would follow immediately, it hit with almost the same impact as the first. It stopped at last, followed by six seconds of silence.

The house had been built in 1925, during the burst of economic enthusiasm engendered by the burgeoning automobile industry. When they were built, each house on the street—in fact each house in the quarter-mile tract—was identical, except for six variations in the windows and dormers in the front, and even these slight variations occurred with predictable regularity proceeding down the street. The first owner had been an accountant at the River Rouge plant. For thirty years the house was home to his growing family, and the Christmases, the tragedies, the hugs, the tears, the handshakes, the triumphs of a generation clung to its walls and pervaded its corners. By the time the oldest grandson could drive, the elms were twice as high as the houses, bridging across the narrow street and giving the

impression that the neighborhood had been there forever. In 1954, the accountant's widow moved to Florida and sold the house to a burly young man who worked at Fisher Body and was somehow associated with the United Auto Workers. For the next eight years, when she made her May visit to her daughter in Pontiac, she returned to the neighborhood, drove up the alley, and paused outside the ancient iron gate to see the dogwood they had planted that first
hot summer.

When the school was 40 percent black, the union official moved to Redford township and sold the house to Benjamin Weiss who had owned the drug store two blocks away for twenty years. The house sold for thirty-four thousand dollars. It would have been thirty-eight thousand, but the Dutch elm disease had finally caught up with Calvert Avenue, leaving stumps and scraggly skeletons. Ben and Rachel Weiss knew and liked their neighbors. They offered credit in the drug store, and still cashed payroll checks on Fridays. When the store had been robbed four times they considered moving, but they liked walking to the synagogue two blocks away. They liked the old house too. The fireplace worked well and the morning sun lit the back porch off the kitchen which had been wisely glassed in so long ago.

When the new freeway was built, Temple Beth El turned out to be directly in its path. When the temple was gone, the little congregation banked the money and met at a high school in Grosse Point, since most of the members had moved there. It was more the loss of old friends than it was the riots in 1966 that finally prompted Ben Weiss to sell the house to D&D properties in 1967. For the next three years, it stood vacant much of the time under the management of D&D. A front window was broken and replaced with plywood. Eventually D&D added some drywall between the staircase and the front hall, changed some plumbing and meters in the basement, and created a duplex in 1971.

The upstairs apartment had been empty for two months, which pleased Sally. The last tenant sold dope and the regular visitors were a bad influence on the children. She had lived there for three years and loved the old bay window, the brick fireplace, the blue and white kitchen caked with layers of enamel. She especially liked the sun porch sticking out into the backyard. In winter the afternoon sun warmed it, even on the coldest days, and a cardinal family always nested under the down spout. In spring she could review the greening process and supervise the foliation of the big dogwood tree. The dogwood reminded her of childhood trips to the park in Baltimore. Each spring her mother would expect a call on the day the dogwood bloomed. But now it was a gray October afternoon, the dogwood was bare, and the only colors in the backyard were the orange rinds and Stroh's beer cans left where a vagrant dog had dumped the trash. She had been sitting at the kitchen table absently watching the minutes flip by on the digital clock when the telephone bell had gripped her so suddenly. Her eyes still fixed on the source of the awful noise, she gradually relaxed from the tonic posture, cringing slightly when the next ring came. She resolved to answer it as soon as the initial shock subsided.

In the summer of 1972, Sally, her husband, and their three-year-old son had moved to Detroit when the Pinto factory outside Wheeling closed. They had found the place on Calvert Avenue after searching the classified section of the *Free Press*. The price was right. They settled in hopeful, but even though he belonged to the union, Sam could not find work for months. The wheels were stolen from their Volkswagen. Sam began to drink a lot and lost his temper often. One November day when she returned from work he was gone. Hours of panic led to weeks of despair, then months of bitterness. She learned to maneuver between welfare and waitressing jobs, and kept up on the rent. Little Sammy grew up in day care centers and neighborhood houses, but the food supply was always adequate and his mother's love abundant. After two years of ceaseless anxiety and hard labor, her loneliness reached its peak and she succumbed to the white bartender at the restaurant. The first time she was consumed with guilt. He was married and she had always held to the simple moral code which she had learned at Baptist Sunday school. But by a simple girl's standards he was a skillful lover; the second time was easier and more enjoyable, and eventually she could hardly wait for Thursday afternoons when he left his home an hour early and arrived at work an hour late.

That affair ended abruptly when the bartender was mugged one night while returning to his Camaro from her house. But Sally had become addicted to companionship, a regular warm body, and multiple orgasms. Soon there were other men—not many, but enough—and Sammy learned to play in the backyard when there was a car parked in the alley.

When she met Kevin Washington all that changed. He came in for breakfast when she was working at a little diner on Livernois. For a month he sat in her section at the counter every day, then he asked her for a date. Two weeks later the transient visitors stopped coming, and shortly thereafter Kevin moved in and began to pay the rent. The old house, or at least its lower half, regained the glow of its youth. They found two big armchairs on a trip to the Goodwill. Kevin put travel posters from Japan on the walls and described to her exciting nights in Hong Kong and endless days in Vietnam. He fixed the casement windows on the porch and put up screens in May. After a rain the gentle aroma of the dogwood filled the sun porch. Sally told her mother about the dogwood, but not about Kevin, nor her pregnancy.

She discovered she was pregnant only a month after Kevin moved in. It took another month to get enough courage to tell him; she was sure he would be gone in the morning. Instead she awoke to a bouquet of goldenrod in a water glass beside her bed, and Kevin was singing loudly in the kitchen. Although it was obvious to everyone that Kevin was not the biological father, he had beamed with pride on the day Rebecca was born.

By the time the dogwood flowered in 1975, Sally was pregnant again. The baby was born in August–another girl. They named her Susan, after Sally's mother. From the beginning Susie had Kevin's broad nose and pensive eyes. When Kevin caressed his new baby for the first time, Sally took his hand and kissed the new wedding band. They planned to be married, though they had to wait on some legal problem holding up the completion of Sally's divorce. Kevin bought the rings just before she went in for the delivery. He had named her and the children Washington to include them in his medical insurance at work. They did the same when Sammy started school.

When the telephone rang for the third time Sally was composed and rose with a sigh. It was Kevin.

"Hey, baby, you're 'sposed to be at work. It's after four o'clock."

"I know. I'm too worried about the girls. Are you at the hospital?"

"Yeah." His voice seemed to choke. There was a pause.

"Kevin?"

"Hey, baby, you gotta come down here."

"What's the matter? Is there a problem?"

"No—I don't know. They don't tell ya nothin'. The doctor here wants to ask you some questions."

"What about?"

"I don't know, but he said he wants to talk to you. They asked me the same questions two or three times."

"What about Sammy?"

"Maybe the neighbor could take him. Or you could just bring him along. I left you the car this morning. It's in the garage."

"I'll come right away. Kevin, how's Susie?"

"She's fine. Just hurry."

* * * *

Beth opened some gauze four-by-fours and pushed them into the cream to hold it in place. Lacking the elastic netting she was accustomed to, she completed the dressing by fashioning a little suit from stockinette and safety pins. She knew that the nurses on the PM and night shift would leave the dressing undisturbed, and she planned to change it before Dr. Greenfield appeared in the morning. She had discarded her isolation gown and sat at the desk to complete the vital sign sheet and record her summary in the nursing notes. She concluded with "Dr. Crane examined patient" and signed her initials followed by a small happy face—a sign that the patient did well during the shift. Instead of going down the back stairs as she usually did, she checked on Jason one last time through the hall window. Down the hall, she noticed the same young black man she had seen earlier in the cafeteria. He was leaving the pay phone and walking toward the pediatric ICU. Curious, she followed him, quickly inventing an excuse for an unscheduled visit, should anyone ask.

There were two doors into the pediatric ICU: one was prominently marked and adorned with a variety of instructions for visitors, the other bore no label. She entered through the latter. The pediatric ICU had space for nine beds. Only five were occupied. The central door through which Washington came entered directly into the cramped nursing station. From the desk she could observe the entire long, narrow room through the wired glass partition. Beth looked over the room, trying to match Washington with one of the patients. Bed one was empty. Bed two was replaced with an isolette holding a baby she guessed to be three months old. The baby was breathing about sixty times a minute–gasping, really. His nostrils flared as if attempting to capture more air. He had the wild-eyed look which comes from unrelenting concentration on the work of breathing. The ageless physiognomy of dyspnea. Every few seconds, as he tried to take a deeper breath, his breastbone sank into his belly and his eyes rolled up and to the right. His lips and fingers were blue. His forehead was dotted with beads of sweat. Beth noticed that each deeper gasp was accompanied by a slowing of the heart rate as displayed on the monitor. It only happened for two or three beats, not enough to trigger the alarm. "Should be intubated," she thought to herself, guessing that a cardiac arrest was two to three hours away.

The shaved head, turban-like dressing, and black eyes identified the six-year-old in bed three as a neurosurgical patient. He lay very still despite the efforts of his mother, who stood beside him kneading his hand. Beds four and six had been removed to accommodate the activity around bed five. Beth recognized the patient as Sandra Hepps, who had gone down for open heart surgery that morning. The operation must have been quite successful judging by the near-empty chest drainage bottle, the smiles and small talk of the people around the bed, and the full pressure wave displayed on the oscilloscope.

Bed seven had been removed and replaced with a makeshift partition made of a tubular frame screen, a laundry hamper, and an isolation table loaded with gowns, gloves, and masks. A printed sign hung slightly askew from the cloth screen. "Reverse isolation gowns, gloves, masks, shoe covers." The screen separated beds eight and nine from the rest of the unit. Two nurses in full isolation regalia moved silently between the cribs, one pausing to scratch her nose by craning her neck and rubbing the cloth mask on her shoulder.

Beth had heard about the two little girls with scald burns admitted the night before, now occupying beds eight and nine. She walked the length of the room ostensibly to read the notices on the bulletin board, which was just outside the little isolation area. She had promised herself not to get involved with burns at Presbyterian Hospital. Four years at the Shriner's Hospital for Burned Children in Galveston had given her a lifetime of experience, but with experience had come understanding and with understanding an intolerance for less than perfect burn care. Taking a stand on these principles had led her into trouble more than once, and she planned to avoid problems by avoiding the subject. But she did get close enough for a better look. She saw what she expected to see. There was one IV bottle near the head and one near the foot of each crib. Dilute yellow urine dripped into plastic collecting chambers hung from the crib rails. Radiant heaters straddled the cribs. The older girl–she appeared to be about two–was wrapped from the chest down with a thick roll of fluffy gauze which had obviously been in place all day. A silver-gray cream oozed through in places, and the dressing over the abdomen and upper thighs was yellow with serum. The girl had curly yellow hair, matted and soaked with perspiration. Intermittently she whined and sucked her thumb.

The other patient was a baby lying face down with her knees pulled up to her chest. A deep second-degree burn extended from her upper back to her heels; the raw, red, swollen tissue was covered for the most part with a layer of creamy ointment. Much of the cream was on the bed, washed away by the streams of fluid coming through the burn. A large patch of intact cream over the sacrum identified that as an area of unburned skin. Beth looked at the foot of the crib and saw that the baby's round bottom and vulva had sustained the deepest burns. Her labia were grotesquely swollen, resembling a huge, ruptured tomato impaled by a yellow catheter which disappeared through the cleft into her bladder. Her doctors had decided to treat her by the exposure method, but it was hideous and obviously painful. Her facial appearance was negroid, although a swollen black eye and large bruise on the forehead made it difficult to tell. Her eyes were closed and she chewed a plastic pacifier. When Beth saw Kevin, mask and hat in place, putting on the paper gown, the emotional scene in the cafeteria started to
make sense.

Kevin entered the makeshift isolation room cautiously, as if he were walking on ice. He edged his way along the wall opposite the cribs, nodding politely to the nurses who greeted him with cold stares–talking to each other but not to him. With the self-conscious-ness of a child in all-adult company, he tried to put his hands in his pockets and, finding them covered with the gown, finally let them hang at his sides. When the nurses were both at Susie's crib, he inched his way over to Rebecca, who seemed to be dozing.

"Becky," he whispered, glancing up at the nurses. "Becky, it's Daddy." The little blond girl jerked in her dream and awoke at the same time. As she opened her eyes she was looking straight at him. She screamed immediately–a piercing, continuous shriek–and pulled herself toward the far side of the crib. Kevin stepped toward her, grasping the crib rail. "Becky, *shh shh.*" He looked again at the nurses who had spun around and were inspecting him carefully. One put a hand on Becky's forehead.

"Now, Becky, it's okay, everything's okay." The screaming merely got louder. The smaller baby, startled by the noise and activity, started to cry also–a squeaky, rhythmic sound like the bleating of a lamb.

"Becky, please, it's Daddy," said the large gowned and masked figure, to
no avail.

"You'd better wait out there," said the nurse stroking Becky's head–motioning toward a rolling stool outside the partition. He tried for his pockets again, backing up and nodding at the pudgy authoritarian nurse. As he turned to sit down he looked at Beth. She thought she detected tears in his eyes, but the expression was one of mounting anger–not the abject fear she had seen in
the cafeteria.

She was puzzling over the nurses' attitudes when Dr. Redford bustled into the ICU, leading a small entourage of two interns and a medical student. They walked directly to the isolation area, peered in, and began talking to one another. They stood next to Kevin, almost touching him.

"This little girl is one and her sister is two and a half. They are about twenty-four hours post-burn–by history–and eighteen hours post-admission. They're fairly stable–urine output's around twenty ccs an hour. The little one has God-awful edema, especially her genitalia." They all looked in the direction indicated by the intern, wincing at the sight.

"Now there's a hot bottom," said the other intern to the student, *sotto voce.* Washington stiffened, his tense jaw muscles visible behind the mask. Redford shot a disapproving look at this crudity.

"So what's the plan for tonight?" said Redford.

Of course he directed the plan, but wanted to see if one of his eloquent lectures on burns that morning had sunk in.

"Just keep running in the Ringer's, keep the urine up, 'crit and lytes at midnight and six," recited the flippant intern. Redford showed agreement. He turned to Kevin.

"Mr. Washington, did you get your wife?"

"Yes, just now."

"Well, good. We need to talk to her. The girls are doing . . . okay . . . so far so good." Redford managed a tight smile.

Washington mumbled, "Thanks." He had innumerable questions, but no explanations were offered and he was hesitant to ask. The doctors were starting to leave. "Say, Dr. Redford," said Kevin, rising to his feet. They turned their heads toward him, but kept leaning impatiently toward bed five. "Will there by any scars?"

"Scars?" Redford repeated, incredulous. Here they were trying to keep these kids alive and this guy's worried about scars. "As of right now, if we get to the point where we're worried about scars, we'll be happy." They left without waiting for a response.

Beth could feel their hostility but she didn't understand it. Pediatric nurses and residents were normally careful and compassionate, but today they acted more like the hard ER team. Washington was slowly comprehending the last remark. He sank onto the stool, making a soft whimpering sound that only Beth could hear. She had made some mental calculations of the burn size and depth based on what she could see. The mortality risk was less than 10 percent. She leaned over in front of him and put her hand on his shoulder. "They'll be fine," she said, "and don't worry about scars." The latter advice was non-committal but honest. Washington smiled, grateful, but unable to speak. Beth smiled back, squeezed his shoulder, and left for the door.

As she waited for the elevator she saw Steven Crane leaning against the wall near the ICU back door, engrossed in discussion with Sue Hathaway and a middle-aged man in a sport coat. She was doing most of the talking, raising her chin and shaking her earrings at regular intervals. The sport coat was black and white checks, identifying its occupant as a drug salesman or hospital administrator. The vinyl notebook under his arm confirmed the latter. They all looked troubled. Steve shook his head frequently as if denying an inevitable fact.

Beth couldn't hear much as the elevator lights slowly braked to the sixth floor but she did recognize "standard procedure," "a little fishy," "abuse team," "protective custody." She was putting this observation together with the episode in the ICU when the elevator door clicked, clunked, and rolled back. Not expecting anyone to be aboard, she started forward, then halted, looking up into the eyes of Peter Blake.

"Hello again." Blake was charming, catching her arms gently to prevent a full collision. Of course there had never been a "hello" the first time, but Blake recognized her immediately and organized his greeting to connote recognition of their eye contact in the cafeteria earlier in the day.

"Hello again," she repeated, rather demurely, allowing him a point for poise and quick thinking. "Excuse me." She smiled and stepped back. He paused just slightly to imply he knew what she was thinking, then grinned, nodded, and escorted the blond woman at his side past her without further comment. The blond woman absorbed this encounter with an open expression of simple but unpleasant recognition, the way one responds to a dentist's description of small X-rays showing carious teeth. Beth entered the elevator, turned, and the door shuttered closed on Peter and Valerie Blake walking down the hall past the freshly painted bear. On the first floor, as Beth exited, Sally Washington got on, each lost in private thoughts.

Sally pushed six, and kept pushing it until the door closed. In the privacy of the elevator, she pulled her T-shirt down and checked her reflection in the stainless steel plate holding the buttons. She found her way to the pediatric ICU and stood anxiously waiting for a response to the bell ("Ring here, wait for Nurse."). Down the hall she noticed a tall doctor with his back to her, an attractive woman with a bright blue scarf, and a thin, balding man in a checkered sport coat. "Nice sport coat," she thought. She suddenly felt conspicuous in her flowered blue jeans and tight white T-shirt with "Nature's Best" emblazoned on its contours.

"Come in, Mrs. Washington." The nurse seemed overly courteous.. "Mr. Washington—your husband?" Her voice went up, implying a parenthetical question. "Mr. Washington is waiting for you. He'll show you how to wash and gown." Kevin was already standing and they embraced for a long moment. She turned her head on his chest and looked at the girls. She had seen them here last night, but it seemed worse now. Susie's crib had been covered with a sheet so that only her bruised face showed. Sally looked away.

From bed two Bill Redford had noticed Sally come in. He waited a discreet interval, directed his little group to finish rounds, and approached the distraught couple. Redford had not seen the Washingtons when the girls were admitted—he was too busy—and he relied on the surgical intern's history from the emergency room. He knew that Becky was Caucasian and that Susie was Negro, but somehow, he had imagined Mrs. Washington as a black woman. Walking down the unit, he readjusted his thinking to address this bleached-blonde, peaches and cream, blue-eyed Sally Washington.

Bill Redford was short, five-foot-seven at best. He had grown a full beard and always dressed well, but he still felt intimidated by tall people. When Sue Hathaway had asked him if he was going to report the burn cases to the child abuse investigation team, he had had some reservations. The intern's note questioned whether severe burns could be caused by tap water. It described the burns as "very suggestive of non-accidental trauma," and, combined with the bruises and contusions, were "probable BCS." Redford had seen his share of battered child syndrome, and Susie certainly had multiple injuries. But he had also spent a month on the busy burn service in medical school in California. He knew that tap water did commonly cause scalding, especially in small children.

Redford had not yet talked to the family himself, which he always did before notifying the abuse investigation team. But Sue was two inches taller and very persuasive; this was such a repulsive injury, there was talk of losing the girls to the burn unit at Children's Hospital, and the burns were typical of inflicted injury. Besides, the team merely investigated and counseled—no judgments involved. He had signed the suspected child abuse form that morning. And now he would meet with the family.

"Mrs. Washington? I'm Dr. Redford. Let's all go to the conference room by the elevator? It's a little more private." They forgot to remove the gowns and the three made a strange procession crossing the main hall. The hall was particularly active at this hour. They waited for the big food cart to pass. It smelled of overdone fish and leaked a trail of some amber liquid. Down near the elevator, Steve, Suzanne, and Mr. Heisal, the hospital administrator in the checkered suit, had been joined by another middle-aged man wearing a brown suit. They approached when the Washingtons came out of the ICU. From the other direction, Peter and Valerie Blake were heading for the elevator.

Blake recognized his acquaintance from the cafeteria. Trying to be friendly, he stepped between Dr. Redford and Washington.

"Hello there," said Blake. "How are your little girls doing?" From Washington only a twitching, fleeting smile in response. "Valerie, this is the fellow I met in the cafeteria. My wife Valerie Blake, Mr. . . ." Blake recognized suddenly that he had never learned the fellow's name.

"Kevin Washington." He bowed slightly toward Mrs. Blake. "This here's my wife, Sally."

There was no camouflaging the reaction to the heterologous match. Kevin and Sally just waited it out. They were used to it.

"Well . . . well . . . Hello Sally," said Blake, perhaps a little too warmly. He still didn't introduce himself. The leaking food cart had passed. Redford started to say something when the man in the brown suit walked up and interrupted him.

"Kevin and Sally Washington?"

"Yes," Kevin said evenly. He recognized the disinterested affectation of a
law officer.

"I am Detective Korinsky, juvenile division." He showed a badge automatically as he spoke. Producing an envelope from his pocket, he gestured and said, "This is an order of the juvenile court remanding Rebecca and Susan Washington to the custody of the county of Wayne, state of Michigan for purposes of their protection from physical and mental harm, until such time as a suitable disposition can be made. You may see the children at the discretion of the court's representative, and must report for a hearing when ordered."

As the detective spoke, the lonely anger, which had been building in Kevin, became fury. Sally clutched his trembling arm. "What is this?" demanded Kevin through clenched teeth. He directed his question to Redford. Redford shrugged. "What is this?" repeated Kevin, looking at Suzanne, who had started to speak. Blake drew back, horrified. "What's happening?" asked Sally, who understood only that something was dreadfully wrong.

Korinsky continued, "You have not yet been charged with willful child abuse. This is only an investigation. However, I must inform you of your right to counsel and your right to remain silent. Anything you say may be held against you."

With one fist Kevin doubled him up and with the other sent him crashing to the floor. Suzanne picked up the protective custody order.

CHAPTER 4

T he village of Hunting Valley is nestled between Franklin and Bloomfield Hills, about fifteen miles from downtown. At one point it had been the five-hundred-acre David Whitney estate, along with the adjacent lake, orchards, and crossroads. Around the turn of the century, a corner of the estate near the lake had been made into the Hunting Valley Country Club, and the rest of the development followed gradually, so that the six hundred homes of the village were a combination of old baronial country houses and newer stone, glass, and timber mansions that blended into the towering oaks on the hillsides. All of the streets were named after places in England, and all were rimmed by stone or wooden fences. The wide trails which ran through the woods now served as many runners as horses. Peter Blake turned off Regents Parkway onto Cornwall Circle. As the electronically operated gates opened into their driveway, Valerie was still talking about their strange encounter at the hospital. "Peter, I don't understand how you got to know that fellow Washington. And walking right up to him in the hall, big as life, and shaking hands with a . . . a child molester."

"Child abuser," corrected Peter. "Besides, placing children in protective custody is a standard procedure. It doesn't necessarily imply wrongdoing. And as for our meeting in the cafeteria, the poor fellow seemed so frightened."

"Well, I can surely understand why. And the way he hit that policeman."

"Yes, that is suspicious." The garage door closed automatically as they walked across the courtyard to the front door. There was a short hallway which connected the back of the garage to the pantry, but it always smelled faintly of grease, gasoline, and old rubber boots. Whenever the weather permitted, Blake preferred to enter through the massive mahogany front door into the grand hallway. The house itself was fifty years old and they had left the basic floor plan intact when they bought it thirteen years ago. The architecture itself was a sort of Tudor-Victorian combination with huge sloping gables and small leaded windows. The pillars, hardware, and drainpipes were black, which gave a stately but foreboding appearance. The central atrium was an extravagant use of space. It was three stories high, all the way to the roof, and the dark wooden staircase wound around the outer walls, reaching the second-floor balcony halfway around and continuing to the third-floor bedrooms, which were the domain of the children. A great chandelier made of walnut, brass, and wrought iron hung from the peak of the ceiling to the level of the balcony. To the left, off the entrance hall, were the living room with its vaulted ceiling and the formal dining room. Straight ahead was the kitchen, rebuilt (according to Valerie's specifications) of old bricks, unfinished cedar from British Columbia, and tiles from Delft. To the right were the music room and the library. The opening of the front door brought Eric and Mary hurtling down the stairs, wondering about Petey, requesting money, reporting on assorted events of the day. Valerie attended each child while Peter inspected the mail on the hall table. Finding nothing more interesting than a bill from Carte Blanche and a postcard from their niece Nancy at college, he retreated to the library while Valerie set off to prepare a late dinner.

The door to the library opened onto a small landing from which three broad steps descended to the main floor of the room. He draped his coat over the railing, loosened his tie, and descended the steps on the thick burgundy carpet. The opposite side of the room was the west-facing end of the house. The small-paned windows had been replaced by a single plate which reached from the floor to the twelve-foot ceiling. One could see a mile down the valley through the oak and maple woods, and now a few lights were visible as twilight closed. One wall of the dark-paneled room was filled with books from the level of the landing up, while the other, facing the leather couch built into the sunken floor, held paintings, treasures, and trophies, a pair of Infinity Quantum 4 speakers, and several cabinets—one of which contained the fittings of a small bar. This one he approached and poured a glass of Bushmill's Irish whiskey. Passing a panel of buttons on his way to the large leather chair, he pushed "Power," then "Tape." The room was instantly filled with Beethoven's F Major String

Quartet. As an afterthought he poured a glass of sherry, put it on the railing near the door, and sank into the armchair facing the huge window. At the end of the scherzo, Valerie came through the door, picked up the sherry, and settled on the couch.

"Pete, I keep thinking about that awful episode at the hospital. How did the police get involved?"

"Well, the hospital is required to notify the county department of child welfare on all cases of suspected neglect or abuse. They get a court order and call the police to put a hold on the children until the question is cleared up. You know, so they won't beat up the other kids or take them out of the hospital. Stuff like that."

"You mean the county can just take over the children? Just like that?"

"Just like that. And of course it's all to protect the children."

"I suppose you're right." She pondered, sipping the sherry. "That young man was so angry. Doesn't that make you think he has something to hide?"

"Well, it sure won't do him any good at the hearing."

"What hearing?"

"These things are usually settled at a preliminary hearing. Child welfare reviews the case, the hospital team has an opinion, usually everything works out and the protective custody order is lifted."

"Who presides at the hearing?"

"Tom Nelson, usually. Either him or Marjorie Weintraub. Tom's been in charge of juvenile court for ten or fifteen years."

"Isn't Tom Nelson the judge who helped out with Billy Williams—and also with Petey?" She was referring to two of the several foster children they had taken in over the years.

"Yes, he's the one. And he's the one who helped cut through the red tape when little Linda died of SIDS."

"What an awful experience that was," she remembered, grimacing. Valerie rose to return to the kitchen. "Well, just so somebody's going to take care of those poor burned children. Do you want peas or broccoli?"

Peter Blake, apparently engrossed in the allegro, responded only with a hand gesture indicating that he didn't care.

* * * *

43

The opening strains of Beethoven's Sixth Symphony bring to mind a walk in the country, gaining the crest of a small hill, and seeing a vista of fields and villages spread out below. The first movement builds slowly as others join the wayfarer at intersecting paths, culminating in a carefree band, frolicking in the splendor of late springtime. At least that was the scene portrayed on the small television screen to match the vibrant opening of Steven's favorite symphony. Steve's roommate from Stanford, Richard Halley, had launched a successful art-nouveau career by combining ancient music and poetry with modern photography. His latest work, *Four Great Symphonies through the Mind's Eye*, was being presented piecemeal on public television. Richard had called Steven from Seattle to tell him that the Beethoven Six movie was scheduled for this night at ten o'clock. Steve had planned their sexual exercise with some care. He stretched and delayed gratification, looking occasionally over Sue's shoulder at the clock, and leading up to a shuddering climax at 9:35, which still left time for a gentle glide back to earth, an affectionate landing, and a quick shower before the program came on. Now, with a pleasurable ache in his pelvis, he lay stretched between the coffee table and the low couch, absorbing his friend's modern day vision of the great master's pastorale.

Suzanne came out of the shower drying her hair and stood behind him, leaning into the couch and the back of his head. Steve stretched out to full length, pointing his toes toward the television and grabbing her with both hands. He arched his back and looked up, providing a sight that, under the circumstances, was more artistic than erotic. Sue smiled and bent forward slowly to lick his chest, her fingers spread out over his taut abdomen, her large soft breasts dragging over his face. Once started she was insatiable. But she was this aggressive only when she knew he was spent or preoccupied, or both, as was his present condition. He remained smothered for several delicious seconds, then dispatched her with a gentle bite, returning his attention to the second movement. Steven recognized the terrain of Mt. Baker on the TV screen.

Suzanne did not like to visit his apartment in the resident's complex across the street from the hospital, but she kept a drawer of toiletries and clothes there, as he did at her apartment in the new high-rise building near the river front. It was this combination of practicality and independence which made their relationship so successful. Tonight it had been rather late by the time Steven had finished rounds and Suzanne had mollified Detective Korinsky. Actually, it was she who had initiated the protective custody order, so she felt responsible for the melodramatic scene which had resulted in Washington's outburst. She had envisioned a more civilized encounter in her office, with herself in charge, explaining the technicalities of the legal procedure. The stressful evening had left her in need of a little personal contact, and so she was waiting with dinner ready in Steven's apartment when he walked in. He was pleasantly surprised. They didn't even discuss the hospital, and had headed for bed before dessert.

The towel was wrapped around her waist as she came out of the kitchen, bearing two mugs of steaming coffee. She sat beside him, their toes touching.

There is no grand ending to the Sixth Symphony, it is simply over. So it was with Richard's movie, which ended with the wayfarer trudging toward the next hill. Steven got up to click off the television and put Klemperer's Beethoven's Sixth on the stereo. He preferred his own mental images. After a discussion of the movie and congenial small talk, Suzanne asked, "Steven, what's the prognosis on those little girls?" Although she didn't specify, he knew exactly which little girls she meant.

"Pretty good, I guess. Scalds are only second-degree burns. They should be all healed up in two or three weeks."

"I just can't imagine someone burning a baby," she said. "I can see how a parent might overreact in a certain situation and hit or spank a child too hard, but burning is so . . . intentional."

"Now, wait a minute. It could have been an accident. Don't you think this whole thing is proceeding a little bit quickly?"

"Now you sound like Bill Redford." She became somewhat defensive. "Haven't you heard about that child abuse case that was sent home from the ER and came back with a skull fracture? The system is designed to prevent that
from happening."

Steve remembered the case very well. "The 'Salem Syndrome,' Browne calls it. We hear about it regularly."

"Children are the greatest natural resource of our society–and the most vulnerable," Suzanne continued. "There are huge agencies that protect the deer and the forests and the energy and the environment—but who looks out for the children? Parents—that's who. Just ordinary people—any two kids who can screw become parents. No training, no experience, no qualification—just sperm and eggs and suddenly they are supposed to be instant experts. Does that make sense?"

"Sounds good to me," said Crane, hoping to derail her familiar speech.

"That's the inane attitude that makes my job so hard," she fumed. "Parents are the custodians of society's resource. If they are inadequate then we must help them out, teach them, and displace them if necessary. We can't let amateurs squander away precious lives. It isn't fair to society and it certainly isn't fair to the little children."

"Perhaps you're right." He sought to change the subject. "Redford was really mad at you, though. He never had a chance to talk to the family, and the doctors should take the history and be the ones to call the abuse team."

"Oh, he let me know he was mad," she said, getting up and putting on her clothes in a business-like fashion. She had planned to stay—which she rarely did—but the warm patina of the evening had been wiped away by the tone of the conversation. "Well, he and you and everyone else will have plenty of chances to talk to the family tomorrow. If it doesn't turn into a street brawl. Do you think I like this job? You know, you're required to report all those cases. It's . . . it's a felony if you don't!" Steve knew that she became emotional about this subject, everyone did. He could also see that there was no changing her decision to spend the night at home.

"I know that, Sue. It's just that it could have been done a little more smoothly." he said cautiously.

"Well, dammit Steven, I do the best I can." Her earrings were shaking violently. "I'll see you in the morning." She wrenched open the door. "Thank you for a nice evening," she said in a softer, more benevolent tone. That took a conscious effort on her part, he thought, and signified her desire to avoid any conflict. He stood, smiled, and kissed her on the cheek.

"Thank you, lovely lady. Be careful."

She closed the door and he listened to her boots clatter down the stairs. Her step was light, and he flopped on the bed knowing that she was really not too upset.

* * * *

Six-year-old boys can be very perceptive. Sammy appeared to be watching television, but he was very sensitive to the tension in the air. His mother had been crying–crying a lot. She was sitting on the window seat by the bay window at the front of the house, looking blankly at the street and sniffing hard every few minutes. Kevin sat at the kitchen table in the back of the house, the car keys lying in front of him where he had tossed them twenty minutes before. He was looking straight ahead at nothing in particular. His hands grasped the chair seat, and periodically he took a deep breath through flared nostrils and exhaled forcibly. Sammy thought he looked like a dragon he had seen on Saturday morning cartoons.

"Sammy, it's past your bedtime," said Sally half-heartedly. Six-year-old perceptions are, unfortunately for adults, matched with six-year-old responses.

"No," he shouted, and turned the television up louder. He knew that something was wrong and he needed some reassurance, not banishment.

"Sammy, turn that off and go to bed!" Sally said sharply.

"No!" he shouted again. "I want a drink." Sally glanced at Kevin through the kitchen door. He had not moved since they came in. He had not spoken since they left the hospital. He had a violent temper on rare occasions, but she had never seen him like this. She was frankly afraid to disturb him. "Come on, then." She turned off the television and went into the kitchen, pouring a glass of milk and putting it at the other end of the kitchen table, looking cautiously at Kevin. Sammy climbed up on the chair and took a small sip, pleased at getting the little family together in one room and hoping to make the milk last as long as possible.

"Kevin looks like a dragon," observed Sammy, louder than necessary. Kevin turned his eyes toward Sammy without changing his expression.

"Just drink your milk, Sammy," said Sally. "Kevin, would you like some supper?"

"No." His voice was measured and raspy because the back of his throat was filled with mucous and tears.

"Kevin, you ought to eat." She was relieved to get the first sound out of him. He cleared his throat and relaxed his grip on the chair seat, moving his elbows to the table.

"I'm not hungry."

"Kevin, I know you're worried about the girls. That other business . . ." With a crash Sammy's glass fell onto the table, breaking into a dozen pieces and sending milk in all directions. Kevin recoiled, almost falling over in his chair. Sally grabbed a towel from the rack by the sink. "Oh, Sammy—now go to bed, just go to bed."

"Look at Kevin, he almost fell over," squealed Sammy getting out of his chair to avoid the milk dripping through the crack in the table. "Kevin has funny hair," he said, trying to regain attention and conversation in the only way he knew how. He danced around behind Kevin's chair and pulled at Kevin's bushy hair with a little thumb and forefinger, once, twice. Sally tried to grab him, but could not react before Kevin spun around, hitting Sammy on the face with the back of his hand. He really intended just to brush him away, but the charge of emotional energy combined with his off balance position made the blow much harder than he intended. Sammy fell to the floor, slipping in the milk and sprawling in the broken glass. He was more shocked than hurt, but started screaming immediately. Kevin reacted first, leaping from his chair and picking up Sammy under the shoulders.

"Oh Sammy, I'm sorry, I didn't mean . . ."

"Kevin, you didn't have to hit him." Sally pulled the little boy away and carried him, screaming, to the bedroom. Eventually the screaming turned to sobbing and the sobbing to the heavy breathing of troubled sleep. Kevin listened as he picked up the broken glass and wiped the milk and blood with a series of paper towels. There were tears in his eyes when Sally finally returned to the kitchen.

"Oh Kevin, what's happening?" She knelt beside him on the floor and they clung to each other, listening to the sobs and breathing.

CHAPTER 5

One of the most unpleasant advances of modern civilization is the ability to measure time. For with that technology comes the concept of being on time which inevitably leads to the practice of going to work before sunrise. Man is a diurnal creature meant to rise with the sun. The fact that we do otherwise, simply because some compulsive hour elapses, is probably at the root of modern man's discontent. These were the thoughts of Edward Browne as he nosed his Cadillac Seville out onto Chatsworth Drive. He pondered this weighty issue each fall on the first morning he had to turn on the headlights as he left the driveway at seven-fifteen. In a few days the change back to standard time would give him a delicious respite of two or three weeks, but then it was four more months of arising before the sun, just because civilization dictated it must be so. As he gained momentum down Cornwall Circle and ran the stop sign at Oxford, he explored the concept of time related to sunrise. Rounds at sunrise plus one, committee meetings at sunrise plus three, lunch at sunrise plus four, the theatre at sunset plus two. After all, the time of sunrise and sunset can be calculated for the next millennium, and some enterprising micro-electronics company could build little watches that convert civilized time to sunrise time. He was beginning to think it could actually work as he joined the incessant stream of headlights heading east on the freeway.

"Any method which avoids driving around like this in the middle of the night has to be progress," he thought to himself, abandoning the idea of the sunrise calculator in favor of the car radio. Like all those who live in the suburbs and work downtown, he had convinced himself that the drive took only twenty minutes and that it provided a welcome period of placid transition between hectic home life and the workaday world. Browne was one of those who actively worked at this concept. He got a new Cadillac every two years. It was always fitted out with every cockpit convenience available. This particular model had maroon velour upholstery, a Nakamichi car stereo system, a digital clock, and a small brass plate embedded in the fake walnut burl stating, "Made expressly for Edward M. Browne, M.D." To this he added a console which held a coffee warmer, a note pad, a cache of fruit, and the Wall Street Journal.

The nine-hundred-dollar sound system he used only to listen to WJR coming and going. The news this morning consisted of another impending autoworkers strike and the information that the tight end for the Detroit Lions would not be ready for Sunday's skirmish. The sun crawled up over the buildings along the river in Windsor, teasing him as he turned off the exit ramp.

The medical office building of the Detroit Presbyterian Hospital was the piece of bait that had, decades before, finally lured Edward Browne from the stuffy security of Harvard to this Midwest outpost. That was when the new hospital was built, and the trustees made a permanent commitment to top quality, full-time medical staff. They recruited the best young clinicians in the country and supported their commitment with the medical office building. The building was actually the original hospital. It had been gutted out, leaving only the high ceilings and the marble floor in the rotunda, then rebuilt from the inside out. The first two floors held the expansive library, conference rooms, and auditorium. The third floor was occupied by the large medical education and audiovisual staff, and the fourth and fifth floors were made over into a set of palatial office and consultation suites for the full-time medical staff. A glass and aluminum fistula connected the fifth floor to the elevator bank in the high-rise hospital complex. The back doors of all six elevators served only one purpose—they opened on the fifth floor to accommodate professional traffic from the office building.

It was this type of foresight and deference to the physician that convinced Browne to join on in 1956. He had never been disappointed. From his large corner office, he surveyed the city coming to life. It was going to be one of those bright, cold, crackling October days. The people bustling through the main hospital parking lot were not yet suited up for winter, but they walked quickly, shoulders hunched, exhaling clouds of frozen vapor. The sun glinted off the bright work of the cars on the freeway below. The big digital clock on the Chrysler Building proclaimed 7:52. He turned from the window to his daily schedule, which his secretary always left under the glass in the center of the massive desk.

Eight o'clock–ward rounds. "Sunrise plus ten minutes," he thought to himself. Ten o'clock–pediatric cardiology conference, eleven o'clock–cystic fibrosis board meeting, twelve o'clock–executive committee lunch. One o'clock–his casual scan of the familiar schedule suddenly required more attention. At one o'clock on Thursday he always played squash in the basement of the medical office building with Harold Abraham, chief of radiology. But "meeting with Abraham" was crossed out and "Child Abuse Committee, Miss Hathaway" penciled in. From two thirty to four were eight appointments with patients, four to five the death and complications conference. His secretary was breaking in a new girl in the office. She needed to be told that squash games always take priority over committee meetings. He scowled, tapping the glass with his pen. Then, remembering the time, he donned a freshly starched white coat from the closet behind the door and walked briskly to the catwalk which carried him to the main hospital.

The sun played on the new frost on the windows, illuminating an iridescent tangle of ferns and spires formed by the ice crystals. Browne always enjoyed walking through the catwalk, five floors above the ground. Because of the windows and the temperature he always felt as if he were suspended in space, traversing time and distance between the oak paneled order of the office building and the spartan intensity of the hospital. An elevator door opened seconds after he pressed the button. The occupants were startled, as they always were, to realize that he had entered through the door behind them. He got off on six east, the pediatrics floor, reaching the nursing station at 8:01. Most of the residents and students were already waiting. "Good morning, all." He scanned the little group noting that only two were absent.

"Good morning, sir." The lounging residents rose hastily. A student was reviewing the scribbling on his note card.

"Where shall we start?" Browne directed his question to Steven Crane, the chief resident.

"You need to see Petey Blake and Lisa. Cynthia Scott came in again last night. Then we have some problems in the ICU."

"I know about Cynthia, her mother called last night and I told her to bring her back. Let's start there."

As they gathered outside the clear plastic canopy, Browne reached through the zippered opening to hold Cindy's hand and feel her pulse. A cloud of water droplets billowed from a port over her head and condensed on the plastic. Cindy looked up, trying her best to smile. With each breath the sinewy muscles in her neck pulled at her upper ribs, in a valiant attempt to make the most of each respiratory effort. She was propped upright, with part of her weight supported on her outstretched hands, the bulbous fingertips appearing strangely out of proportion to her spindly arms and legs. When she started coughing it seemed as if she would never stop. It was a deep, throaty, barking cough which made the veins on her neck and forehead bulge and her lips became a darker blue. Even the students who had not seen her before recognized cystic fibrosis.

"Cindy was discharged two weeks ago following a bout of pseudomonas pneumonia. Two days ago she became increasingly dyspneic, febrile, and developed a productive cough," reported Mike Chatterjee in a clipped English accent. His name was actually Mysore Chatterjee but he had gone by the name of Mike since his parents moved to Southampton when he was an infant.

Cindy waved to interrupt him and corrected, "I always cough."

"She always coughs," amended Chatterjee, "but the coughing became worse and more productive." Cindy nodded agreement at this correction.

Chatterjee continued, "Her chest X-ray shows a new infiltrate in the lower left lobe. We started her empirically on another course of Gentamicin."

Browne nodded and turned to the patient, still holding her hand. "How are you doing this morning, Cindy, any better?"

She was still coughing but nodded vigorously, holding up her other hand to indicate she was about to speak. "I'm much better, Dr. Browne (coughing) I don't even need to be in the hospital. Can I go home tonight?"

"We'll see, Cindy. I hope so." Knowing glances passed between Browne and the older residents.

"Dr. Browne," She motioned for him to come closer, to speak in confidence. "I have a date this weekend. It's my first real date. Please can I go home?"

"We'll sure work on it. That's a mighty important reason to get well." Cindy was fifteen. She wouldn't live past eighteen. Browne had known the family for fifteen years. They moved to the next room.

Todd and Billy were throwing crayons back and forth between their beds. Most of the crayons were on the floor. The ninety-fifth rerun of "Fred Flintstone Invents Bowling" was on TV but no one was watching. "Okay, okay, shape it up in here," directed Steven, who was leading the rounds.

"These boys are both five days post-appendectomy. They're going home today," said Muhammad El-Azir. Although his nametag said Muhammad, everyone called him Moe. Moe was short, rotund, and balding prematurely for his twenty-eight years. He had a thick mustache, thick lips, and a thick tongue which made him lisp and spit when he spoke. Browne was not inherently xenophobic, but try as he might, he just didn't like Azir.

"They certainly look ready to go. Are their temps all right? Eating? Rectal exams?" He glanced at the vital sign sheet hanging from the end of the bed. Muhammad stammered sheepishly, "Temps okay, I have not done rectal."

Browne commented to Steven rather than Azir, "Come on, Steven, all appendices get rectals before they go home, you know that."

"I did it yesterday," said Crane. "They were both negative."

Todd had stolen the stethoscope out of Bill Redford's pocket and had it in his ears, trying to listen to his own heart. Billy found this particularly amusing. "Todd's the doctor now," he said, firing another crayon across the room. The white coated party moved into the next room, with Redford to explain to the medical students that the first signs of a pelvic abscess would be detected by the routine pre-discharge rectal exam.

The next room held Petey Blake and Lisa Emmons. Browne moved to Petey's crib first, as he knew the situation at Lisa's bed would be unpleasant. "Hi there, Petey." Browne tousled his hair. "How's that arm doing? Should we get you out of here?"

"Ball," proclaimed Petey, scoring a strike with the Nerf ball, dislodging Browne's glasses.

"Yes, so it is," said Browne, ruffled. The residents smiled. It was good for them to see that the omnipotent chief was basically human.

"The fracture line is stable. His hand still works well. He is to go home today." Muhammad El-Azir tried to enunciate very clearly.

Sam Schulman, the second-year resident, decided it was time to make a few points. "Dr. Browne, this little boy has a small hydrocele. I called for his old records to see if it was present at birth, but the record room doesn't have anything. The mother said that he was born in this hospital, so we should have records." Browne admired thoroughness in his residents.

"Well, good for you, Schulman, good for you. That hydrocele was not present at birth, but I have been following it for about a year. And the reason that the record room can't find his old chart is because this baby was adopted just a few months ago."

"Oh," said Schulman. He thought for a moment. "But the mother talked as if she'd had the child from birth. I didn't even ask if he was adopted."

Browne smiled. "Right again, Schulman. You see, the natural mother gave the baby up for adoption at delivery. She never saw the child. The Blakes took the baby as a foster child. Many foster families do that to avoid institutionalization, do you see? In this case they decided to apply for adoption, and they were successful."

"Isn't Mr. Blake a rather affluent businessman or lawyer or something?" asked Redford. Browne looked at Bill Redford quizzically, as if his question had no relationship to the matter under discussion. "I mean, most foster parents do it for the money. Like a business."

"Quite so, Redford," said Browne, standing just a little straighter. "But the Blakes . . ." He paused. "First of all, Redford, the Blakes are good friends of mine, neighbors actually." He said this to prevent Redford from embarrassing himself. "The Blakes are well off to be sure, but they have a real love for children. They've had such tragedies with their own children . . ." He paused, realizing that both Petey and Lisa were listening. "I'll tell you out there." He pointed toward the door.

The news at Lisa's bed was indeed bad. It was presented in code (thrombocytopenia, marrow fibrosis, exacerbation), but Lisa had learned long ago to read the forlorn attempted smiles and the lingering touch on her forehead. As they left, she said, "Thank you, Dr. Browne," in her faint, squeaky voice, as she always did. Browne merely waved, afraid to try his voice for a moment.

The group paused in the hall outside isolation number one. Beth Bonnell came to the door to assist with the gowns and masks, but they were engaged in discussion. Dr. Browne was explaining, "The Blake family was among my very first patients when I moved here twenty years ago from Boston." He had learned long ago not to say "from Harvard," but couldn't help making reference to his heritage from time to time. "Blake was a young lawyer in a big firm downtown. They had two children, a little boy, Peter, and an infant girl. On Christmas day–it was twenty years ago this Christmas–the baby was found dead in bed. A crib death. The parents took it awfully hard. They compensated by taking in foster children, usually infants. They adopted four of them over the years–they never had any more of their own. They have a delightful family." He mused for a moment, and then continued. "They had another crib death, a foster child, about ten years ago. I remember because Pete–Mr. Blake–called me over when he found her. No one knows what causes sudden infant death syndrome, you know."

Schulman had been pondering since the beginning of Browne's discourse. He thought he must have misunderstood. "I mean, isn't it unusual to have two sons named Peter?" he asked.

"Oh, that's the worst part," said Browne, who had forgotten to finish the story. "Peter Jr. was killed in Vietnam several years ago. That family has had more than their share of problems. I think that led them to adopt little Petey here."

All of the residents–at least the American residents–had friends or brothers who died in Vietnam. They all felt an instinctual empathy and automatic affection for the Blakes.

"Well, let's see how Jason Hartman looks today," Browne said gaily, breaking the somber mood. As they pulled on the isolation gowns, Chatterjee summarized the progress. "This little boy is doing much better. His white count is up. He's eating well. His bone marrow was normal."

"Just a good old case of chicken pox," interrupted Browne, relieved at the good news. Jason was, indeed, much improved. He was sitting up in bed eating the last of his poached eggs and soggy toast. Beth took the spoon from his hand and moved the tray away. As she was taking off his bib, Benjamin Greenfield bustled in. Dr. Greenfield had a busy practice at a new hospital in the suburbs. For the last two years he brought only his most complicated patients all the way downtown to Presbyterian.

"Hello, Ed. Gentlemen. Good timing, I'm glad you are here. This little fellow has me worried." He paused to look at Jason. Where he expected to find raw thickened skin, he saw only a few red scabs.

"Just a good old fashioned case of chicken pox, Ben," repeated Browne. "You must be getting rusty with all that well baby care out there in the martini and manure belt." Greenfield ignored the jab.

"Oh, this is good, this is really good. What did you do to him, Miss . . . Miss . . . ?

"Bonnell. I just cleaned it up, Dr. Greenfield, as you suggested."

"Whatever you did, do it again." He headed for the door. "Say Ed, I'm going to send you a real interesting well baby for consultation." He was gone before Browne could mount a rejoinder.

Steven waited as the group left the room. He stood, stiffly imitating Dr. Browne, and lowered his voice. "Carry on, Miss Bonnell, just do what you did before, but don't get it wet."

"Whatever you say, sir." Her eyes sparkled. Yesterday Steven thought she was wearing eye makeup, but now he perceived that her eyes were naturally large and attractive. The rest of the entourage had left. "How do you keep the white part of your eyes so white?" he asked, nudging very close for a definitive examination.

"Pepsodent," she said, turning him around and aiming him for the door. "Say, Dr. Crane," she added, as an afterthought while he was taking off the gown, "are those girls with the burns on your service, the girls in the ICU?"

"No, they're not. Why do you ask?"

"I was in there yesterday and everyone seemed so . . . hostile to the father."

"He's a suspected child abuser. Apparently his story doesn't quite ring true. The kids are in protective custody."

"Oh, I see," she said. Suddenly many of yesterday's events fell into place.

* * * *

There was one all-purpose conference room on the pediatric

56

floor. It was called the residents' conference room, but it served as nurses' lounge, classroom, lunchroom, cloakroom, and a place to talk with families under special circumstances. Periodically some compulsive soul would clean it up, or at least push the various piles of things into some semblance of order. The green metal bookshelves along the back wall held a dog-eared copy of Nelson's Pediatrics (1965 edition), a few other textbooks that were never used, and stacks of discarded journals. The *New England Journal* at the bottom of the stack was seven years old. The green "blackboard" always bore some formula or balance diagram. The pieces of chalk were never more than eight millimeters in length and yellow chalk dust covered the baseboard and the screen which pulled down from a roller above the blackboard. The bulletin board held all manner of notes and important messages, including the list of students on rotation from the university and the patients who were assigned to them. This was the only notice which received any attention. The others were what to do in case of fire, the new autopsy consent form, the dress code, and a variety of eight-year-old Volkswagens that were for sale. The central table had been a fine piece of woodwork at one time, but it had long ago lost the hue of the grain and gained instead the rings from a thousand Styrofoam cups. The lockers along the other wall held the nurses' purses and their street shoes. The shoes–combined with the large trash can full of rotting apple cores and banana skins and the smoke of a decade of cigarettes–gave rise to the odor so characteristic of that type of room. One of the orderlies, a solid black man named Jim, was alone in the room eating the remains of his lunch when Suzanne ushered in the Washingtons.

"Jim, we need this room, would you excuse us please?" Suzanne plunked down the handful of papers at the head of the table and arranged her coat on the back of the chair. Her question to Jim was obviously more of a directive than an inquiry.

"Why sure, Miss Hathaway, sure enough." He took one more bite out of his apple and tossed the paper bag, then the apple core, into the trash can; still munching, he walked past Washington and through the door. He would have said, "Hey, bro" and offered five, but the air was electric with tension, and he substituted a slight nod instead. Two years ago he had offered a hearty greeting to a black family in that same room, only to find out their child had just died. Jim had become more cautious since that time. He closed the door softly behind him.

Suzanne was now seated at the head of the table. She indicated chairs near where the couple was standing and said, "Please sit down. The others will be here in just a minute. I think we should wait until everyone's here so we don't have to repeat ourselves." Awkward waiting was exactly what Suzanne did not want. They sat silently, looking at each other. Sally smiled weakly from time to time, patting Kevin on the thigh, trying to calm him. His face was devoid of any emotion. He sat very still, grasping the seat of the chair, head straight ahead–looking at Suzanne and Sally, and across the room, and at the door, all by moving his eyes very deliberately. To keep from looking at them, Suzanne began shuffling through the folder of papers before her. The papers didn't amount to anything, but to the Washingtons they represented the case that the professional and legal establishment was building. How did it get so thick so fast?

At three minutes after one, Suzanne moved her chair to the corner and picked up the telephone. Dialing the hospital operator, she said in a quiet but very annoyed voice, "Would you please page Dr. Crane, Dr. Redford, Mr. Heisal, and Dr. Browne and tell them that the committee"–she emphasized "the" so that the hospital operator would understand some secret connotation–"the committee is meeting on sixth north, resident conference room at this time." As she finished explaining this, Steven and Dr. Redford came through the door.

"You folks are right on time," said Bill Redford, trying to be friendly. He was still embarrassed about the events of the night before. No one offered a response, and the two doctors seated themselves uncomfortably opposite the Washingtons. Suzanne turned to the chief residents.

"Dr. Browne and Mr. Heisal should be on the way. I had hoped we could all be here promptly to avoid duplicating discussion and–" Steve Crane's beeper went off loudly. Steve had one of the older beepers that did not talk to him. He preferred it that way. He turned it off and walked over to the telephone. Suzanne waited impatiently.

"This is Dr. Crane." Someone on the other end obviously started to explain something and Steven interrupted, "Wait, wait, that's okay–that's okay. That's where I am. Yes, I've got that." Steven sat down. Just as Suzanne cleared her throat to begin again, Redford's beeper started up. His was one of the newer types that started slowly, got faster and louder, then delivered a brief message from the caller. Everyone in the room waited for the fifteen beeps to conclude then the static, then the announcement, "Dr. Redford, please go to the child abuse meeting, residents' conference room." More static.

Washington was beginning to get that feeling in the pit of his stomach again.

Mr. Heisal and Miss Whitely arrived together. Suzanne lifted her chin, shook her earrings, and said, "Well, I think we can begin. First of all, Mr. Washington, we are all very sorry about last evening. We could have done better. There are easier ways to inform a family about protective custody. Nonetheless you must learn to control your temper so that we can all help you work this thing through. You're very lucky that Detective"—she felt for the name—"Korinsky didn't arrest you right on the spot. He was very understanding." Suzanne had developed the habit of smiling slightly at the end of each sentence when talking to those whom she considered dependent or disadvantaged. She thought it softened her image and made her seem less institutional. Kevin showed no facial expression, but he was just beginning to comprehend the implication of her choice of words. "We" are going to "work this thing through" assumed that there was a problem to be worked upon, that time and meetings and little lectures would be required, and that he had been plunged into a game in which only the opposition knew the rules.

Only Sally could tell that he was about to explode. She put a gentle hand on his leg under the table, smiled politely at Suzanne and said, "Yes, ma'am. How are my little girls today?" Assuming that everyone who represented the hospital knew the minute-to-minute condition of the patients, she directed her question to Suzanne.

Suzanne looked at Miss Whitely, who said, "Well, actually, Dr. Redford?"

"They're doing fine," he said, smiling at the Washingtons. Redford always felt uneasy with social problems. "So far so good," he added, to indicate that the critical condition continued.

Suzanne started again. "All cases of suspected—" She paused looking for softer words. "All suspicious injuries must be reported to the Child Welfare Division of the County Health Services Agency. They routinely place a hold on all children whenever the circumstances indicate." She was trying to avoid stating the obvious. "Well, it's routine. You can understand." She ended with a little smile, nodding affirmatively. Sally nodded back as if she did understand.

Mr. Heisal, the assistant administrator, didn't want any more violent scenes like the one that occurred in the hall the night before. "It's just a routine," he affirmed. "Becky and Susan need to be in the hospital for the next two or three weeks." He looked at Redford and Crane for confirmation.

"Two or three," agreed Redford.

"Right," said Heisal. "So they'll be here anyway. And the hospital is covered in case–" He stopped abruptly. "Of course you can visit as much as you want."

"As much as you want during visiting hours," said Miss Whitely. She made no attempt to be sweet or tactful.

"Of course, during visiting hours. And this whole thing should be settled by the time of the hearing." Heisal pressed his chubby lips together in a little grin as if to say "that's that."

"What hearing?" Kevin turned from Heisal to Suzanne. He knew that she would answer.

"There will be a preliminary custody hearing in juvenile court in a couple of weeks. It's just routine. That gives us plenty of time for. . . for discussion and counseling."

"Until then?" Kevin's voice was soft. He was struggling to keep his composure.

"Until then, Miss Johnson at Child Welfare is the court-appointed custodian." She avoided the actual term, which was "guardian." Sally started to speak but was interrupted by the entrance of Dr. Browne.

"Sorry I'm late." The only chair left at the table was at the end, near the door opposite Suzanne. Browne assumed that this chair had been left for him and, as was his habit, assumed that he was in charge of the meeting. He looked over the group as he sat down. He had seen the Washington girls on rounds that morning and had been informed of the situation by the residents. He knew that the pattern of the burns was textbook-perfect for child abuse. He knew that the smaller girl had been beaten up as well as burned. He knew that several hours had elapsed between the injury and the time the children were brought to the hospital. And when he asked little Becky what happened, she had said, "Kevin put me in the hot water." He had been told that the father was black, and had attacked the policeman who delivered the protective custody order. In his twenty years of practice in Detroit, Edward Browne had as much experience with child abuse cases as anyone in the city. He had learned to effect external control of the anger and revulsion that boiled up within him. He had learned that emotionally disturbed parents could often be helped. He was one of the advisors to Abusers Anonymous–a group therapy session of parents who had recovered from that heinous compulsion. But the burns always bothered him the most. He had been thinking about those little girls all through the other meetings of the morning. He was barely in control as he sat down, but he appeared calm and cordial. "Let's see, I know everyone here except you folks. You must be Mr. Washington?" Browne did not extend his hand. Kevin started to, but withdrew.

"Yes, sir," said Kevin.

"And you are from County Welfare?" asked Browne, looking at Sally.

"Oh, no." Sally was surprised. "I'm the babies' mother."

"Oh, I see," said Browne. He smiled at Sally, a gesture of sympathy.

"My name is Dr. Browne. I'm sort of in charge of things around here and I am taking care of your little girls, along with Dr. Redford here and the other members of the staff. I'm sorry I haven't had a chance to talk with you before, but I was out of town yesterday." His congeniality brought a rushing sense of relief to both Kevin and Sally.

"Dr. Browne," said Sally, looking quickly at the others as if they would move to restrain her. "Dr. Browne, please help us, we don't understand what's happening." Browne looked at Suzanne and the hospital staff.

"Haven't you explained . . ."

"Nobody told us anything, except we can't see our little girls," Sally said urgently.

There was an awkward silence. Suzanne spoke, trying to regain command.

"The burns are very suspicious. They don't match your husband's description of the accident, and the little girl has obviously been beaten up. Now, there may be a perfectly good explanation . . ."

Browne took over, prompted by the bewildered look on Sally's face.

"People . . . parents sometimes just fly off the handle, overreacting.

61

We can often help these parents once we find out what actually happened from Mr. Washington here–"

"In the meantime we have to protect the children from further injury," interrupted Suzanne. For the first time, Sally was beginning to comprehend. "Kevin," she said, "is that true? Oh Kevin, could you do that?" Kevin sat speechless, tears of anger welled in his eyes. "I . . . I . . . I" his voice choked and ended in an agonizing gurgle.

Browne continued. "I've been through this more times than I like to remember. I'm sure we'll be able to help. The girls should be fine. Actually, we're lucky to pick up this problem before anything really serious happened."

"No, that's not true!" Kevin exploded, smashing his fist down on the table. He glared at Browne. His action reminded Sally of the previous night.

"What can we tell Sammy?" she said to Suzanne.

"Who is Sammy?" asked Redford.

"Sammy's my son." She dissolved into tears, hanging on Kevin's shoulder.

"We'll tell Sammy the truth, just like I already did," Kevin shouted at her, which made her cry all the harder. The others sat still, looking at her. "What is this? This is crazy!" He hit the table again.

After a silence, Suzanne looked at Browne, then Redford and said slowly, "I didn't know you had a son. Where was he during the . . . accident?"

"He was playing outside," said Kevin, still preoccupied with the futility of the inquisition.

"And where is he now?" Suzanne asked deliberately.

"He's in school," said Sally.

Kevin detected the glances between the others at the table. He thought about the cuts and bruises on Sammy's face. Before anyone could react, he stood, dragging Sally by the hand. "Come on, baby, quick." He dashed for the door and closed it behind them. Seeing three people waiting for the elevator, he opened the door marked "stairs" and ran down six flights and into the parking lot as fast as he could pull Sally behind him.

The group in the conference room sat, stunned. "Wow," said Bill Redford. Suzanne picked up the telephone and dialed the number for Child Welfare. When someone finally answered, Suzanne said, "Miss Johnson, please."

CHAPTER 6

In 1954 Hamtramck beat Pershing High School sixty six to sixty-five to win the city basketball championship. The margin of victory was provided by Gus Korinsky, who sank eight shots from the field, the most important of which was a twenty-foot one-hand jump shot from the baseline which bounced high off the rim, then dropped through the net as the final buzzer rang. He made the second all-state team. He went to Michigan State on a basketball scholarship, but quit after the first year to join the police department like his uncle and his father. Those who remembered the glorious season of '54 still called him "Clutch" Korinsky.

Gus Korinsky (now twenty-two years older but still the wannabe athlete) wadded up the glassine wrapper from the egg salad sandwich, leaned back on the rear legs of the chair, and aimed a hook shot at the wastebasket in the corner. The paper ball ricocheted off the wall and dropped in. "Two," he exalted, as he always did when he hit the basket.

Mavis Johnson tried not to notice. She sat across the desk–her desk–slowly turning pages in a folder with a long red fingernail. Whenever Korinsky was in the Department of Child Welfare in the early afternoon he would find Mavis Johnson, offer to buy her lunch, and then produce two egg salad sandwiches. Usually she would politely refuse, in which case he would eat both. They didn't particularly like each other, but she was indebted to him for several favors and he was fascinated by this young black woman who spoke such perfect English and always addressed him in a courteous but condescending tone. She was a big woman, not at all fat, but turgid without a wrinkle in her smooth brown skin. He wondered if she would maintain her aloof disdain in bed.

"Gus, you didn't tell me what happened to your lip." She smiled, exposing perfect white teeth. He licked the swollen bruise carefully.

"My lip ran into that fellow Washington that you gave me

yesterday."

"You mean the protective custody case at Presbyterian Hospital?"

"That's the one. I stopped by the hospital on the way home to put the hold order on those kids and I ran into the parents. I figured I could kill two birds with one stone so I talked to the family right there. And the father hauls off and slugs me."

"Gus, that's awful. Did you arrest him?"

"No. I should have, but that good-looking social worker talked me out of it. I'll tell you though, that guy's a mean dude. Those child beaters deserve everything they get." He licked his lip again, touching it gently with his index finger.

"Do you have anything on him yet?"

"Yeah, quite a bit." He pulled a notebook from his pocket and reviewed the notes. "He grew up here. Doesn't have a record. Discharged from the Marines three years ago. Works for Metro Buick on Livernois. Lives on Calvert Avenue. He's in the phone book. The wife–" He thought for a moment. "The wife's a white girl." Mavis showed no reaction. "I can't turn her up anywhere; I have a hunch they might not be married."

"That figures," said Miss Johnson, pulling a pencil out of her Afro and drumming restlessly on the desk. "Have you been to the house yet?" she asked.

"Not yet, I'll probably–"

The ring of the telephone interrupted his sentence. She stuck the pencil back into her hair and picked up the phone. "Hello, Mavis Johnson speaking." Then she listened, pointing her finger at Korinsky.

"Oh, hello Sue, we were just talking about you." She paused, listening. "Yes. Detective Korinsky is here. He tells me that you protected him from a nasty bully." She mugged at Korinsky. He rendered an obscene gesture. "Korinsky, the detective that brought over the hold order on the Washington children. Yes." After a pause, she put her hand over the mouthpiece and said to Korinsky, "Sue says to thank you for not running him in."

"Well, tell Miss 'Suzy-Q' I'll get him better on the outside," said Korinsky, rubbing his lip again.

Mavis returned her attention to the mouthpiece. "He says you're welcome. What can I do for you?" She listened for almost a minute while Suzanne recounted the events of the meeting. The smile on Miss

Johnson's face darkened into a scowl. "Well, that figures, that figures." Then she listened more intently. "Really? You didn't tell me that yesterday. What's his name?" She wrote "Sammy Washington" on a piece of paper. "Which school? Well, how can I pick him up if you don't know which school or even how old he is?" A longer pause. "Well, thanks for letting me know, all I can do is have some one go over to the house. Well, I know, I know. You don't have to tell me how violent he is, I can see that by looking at Lieutenant Korinsky's face." She flashed her white teeth again. "Yes, thanks Sue, I'll take care of it." She hung up the phone. "Gus." Her attitude was suddenly sugary. He could always tell when she wanted something. "Gus, there's another child in that family, a boy in school. Miss Hathaway's afraid something might happen to him."

"Well there's nothing I can do about it, till you get a court order."

"I can get an order in an hour," she said. "Couldn't you just try to find the boy before the father does? I'll cover you."

"Bullshit, Mavis. I wouldn't lift a finger without an order, and besides they live over near Division Twenty-Three. Call over there and get them to serve it." Korinsky was standing up, stuffing the notebook in his pocket, and picking up his coat from the back of the chair.

"Why Detective Korinsky." Her wry smile returned. "I think you're afraid of that man." He leaned over the desk, close to her face.

"I'm afraid I'd kill the son-of-a-bitch," he said, and stamped out of the room.

* * * *

Tom Hurley was six feet tall and husky, but he felt puny next to his partner John Jefferson. Big John had fifteen years in the Detroit Police Department and each year he seemed to get bigger. On this cold October night he was still wearing a short-sleeved uniform, his big black arms nearly bursting the seams as he wheeled the cruiser between Woodward and the side streets. Tom had been on the force for six months, and had spent two months at Division Twenty-Three. Most of this time he had been paired with Jefferson, for which he was grateful. A white cop was always tense riding out of Twenty-Three, but there was rarely a problem when Big John was along. No one ever accused Big John of racial favoritism. He was equally mean to everyone regardless of race, but there had been a noticeable decrease in street crime in Division Twenty-Three during the four years he had been assigned there. He was particularly good at intimidating rookie cops–black or white–but Hurley had been assigned to him for training, not for discipline. This evening had been unusually quiet: a family fight over drinking, one MVA with injuries, a group of kids smoking pot behind the grade school. With only one hour to go they pulled in behind the station, hoping for a cup of coffee and an early replacement. When they passed the desk sergeant he called them over. "Hey Hurley, Jefferson. I want you guys to go pick up this kid. Now this damn thing's been here for two hours and everyone's got some reason why they can't do it." Jefferson picked up the folded paper.

"Well what the hell do you expect, Sarge?" His bass voice seemed to rattle the windows. "This is a pickup on a protective custody order. Who the hell's gonna serve that at ten o'clock at night?"

"I didn't ask you if you like it, Big John," said the sergeant in businesslike fashion, "I only asked you to do it. Now, someone's gotta do it tonight." He looked aside as if the matter were finished.

"Why tonight?" asked Hurley.

"The guy that brought it over from welfare said the kid's in with a child abuser. He burned two little girls a couple of nights ago and they're worried about what he might do to this boy tonight. Somebody's gotta get over there and do it."

Hurley picked up the document from the counter. "We'll do it," he said. "Come on, John."

"Oh, there's one more thing," said the sergeant, as they retraced their steps to the back door. "This guy took a swing at Korinsky when he tried to serve him last night."

"He won't tonight," rumbled Big John.

* * * *

Both Kevin and Sally pretended to be sleeping, but neither one was. They had gone beyond talk. They had reviewed the events of the day over and over, trying to make some sense of this new torture which had been forced into their lives. Once they got Sammy home from school, and the door locked, they felt more secure. They had rationalized most of it away. There must be some misunderstanding.

66

Tomorrow Sally would contact the lawyer that had been working on her divorce. Becky would tell what really happened as soon as she felt better. Only once did Sally give voice to her growing concerns about the actual circumstances of the accident. Kevin became so furious that she quickly dropped any discussion. But the thought grew larger in her mind as they lay, back to back, staring into the darkness.

Sally heard the creak of the front step first. "Kevin, listen." Heavy steps were heard on the front porch followed by loud sustained knocking on the door. They scrambled out of bed, pulling on clothes.

"Who is it? Who's there?" shouted Kevin. The knocking continued. A path of light flitting from object to object in the living room indicated that someone was shining a flashlight through the front window.

"Kevin, what is it?" Sally joined him in the living room, trembling hands pulling at the tie on her terry cloth robe.

"I don't know, baby. Who's there?" he shouted.

"Open up. Police!" The flashlight caught them both in the eyes, dancing from face to face and blinding them, transfixed like deer in the center of the room.

"Open up!" the deep voice rumbled again. Kevin went to the door and looked out. Turning on the porch light he saw the huge figure of John Jefferson filling the doorway. His badge was at Kevin's eye level. With Sally still clinging to his elbow, he opened the door. A white officer about his size stepped in.

"Mr. Washington?"

"Yes?" Kevin was getting that sinking feeling in his chest again, the feeling triggered by a sense of bitter authority.

"I'm Officer Hurley, this is Officer Jefferson." The young man's jaw was set and he was squinting slightly, giving the impression of anger. "We have been directed to serve a protective custody order on"–he glanced at the paper– "Sammy Washington."

"What?" Kevin made a pathetic sound somewhere between laughing and crying. "Okay, Officer. Well, you've done it." He took the paper from Tom's hand. "Now get out of my house. Jesus! Coming in the middle of the night, scaring me and my wife half to death." He stepped past them and opened the door. The policemen did not move. "Get on now," repeated Kevin.

"We're here to pick up Sammy Washington–now."

"No, no, you can't do that." Sally tried to push him toward the door. "Not my Sammy, not my Sammy." She turned and ran toward the bedroom.

Sammy, awakened by the commotion, had been crouching wide-eyed by the door, and he dove back into bed when he saw his mother coming. She stationed herself in the doorway. "Please . . . He's not here. He's . . . staying over at a friend's. He's not here." Tom Hurley gently but firmly pushed her back into the room with a hand on her shoulder. He flipped on the light.

"Oh my God," he said. He pushed Sally out of the way, roughly now, and advanced toward Sammy in the bed. His black swollen lip and eye looked worse than it actually was. His right forearm was covered with long scratches. Kevin tried to run to Sally but Jefferson grabbed him by the wrist and easily flipped his arm behind his back, holding him in a hammerlock that stretched the ligaments in his shoulder. Tom leaned over the bed. "Hi Sammy, I'm Tom." Sammy grabbed onto the bedpost as Tom reached out to touch him. "Hey, it's okay, little buddy. What happened to your face, little buddy?" As he put both arms around the little boy to pick him up, Sally grasped at his feet, shrieking.

"No, you can't take him! You can't do it!" She fell to the floor in a heap of tangled sheets and blankets.

When Jefferson saw Sammy's face, he pressed the hammerlock a little tighter, causing Kevin to rise on his toes. He released his grip to get a better look at Sammy, cupping the little face tenderly in his huge hands.

"What happened to you, little guy?" Sammy stopped shaking but still looked terrified.

"He fell down the stairs," said Kevin. "He fell down the stairs in the backyard and . . . and . . . he hit his face. Isn't that right, Sammy? You fell down the stairs?" Sammy twisted around to look at his mother who was on the floor of the bedroom, weeping.

"He fell down the stairs," she said without much conviction.

"I fell down the stairs," said Sammy, looking back at Kevin. Lying to police was a fact of life that Sammy had learned from the other street children years ago.

"Yeah, sure you did, kid," said Jefferson.

"How would you like to go for a ride in a real police car?" said

Tom.

"No, you can't take him!" Sally came running from the bedroom. Jefferson stepped in her way.

"Now ma'am, we're just doing what we have to do. He's going to juvenile hall. He'll be just fine; they'll take good care of him. Just as soon as your lawyer and your social worker get this thing straightened out, he'll be right back." Kevin tried to block the door.

"You can't do this. You can't just come into a man's house in the middle of the night and take his child out of bed. You don't have the right to do this."

Jefferson pushed him aside while Tom carried Sammy out the door. "A little late for you to think of that now, isn't it, fella? These kids are lucky that somebody cares. There are places where kids don't have rights, y'know. There are places where the government doesn't give a damn."

CHAPTER 7

When the new Wayne County Hospital was built in 1914, it was said to be the largest and most advanced mental health facility in the Western Hemisphere. The site, in fact the concept itself, was wisely selected by a small group of shrewd politicians who rode to re-election on the wave of state-provided health care for the disadvantaged that concentrated on the insane, the permanently maimed, and the idiots, imbeciles, and other mistakes of nature which were never meant to survive the newborn period. The selection of this group of unfortunate patients came out of careful deliberation. It did not antagonize the free enterprise community of physicians; on the contrary, they supported it. Both the right wing scientists and left wing socializers lauded the plan because the care and study of diseases of the mind was then (as it is now) more social than scientific. The local politicians in Saginaw and Mt. Clemens and Marquette loved it, because each had fifty, or eighty-seven, or sixteen demented souls stashed away in jails or county hospitals which were grudgingly supported by their local constituents. Of course they built it in Wayne County, where it provided tens of thousands of jobs for the blue-collar voters in the burgeoning industrial city of Detroit. They built it in the cornfields in the far west corner of the county; even the most altruistic public-spirited citizen wouldn't want all those lunatics and funny folks too close to home. Then, of course, that imposing–even monumental–procession of six-story red brick buildings was situated on the main road from Detroit to Chicago at the only place where it could also be seen–from a safe distance–from the railroad. Every politician, businessman, and taxpayer who traveled through Southern Michigan for fifty years had to look at that foreboding home of ten thousand tortured souls and conclude that the governor was a very wise man.

For two generations the brooding institution provided domiciliary care–not just to the Mongolian hoards, but as necessary to the veterans, the alcoholics, the criminals, the lunatics, and the unfortunate social residual of influenza, polio, tuberculosis, apoplexy, rheumatic fever, even LSD and PCP in their time. But in the third generation came Thorazine, birth control and abortion, less congenital idiots, and the desire of local constituents to keep the now-sedated psychotics of Saginaw, Mt. Clemens, and Marquette right there at home. The big buildings closed more rapidly than they had opened. The unlighted windows, rattling doors, and unkempt lawns now presented an even more chilling aura than they did when they were full. Empty ghosts holding the ghosts of empty heads.

Two years before, there were four killings in the downtown juvenile hall. One of the victims in that particular year was the fourteen-year-old daughter of a state senator from Grand Rapids. She had become separated from friends at a rock concert, lost her purse, and was picked up at one in the morning wandering through a tough section of town. Lacking proper identification and unable to reach anyone at home by telephone, she was consigned to juvenile until morning. She never saw the morning. Both the *News* and the *Free Press* carried the ragings of her father, the governor, and the other senators for a week and a half. The result was the reopening of one of the old buildings on the grounds of the County Hospital as a holding area for children who were not charged with crimes. The drafty old wards were far from code, but the plan solved many problems and was generally successful.

It was to this place, building D of the ancient County Hospital, that Sammy arrived on that cold October night.

The desk sergeant at Division Twenty-Three had called Gus Korinsky at home. Even though it was late, he was sure that Korinsky would want to see the scrapes and bruises before they were treated. Korinsky had photographs taken and appropriate first-aid given. This big, rough detective who seemed so concerned reassured Sammy. After the usual paper work, Korinsky offered to take Sammy out to the campus (the euphemism for the old county hospital), since he lived in Livonia and was going that way. Sammy enjoyed the ride. He listened to the police radio and talked into the inactivated microphone. Korinsky bought him a McDonald's burger and seemed to know all about kindergarten and his mother and the kids on Calvert Avenue.

Korinsky explained the campus and what fun it would be. There were lots of other kids, they only went to school for two hours a day, the food was good, and his mom would visit often, probably the first thing in the morning. It sounded satisfactory to Sammy and his fear resolved to a simple question. "Why do I have to go there, Gus?" he finally asked.

"Well Sammy, we think that your daddy maybe hurt your little sisters, y'know."

"You mean Kevin?"

"Yeah, your daddy."

"Kevin ain't my daddy."

"Well, of course, of course. I meant to say, we think Kevin hurt your sisters and some folks are afraid he might try to hurt you. You're such a neat guy nobody wants to see you get hurt, y'know?" Korinsky looked over to catch Sammy's reaction, but there was none.

"Kevin wouldn't hurt no one, Gus."

"Gee Sam, he sure banged your face up pretty bad." The detective seemed to know the family so well that Sammy assumed that his information had come from Kevin.

"Mommy said he didn't mean to. I was the one who spilled the milk." Korinsky was the one who reacted.

"Aw, Sam. He beat ya up like that, just for spillin' milk?"

"He didn't mean to, Mommy said."

The sign over the entrance to the old county hospital was illuminated by a sixty-watt bulb. Driving through the massive, darkened buildings was frightening to Korinsky, who knew their history, but not to Sammy. They finally reached building D, roused the night attendant from her crossword puzzle, and got Sammy signed in. Korinsky asked casually, "Sammy, what's your daddy's name, your real daddy's name?"

"Sam Flynn, just like me," he said proudly. Korinsky wrote "aka Flynn" after "Sammy Washington" on the more important papers. Then he addressed the night attendant, a chubby, sleepy-eyed, fortyish woman.

"Now, Mrs. Aldrich, I want you to take special care of my friend Sam here, 'cause he's had a tough time of it, as you can see. Get him a nice room all for himself and a special good breakfast in the morning." Korinsky had told her privately that he didn't want to risk any of the bigger boys beating up on him until everyone had a chance

73

to examine the bruises.

"We certainly will, Lieutenant. Come on, Sammy, let's find a great place for you." She took him by the hand and headed down the dark hallway.

"Are you coming, Gus?" Sammy was suddenly losing his newfound security.

"No, Sam, I got to go home. I have boys to look after there too. I'll see you in the morning. Don't worry."

Sam and Mrs. Aldrich walked down the dimly lit hall, took a rattley elevator up two floors, and proceeded down a darker hallway. Mrs. Aldrich yawned, but didn't speak. She opened a solid metal door and ushered him into a small room. The moonlight threw shadows from the bars on the window against a cot. "There's your bed, have a good sleep, breakfast at seven." The sound of the heavy door closing echoed down the empty hallway. The metallic clunk that followed told him he was locked in. Mrs. Aldrich shuffled back to the elevator, oblivious to his terrified wail.

* * * *

"I think your hours are worse than the doctors'. Sugar or cream?" Suzanne was trying to accommodate Korinsky and Mavis Johnson in her little office.

"Black, thanks. I work the same hours for less pay."

"Cream and sugar, isn't it, Mavis?"

"Yes, thank you, Sue." She sipped, then glanced at Gus. "You earned your money last night, Gus," she said without any sarcasm.

"He's a nice little boy, that kid. He said his father's name is Sam Flynn. He said his mother"—and he was about to say "and the black guy," but he thought better of it-"and Washington are not married, so we've got em both on falsified records. I told you about the father saying how the boy fell down the stairs. Not to mention striking a law officer."

Mavis Johnson had requested this meeting. She wanted Suzanne to hear the new information from Korinsky himself. She saw no reason to bring in the whole child abuse committee. The others tended to get off on tangents anyway and these decisions were best made by the key individuals. She had decided that she had a good case for felony child abuse, but wanted to check with Suzanne on the burns. A judge would probably discount Sammy's injury to misdemeanor level, even if they got a conviction. Mavis wanted it all put together before she went to the district attorney's office.

"Do you have the pictures of the girls?" asked Mavis.

"Just the slides," said Suzanne. As chairperson of the child abuse committee she held all the evidence in cases under consideration. She opened the locked lower drawer of her desk and withdrew an envelope from the file marked "Washington." They passed the slides around, holding them up toward the light from the window.

"Oh that's awful, isn't that awful," said Mavis Johnson. "Look at the cutoff lines–and the skip areas–and the watermark on the older girl."

"How come the little one's burned so bad on the back and the bottom, but not right here?" asked Korinsky, holding the slide toward Mavis and pointing.

"That happens when they're held down against the bottom of the tub," she explained. "That spot touches the cold tub and the rest is burned by the hot water. See the burns on the back and the bottom and the heels?"

"Oh stop," said Suzanne. The thought caused her to shiver.

The door opened abruptly, shielding Mavis and Korinsky. "Good morning, lovely lady," said Steven Crane. "Did you ring for medical care or a roll in the hay?"

"Steven!" Suzanne was acutely embarrassed. She recovered her voice but remained bright red. "Doctor Crane, this is Miss Johnson from Child Welfare, and I believe you remember Detective Korinsky. Your little attempt at crude humor is not appreciated." She tugged at her blue scarf.

Korinsky grinned widely and rose to shake hands. "Hi Doc." Miss Johnson merely nodded.

"I called for Bill Redford actually," said Suzanne. "Are you taking his calls?"

"I'm taking his calls, his service, and everything else. He's on vacation for
two weeks."

"Good," said Mavis Johnson. "Then you can tell us what we need to know about the Washington girls." Steven had an old-fashioned

reverence for the doctor-patient relationship that made him cautious about discussing his patients'
conditions.

"They're stable. Still critical." He resorted to the official doctrine that would be told to anyone.

"Oh, we know all that. We need to know if they said any more about the injury, about their family. Do they have old fractures on their X-rays, that sort
of thing?"

Steven was surprised. "I've only taken over today," he hedged, waiting for more information.

Suzanne knew this idealistic side of his personality very well. "It's perfectly okay, Steven, they know the whole story. They're trying to decide whether to prosecute the father." Suzanne thought she knew him, but had actually overstepped her prerogative slightly. He remained silent.

Mavis Johnson missed this subtle interchange. "What does the burn expert say?" she asked. She had decided that she was wasting her time with a resident. "Have you had them seen by a burn expert?"

"They're both assigned to Dr. Browne, Dr. Edward Browne, chief of pediatrics," Steven said evenly. Suzanne could tell that Mavis was on the wrong track.

"Oh I know that," Mavis dismissed. "I mean, a surgeon, a real burn expert, someone who's used to testifying in cases like this. We usually use Dr. David Lower of Children's Hospital."

"I'm sure Dr. Browne will invite consultants if he thinks it is necessary. Is there anything else?" Steven turned to go.

"Yeah, Doc, take a look at this, will ya?" To Korinsky, one doctor was the same as another. He indicated his lower left cuspid tooth. "This tooth has been loose since that son-bitch hit me the other night. Do you think it's okay?" He wiggled it back and forth. Steven examined the tooth. It moved slightly.

"It'll be fine," he said. Steven liked Korinsky in spite of—or perhaps because of—his rough and ready approach.

"Thanks, Doc." He felt the tooth again for reference. Seeing that his coffee was gone, he reflexively crumpled the Styrofoam cup into a little ball and fired it into the wastebasket across the room. "Two," he whispered to himself. Miss Johnson looked disgusted and recrossed her legs, leaning away from Korinsky.

"Suzanne, I'll see you later." Steven closed the door behind him.

"He seems a little edgy, doesn't he, Sue?" asked Mavis after Steven was gone.

"He's one of our very best residents," said Suzanne. "He's probably been up all night." They all smiled at one another politely, glad to let the subject drop.

"Well, I think we'll wait a day or two until we see what else Gus here can turn up. And perhaps I should talk with Dr. Browne," said Mavis, rising and picking up her briefcase.

"Yes. Thanks so much for coming over." Suzanne led the way to the elevators. After she delivered her guests to the parking lot, Suzanne turned back toward her office. Steven and Beth Bonnell were coming out of the ICU, going over some orders. When Steve saw Suzanne he excused himself and, taking her elbow, steered her to the opposite wall.

"Suzanne." He called her Suzanne only when he was very perturbed with her. "What the hell was that about?" Suzanne removed her elbow from his grasp and backed up a step.

"I might ask you the same thing. Those people came over here specifically to get the medical information. They're carrying out an important investigation."

"It sounded more like a prosecution than an investigation to me." Only the slightly rising pitch of his voice indicated his inner excitement. "And why is some . . . social worker telling me what consultant to get? I hate people who say they 'use' Dr. so-and-so."

"I know you do, Steven." Her chin was up to maximum and her earrings were trembling continuously. She brushed by him without giving him a glance. "Honestly, Steven, some days I do not understand you." She was gone. Steven gestured as if to follow her, then reconsidered and turned around. Beth was
still watching.

CHAPTER 8

When Steven Crane had been a medical student on the cardiac surgery service, he had been assigned to the case of Otto Steigler. In addition to having coronary artery disease, Mr. Steigler had the biggest Porsche dealership in San Francisco. Of the many doctors on the busy team, Steven was the one that Mr. Steigler remembered. They often visited together early in the morning and late at night, and they would discuss the finer things in life—the Vienna Philharmonic, Oktoberfest beer, Danish pipes, and Porsches. So when an executive from Mill Valley decided to trade in his carefully preserved 1958 model for a new Turbo-Carrera, Mr. Steigler let Steven have it for six hundred dollars. Automobile fanciers can be classified into round car and square car types; the 1958 Porsche is undeniably round in every dimension. It was running better than ever now, thought Steven, as he dropped into fourth gear, purring along the freeway out of town toward Birmingham. The Porsche was black, of course, and just beginning to show the signs of three winters in Detroit. He liked the feel of it on the road, the precision of its fittings, but most of all he liked the ambiance of the leather upholstery. When he got the car he had removed the seat covers and discovered the vintage leather work, mellowed into a cordovan glow. Climbing into the spacious seat was like putting on a custom-made glove. The sun made it warm to the touch, although the temperature outside was only forty-five degrees. This being Sunday morning, the freeway was virtually empty and Steven couldn't resist the temptation to blow some of the carbon out of the engine.

The weekend football games were always in Birmingham because one of the urology residents had played football in high school there many years before, and he was always able to find a suitable field. Steven geared down as the freeway climbed out of its concrete chute onto the busier surface streets.

Eisenhower Junior. High School abutted the woods which were owned jointly by Birmingham, Bloomfield Hills, and the Northwest Riding Club. Most of the oaks still had their leaves, giving a waxy brindle brown sheen to the hillside, dashed with splashes of gold and crimson where an occasional maple had been sheltered from the wind. There was still a small farm across the creek to the west of the school. Nowadays the farmer put all his cornstalks through a shredder to mix with the pig feed, and burning the stubble was prohibited by law. But each year he gathered two great armfuls of cornstalks, baled them upright, and stood the shock in the middle of the field until Thanksgiving, to educate the children at the school and remind the neighborhood of simpler times. The farmer had chosen this Sunday morning to violate the law and burn a large pile of oak and maple leaves so that he might mix the ashes into his wife's compost pole. The bluish haze from the smoldering decidua curled lazily across the playing field and floated on its back off into the woods. It was a morning of cold air and bright sun, black trunks and golden crowns, the brittle taste of well water and the velvet smell of smoke; delicious contrasts which are unique to autumn in northern North America.

Pumpkins, cider, and honey were for sale at the weather-beaten stand on the farm next to the school. Steven decided to stop there on his way home. He directed the Porsche into the school parking lot. Either he was the first to arrive or he was in the wrong place. He examined the photocopied map again. No, it was the right place, even down to the creek and the farm. He was pleased that he had preceded his surgical friends. He took the football from behind the seat and closed the door, softly so as not to interrupt the chipmunk on the picnic table. Stu Howards was right. The field was perfect, freshly mowed and limed. In the shadows of the oaks it was still heavy and wet with dew.

Even with his hooded sweatshirt, (marked Stanford Track in faded letters) he was cold. To get warm he punted the football and loped after it down the middle of the field. The ball settled on the forty-yard line. He picked it up, dodged imaginary tacklers for twenty yards, and punted it again. It careened off the goalpost toward the woods. He concentrated on stretching his hamstrings as he ran, planting his toe and pushing off hard, sending small divots behind him. He retrieved the ball and kicked it back to the field. More cars arrived in the parking lot. Soon there were eighteen men running around the playing field. Some brought wives and children. For most residents, family life consisted of every other Sunday, and all domestic activities must go on simultaneously.

Steve knew about half the players. Jim Bishop and Stu Howards were the organizers. There was the usual group of eight other residents. Some of these brought neighbors, friends, or medical students. The game was two hands anywhere, six downs for a touchdown, no first downs, no pads or helmets. Other than that, regular rules applied but there were no referees so holding, clipping, and pass interference were part of the game. Several of the hard-core members took the game very seriously, wearing cleats, taping their wrists and fingers before the game, and practicing forearm shivers on walls and door jambs. It was a sort of football-rugby combination that satisfied everyone's need for an aggressive contact sport. Today was a perfect day for it.

Two teams were established by segregating lighter and darker shirts. There was some trading back and forth to equalize the numbers. Richard Hicks, the chief surgical resident, had brought along his next-door neighbor who was obviously a ringer. They both wore white sweatshirts. The neighbor–his name was Walter Reed–was allegedly a lawyer who bore an amazing resemblance to O. J. Simpson. Jim Bishop kicked off and Hicks ran it back to the thirty-yard line behind Reed's blocking.

The quarterback for the dark shirts was a senior medical student named Paul Ramsey. Ramsey had played four years at Albion College and quarterbacked the 1973 team which won the MIAA championship. Jim Bishop had discovered Ramsey when he rotated through the orthopedic service the year before. He had a fair arm, and he was extremely accurate. No matter how hard he threw the ball, it always seemed to arrive to the receiver at exactly the right time, nose up slightly, and settled in as gently as a hen sitting on eggs. Steven Crane appreciated this more than anyone, since he was the primary receiver in a game that depended on routinely successful intermediate range passes. They had worked out the timing on three basic patterns performed twenty yards down field, which were working well today. After about forty-five minutes of play, the dark shirts were leading twenty-one to fourteen when Stu Howards lost a contact lens and

Bishop's beeper went off at the same time. They declared halftime and sat down on the sidelines.

The sun had warmed the red brick buildings of the school and the steely water from the ancient outside drinking fountain tasted good to the sweating neo-athletes. Hicks and Reed were busily occupied drawing diagrams in the sandy soil around home plate. When play resumed, Steve found Reed lined up in a linebacker position on his side of the field. They ran the down-and-in pattern successfully twice. The second time Reed was right behind him and Steve had the feeling that Reed let him catch the ball. Two plays later they tried the down-and-out. After his fifteen-yard sprint Steve had Reed running next to him, watching his eyes and smiling. When he planted his right foot, Steve knew that Ramsey had already released the ball. He faked inside and turned toward the sideline expecting the ball to be three steps away. Indeed it was, but between him and the hanging spiral was Walter Reed, who had slipped his fake and gathered the ball in with a chuckle. Steve's momentum carried him skidding across the sideline. When Reed circled around in the end zone he was laughing aloud. For Steve, the rest of the game boiled down to a losing duel with Reed, which made the game twice as interesting for both of them.

When Steve discovered how he had telegraphed his fake and corrected for it, Reed adjusted in return. All this jostling removed Reed from the rest of play, making it easier for Ramsey to score, running around the other end on the last play of the game. It was declared the last play because Pete Strock dislocated his finger somewhere in the interior line. Jim Bishop popped it back in easily, but the combatants were exhausted and no one objected to the final score, which was tied. Taking a cold beer from the ice chest and handing it to his counterpart, Steve introduced himself.

"Hey you're good. You stuck all over me in that second half. I'm Steve Crane."

Reed shook his outstretched hand. "Walt Reed. You're pretty good yourself. Now that was fun." They turned and watched the children imitating their efforts on the field. "You must have played in college," said Reed.

"No, I ran track. A guy can get hurt playing football." They both smiled. "Where did you play?"

"I played some at Penn State before I went to law school."

"Are you practicing now? Here in town?"

"Yes, in a manner of speaking. I've been working in the public defender's office downtown since I graduated. It's pretty good."

Rich Hicks walked up between them, throwing his arm around Reed. "What a team, what defensive strategy. Walter, my man, you covered old sticky fingers like the proverbial glove."

"He sure did that," said Steve. Hicks lopped his other arm around Steven.

"Don't feel bad, Steven my man. Walter here would still be playing for the Vikings if it weren't for a little matter of a medial meniscus problem" Steven looked blank.

"Speed Reed. Almost rookie of the year, 1971." Hicks smiled his famous "gotcha" smile and took off cackling around the field as Steven chased him, trying to pour beer down his back. They were both too tired to continue it for very long. They returned to where Reed was standing. He was grinning.

"I wasn't very good," he said, but Steven remembered newspaper stories to the contrary.

"Well, at least I don't feel so bad," he said.

"My friend Steve here is a baby doctor," explained Hicks to Walter. "During the week he takes care of boo-boos and owies in the tum tum and on weekends he comes out to play with the big boys."

"That's funny," said Reed. "He doesn't look like a baby doctor."

"You're just jealous because you have to get up at five o'clock every morning," Steve said to Hicks.

"Ah, my man, perhaps you're right. It's getting a little old, lo these six early-morning years." Hicks did look older than thirty-two. He was partially balding and looked pasty white, as surgical residents always do.

"Say Steve, do you know anything about two little girls with scald burns at Presbyterian?" asked Hicks casually.

"Sure, they're on my service. Why do you ask?"

"I'm on rotation over at the Children's. Somebody called over to ask Dave Lower about those kids and he was sounding off about it on rounds yesterday. Is there a surgeon involved with those cases?" The questions were not accusatory.

"Dave Stone is the senior resident now. He's been by to see the kids a couple of times. He must have an attending, but I don't know who it is this month. They're just second-degree burns. We haven't had any problems."

"You know the guys at Children's; if they're not doing it, it must not be right. Especially when it comes to Presbyterian with that high horse pediatrician who runs the service. What's his name?" Hicks asked candidly. Steve knew he meant no offense by addressing him in confidence.

"Browne," he responded. "He does run a tight ship." The conversation was interrupted by Jim Bishop who walked up with his wife and two little boys.

"Hey, Steve! Some great game old buddy." They slapped at each other's hands. "I see you met the ringer." He grinned, indicating Reed.

"I met him all through the second half," said Steve, smiling at Reed.

"So I noticed," said Bishop. "I hope you can join us again. It was great to have you. We play almost every other weekend."

"Thanks very much," said Reed. "I had a great time."

Kathy Bishop was a petite, vivacious blonde who seemed to always be pregnant. She herded her tow-headed boys over to Steven. "Hi Steve," she said. "Would you take a look at Jimmy? I think he has a fever." She clasped her palm over the little boy's forehead in the classical tradition of a maternal thermistor. Steve dropped down to his haunches to be at eye level with the little boy. His red face, dull swollen eyes, and lethargic attitude were, to Steven, confirmation of his mother's suspicion.

"Hey Jim, you don't look so hot," said Steve, feeling his neck for lymph nodes. "You hurt anywhere? How 'bout your ears?" Jimmy was four years old. He was used to curbside consultations with Dr. Crane, or other of his parents' friends.

"It hurts when I swallow," he croaked. He swallowed to demonstrate, showing a pained expression. He scratched his chest through his Tigers T-shirt.

"Let's see," said Steve. Jimmy opened his mouth and stuck out his tongue without further prompting. When he said "Ah," his palate and uvula rose up to expose a mottled pharynx. Steve smiled, pulled out the neck of the Tigers shirt and looked down at Jimmy's chest. He had seen Jimmy playing with all the other children throughout the morning. Now he called them over. "Hey kids, wanna see something interesting? Come on over here. Look at this." A collection of boys and girls from age seven down quickly assembled. Mothers brought other toddlers. When they were all gathered around, he said, "Look what Jimmy Bishop has. It's very special."

"What is it? What is it?" They crowded closer.

"Would you like some too?" Steven teased them even closer.

"Yes, yes."

"Then you can have some. And here it is." He lifted up Jimmy's shirt to expose a flat red rash.

"Ohhh! What is it?" asked Jimmy's little brother, rubbing his own belly.

"Measles, and you can all have some."

"Steven Crane!" Kathy pushed him on the shoulders, knocking him onto his back. The children pounced on him and they rolled around in the grass.

* * * *

Everything about Becky looked better. Her eyes were clear and bright and she laughed easily. She ate all of the chicken and mashed potatoes on her lunch tray. When she saw Kevin putting on the hat and mask, she crawled to the corner of the crib, pulled herself up, and said, "Daddy's here, Daddy's here."

Kevin had not visited the hospital since the meeting with Suzanne and the committee. Every time he confronted someone in authority he seemed to dig himself deeper into a hole. He had decided to avoid such contacts altogether until Sally's lawyer could tell them what to do. They had an appointment with the lawyer on Monday, but Kevin missed the girls so much that he chanced a Sunday afternoon visit. His guess was correct. The halls were nearly empty, aside from a few parents. The ominous offices in the old solarium at the end of the hall were dark. Dr. Schulman was the only doctor on the floor and he was absorbed in the televised football game. Kevin slipped into the ICU almost unnoticed. Becky's enthusiastic greeting convinced him that he had done the right thing.

"Hi Becky," he whispered, to avoid attracting attention. The tension that had been burning in his throat melted away as he saw the joy in her face. "I'm so glad to see you. You look wonderful." There

85

were no nurses in that end of the ICU. Little Susie appeared to be sleeping. Kevin walked over to the crib and Becky hugged him around the neck. He pried her loose and held her out at arms' length. "You look so good, so good. Pretty soon you'll be ready to come home."

"See the book!" she squealed, picking up a "Tommy Visits the Hospital" coloring book.

"I see, did you do these nice pictures? My that's good work."

"She's getting to be quite an artist." The feminine voice startled him. He had not seen the nurse return to the cubicle. Kevin turned toward her, expecting another confrontation. Instead he recognized the nurse with the large, dark, sympathetic eyes who had spoken to him kindly on that first fateful day. She spoke with confidence.

"Becky is doing very well. She shows signs of healing already and she's in very good spirits."

"She sure looks good to me," said Kevin, caressing Becky's forehead.

"Little Susie." She paused. "Little Susie looks like she might be heading for an infection problem. She has a deeper burn." Kevin nodded, not knowing an intelligent question to ask. "Her bruises are better. How did she get those bruises,
Mr. Washington?"

The glow disappeared from Kevin's eyes, leaving the steely chill of suspicion. He had been lulled into security by her gentle approach, he thought. She was trying to trick him. After the episode with Sammy, he decided that he must be very careful answering questions. Telling the truth didn't help. Making up excuses was even worse. They all assumed that Susie was beaten up–Miss Hathaway had even said so. But no one had ever asked Kevin about the bruises. He would have to be very careful, he thought.

"Haven't they told you about the bruises?" He expected another contrived accusation, but she surprised him.

"I've heard what other people said; I wanted to hear it from you." Her tone was business like but not abrasive. Perhaps this was his chance to tell his version of the incident. His hopes raced forward for a moment, but he stopped himself. It's just another trick, he thought.

"When I picked her up out of the hot water, she slipped and fell on the edge of the tub." He recited this in a flat unemotional tone. He had decided that this would be the best approach to further questions.

86

"Oh, I see. That must have been terrible," Beth responded with genuine concern. Kevin reminded himself not to be fooled.

"It was," he said in the same flat tone. To satisfy her own curiosity, Beth wanted to ask about the burns also, but Kevin had become so cautious and hostile when she asked about the bruises that she decided to change the subject. They talked about the Lions game, when the snow would come, and Becky's coloring book. Gradually Kevin relaxed. Beth left him alone with the girls while she busied herself with something at the nurses' station. While she was gone Kevin put his hand through the crib bars to touch Susie's swollen cheek. She grasped his index finger and made a soft affectionate humming noise. He wiped the tears from his cheeks. He gave Becky another kiss and read her the captions under the line drawings in her coloring book. Visiting hours were over at four, but Beth didn't say anything. He left at four-thirty, explaining that he had to pick up his wife. He did not explain that his wife was visiting Sammy at the campus—a term that she had picked up from one of the social workers. "Thank you, miss," he said, taking off the mask and gown. "I hope you take care of my girls again."

"I usually don't work in the ICU," she explained. "This is sort of an extra weekend shift. But I hope I can do it again too. They're very nice girls." She smiled, and he smiled in return. As he was driving out to the old county hospital he thought to himself, "Damn they're clever. I must be more careful."

For the rest of the shift Beth was too busy to reflect on this conversation. She was worried about the smell and the blackish green spots on Susie's legs. It took almost three hours just to be sure that they both ate all of the diet that was offered. When she sat down to summarize her activities in the nursing notes, she read back through the accounts of her predecessors. Kevin Washington certainly seemed different than his description in the notes. She concluded her comments with "Father visited. Seems loving and concerned. Children also loving. Father states facial bruises occurred when he dropped the baby by accident."

She had rented half a duplex on Outer Drive when she moved back to Michigan. Her family and friends still lived in that neighborhood. Most of her books and clothes were still in the boxes she had packed in Texas.

There would always be time to complete the unpacking. On this cold night the sheets felt very good. She finished two more chapters of Chesapeake but she had to read the last paragraph three times as her eyes became heavy with sleep. She turned off the light. She thought about Kevin's response and wondered what actually happened to the Washington girls, just before her mind slipped below the horizon of consciousness.

CHAPTER 9

The fake pecan plywood paneling had warped away from the wall in several places and it was scratched where someone had leaned back in the desk chair. There were indelible coffee stains and cigarette holes in the faded gray carpet. The print on the wall—a modernistic black on blue version of the New York skyline—was slightly askew. "This place looks like a used car dealer's office," thought William VanPelt, Jr. to himself as he sifted through the mail. William VanPelt, Sr. had always said, "An automobile dealership does not have to look like a used car shop." When he died of carcinoma of the pancreas at Presbyterian Hospital six years ago, he had left the downtown Buick dealership and the Cadillac dealership in Grosse Point to his son. Bill had kept all the amenities in the Cadillac enterprise. In fact, he had added to them. There was now Astroturf on the floor of the showroom, Fortune magazine and the Wall Street Journal in the big comfortable waiting room, free loan cars always available in the service area, and classical music tapes which played automatically in the demonstrators. The same customers came back year after year. But the Buick franchise on Livernois couldn't compete with the Ford, Toyota, and Chevrolet operations just down the street. The neighborhood was changing and the method of selling cars had to change with it. Bill changed the name from VanPelt Buick Motor Cars to Metro Buick, Inc. He moved the most senior salesmen to VanPelt Cadillac and fired the others. He hired the fast-talking sales director from the Ford dealer, and he, in turn, hired the sleaziest, slickest group of college dropouts ever to sell cars. They tightened up the credit policies, increased the charges for service, and advertised on the late-night movies on TV. Sales had doubled in the last three years, but the place definitely looked like a used car lot.

VanPelt visited here only on Tuesdays and Fridays to go over the books and review the mail. Gus Korinsky had found that out and timed his Tuesday afternoon visit to coincide with VanPelt's. VanPelt observed that Gus fit right in when the secretary ushered him into the office.

"Sit right down, Lieutenant Korinsky. What can I do to help?" Bill VanPelt was expecting a complaint about service overcharges or foreclosure on a time payment. He was pleasantly surprised.

"Mr. VanPelt, I know you're a busy man and I appreciate your taking the time to talk to me. I'm here to get some information about one of your employees, a Kevin Washington. He's a mechanic in your service department." VanPelt pressed a button on the intercom and said, "Miss Jackson, please have Mr. Sweeney come to the office right away." He turned to Korinsky. "I don't know Mr. Washington, Lieutenant, but we have almost sixty employees here. Mr. Sweeney is the director of our service division; he'll supply the information you need. What's it about?"

"Just a routine investigation, routine," said Korinsky. "Boy, that's some beautiful machine," he said, looking through the glass partition at a Riviera on the showroom floor. "What do you get for a car like that?"

"The sticker price is around twelve thousand dollars," said VanPelt, guessing, "but for you, Lieutenant, we can make a very special deal." He smiled widely to suggest that he was kidding, but just in case the lieutenant was really in the market, he added, "Would you like to take it home for a day or two?"

"Oh, no sir, no sir, I'd be much too tempted to buy it. My wife wouldn't let me, understand, but I sure would be tempted."

The service director was an intense little man with a carefully trimmed moustache. He was wiping his hands on a greasy towel as he entered. "Yes sir, Mr. VanPelt, what can I do for you?"

"Mr. Sweeney, this is Lieutenant Korinsky from the police department. He's investigating a fellow named Washington. Do we have a Washington on our service staff?"

"Yes sir, we have a couple," said Sweeney, eyeing Korinsky.

"Kevin Washington. He's a colored man, about twenty-five years old. Works your day shift." Judging that Sweeney was about fifty-five, Korinsky figured he would feel more at home with the description "colored." Sweeney seemed to relax.

"Yeah, Kevin Washington, he's here now. He's a good boy—a good mechanic. What did he do?"

"This is just a routine investigation. There are no charges against him," said Korinsky. "Is he a good worker, is he a trouble maker, does he get into fights, does he drink? Anything you can tell me would be helpful."

"Well, he's been here almost two years," thought Sweeney aloud, squinting up at nothing in particular. "He knows cars. He worked as a mechanic in the army or marines or something. Spent time in Vietnam. He's a quiet fellow, keeps to himself mostly. I can't recall any fights or problems. I've never seen him drunk." He turned to VanPelt. "God knows we have enough fellows who show up sauced up. It is a problem."

"Do you know anything about his family? He has three kids, does he ever talk about his kids?"

"No, I can't recall hearing anything about his family. Does he have some money problem?" Sweeney was becoming increasingly curious.

"No, it's not a money problem. He's married to a white girl." Korinsky paused. Sweeney sucked at his teeth, but didn't comment. "At least, he says he's married. We're not quite sure . . . well, if you don't know anything more, I'll move on. Thank you very much the your information."

VanPelt spoke up. "Lieutenant, I think you should let us know what this is all about. I mean, if we have a man on our staff who's in trouble with the law, we need to know about it. We give these fellows a lot of responsibility, delivering cars and such. If he's in trouble, I need to know about it."

Korinsky thought the businessman had a right to know. After all, he had good evidence of Washington's violent temper. Suppose he blew up at a customer or a neighborhood kid. "Well sir, the investigation concerns child abuse." Korinsky knew he had planted a devastating seed. "His kids had some accidents which are . . . sort of questionable and we're investigating it, that's all." He recognized the look of revulsion on the faces of the two men. It is the natural response to the thought of child abuse. Korinsky rose to leave, repeating his gratitude.

* * * *

Kevin had been working harder than usual. He pushed through

three or four cars a day in an effort to submerge his personal problems in work. This morning he was repairing the carburetor on an old Roadmaster when he noticed a crack in one of the radiator hoses. He knew that Sweeney would okay replacing it, but he thought it best to check first. He was told that Sweeney had gone to see Mr. VanPelt. Kevin had to stop in the main office anyway, so he walked over to the showroom and went through the swinging doors to the back offices. He looked through the glass partition just as Gus Korinsky turned to come through the door. Both froze for a moment. Korinsky unconsciously rubbed his lip.

"Well, speak of the devil," he said, without taking his eyes off Washington. Kevin looked at Korinsky, then at Sweeney, then at VanPelt. The icy glare from both his supervisor and his boss told him why Korinsky was here. It was the look of hatred that he had seen on the hospital staff and on the policemen who came to take Sammy away. Telling himself to be calm, he turned and walked away, forgetting the question he had planned to ask Sweeney. Korinsky came through the door and walked past him without a word. VanPelt and Sweeney looked at each other. VanPelt turned to his intercom, pushed the button, and said, "Miss Jackson, please find me the personnel file on Kevin Washington, especially the health insurance."

* * * *

The little office of Brian Jennings, attorney-at-law, indicated just the right amount of success. It was in the middle of a two-story office building that had originally been constructed as a motel. When the interstate had taken most of the traffic from Telegraph Road, the motel had folded, and eventually the office building had taken over. Most of the occupants were osteopaths, dentists, and accountants. There were only two attorneys. It was a long way from the courthouse, but Jennings rarely got involved with trial work, so it suited him just fine.

Sally got Jennings's name from another waitress. Jennings had handled the woman's divorce and she came out with a good settlement. She had suggested that Jennings fee was, well, negotiable. Jennings had been working on Sally's divorce for almost a year. He had explained the procedure regarding desertion, and filed a missing persons search. She had visited Jennings's office twice and he had only charged her fifty dollars so far. There was no one else in the waiting room. Sally thumbed an old issue of Time while the secretary filed her nails. Presently Mr. Jennings opened the door to the inner office. He wore a Jersey turtleneck sweater that made him look paunchy. "Come right in, Sally. It's nice to see you again. Mrs. Nichols, hold my calls." He ushered Sally into the little office. After the door was closed, the secretary mimed "hold my calls" and continued filing her nails and chewing her gum.

Jennings openly looked her up and down as he riffled through a file folder. "Now Sally, we've had no response to the missing persons search either locally or nationally. It seems that Samuel Flynn just walked off the face of the earth. He must be a disturbed person to leave such a beautiful wife. I mean, a disturbed person." He smiled with one side of his mouth and pushed the hair out of his eyes. "But there it is. Now, once this search has been underway for six months, we can start to process all of these complicated legal forms." He examined a series of papers in the folder.

"Mr. Jennings," she interrupted, "I know you're working on that, but I came to see you about a different problem. The social worker said I needed a lawyer. You're the only lawyer I know and you've always been so nice." She seemed close to tears.

"Well, Sally, if it's a welfare problem, you should see the folks in the welfare office." To Jennings, social workers meant welfare. He began to write a name and address on a pad of paper.

"No, it's not that." She fought for composure. "You see, my children . . . my husband, that is, my boyfriend . . . it's gotten so confusing." Jennings paused, pencil poised. "My little girls got burned when Kevin was giving them a bath. I was at work. When I got home we called the paramedics and they took them both to Presbyterian Hospital. All the people there say that Kevin did it on purpose. But I just can't imagine that. Then the police came in the middle of the night and took Sammy—my little boy, Sammy—just took him away. He's in the County Hospital and they won't give him back. Miss Johnson from Child Welfare said that I could probably get the kids back after the hearing, but I want Sammy back now. It's awful. They lock him up out there. The other boys—" she was crying too hard to continue. He handed her the box of tissues from his desk and puffed at his smoldering cigarette.

"Now Sally, this sounds to me like a boyfriend problem. The people at the hospital are experts. They wouldn't say anything unless they knew something that you don't. I can't believe that the police would come in the middle of the night–"

"They did," she interrupted, still crying. "They came and took him away. Right out of his bed. And our girls too. They say they're in protection."

"Protective custody?"

She nodded, and then continued. "I want to do everything." She started again. "Kevin and I want you to do everything you can to help us. Nobody believes us. Nobody even listens. Whatever it costs."

The disjointed story was too much for Jennings. "Sally," he said, "tell me the name of the social worker who sent you here."

"Her name is Miss Johnson." Sally rooted through her purse and came up with a bent business card bearing the name Mavis Johnson, M.S.W. and a phone number. She offered it to Jennings. He left her crying and turned to the telephone. After a series of false starts he was patched through to Mavis Johnson.

"Miss Johnson, my name is Brian Jennings. I represent Mrs. Sally Washington. She is here in my office, telling me that her children are being held in protective custody. Now I am sure there is some misunderstanding or a simple explanation–" Miss Johnson had obviously cut him off in mid-sentence. He puffed his cigarette and said, "Yes, I wish you would," leaning back in his squeaky chair. As he listened, his aggressive demeanor vanished and he slowly swiveled the chair so that his back was turned to Sally. He listened for almost two minutes, interspersed with an occasional "I see," or "You don't say?" When he finally turned the chair back toward Sally, he was saying, "Thank you so much, Miss Johnson, you've been extremely helpful. Yes, I'll see what I can do. Thanks again." He hung up the telephone and stared at Sally for ten seconds before speaking. "Mrs. Washington, I don't like child abuse cases. You'd be better off with another lawyer. Any other lawyer." Sally was shocked.

"I don't know any other lawyer," she said meekly. "Please help me."

Jennings rubbed out his cigarette viciously, taking out his feelings on the Kiwanis ashtray. "I can get your kids back–easy–but it's gonna

94

cost you. I hate these cases."

"We'll pay anything, we'll do anything, just help us." She pulled her wallet from the bulky purse.

"Five hundred dollars up front and two dollars a minute, starting now."

"Oh, I don't have that kind of money–we have a few hundred dollars." She sighed audibly.

"It's up to you," he said brusquely. "I hate these cases."

"Oh, I'll borrow it or something. Are you sure you can get my children back, are you sure?"

"Look, Sally, let me save me some time and you some money. You want your kids back? You can have them tomorrow. All you have to do is kick that bastard out of your house, tell the folks at Child Welfare what really happened, sign up for counseling, wear a dress, smile pretty, and tell them you'll never let it happen again." He counted up the salutary measures on his fingers for emphasis. Sally sank back into the chair.

"But that's not true. Kevin would never do that. It was an accident." She said it as if she was not entirely convinced.

"Yeah, the Child Welfare folks know all about the accident. And was it an accident when he hit your little boy for spilling his milk? And was it an accident when he lied about that to the police? And was it an accident when you lied about how it happened? Right now, sweetie pie, you're in this just as deep as he is. They're gonna charge you too, y'know. Now do you want five to ten years for child abuse? Or do you want this thing to be over and your kids back under your roof? It's up to you."

Sally released a long sigh. It occurred to Jennings that she looked defenseless and pathetic. Finally, she said, "It can't be right, there must be another way."

"Lady, they hold all the cards," said Jennings, growing exasperated. "They play the song and you dance until they like it. If you have half a brain in that pretty little head, you'll get your ass down to Child Welfare and start dancing. Now that's the end of the free advice. From now on the meter's running, God dammit." He slammed his desk. "Christ, I hate these cases."

Sally rose. "I'll try to get the money. Thank you," she mumbled on her way out.

95

* * * *

In her three years at Presbyterian Hospital, this was the first time that Suzanne had been on the upper floors of the medical office building. She sank more than an inch into the dark blue carpet in the hallway. The oak door with the brass nameplate "Edward Browne, Chief of Pediatrics" was closed and locked, but the next door stood ajar. Through it she could see Dr. Browne, sitting behind his large desk, back to the door, silently studying the gathering shadows of evening. Suzanne adjusted her scarf and knocked at the open door. "Excuse me. May I come in?" Browne turned from the windows.

"Of course, of course, Miss Hathaway, please come in." He took off the half glasses that he used for reading and moved to the plump leather couch. "It's getting dark early now," he said, continuing aloud the thought he had been pondering before she arrived.

"Yes," she said. "I like this time of year."

"Hmm," said Browne, in noncommittal response. "What can I do for you, Miss Hathaway?"

"First of all, thank you for seeing me." She smiled demurely. "I wanted to bring you up to date on the Washington case, the girls with the burns—" Browne nodded, listening. "There's a six-year-old boy in the family. He's in protective custody out at the campus. He had a lot of bruises on his face when they picked him up. The father said he fell down the stairs, but the little boy said his father hit him for spilling a glass of milk." Browne winced. "The couple's not married but they claimed to be to get medical insurance. There may be a problem paying the girls' hospital bills."

Browne waved off any concern. "They'll be eligible for Crippled Children's," he said.

"Yes, that's what I thought. The family's acting very defensive. They contacted a lawyer. We had hoped to get everything solved at the custody hearing but that might be more involved than we had planned. Of course, if welfare decides to bring a felony child abuse charge, that goes to superior court anyway."

Browne was only half listening. Part of his job was to provide an audience for members of the hospital staff who considered their particular problems to be the highest on the hospital administration priority list. This was the fifth such meeting he had had today—the others involved signatures on medical records, some multi-thousand dollar piece of radiologic gadgetry, and a dispute over charges for respiratory therapy. He was hungry and he still had a long list of calls to make. He decided to make some from home. Miss Hathaway was still talking. His wandering attention settled on her long graceful neck. He decided it matched her high cheekbones, long narrow nose, and slender fingers. A few strands of her hair had come out of her pony-tail and curled around her ear, impinging on the gold earring. He suppressed a transient impulse to reach out and place them back into proper position. He already knew everything that she was telling him, and he waited for the purpose of her visit to become clear.

"If the case goes to court, we might have some problems with the consistency of our own records." Now she paused.

Here it is, thought Browne.

"Some of the nurses' notes are . . . contradictory. There's one that describes the father as loving and warm, but that's the exception."

"That's not unusual. Nurses come and go. They all see different things." He smiled.

"Also, Miss Johnson and Detective Korinsky from the Department of Child Welfare thought it might be wise to have a note from a burn specialist. She suggested the name of a surgeon that they often . . ." She was about to say "use," but she changed her mind to "consult." Her neck became slightly blotchy and she shifted in her chair, pulling at the yellow scarf. Although this was the purpose of her visit, she was obviously uncomfortable. Browne's immediate reaction was the same as Crane's had been two days before, but he covered it up better.

"David Lower?"

"Yes, I think that was the name," she said, relieved at his apparently
favorable reaction.

"Miss Johnson from Child Welfare called me this afternoon and told me some of the same information. We discussed Dr. Lower; he's on my list of people to call this evening." He pointed in the general direction of his desk, suggesting that such a list was lying among the papers. "I must say Miss Johnson was a little pushy. I like your approach much better." He smiled and leaned toward her slightly. He almost reached out to straighten her hair again. She rose with a satisfied sigh.

"Thank you so much, Dr. Browne. I won't keep you any longer. I wish all of our residents understood these problems as well as you do." They walked toward the door.

"Have you had a problem with the residents?"

"No, no, nothing important. Sometimes Steven's idealism gets in the way of practicality, that's all."

"Steven Crane? Steve's always been our best resident. Didn't he bring you to the department picnic last summer?"

"Steven's a fine person and I was just thinking out loud. I'm sorry. And, yes, he did bring me to the department picnic. You have a wonderful memory." She had turned in the doorway and was standing very close. He reached out and gently disengaged the strands of hair from her earring, a gesture which she interpreted to be primarily paternal.

"Thanks again," she said.

"Any time," said Browne. He returned to his desk as she disappeared down the hallway.

Although his heart was not in it, he forced himself to dial the number of Lower's exchange. He rationalized that it would save him a day in court. Lower finally came on the line with his best radio announcer voice. "Hello, this is Dr. David Lower." Browne tried to be cordial.

"Dave, this is Edward Browne from Presbyterian Hospital."

"Well, Ed! This is a special occasion. What can I do for you?"

"I'm calling about two little burn patients we have over here. It seems that—"

"Are you guys still holding onto burn patients? Honest to God, Ed, why don't you just send all those kids over here where we can do it right?" He had a smile in his voice, but over the telephone it was impossible to tell if he was kidding or just amazingly tactless. Browne decided to ignore the remark. "It seems that you're a popular man with the Department of Child Welfare, Dr. Lower. These little patients have the typical pattern of inflicted burns. We would appreciate it if you would—"

"Oh, great. Another child abuse. Look, Ed, why don't you just transfer them over here, send them tomorrow. Then I can talk to the family and get a look at the kids—do it up right, okay?"

Browne gave up any pretense of being congenial. "I didn't call to discuss a transfer. I called to get your opinion–"

"So I could testify and get you off the hook. You want me to look at the burns and say it's child abuse. No way! Sometimes it takes me a week just to get to know the family. Why don't you just send them over here in the morning, okay, Ed?"

"Nevermind, Lower. I'm sorry I bothered you, very sorry. Good night." Browne hung up without waiting for an acknowledgment.

He looked out the window for a few minutes, occasionally shaking his head, as if trying to awaken from a bad dream. When he had calmed down enough to move, he grabbed his briefcase and his overcoat and sought solace in the cockpit of his Cadillac. WJR was broadcasting an orchestral transcription of "Sheep May Safely Graze." Browne didn't recognize the piece. He didn't even know it was Bach. But it restored his sense of order. When it was over, he took a small tape recorder from the glove compartment and dictated a memo: "Dr. John McNamarra, chief plastic surgery, Presbyterian Hospital. Dear John, There are two little girls on my service named Washington with scald burns. We suspect they are victims of child abuse. Would you kindly see them in consultation and give us your written opinion? Thanks. Edward G. Browne, M.D."

CHAPTER 10

The rain had stripped the dogwood of its leaves and formed muddy puddles between the trash buckets. It was still raining hard when Korinsky parked in the alley. From the dry shelter of his Plymouth he surveyed the backyard. The car was gone from the garage. Good. There seemed to be no one at home. He knew Sally was visiting the hospital and Kevin should be at work. The rain came in such strong sheets and bursts that it seemed the windshield would break. He examined the keys he had picked up at Big D Realty. The brass keys were for the front and rear doors of the Calvert apartment and the big silver "Yale" key was for the padlock on the cellar doors. He selected the latter and waited until there was a lull in the storm. Squinting against the slanting rain, he ran to the cellar door hatch. The back entrance to the cellar was a pair of slanting steel doors covering a cement stairwell. He fumbled with the lock which was gritty with sand. Finally it released and he creaked open the door, hurried down the stairs, and let the door close behind him.

The air in the basement was heavy, and smelled of mildew, old newspapers, and coal dust. He turned on his flashlight and inched out onto the floor. Shining the light around the room he identified the wash tubs, and followed the galvanized pipes to the meters against the back wall. From the meters he followed pipes another direction until he came to a pair of water heaters, side by side near the corner. He inspected each one with his light. They were designated "No. 1, lower" and "No. 2, upper" in crude marking pen on the white enameled surface. There was a stack of boxes and paint cans in front of the water heaters. From the dust on the boxes, Korinsky guessed they had not been moved for some time. That was good, he thought, because it had been more than a week since the accident, and he should have come over to measure the water temperature sooner. Without disturbing any of the boxes he moved closer and inspected heater number one with his light. There was a small aluminum box on the outside of the tank connected by gas tubing and wires to the inner workings. On top of the box there was a red plastic knob which controlled the water temperature. It was set three-fourths of the way toward hot. Korinsky was pleased. The water from the bathtub today should be the same temperature as it was the day of the alleged accident.

He turned on the light on the opposite wall and was looking for the stairs up to the house when he heard a door opening. Korinsky turned off his flashlight and pulled back into a corner behind the old coal-to-gas furnace. Heavy feet scraped the top stair. With the click of a light switch a single bulb over the stairwell ignited, providing faint illumination to the corners of the basement. Kevin Washington came down the basement stairs slowly, squinting and blinking and trying to accommodate to the darkness. He didn't hesitate at the foot of the stairs, but walked directly to the water heaters. He looked at them briefly, and then moved away the boxes and paint cans in front of the one marked "No. 1." He put his hand on the side of it as if to feel the temperature, then looked around. To the side, in the shadows, he located the box. He knelt and blew the dust off the surface. A particularly hard gust of rain splattered against the basement windows and the steel outside cellar doors, causing him to hesitate and look up. The lone bulb dimmed, then glowed again as the storm played with some electric line outside. He returned his attention to the thermostat. Just as he leaned over to touch it a loud voice came from directly behind him.

"Don't touch it, Washington." He stood and spun around with his knees and elbows bent, hands and arms outstretched in the defensive position he had trained into instinct in the marines. Korinsky was three feet away. He also went into a crouch and raised his heavy flashlight to use as a weapon. He sneered at Washington. "Just make a move, buddy boy. I'd just love to crack your head with this." He brandished the heavy flashlight.

Washington experienced an emotion that was becoming familiar—a combination of fear and rage. His fingers clenched into tight fists, and he shook with isometric spasm as he fought for control. Finally, he said, "What are you doing here in my house?"

"I'm here to check the temperature of the hot water. It looks like

I got here just in time. What were you doing fooling with that water heater?" Korinsky suddenly turned on the flashlight and held it in front of Washington's face for the interrogation.

"I, I, was checking the pilot light," Washington stammered. "The, the water's cool, I had to see if the pilot light went out."

"Well, take a look, buddy boy, take a look." He waggled the flashlight back and forth. Washington clamored down to his hands and knees and opened the little door at the bottom of the tank. They could both see the blue-white flame of full burning gas jets. "I guess it's working all right," said Korinsky. He grabbed Washington by the collar, pulling him up to his feet. "Let's go up and check that cool water temperature, buddy boy." He pushed Washington ahead of him across the basement to the stairs. They went up the stairs into the entrance hall. The door to Washington's apartment stood ajar where he had left it open. "Where's the bathroom?" asked Korinsky.

"It's back here." A sullen Washington led the way to the only bathroom. The tub was an aged porcelain structure supported on rugged feet. The plumbing itself had been replaced by Big D Development a year before. They had arranged an unusually good deal on a truckload of bathroom fixtures.

"Sit there," said Korinsky, indicating the toilet. Washington obeyed. "How do you work this thing?" he asked, examining the concentric rings and handles which controlled the water.

"Turn it on in the center," said Washington. "The outside handle, sets the temperature." Korinsky turned the inner handle resulting in a blast of water from the spigot which stuck several inches out over the spacious tub. The water splattered up onto his overcoat. He stuck his fingers into the flow. Finding it cool, he reached for the outer handle. The outer handle stuck out at about one o'clock. He turned it clockwise slowly. It took some force until he reached four o'clock, then it dropped abruptly to the straight down position.

"Jesus!" he said, and jumped back, pulling his hand from the water which had suddenly become hot. He glowered at Washington. "Cool, eh?" He left the water running while he rummaged through his pockets until he found a black cardboard tube containing a yellow and white laboratory thermometer. It was graduated from 32 to 212 degrees Fahrenheit. He held the tip of the thermometer in the rushing water until the silver column no longer rose. "One hundred forty-two degrees," he read, holding the thermometer at arm's length and rotating it to get the right light on the thin ribbon of mercury. "It's only 142 degrees. Not very hot, Washington. Is that the water that you say burned those little girls? Is it?"

"It was hotter. The water was hotter."

"What makes you think it was hotter? How do you know it was hotter?" Korinsky held the thermometer up for him to see.

"It was steaming when it came out of the faucet. It's not steaming now, that's how I know."

"Oh yeah," said Korinsky, "and that's why you were down there trying to change the thermostat to make it look steamy? Is that it, fella, is that it?"

Washington was trembling. "I thought the pilot light was out," he said through clenched teeth.

"Now let's go over your story one more time," said Korinsky. "Just like you told it to me at the station a few days ago."

"It hasn't ever changed," said Kevin.

"Okay, you said you put the girls in the tub, the water was running," Korinsky pantomimed the movements as he spoke. "The phone rang, you went to answer it–where's the phone, Washington?" He went in the direction Washington pointed, finding the telephone on the kitchen wall. "You answered the phone, you talked for awhile, the girls screamed, you dropped the phone, you ran back in here." He clomped into the bathroom, switching to the present tense for narration. "You reach in and take one out. You reach in for the other one and she falls on the edge of the tub, you pick her up again and wrap 'em up in towels. Is that right?" By now Korinsky was kneeling on the floor, having pulled an old towel from the rack next to the tub.

Kevin had his head in his hands. "That's right, that's right," he said, not wanting to relive the scene another time.

"Well, Washington, it doesn't hang together. How could the water get so hot so fast?"

"I don't know. Becky pulled the handle, just like you did." Korinsky ignored him.

"And how could anyone get burned in water that's only a hundred and forty-two degrees?" Kevin started to answer but Korinsky interrupted. "Most of all, Washington, why didn't they just get out? They can walk, they can crawl, they can shout for help. Do you expect me to believe they just sat there in the hot water? It doesn't hang together, Washington."

"Well, that's what happened," Washington shouted, unleashing his rage. He reached out and grabbed Korinsky with both hands, making himself hold onto his coat and trying not to hit him. That was all Korinsky needed. He was still very agile for a big man. He shot to his feet and in the same motion delivered a powerful blow with the back of his hand to Washington's neck. The sudden pain and an inability to breathe caused Washington to release his grasp but Korinsky continued, grabbing a full fist of Kevin's hair and wrenching his head back while he struggled for air.

"Try me again, Washington, just try me again." Kevin made a series of crowing noises and clutched at his throat. Korinsky held him for several seconds, then threw him toward the tub. Washington lurched across the room and fell, hanging with his hands in the water pouring from the faucet. Gradually he drew himself up, still gasping for air. When he got to one knee, he looked at Korinsky glowering over him. In a very hoarse whisper, he said, "It was hotter than this," his hand still in the water.

* * * *

Muhammad El-Azir had studied English–in addition to French, German, and Arabic–since he was six years old. The Greco-Latin-based languages followed a general set of rules, derivations, and etymology. German had a sort of back-of-the-throat guttural quality that was similar to his native language, but English–borrowing as it does from all of these sources–was the most difficult to learn and–once learned–the most difficult and least appealing to use. *Pseudomonas auriginosos septicemia* was a typical example, he thought, as he reviewed the laboratory slips in Susie Washington's filet. He wondered what "monas" meant to the microscopist from Vienna or Leyden or London who named this bug. If this was "pseudo"-monas, then there must be "monas" and "eumonas" and "neomonas." If "auriginoso" meant yellow, then why not "aureus"? Or "verde" for green, since the cultures were basically green anyway. Why use a vague term like "septicemia" when more specific words like "bacteremia" and "fever" and "hypotension" could be used?

105

While Azir was puzzling over the vagaries of Anglo-Saxon semantics, Beth Bonnell was more concerned with the practical aspects of that saprophytic little plant. The rotten musty smell permeated halfway down the hall. The pus, which dripped on the bed from the dressings, had a bluish-green hue. During the last several days, the treatment of little Susie's burns had ranged from dressings to exposure and back to dressings again. When Beth came on duty, there were loose spirals of Kerlix gauze hanging at irregular intervals around her torso. She was lying on her back, an intravenous catheter entering the left side of her neck held in place with a heavy suture of black silk. Her face looked like that of an old man, except that her eyeballs had fallen back into the space where the supporting fat in the orbit had been. Although she was emaciated, her belly and feet were swollen. She had grown into a sort of symbiosis with the nation of pseudomonas organisms. They both had roughly the same number of cells, and both were sustained by the same metabolic sources. There was a fight for the available calories, with the bacteria and the little patient at a stalemate. Of course, the bacteria could thrive on the dead burned skin, which afforded an advantage for awhile, but the feast of the eschar was no longer adequate, and the bacterial army sent battalions into the dermis and the fat and the capillaries, killing tissue as they spread so that their multiplying progeny could feast on the wasteland.

Beth had removed all of the dressings and washed the surface off as best she could. The burns on the heels and the front of her abdomen were healed–covered with a delicately thin but intact sheet of new skin. Those areas were reddish purple in color, unattractive to the uninformed observer, but destined to return to normal in time. The back, thighs, and perineum now looked much different than they did when Beth last saw them over a week ago. Where there had been raw, red, painful open wounds, there was now a yellowish white mat, pockmarked with greenish-black holes and irregular crevices. She had seen only a few cases like this in Galveston, and those were always children who were transferred in weeks after the initial injury. At that institution, such patients were whisked off to the operating room for removal of the dead tissue, eschar, it was called. Cautiously, she pushed her gloved fingertip into the biggest of the black craters. The hole ran for an inch or more under the leathery covering, leading to a small hidden lake of greenish pus.

106

The door to the ICU opened abruptly, almost hitting Azir. Dr. Browne and Steven Crane entered, followed by the usual entourage of pediatric residents and students. They gathered outside the screen that signified the isolation area. Crane looked at his watch. "Dr. McNamarra and the surgical residents said they would meet us here at ten, after their conference. Dr. McNamarra saw the patients last week. He left a note in the chart and he's been by to see them each day since. He's not particularly happy with our management."

"I know, I know," said Browne. "I asked him to consult on these patients personally. When I saw him in the doctors' dining room yesterday, he told me that none of his suggestions were followed. That's why we're meeting here this morning." Browne looked over the top of his half glasses at the group of residents. He was clearly not pleased with the course of events.

"We're already doing most of the things he suggested," said Schulman. "IV gentamicin, cultures from everywhere, Kerlix dressings, aspirin for fever, all
those things."

Steven Crane interrupted. "He suggested we do an LP to rule out meningitis, but the child has no signs of meningitis, and it seemed unwise to run the risk of puncturing through the burn." Browne suppressed a chuckle and dug his hands into the pockets of his long white coat. He cleared his throat.

"Many years ago, Dr. McNamarra lost a little cleft palate patient to meningitis," he explained, almost apologetically. "Ever since then he asks us to do a spinal tap whenever a baby has a fever." A smile flickered across his face. "Of course it's not a bad idea–usually–and we do it whenever it's indicated." He looked again at the group over his half glasses, this time with a fatherly nod and a wink in the direction of Crane. It was a look the residents knew well, and was meant to connote, "It's a good thing we are here to keep those guys out of trouble."

John McNamarra, David Stone, and two other surgical residents came in the back door of the ICU and walked the length of the long ward. McNamarra–Dr. Mac–was a legendary figure in Midwest surgery. As a dashing young general surgeon in World War II, he had been befriended by Gilles in England. Mr. Gilles then, Sir Harold Gilles in later years. McNamarra had remained in East Grinsted for a year after the war was over, and then returned to Detroit to start his practice of plastic surgery before there was such a thing as plastic surgery. For over thirty years he had practiced 1947-vintage reconstructive surgery. For twenty of those years it was the best to be found anywhere. He eschewed cosmetic surgery, although some of the younger associates in his office had become very wealthy by doing it. He was meticulous to a fault, and took six hours in the operating room to do what others would do in two hours. His unique and ingenious method of using the skin and muscles of the neck to reconstruct the lower lip and chin (the McNamarra flap) was used throughout the world. His practice consisted almost exclusively of head and neck reconstructive operations for harelip, cleft palate, trauma, cancer, and infection. He had been the chief of plastic surgery at Presbyterian Hospital ever since anyone could remember. Although there were many more artistic and modernistic young plastic surgeons in his office and on the staff, Dr. Mac was still treated with deference, even reverence, by his colleagues. However, to a group of young upstarts who lacked the amenities that come with a sense of history, like pediatric residents, he was just another old surgeon who didn't understand modern pediatrics. It was true that he had not cared for an acute burn patient for more than ten years.

"Good morning Dr. Browne, gentlemen." Dr. Mac felt it important to address everyone by his proper title in front of patients and nurses. "Thank you for meeting with us. We're making a little progress. Do you see that tissue forming at the edge of the eschar?" He pointed toward Susie. The pink tint of the lumpy fat which was exposed where Beth had pulled away some of the leathery covering was obvious only to McNamarra. "That's what we used to call 'proud flesh' back in World War II. That's a sign of healing, a sign of a healthy wound. When it's all like that it'll take a graft just as sweet as you please." Browne had observed that Dr. Mac was given more to little homilies and references to World War II in recent years. McNamarra continued. "As long as those bugs stay out of the blood stream, they're helping us out."

Muhammad El-Azir interjected. "She has septicemia," he said, lisping over the s. "Pseudomonas auriginous septicemia," he specified, spraying little droplets that caused Browne to move back a step. "Blood cultures are positive."

"Well, there's a fine kettle of fish," said Dr. Mac, rubbing a hand through his short white hair. "I remember when we got our first batch of Achromycin. It would clean up a pseudomonas sepsis just overnight. It was much better than sulfa–much better–and of course the penicillin wouldn't touch those gram negatives. What's that new pseudomonas drug you use nowadays?" He was still looking at Moe Azir, so he responded.

"Gentamicin, sir, gentamicin. She's been on it for five days."

"And she has positive blood cultures on gentamicin? Maybe we ought to try Achromycin; it's a good old drug. We don't seem to use it much anymore." Schulman rolled his eyes, as if to say "Oh brother," and looked at Crane.

"It's an interesting thought, Dr. Mac, an interesting thought." He rubbed his chin with his palm as if he were giving serious considera-tion to this suggestion. The residents knew he was just being polite. Beth caught Steven's eye and nodded to him almost imperceptibly, as if urging him to comment. The two of them had discussed Susie's infection over coffee in the cafeteria the day before.

"What about excising the eschar?" Crane asked cautiously. "Taking it off under anesthesia–in the operating room?" McNamarra broke into a laugh–a deep rumbling chuckle that caused his nose to become even redder.

"Well, that's coming full cycle, young man." He liked Crane's naive but straightforward approach. "We did that, you know, back in World War II. Oh, we excised a lot of eschar back then." He became serious. "And we killed a lot of fine young soldiers. That's all there was to do, mind you, cut off the eschar–but we surely proved it was a bad thing to do. Take this little girl. Now you'd have to intubate her to turn her prone, then you'd give her ether, or Fluothane or one of those anes-thetic poisons to make her temperature drop. Then you open up the capillary bed so you'd have to give three or four transfusions. Then all those capillaries fill up with bacteria; why it's just like a big intravenous infusion of pseudomonas." He shook his head. "Then what do you do with all that raw fat? You can't graft it, so you put on Scarlet Red or Tulle Gras and it gets infected all over again. It's a good theory, young man, but we've made that history before. No, just wait for the separation and the proud flesh." He chuckled again, looking wisely at the surgical residents who grinned politely to support his analysis.

Bob Kline, the plastic surgery fellow-in-training with McNamarra's group, was older and more experienced than the other residents. He had completed his general surgery residency at Cornell, and spent a year on the trauma service in Dallas. He had seen the girls with Dr. Mac for the past few days and was growing increasingly concerned about Susie. "At Parkland, we used to treat this problem with sub-eschar clysis. We put the antibiotic right at the interface between the septic wound and the granulation tissue. It seemed to work pretty well. As long as you have to give the antibiotic, you might as well use it where it'll do the most good."

"Now that's a worthwhile idea," said Browne. "How do you do it?"

"Well, back there, they'd take a whole set of spinal needles and IV tubing and run in the fluids with antibiotic under the eschar. You have to put in a lot of needles, ten or fifteen, I'd say."

"What do you think, Dr. Mac?" asked Browne.

Privately McNamarra thought it sounded cumbersome and ineffective, but he was pleased that his new fellow had come up with an idea that was obviously intriguing to the pediatricians. "It's not a bad idea, not a bad idea at all," he said. "Why don't we give it a try? Dr. Kline can show us how to do it." All nodded agreement. After a few more comments the group split up, each to pursue his or her own set of problems. Beth was disappointed. No one had bothered to examine the wound she had so carefully prepared.

CHAPTER 11

The publicist for the Detroit Symphony Orchestra was experimenting with cute little titles for each program. The classicists and the music director objected, of course, but it did seem to improve the series ticket sales somewhat. The first two programs in the Thursday night series were titled "The French Connection: Berlioz to Boulanger" and "Beethoven's Bombastic Best." The program of the evening was titled "Music for Unashamed Romantics." Steven was admittedly an unashamed romantic, but he thought the idea of naming the concerts should be consigned to the summertime pops orchestra. True to its billing, the program was luxurious to the point of overflowing, but it included an intelligent blend of old world and new world selections that made for a better evening than the title would have suggested.

The program notes described Chadwick as a turn-of-the-century Bostonian. His *Symphonic Sketches* opened with a racing fanfare and evolved into a lyric section of surprising strength and beauty. Chadwick was new to Steven Crane. He was enthralled, but Suzanne found it overbearing and heavy. The guest conductor was Zubin Mehta. Although the Chadwick was very good, Mehta's *Don Juan* was superlative. Both the conductor and the orchestra seemed at home with Strauss. The expansive Mahlerian chords and the soaring heroisms brought some of the unashamed romantics to their feet. There was another piece listed before intermission, and Suzanne commented that anything would be anticlimactic after Strauss. The orchestra seemed to agree, as all except the string section left the stage. Mehta waited a long time. Twice he turned toward the audience, smiling gently, waiting for quiet. Finally the huge hall was absolutely silent.

The *Adagio for Strings* begins, pianissimo, on a single note from which it winds and intertwines continuously, gathering tension and complexity at each turn. It is a work of clever deception because the listener is caught up in a dizzying spiral of emotional intensity, given the impression of events whirling through time and space so fast as to become blurred, then jettisoned into silence just when it seems the spring has been tightened to its limit–all of this created without deviating from the glacial tempo. Everyone in the hall was awestruck, even Suzanne. She was sitting in the same position several minutes after the house lights went up and most of the audience had left to cloud the lobby with cigarette smoke.

Steven stood up to stretch. These seats–in the third row of the first balcony–were one of the true luxuries he allowed himself. Two Thursdays a month, from October through May, he communed with the masters of music, oblivious to the hospital, the practicalities of life, the seething city outside. Suzanne had recovered enough to read about Samuel Barber. Steven moved to resume his seat when he heard a voice nearby.

"Dr. Crane? Aren't you Dr. Crane?"

"Yes," said Steven. He turned back toward the stage and was facing an attractive middle-aged woman with perfectly kept blond hair.

"Dr. Crane, I'm Valerie Blake. Petey Blake's mother," she added when his face registered no recognition.

"Oh yes, of course." He smiled as they shook hands. "I'm sorry. I didn't recognize you in this setting. How's Petey doing?"

"Oh, he's fine. The cast comes off next week." She turned and called to her husband, "Peter, look who's here. It's Dr. Crane. He took care of Petey." Blake looked up from his program and smiled in recognition. He joined them, extending his hand to Steven.

"Well, Dr. Crane, this is a pleasant surprise. We were just talking about you last night, weren't we, Val?" Valerie nodded.

"Nothing bad, I hope," said Steven.

"On the contrary, all very good," said Valerie. "We were at a cocktail party with the Brownes–Dr. Edward Browne–and we were discussing little Peter's last trip to the hospital."

Blake had noticed Suzanne when he first stood up. Her long hair was released from its usually austere restraints, and she wore a tight black knit dress decorated only by a single gold pin of modernistic design. ("Asserted by a simple pin," Steven had commented when he picked her up, quoting Eliot.) Now she stood slowly, privately enjoying Blake's analytical gaze. It occurred to Blake that the combination of

Suzanne and the dress should be recorded in some lexicon to define the word "statuesque."

"Is this . . . Mrs. Crane?" asked Blake.

"No. I'm sorry." Steven hastened to introduce Suzanne. "This is Suzanne Hathaway, Mr. and Mrs. Blake." To Suzanne he explained, "The Blakes had a child in the hospital recently."

"Yes, I remember," said Suzanne. "It's so nice to see you again."

"I thought we had met you in the hospital, but I can't remember where," said Blake. "Are you a nurse?"

Suzanne smiled. "No, I'm a social worker in pediatrics."

"*The* social worker in pediatrics," corrected Steven. "And you met one another in the hallway during a sort of unfortunate scuffle . . ."

"Oh, now I remember," said Blake. "Remember, Val, when that young fellow I saw in the cafeteria hit a police officer? Yes, you were there, Miss Hathaway. That's where it was."

"Oh, I remember it well," said Valerie.

"What happened to that fellow? Yes, and how are the little girls? They were burned as I remember." Crane seemed reticent and Blake understood immediately.

"Oh, I'm sorry." He put a pacifying hand on Steve's arm. "You don't want to talk shop. I'm a lawyer, you know, and I never discuss cases out of court." Steven was unconcerned.

"The girls are doing fairly well. The older one's ready to go home. As for Mr. Washington–" He looked at Suzanne with a here-we-go-again grin. They had resolved to leave the Washington matter up to Child Welfare and not discuss it at all. She smiled back, indicating a truce.

"There was a question of child abuse," she explained, cautiously. "That was the reason for the scuffle," she nodded at Crane, acknowledging his choice of the word, "that evening when we met in the hallway. Child Welfare is looking into it."

"I see, I see," said Blake, slightly embarrassed at having started the discussion. "What do you think of Zubin Mehta?" he asked, changing the subject. "Doesn't he look like he's having fun?"

"That string piece was marvelous," said Suzanne. "I've never heard anything quite like it."

"It was beautiful," agreed Valerie. "The whole program is an interesting combination of pieces. I wonder if Mehta selected it?"

"I'm sure he had something to say about it," said Blake. As the conversation rambled through other subjects, the younger couple felt more at ease with their older counterparts. They discussed the horn section, the acoustics, the rapidly developing riverfront complex, and Dr. Browne. The sippers and smokers were starting to return when Blake turned to Suzanne. "You must have a very interesting job, Miss Hathaway. Do you get involved with all the cases of child abuse?"

"Yes, I do. But, fortunately, it's a very small part of my responsibilities."

"It must be awful," said Valerie. "I don't know how you do it." She was addressing Suzanne, but Steven spoke.

"Suzanne is chairman of the Child Abuse Committee at Presbyterian," he said. "It's such an inflammatory subject that it takes someone with a level head and a sense of fairness. Sue does a very good job."

"I'm sure she does," said Valerie. "I remember how she handled the episode with that policeman and the young couple. I'll never forget the look on that young man's face. Such . . . rage and violence." Suzanne appreciated the recognition of her efforts, especially in front of Steven, who was teasing her with his talk of fair play.

"Thank you," she said. "He is a dangerously violent man. He beat his son for spilling a glass of milk. He attacked the detective again–Lieutenant Korinsky. He's going to need a lot of help." She sent a sidelong glance to Steven as if to say, "I know what you're thinking, but this needs to be told."

"Did he actually burn those little girls?" asked Blake. His face took on a troubled attitude and he folded his program over and over, creasing it vigorously. "How could he do that? How could a man do that?" Steven and Suzanne began to speak at the same time. Steven's tone was cautionary, but Suzanne persisted.

"It certainly looks like he did. But the courts will have to decide that. You should know more about that than we do, Mr. Blake," she said.

"I try to avoid those cases," he almost growled. He had kneaded the program into a ball and was venting his internal emotion by squeezing it in his fist. He looked up suddenly, realizing that the others were watching him. He intentionally lightened his tone. "Most lawyers do, so do the judges. We should have a better way of dealing with those people." The orchestra had returned and was warming up. Another couple was waiting for the Blakes to move so that they could occupy their seats. Valerie sighed and said, "Well, let's not discuss that subject anymore. Come on Pete, we'd better get back to our seats. It was so nice to see you." She smiled sweetly at Steve.

"Dr. Crane. Miss Hathaway. I hope the second half of the concert will be as good as the first was." Blake nodded and smiled, having regained his urbane composure.

As they settled in on the velvety seats, Steve said, "I thought we weren't going to discuss the Washington case anymore."

"Well, I didn't bring it up. And besides, people have a right to know the truth." Her chin was up and she swept her long hair behind her shoulder. The house lights had dimmed and the handsome Indian was walking to the podium.

"Let's forget it," said Steven, as the applause began. The second half of the program was the Rachmaninoff Second Symphony. Steven had purchased the Thursday night B series specifically because this symphony was on the program. This was "their" personal piece of music. They saved it for making love on special occasions, floating and rolling on the lavish emotional bed of Rachmaninoff's richest of the rich. When the beautifully simple melody was introduced in the first movement, Steven took her hand and intertwined their fingers. Her hand was warm. She was not very upset.

In the Rachmaninoff Second Symphony, the melody is treated coyly in the second movement and then brought to full flower in the incredible third. Mehta was working hard to get a feeling of lyricism from the brassy young orchestra, but the adagio had had its effect on the string section and when they arrived at that singular glorious moment, Mehta simply stopped conducting, put down the baton, threw back his head, and held out his arms as if he were basking in radiant sunshine, letting the orchestral swells roll over him and recede, finally pulling himself and the audience deliciously into the diminuendo undertow. It was a magical performance. Nothing could end in such a perfectly sensuous dream, which is probably why Rachmaninoff added the bustling final movement.

While the audience was standing and shouting bravos, Steven hustled Suzanne down the row and toward the door. He rarely demonstrated such improper concert manners, but he was inspired to consummate the tender moment engendered by the Second Symphony. As they hurried up the darkened aisle, he waved briefly to the Blakes; both were applauding and smiling. The crumpled program lay in the aisle at Peter's feet.

CHAPTER 12

Achill wind skittered old leaves across the porch as Mavis Johnson mounted the steps at 929 Calvert. Sammy followed behind, on his first trip home since he left under the arm of the DPD. She pushed the button over the card reading "Washington." She took Sammy's hand and waited with her back to the building, looking uneasily up and down the street. After thousands of home visits in the sprawling ghetto, she still felt herself to be a venturesome stranger on hazardous duty. Mavis Johnson had grown up in a middle-class neighborhood in Midland, where her father worked as a research chemist. Armed with a bachelor's degree in sociology from Central Michigan, and MSW from the University of Michigan, and being black and female, she had her pick of jobs across the country. She had chosen the Human Services Agency in Wayne County because she thought it presented the greatest challenge and the greatest opportunity. But now, after five years, she was convinced of the challenge and unsure of the opportunity.

Charles Johnson wanted his daughter to go to law school. She argued well, and spoke strangely impeccable English without a hint of the rolling drawl so characteristic of the black American. This was partly because her grandfather and her father permitted nothing else in the home, and partly because her mother had immigrated from the Bahamas. Of necessity, she learned to comprehend Motown jive, studying it as one would a foreign language. But she never spoke it. She considered it to be a reversion to uncivilization rather than a subset of society seeking identity. Many law schools had courted her, but she had decided on social work instead, a decision which had precipitated long arguments with her father. She rang the doorbell again. This time Sally Washington opened the door.

"Mommy," squealed Sammy, pushing past Mavis and grabbing his mother above the knees.

"Hello, Sam. Oh, it's good to have you home." She stroked his hair and bent over to kiss him. "Hello, Miss Johnson," she said sweetly. "Won't you come in?" Sally led the way into the living room while Sammy broke loose and ran from one corner of the house to another, touching familiar objects to verify their reality. Mavis followed Sally into the room and made a quick mental inventory.

The house was reasonably clean. No pets, no beer cans, no clothing on doorknobs. Secondhand furniture, but adequate. Oriental travel posters on the walls. A large television set was standing on a table in front of the fireplace, which indicated to her that the latter was used rarely, and the former continuously. No records, no books.

"Won't you sit down, Miss Johnson?" asked Sally, gesturing toward the special Goodwill chair.

"Let's see where Sammy's gone," said Mavis, walking toward the back of the house. The two bedrooms had been staked out in the old dining room with a series of partitions. In the smaller one, Sammy was rummaging through a large cardboard box filled with toys, jackets, and assorted sports equipment.

"What are you looking for, Sammy?" asked Mavis.

"Here it is, here it is." He stood up and turned around with a plastic machine gun. *Brrrrpppp*. The ratchet noisemaker clicked over cogs as he sprayed them both with imaginary bullets. "I'm gonna take this gun back to the campus to show Ralph." *Brrrrpppp*. Sally moved forward to interrupt him.

"Now Sam, we never aim the gun at people. You know that." She held the barrel of the plastic gun aside and looked uneasily at Mavis Johnson. "It's one of his favorite toys. You know how it is with boys."

"Of course," said Mavis, walking into the other bedroom. "And this is your room?" she asked, studying the double-bed-sized mattress lying on the floor. "Where do the girls sleep?" she asked, without waiting for an answer to the
first question.

Sally hurried past her and self-consciously smoothed wrinkles in the blanket covering the mattress. "Here. The girls go to sleep here, and then we move them out onto the couch when we are ready to go to bed. Susie used to sleep in here with us,"–she pointed to a chrome and vinyl baby carriage in the corner of the room–"but she's bigger now." She smiled again, unnerved by the importance of Miss

Johnson's visit.

Mavis walked into the kitchen. Not too dirty, better than most. A faint smell of deep-frying oil. Two scraggly plants on the windowsill. No dirty dishes. She opened a cupboard door abruptly. No roaches. She opened the old refrigerator. Needed defrosting. No milk. Two six packs of Stroh's beer and assorted containers full of leftovers. The lingering odor of onions.

The telephone was on the wall next to the refrigerator. Mavis learned the most about a family by examining the surroundings of the telephone. The more cluttered the better. One point for a notepad, two points for a bulletin board, three points for a blackboard, four points for a calendar scribbled full of family activities. None of the above, she thought, noting only two business cards stuck under the black plastic phone: hers and Brian Jennings, Esq. Sally watched this professional perusal of her kitchen with concern. Miss Johnson's face registered nothing.

"This is my sun porch," Sally said. "Isn't it, Sammy?" She led the way into the windowed porch off the kitchen, and sat deliberately in a wicker chair, hoping Miss Johnson would do the same. She did. "Of course there's not much sun today." She smiled again. "But in the spring our backyard is beautiful, just beautiful. Isn't it, Sammy?" Awkward silence. "Sammy, talk to Mommy when she talks to you." *Brrrrpppp.* With a nervous laugh, she wrenched the plastic gun away from Sammy as if Miss Johnson would not notice.

"I want the gun, I want the gun," said Sammy, tugging on the handle.

"All right, but don't shoot it anymore." Mavis appeared to ignore the repartee.

"Well, you have a very nice house here, Mrs. Washington—or should I call you Mrs. Flynn?" Sally flushed. She was aware that her marital status was well known.
"Just call me Sally," she responded.

"And what's the status of Mr. Washington? I take it he's still living here?"

"Well, ah, yes, ah, for now, ah, y'know, he lives here now."

"I see. Well, you must have things to do, so please go right ahead. Sammy and I can stay for,"–she looked at her watch–"another hour or so."

119

"Can I go outside, can I go outside? Can I see my fort?" Sammy was asking his mother, but looking at Miss Johnson.

Miss Johnson responded, "Of course, Sammy, as long as you stay in the yard. You may go with him." She nodded to Sally, encouraging her.

"Oh good, let's go, Sam." Sally looked relieved at the thought of avoiding further conversation. She pulled on an old coat–Sammy had never shed his–and soon they were poking around the corner of the garage. They giggled and shouted together, climbing in and out of the clearing under the lilac bush. Mavis watched, aligning adjectives for her report. Today she was not the conscience of society, she was its eyes and ears. Her perceptions would be used to measure shelter, care, mothering, love, warmth, maturity, understanding, and a dozen other immeasurable qualities that society had seen fit to assess on behalf of the three little Washington children. Quantifying these elusive variables required value judgment, which in turn required a reference standard. The standard against which Sally Washington was to be measured was society's concept of what motherhood, maturity, concern, etc. ought to be and society's concept in this case was Mavis Johnson's concept. Usually the business of social service was to conform the benefits of society to match the needs of a misfit or straggler. In this peculiar turn of events, it was Sally who would need to conform to society, and the business of social service to decide if and when she had. Neither woman felt the weighty impact of the phenomenon, as they occasionally eyed each other through the windows of the sun porch.

* * * *

"What the hell is this?" said Bill Redford, looking at the series of long steel needles. "This baby looks like a barbecued pig." Redford was just back from vacation and full of energy.

"Sub-eschar clysis," said Schulman. "We've been doing it for a week. Actually, it's helped a lot."

"How do you know it's helped?" asked Redford. "I never saw so much soupy pus in all my life." Redford poked at the slimy surface, forcing a small geyser of cloudy antibiotic fluid from a crevice several inches away.

"I guess I mean she's still with us," said Schulman.

"Well she's *barely* with us," said Redford. "What's wrong with the surgeons? Why don't they get this cruddy stuff off here and put on some skin grafts? At least they could clean it up."

"Dr. Mac thinks that would be a bad idea," said Steve, who had been listening. He was turning half of the service back over to Redford. "There's a plastic surgery fellow named Kline who seems to know something about burns. He suggested this clysis stuff. You could probably talk him into debriding it if you wanted to."

"Why don't we just send the kid over to Children's where she belongs?" asked Redford, under his breath. The residents rotated through all the major hospitals in the city, and they were more loyal to good patient care than any specific institution. Bill Redford had the perspective of an informed observer who was suddenly dropped into the middle of a complex problem. That vantage point often afforded a much better view than that of the day-to-day and night-to-night bedside physician. In this instance, Redford was correct. "Okay, look," he directed. "This kid needs, number one, food–put a tube in her stomach if you have to, or start her on hyperal; number two, wash her up, get her in a tub, I don't care how you do it; number three, get that pus poultice off of there. I'll call Kline about that myself. Number four, let's get the surgical residents from Children's or Lower to give us a hand with this kid. Christ, this is sickening."

Schulman turned to Steven and whispered loudly, "Where did he go on vacation, Vic Tanny's?"

"He's right," replied Steven, "but Browne will never buy it. You know how he is about child abuse cases, and Children's Hospital, no way."

Redford nodded agreement. "Well, let's do the best we can. How's the other one doing?" They moved to the other crib where Becky Washington was sucking her thumb, watching television, oblivious to the precarious condition of her sister.

"This little girl's all healed up and ready to get out of here," reported Schulman. He pulled back the covers and helped Becky to her feet so that all could see the shiny red skin of freshly healed second-degree burns. "She's been up walking for two days. We're just waiting for disposition."

"Let's just send her home," said Redford. "Get the family in here and teach them how to do whatever needs to be done."

"She's in custody," Schulman reminded.

"Oh, that's right," recalled Redford. "Well, get her out of here anyway. Send her to juvenile hall or a foster home or something like that. You don't want her to watch her little sister." He gestured, indicating a fatal nosedive. "Get Suzanne, the social worker working on it. You can arrange that, can't you, Steve?" He grinned at Crane.

Crane smiled and blushed slightly in response. "Sue and I have had a little disagreement over these cases. I was sort of hoping you'd return from vacation and solve all the problems."

"You're asking me to solve sociable Suzanne's social problem?" He rolled his eyes and licked his lips. "Crane, you are a most benevolent friend, most benevolent."

"You work on the disposition of these little girls," said Crane. "I'll handle Suzanne's social problems."

"Oh, I'm sure you will, I'm sure," leered Redford. "Let's move on."

* * * *

Despite the righteous indignation of club handball champion Gordon Vineyard, racquetball was now permitted on two of the four handball courts at the Hunting Valley Country Club. Edward Browne was much less of an athlete than his agile opponent, but he needed the exercise more. This particular evening he was getting it, running from the front to the back, from side to side, while Blake seemed to be standing still in the middle of the court. The score was fourteen to six when Browne finally got the serve back. He gave up on smashing the ball and aimed it carefully, trying to gently arc it along the wall toward Blake's backhand. He was successful three times in a row, firing Blake's weak return into the far corner.

"Ed, you keep doing that and you're going to win this game," huffed Blake.

"That's my intent," said Browne through clenched teeth. He regularly lost to Blake at every sport except chess, which is probably why they remained friends. Browne bounced the ball on the floor, preparing to roll another serve along the wall. "Say Pete, have you and

Val given any thought to taking in more foster children?" Blake waited for the ball to come off the back wall, but it never did, just drizzled into the corner.

"Come on, damn it, Ed serve like a man."

Browne chuckled, bouncing the ball on the floor. "Fourteen–ten," he said. "You didn't answer my question." He looked at the wall behind him, but fired a Z serve into the high opposite corner which came down near Blake's feet. Blake hopped out of the way and played it off the back wall, firing down the alley and leading into a prolonged rally. Finally the ball snuffed to a stop in front of Browne.

"Hinder, hinder!" exclaimed Blake.

"Hinder, my ass. Fourteen–eleven," said Browne, rolling another sucker serve along the wall behind him. But Browne was off balance and this one bounced off the wall. Blake hit it off the front wall two inches above the floor and took over the serve.

"Seriously, Pete, I sure could use some help. I have two little girls headed for juvenile hall. They're in protective custody. I sure would like to find a family that would take them in for awhile." *Pong! Splat, splat, splat, splat.* Blake hit the ball with such power that it carried all the way to the back wall only one foot off the floor. Browne didn't even try for it. "They're nice little girls, Pete, but they come from a mixed racial background." The next three serves were equally ferocious. All went unanswered. At the end of the rally which defined Blake's nineteenth point, the ball broke. Browne pulled another out of his pocket and tossed it to the sweating Blake. Browne sensed defeat and vowed to go all out for the next return.

"Ed, I don't think we could take any more for awhile. Petey's still recovering from that broken arm, you know." He prepared to serve again.

"I know, I don't blame you, Pete. But I promised Sue Hathaway I'd try."

"Sue Hathaway? Suzanne Hathaway? The lady who works in your hospital and goes out with young Dr. Crane?" Blake came up out of his crouch, his arms hanging at his side.

"Yes, Sue Hathaway, the social worker in pediatrics. Do you know her?"

"We met last week at the symphony." He seemed pensive as he bounced the ball, preparing to serve. "She's a good looking woman."

"Yes, and bright, too . . ." *Splat. Splat.* "Damn."

Blake bounced the ball. "Game point," he said. "What's the name of those children you promised you'd place for Miss Hathaway?"

"Washington. Two little girls named Washington." Browne took a swing, but didn't come close to the ballistic serve. Although he had won the game, Blake intercepted the bouncing ball and flailed it against the front wall, two, three, four times with increasing intensity. Finally he smashed it into the far corner.

He stood up, sighed, and said, "I might consider it, Ed. Let me talk to Val."

* * * *

Although she was trying to be fair, Suzanne could not look directly at Washington without a sense of loathing. Three weeks of watching the pain and agony of the little girls had overcome her sense of reason. Consequently her comments were all addressed to Sally, although both the Washingtons sat stiffly across from her small desk. "And so Becky will be staying in juvenile hall until the hearing or some other settlement." Suzanne smiled at the end of this grim news, as she had trained herself to do.

"But she's my baby, why can't she come home just for awhile?" Sally was on her sixth Kleenex.

"Now, Sally, we've been through this before, you know all about protective custody and I hope you understand the reasons for it. I know you wouldn't want this to happen again." She ventured her first disapproving look at Kevin. He sat very still, only his tense jaw muscles indicating the degree of his emotional response. During the last week he had practiced saying nothing, even in the most stressful circumstances.

Sally continued, her voice shaking. "But it was just an accident. Wasn't it, Kevin? We keep telling you."

Suzanne reached across the table and pressed Sally's hand.

"Sally, we can't help you unless you start to help yourself. Didn't your lawyer tell you—"

"We don't have a lawyer," said Kevin in the controlled monotone he used to fight back his instinctive reaction.

"I thought you had engaged a lawyer. Some lawyer called up Miss

Johnson in Child Welfare." Suzanne was secretly pleased at the news.

"Mr. Jennings was our lawyer," said Sally, sniffling. "He made some phone calls and several suggestions." She looked sympathetically at Kevin.

"He suggested that I confess to something I didn't do. For that he charged us five hundred dollars. When we couldn't raise any more money, he said he couldn't help us any more. Five hundred dollars," Kevin muttered, shaking his head.

"Mr. Jennings sent us back to Child Welfare, and Miss Johnson suggested the public defender. We're going to see him tomorrow." Sally pulled out another Kleenex, her damp and rumpled one still held tightly in her fist.

"Maybe you got your money's worth," said Suzanne, cautiously. "These things happen in all sorts of families. You have to recognize that you need some help. Once you've reached that point, you're 90 percent of the way there." She looked at Kevin again, quickly, and perceived that she was getting nowhere. She concentrated on Sally. "At counseling sessions, you'll meet many parents of abused children. They can help you through this. They've done it before. Once you start into counseling, I'm sure you'll get your children back soon."

"Miss Hathaway." Kevin was straining, trying to be calm and tactful. "Miss Hathaway, we'll go to counseling, we'll do anything you say, just let us have our girls back. We don't want Becky to go to juvenile hall."

To Suzanne he seemed sincere. Perhaps he was finally going to crack and confess. "We don't want to send her to juvenile hall, either, Mr. Washington. I've kept her in the hospital just as long as I can, hoping that you'd help get this settled." She smiled involuntarily and shook her earrings. Kevin showed no response. "We would prefer to place her in a foster home. We are working on it. Especially after the custody hearing, it would be a shame to have to keep her in juvenile hall."

"What do you mean, after the custody hearing?" asked Kevin, leaning forward on the desk. "The custody hearing is when we get our children back, not when they go to a foster home. Isn't it? Isn't it?"

"The custody hearing determines the conditions for returning the children to the home. I don't know if you two will be ready to meet those conditions, frankly. Anyway, that's up to the judge and Child

Welfare. In the meantime, Becky's going to juvenile hall. We'll take her there in the morning and the nurse there will check her every day. You can visit her in the evenings. It's really not that bad." She ended with another involuntary smile.

Kevin tried one more time. "Miss Hathaway, what can we do?"

"I've told you what to do. Now it's up to you." She handed them a brown and white plastic bag with a picture of Teddy the Bear holding a sign which said, "Going home from the hospital." The bag contained some stuffed animals, coloring books, and the nightgown Susie had worn on the ambulance ride, which now seemed long ago.

"You might as well take these home with you," said Suzanne.

CHAPTER 13

Sweeney had taken to calling Washington "boy." Kevin was the last mechanic left in the shop when Sweeney entered at quarter to six. Seeing no one else around, Sweeney called out, "Hey Washington. Hey boy."

"Yes sir," Kevin responded.

"Mr. VanPelt wants us to deliver this car tonight." He tossed Washington a set of keys. "It goes to a Mr. Jensen at Riverfront Apartments. Take it down there now—we promised it at six. You can take the bus home from there." He turned and walked out without waiting for a reply. Washington was pleased. He hadn't been given a delivery job since the detective visited the dealership. Everyone in the dealership had been treating him like a leper. His friends in the shop stopped loaning him tools. Millie in the front office refused to let him use the telephone. He had received a notice in his box by the time clock saying that his medical insurance was under review. He was afraid to follow up on that. He refused to believe that all this animosity resulted from the short visit of one detective. Maybe the delivery assignment was a turn for the better.

He found the car—a maroon Riviera—in the service lot. Removing his coveralls and adjusting the paper floor mat, he directed the big machine out toward the freeway. Mr. Jensen ought to be good for a five dollar tip, he thought, turning into the parking garage at Riverfront Apartments. The Riverfront Apartments towered twenty-two stories above the northeast side of downtown. Kevin had heard you could see Lake St. Claire from the top. The restaurant up there had done a booming business until the Renaissance Center opened. Now the bar catered to the building residents only. Although it was only six thirty, it was dark when he left the Riviera in its parking stall and ascended to the small lobby.

He looked down the list of tenants until he found Jensen–1216. He was turning toward the intercom beside the locked door when his attention was riveted on another name–Hathaway, S.–1202. He stood still for several seconds. Could it be Suzanne Hathaway? What a stroke of fate. That afternoon he suddenly realized that Miss Hathaway's advice was solid. He would admit that the accident was his fault and could have been prevented. He would attend the counseling sessions. A small price to pay to have the matter settled. Sally would like that. Even Miss Hathaway would like that. He had resolved to call her first thing in the morning. It's probably another Hathaway, he thought, shrugging and pushing the button on the intercom. When Mr. Jensen answered, he said, "Metro Buick with your car, sir. I'd like to give you the keys."

"Fine. Come on up." A loud buzzer rang in the lock of the aluminum door. Kevin pushed and the door opened, giving him access to the bank of elevators. He ascended to the twelfth floor and delivered the keys to 1216. Mr. Jensen, shirtless, met him at the door. Soft music and the stale smell of cigarettes and perfume came from the apartment. Mr. Jensen had a half-consumed martini in one hand and a ten-dollar bill in the other. He traded the bill for the keys.

"Thanks, fellow, thanks a lot. Is it running okay?"

"Yes sir, it's running just fine. I drove it all the way down here myself. Just a matter of adjusting the transmission."

"That's terrific. Thanks a million. Have a good night now, you hear?" Jensen closed the door. Kevin was alone in the darkened hallway. He walked past 1208, 1206, 1204. There was a name card on the door of 1202. He stepped close to read it in the dim light–Suzanne Hathaway, MSW.

He began to reconsider. She probably wasn't home yet. She might consider his visit an intrusion. She might disagree with his plan. He turned toward the elevator, walked a few steps, then spun resolutely, walked directly to the door, and knocked loudly. When there was no response, his spirit sagged again. He knocked one more time. This time a cheery voice responded, "Just a minute, Steve, I'm coming. You don't have to knock it down." Presently the door opened widely.

"Steven, this is your lucky . . . Oh my God, oh my God!" The pitch of her voice rose, rapidly reaching a shrill cry. Her hair was folded into a towel and another was wrapped around her waist. She had opened the door with a seductive pose, but, recognizing Washington, tried to grasp at the towel and her bare bosom at the same time, leaving no way to close the door. As her shrieking became louder, Kevin became scared. He looked anxiously down the hall.

"Shh shh, please Miss Hathaway, I just wanted to talk to you."

"Oh my God!" She was at siren level now. Kevin contemplated running for the elevator, but down the hall he heard activity and two doors clicked open. Quickly he stepped into 1202 and closed the heavy door behind him. He put a large greasy hand over her mouth to silence her shouting.

"Please Miss Hathaway, I'm so sorry. Please be quiet." Her screaming dissolved into a terrified whimper. Both towels had fallen to the floor. She clutched at herself, trembling.

"What are you doing here? Please don't hurt me. I thought it was Steven, please don't hurt me." His own fear gave way to embarrassment as he started
to explain.

"I was delivering a car here." He covered his eyes, and then turned his back. "Do you know Mr. Jensen, 1216? I saw your name. I just had to talk to you. I'm, I'm so sorry. Please be quiet. I'll go; I'll go right now. Please be quiet." Suzanne took advantage of his confusion to run behind a high counter top in the small kitchen. She grabbed a brass frying pan from the wall for defense.

"What are you doing here? Get out of my house. Oh my God."

"I'm sorry, I'm sorry. I'll go. Please be quiet," Washington mumbled, feeling for the doorknob, keeping his back to her. Gradually she became aware of his confusion. He was obviously not here to attack her. The poor fellow was shaking from head to foot. He was more scared than she was. Suddenly swept with the inappropriate euphoria that follows a close brush with disaster, she began to laugh. Washington was bewildered. The more she thought about the scene, the more she laughed. Her pose at the door and her compromised crouching position touched her sardonic sense of humor. Her laughter was infectious, and Washington smiled and chuckled without knowing exactly why.

"Mr. Washington, would you be so kind as to throw me that towel, then explain yourself again?" she asked, putting down the frying pan but keeping her chin on the counter. "Don't turn around. Oh, I'm so embarrassed."

"Yes ma'am, yes ma'am," said Washington, bending over and tossing the towel onto the counter. She wrapped the towel around her like a mini-sarong. It was not a wide towel and barely provided coverage. "Mr. Washington, how did you get in this building?" she asked, cradling her large breasts in her folded arms.

"I was delivering a car for the place where I work—to a man down the hall. I came up to bring him the keys and I saw your name on the door. I'm so sorry. I shouldn't have bothered you." He chanced a look at her, then quickly turned away again. His cheeks darkened. "I'm so sorry." He moved to the door.

"Just a minute, Mr. Washington. You must have had something very important on your mind. Please wait here just a minute." Suzanne was also embarrassed at her terrified reaction. She had lost control, something she tried hard never to do. She was giving herself a poise test to regain her self-confidence. She went to the bedroom, moving backward with the towel in front of her. "Wait just a minute." She closed the door. A moment later she returned, wrapped in a white terry cloth robe, well covered, with her damp hair drawn back and held with a rubber band. "Now, what did you want to tell me?"

"Nothing that can't wait, Miss Hathaway. I'll call you tomorrow. It was just about the counseling."

"What about the counseling?" she asked, ending with the customary smile.

"I . . . I thought the counseling might be a good idea. I . . . wanted to know more about it."

"Mr. Washington, I'm glad you decided to come to me about it, even at this unusual hour. And I'm sorry for the way I greeted you at the door. I thought you were someone else." She stifled a giggle, again thinking of how she must have looked to the startled Washington. "I'm just getting ready to go out for the evening," she said. "I'd be delighted to discuss counseling with you, but do you mind if I get dressed?"

"Oh, no ma'am, no ma'am. Look, I should just be going."

"No, no. I'm quite all right now." She turned and walked back toward the bedroom, talking over her shoulder. "Have a seat." She indicated a blue brocade chair as she walked by. "I'll just be a minute. God, now that you're here, we might as well have a talk. Sit down, sit down." She disappeared into the bedroom, leaving the door ajar.

"How do you get home when you deliver a car?" she asked, her voice accompanied by the sounds of drawers sliding in and out.

"I take the bus. It's not far. I make good tips delivering cars." Washington sat awkwardly on the hard armchair. As he spoke he looked toward the bedroom and his voice trailed off. Through the crack in the door he could see the full-length mirror which formed the closet door. Reflected in the mirror Suzanne came in and out of view, dressing. Washington tried to look away, but could not for very long.

The voice from the bedroom continued. "I'm certainly glad you decided to help us. That will make things much easier on Sally. And of course on the girls. It's definitely a wise decision on your part." He wondered if she realized he was watching. He decided she didn't.

"What decision, Miss Hathaway?"

"Your decision to finally tell us about the burns. Once you admit the problem, you're halfway toward rehabilitation."

The familiar feeling of bitterness welled up, extinguishing any subconscious sexual arousal. "She's playing me along. Nothing's changed," he thought to himself. She had turned her back to the mirror and stepped into a pair of black panties, fitting and smoothing them over her hips with her palms.

"Many parents get over-emotional and over-reactive," she was saying. "As long as you recognize that we can help . . ." Her voice was becoming more businesslike as she tired of her own self-confidence game.

"That's not what I meant, that's not what I meant at all," said Washington in a low voice, talking more to himself than to Suzanne.

"Child abuse is a big problem, bigger than most of us realize." She turned, settling into a black lace bra.

Trembling under the influence of a combination of hormones, he thought, "I never should have come here. She's just trying to get me to say I burned the girls."

"Of course, hitting a child is one thing," she continued, pulling a dress over her head, her tone becoming more metallic. "But burning a child is hideous–hideous." As she said this she opened the door, adjusting a bracelet, talking directly to Washington. He was sure she was taunting him. He reached the bedroom in three strides.

"I didn't do it!" he shouted. "I didn't do it. Don't you ever say that."

"Why, Mr. Washington." She was smiling uneasily.

"You bitch," he said through a tetanic jaw. In frustration he threw her onto the bed, holding her down by her long hair.

A key turned in the lock and the door opened. "Sue? Ready to go?"

"Steven!"

Steven ran to the bedroom and stopped abruptly in the doorway, shocked.

The appearance of Steven Crane brought Washington back to reality instantaneously. He looked down at Suzanne and up at Crane, realizing that explanation was hopeless. Flight now was his only thought. He took advantage of Crane's momentary disbelief to throw a crushing block into Steven, knocking him sprawling into the middle of the living room. Without breaking stride, Washington hurdled over him, opened the door, and disappeared down the hall. By the time Crane regained his feet, the door was closed and Suzanne was calling his name again. He decided to forget the chase and went into the bedroom. Suzanne was sitting on the bed. He gathered the blanket around her and sat on the bed holding her tightly, kissing her forehead, and muttering, "It's okay" until the shaking stopped.

After a minute, Steven reached over to pick up the telephone. "What are you doing?" she asked.

"I'm going to call the police, of course." He began to dial. She pushed down the button.

"No, Steven, wait." She sighed several times and began again when her voice was stable. "It was my fault. I let him in. I thought it was you. I was . . . in my bathrobe. He came to talk about the burns. He said he was sorry and he wanted counseling. He was in the living room and I was getting dressed. We were having a good talk. Then all of a sudden he was in here. He was just furious, seething. Oh Steven, it was awful." The shaking began again.

"Well whatever it was, he should be picked up and locked up. That guy's a menace." Crane started dialing again.

"No, Steven, don't. I never should have let him in. We know where to find him, he won't run away. Please Steven."

"Honestly, Suzanne, sometimes I do not understand you." She recognized her own rejoinder coming back to cheer her up. She smiled in recognition.

"Just hold on to me," she said, pulling him down onto the bed.

* * * *

The offices of the Wayne County District Attorney occupied two floors in the county court house. There was a definite hierarchy of offices based on an unwritten formula which combined seniority and accomplishment.

Deputy District Attorney Norma Baldridge had moved from the inner core (no windows), to the west side (hot in summer), to the east side. The next and final step would be the north end. Few of the deputy DAs ever made it to the north end; most went from the east side to judgeships, public office, or full-time teaching at the University of Detroit Law School. By chance, the day that Mavis Johnson and Gus Korinsky had an appointment was also her forty-ninth birthday. Just before they walked in, she had her fourth unmistakable hot flash. Mavis had observed that female prosecutors got the most convictions and the heaviest sentences in child abuse cases, so she had arranged through secretarial friends in the main office to get either Rollins or Baldridge. They had worked together before, and Norma Baldridge knew what was coming.

"Hello again, Miss Johnson, it's been some time hasn't it?" She stood as they exchanged greetings.

"Yes, Mrs. Baldridge, it's good to see you again. This is Lieutenant Gus Korinsky from the police department juvenile division. He's been investigating the case we'd like to discuss."

"Could it be another child abuse case?" asked Baldridge. Mavis smiled, putting the thick folder in front of the prosecutor.

"Why else would we come to see you?" she asked. "This is an interesting case. There's no question of the child abuse. The problem is whether to go straight to felony charges. We have a man with recurrent violent behavior, but nothing to support a conviction aside from the episode itself." Baldridge remembered that this was the social worker who spoke in legal terms and always did her homework.

"Tell me about it," she said, leaning back in her chair and subconsciously fanning herself with a note pad.

Mavis recounted the story in precise sentences. She included the home conditions, the fraudulent marriage, and the recent encounter in

Suzanne's apartment. She described Sally as a naive, simple girl with a flat affect who lacked the foundation to function as an independent mother. She reported the score of minus six on the Manifestations of Parent Responsibility Index as "embarrassingly low–indicative of inadequacy at coping with ongoing dynamic social interaction."

Korinsky described his encounters with Washington and Sammy, and the results of his various investigations, ending with "and finally, there was some note in his military record about an automobile accident involving children. We've called for the full details." Baldridge had listened to most of the description, but this was a familiar story and her mind wandered into concern over advancing age, and dreading the inevitable birthday dinner at home.

"Well, it all centers on that burn injury," she said, zeroing in on the critical issue in characteristic fashion. "The rest is all corroborative. Some of it's very strong, but it doesn't amount to a felony charge. But if the burn evidence is solid, then we have it. Tell me again what happened?"

She yawned and read the top page of Mavis' summary while Mavis spoke.

"Washington says he was giving the girls a bath. He left the bathroom to answer the telephone or something and when he returned the hot water was running on the children. Several hours later, when he got worried about the blisters, he called the paramedics. The paramedics said the little girl looked awful when they arrived. She had signs of a beating around the head and neck, and burns that were six to twelve hours old. All the doctors say the burns are typical inflicted scald burns that had to be caused by prolonged immersion in very hot water. Gus measured the water from the tap. It was a hundred and forty-two degrees. Not very hot."

"When did you measure the water temperature?" interrupted Baldridge. "On the night they were admitted?"

"No, it was later. About a week later," admitted Korinsky.

"That won't stand up on a cross examination. We'll have to be careful how that gets presented." Mavis felt a surge of optimism. Baldridge was going to take the case. "If he did submerge them, where did he do it, in the tub?"

"In a tub," said Mavis. "The little one has an island of normal skin on her back. The only way that can happen is if someone's holding her down in hot water against the bottom of a cool container like a tub. The older one is an obvious immersion burn with water lines just below the knees. Gus found a big metal trash can in Washington's apartment that he might have used."

"Damn, that's horrible. Any witnesses? Where was the mother?"

"The story is that the mother was at work. No witnesses except the victims."

"How old are the girls?"

"Thirteen months and two years."

"What does the two-year-old say?"

"She says, 'Daddy burned me in the tub.'"

"That could mean anything from a two year old," said Baldridge, "but it'll only mean one thing to a jury. Is there any defense?"

"They had a lawyer but ran out of money. The last word is the public
defender's office."

"Who's taking it?" Baldridge waved it off as soon as she had said it. "Nevermind, nevermind. It doesn't matter. We can deal with anybody down there. How 'bout experts and documentation?"

"That's up to you," said Mavis. "We tried to get Dr. Lower involved, but there was some sort of conflict with the physician in charge."

"Really? Who's the physician? Is he trying to hide something?"

"It's a Dr. Edward Browne. He's chief of pediatrics at Presbyterian. I think he's all right, just some cross-town rivalry."

Baldridge smiled. The damn doctors are worse than the lawyers, she thought to herself. "Did Browne report the case?" she asked.

"No. The case was reported by a Dr. Stone. He's the surgery resident who saw the babies on admission."

"Anyone else involved? Any other doctors or family members? Anyone who'd give us trouble on the stand?"

"Lots of other people in the hospital, but they're all very supportive. All except for a pediatrician named Crane. He seemed a little arrogant. But everyone else is fine."

Baldridge fanned herself and looked through the stack of papers once again. "It's a good case," she said. "Let's go for it."

"I'm for it," said Korinsky, speaking up for the first time in minutes. "But I've got some loose ends. Motive, first of all. Oh, I know those child abusers are all crazy, but we might be able to turn up something a little more specific. Then there's the matter of a real expert witness. We could get shot down on that one. I'm still waiting for the records from the Marines. And on top of that, the guy's getting crazier every day. I think he'll flip out or confess at the custody hearing and that'll save us all a lot of time in court."

"Makes sense, Lieutenant," said Baldridge. "If you line him up against the mother at the custody hearing he just might do that. When is the hearing?"

"Next week."

"Terrific. Let's get the papers together, but we'll hold any charges until after the hearing, then we'll know which way to go." She stood with a sigh. "Now I'm going home to a birthday party. I'd just as soon forget it, but my family won't let me. Thanks for coming by. That's a very nice job," she said, tapping the thick folder on her desk. "This is the way the system ought to work."

* * * *

Sally was awakened at quarter after eight by the persistent nudging of a full bladder. She stumbled in and out of the bathroom without getting her eyes fully open. Only when she climbed back into bed did she realize that Kevin was still there. "Kevin, Kevin, wake up, you're late for work." He wasn't sleeping.
"I'm not late for work," he said softly.

"Of course you are, it's eight fifteen. Hurry up. You can take the car."

"They fired me yesterday."

"Oh no, Kevin." She flopped back onto the bed looking at the ceiling. "Was it that social worker? Is that what that trap was all about?" Kevin had told Sally a modified version of the episode in Suzanne's apartment.

"No, they didn't even know about that, at least they didn't say anything about it. Sweeney said VanPelt wanted me fired. He said it was because I lied about the medical insurance. I don't know why, they just fired me."

"But Kevin, they can't do that. They have to give you notice or something. And what about the union?"

"They gave me two weeks extra pay. The union guy said he heard I was in trouble with the law; he wouldn't have anything to do with it." They lay without moving, listening to the refrigerator hum to the freeway. Finally Kevin said, "You know, baby, I've been thinking that I should just move out of here. Make a big deal, y'know, like we've had a fight. Then you could get the kids back right away and I'd come see 'em, y'know, at night or sometime. And when this whole thing's quieted down, then we'll get married like we planned." In the past when Kevin had suggested this, she had remonstrated loudly. This time she was silent.

A minute passed, then Sally said, "I guess you're right, it might be best for the children. It just kills me to see Becky in that place." More silence.

Kevin sat up. "Well, let's do it then." He sighed. "You call that Miss Johnson this morning and tell her what a bad guy I am. Tell her we had a big fight and I'm gone forever. You'll have the kids home by tonight." He rolled his feet over the edge of the bed.

"Wait, Kevin, not yet." She held his arm and he sagged back onto the pillow. They were both beyond tears.

CHAPTER 14

Petronella Batts was much more than the average dietitian. Her uncle had been a chef on the *SS France*. In fact, he personally prepared the sensuously subtle chestnut purée that accompanied the pheasant on the very last captain's table. After a short tour in a posh Caribbean resort hotel, he was called to direct the kitchens of the venerable Harvard Club on Commonwealth Avenue–with the opportunity to prepare special dinners at the Tavern Club downtown. The former appealed to his economic needs, and the latter to his sense of culinary art. His English composure matched the staid security of the Back Bay like mint sauce on mutton. Petronella learned to cook at his knee, then at his waist, then as salad cook and serving girl to the tweed-covered, horn-rimmed, boiled-potatoes-and-schrod Harvard alumni. And on those evenings when they would slip down the back stairs and travel to the warm and cluttered kitchen of the Tavern Club, ah, there she learned how to drain and chop tarragon, put a dash of dry bordeaux into thick onion soup, and bone a Chesapeake Bay duck. A kindly old cardiologist who frequented the Harvard Club helped to get her into the dietetic school at the MGH, and the butcher who supplied the Tavern Club introduced her to Stanley Widenfelt.

In his day, Stanley Widenfelt was the premier hotel steward in Boston. He could keep chefs and waiters and hotel managers happy all at once. He could run a kitchen under budget for months at a time. He could get more income out of a side of beef than anyone else, and still have it taste good–not great, but for a hotel, very good. But most of all he could write menus. If they gave Pulitzer Prizes for menu writing, Stanley would have won five or six; "Crème Royale," for example, was a Widenfelt original. To this day, every soft, slippery dessert served at the Parker House or the Copley Plaza or the Pilgrim Coffee Shop at the Hilton is called "Crème Royale." Petronella tried to bring all of this gastronomic background to her dietetic internship at the MGH, all to no avail. "Hospital menus should sound like good nutritious food, that's all," she was told, as the hospital pandered macaroni and cheese, tuna casserole, and desiccation of pork chop to its anorectic captive clientele.

The administrator of Presbyterian Hospital had no idea what he was getting when he hired her in 1969. Gradually, "fluffy baked Idaho potato" replaced "potato" on the hospital menu. "Atlantic rock cod in whole grain batter" replaced "fried fish," "Delicate pasta in sauce fromage" replaced "macaroni and cheese." Oh, the food was the same. No amount of tarragon, dill weed, or Madeira can improve the cuisine that comes out of number ten cans, commercial bakeries, or roast beef prepared for, 1342 guests. But two or three times a year the executive committee of the medical staff or the board of trustees was treated to a lobster bisque or a veal pâté or a sauce bordelaise which was, unbeknownst to them, straight out of the secret files of the Tavern Club. And the patients loved the menus. They ate better, healed better, and wrote fewer letters to the administrator.

This subliminal influence extended even to the felt board in the cafeteria, so that when Steven Crane finished his "charbroiled Kansas City steak with American cheese on a Kaiser roll" and dug into his "Crème Royale Chocolate," he was quite satisfied.

"Why do you suppose it is," he asked Suzanne, "that chocolate pudding tastes better in the hospital cafeteria than it does from a little can in my kitchen?"

"I don't see how a perfectly intelligent doctor could eat that stuff," said Suzanne. "Why don't you have a sensible, nutritious dessert like an apple or an orange?" She maintained a straight face.

"Sue, you get more like my mother every day," he responded.

"That's why you love me." She smiled and sampled the chocolate pudding. "Tastes like the stuff out of a can to me." Steve had been more attentive to Suzanne since the episode with Washington in her apartment. She seemed to be remarkably stable, aside from overre-acting to unexpected noises and minor irritations. She was afraid to stay alone in her apartment, and he had spent the last two nights there. But tonight he was on call.

"Sue, would you like to stay in my apartment tonight? Or perhaps you'd like to join me here in the on-call room." He raised his eyebrows and waggled an imaginary cigar in the universal Groucho salute to a semi-serious proposition.

"No, Steven, I'll be perfectly fine. But thank you anyway." In discussions of the event itself, she seemed unusually tolerant. They had verified Washington's explanation with Mr. Jensen down the hall. Crane could understand his impulsive decision to talk to Suzanne. Since the security in the building was tight and Steven had a key to the main door, it was reasonable for her to assume that it was he who knocked. Given her headstrong independence and devotion to amateur psychology, he could even understand why she invited Washington in while she was wearing only a bathrobe (which was how she described it). But he could not dismiss from his mind the image of Washington standing over her in the bedroom, and the concern of what might have happened if he had not come in. He decided to bring it up one more time.

"Sue, I still think you should consider filing a complaint against Washington for the other night."

"Complaint about what, Steve? I let him in. I sat there like a fool with nothing . . . in my bathrobe and talked to him. I was actually making a lot of progress when he got so upset." She shrugged. "Besides, I told Korinsky and Mavis Johnson about it. They'll know how to use it."

"I hope so," said Steve. "How'd you like to go to the Red Wings game this weekend? They'll be in town on Saturday and Sunday."

"I'd love it." She smiled. Intentional efforts at being considerate were unusual for Crane and she was enjoying it.

"Dr. Crane, Dr. Steven Crane." The voice of the paging operator interrupted a Muzak rendition of "How Are Things in Glocamorra."

He dialed the paging operator. "This is Dr. Crane."

"Please hang up for an outside call." This contradictory statement was an instruction to hang up so that the operator could patch the call through on that line, thus getting it off her switchboard. Crane had lost enough outside calls to know the routine.

"Wait, wait, operator, tell me who it is so I can–" Click. Too late. He hung up hoping the call would come through. It did.

"Hello, this is Dr. Crane."

"Hello, is this Dr. Steven Crane who sometimes plays football with Richard Hicks and friends on the weekends?"

"Yes it is."

141

"Oh good. I'm glad I found you. Steve, this is Walt Reed. We met at one of those football games a few weeks ago. Do you remember?"

"Speed Reed, formerly of the Vikings? How could I forget? What can I do for you?"

"Steve, I work in the public defender's office. I'm working on a case that involves one of your patients. Could you give me a little information?"

"Sure," said Crane. Crane would have cooperated even if it had not been for their personal acquaintance. Hospital physicians–especially residents–and public defenders share the camaraderie of the low-paid public servant. Any other lawyer would have to come with release-of-information papers in hand and wait hours or days until it happened to be convenient for a resident to grant an audience. "Who's the patient?"

"There are two little girls named Rebecca and Susie Washington."

"Yes, I know all about the case; how did you get involved?"

"The children are in protective custody. There's a custody hearing next week. The mother's entitled to legal representation and she can't afford a lawyer, so Child Welfare sent her to our office. It seems fairly straightforward to me. The boyfriend that was involved with the injury has moved out of the house. The mother has a job and seems fairly responsible. I'm sure that Child Welfare will return the children as soon as they're sure the home situation is stable."

"When did the husband–or boyfriend–move out of the house?" asked Steven. "He was still there just a few days ago."

"It sounds like the mother sent him packing–but only two days ago. That's the only weak spot in my case, but I can deal with that."

"What do you need from me?" asked Steve.

"First, I might need you to testify. It wouldn't take long and I could get you in and out whenever you could get free on Monday. Then second, I need to know who took the history and what the family said about the injury."

"That should be easy. As I recall, it was Dr. Stone and Dr. Redford."

"I can't be sure from the records I have. Would you mind checking it over?"

"I'll be glad to. Are you going to play football this weekend?"

"I'm planning on it."

"Then I'll see you there."

"Hey, thanks buddy. And sorry to bother you."

"No problem."

Suzanne had finished her coffee and started on his. "Don't tell me," she said. "Jason's mother again."

He laughed. "Not this time. Actually, you may be right about Washington. That was a fellow I know from the public defender's office. He's representing Sally Washington at a custody hearing. Apparently she kicked Washington out and she's going it on her own. So you must have gotten through to at least one of them."

"I'm glad to hear that. The mother's not a bad person, really. That hearing is next Monday."

"I know, I might have to testify."

"The public defender asked you to testify? Steven, you wouldn't do that."

"Why not?"

"Why . . . you'd be testifying for the family. They'd try to get you to say that those little girls should go back where they might get hurt again." She was indignant.

"Well, first of all, Sue, the family now consists of the cute little mother . . ."

"You don't believe that, do you really, Steven? Sometimes you are so naive."

". . . and in the second place, it's not a trial, it's a hearing. It's just a matter of getting all the facts before a judge and he makes a decision. It's not an adversary proceeding."

"Steven Crane. How many custody hearings have you been to?" she challenged him, chin up and eyes flashing.

"Well . . . not any, but that doesn't change the fact that—"

"You come and testify. Then you tell me it's not an adversary proceeding." She had risen from her chair and held the tray in her hand, a signal that the conversation was over.

* * * *

"Every intern and every nurse should go to court and be cross-examined about what they write in charts" was the standard opening at the orientation lecture delivered by Edward Browne every year.

"Now, here are a few current charts I pulled at random. Pick any page." He would let a chart fall open and read, "'Baby looks pale.' Did you write this note, Doctor? What does pale mean to you? Did you think the baby was anemic, Doctor? Did or did you not order blood tests? Did you order a transfusion, Doctor? Did the baby look pale or not? Well if the baby was pale, why didn't you do something about it? Do you think this is related to the baby's death? Why not, Doctor? Was the baby anemic at the time of death? Then doesn't the fact that he was pale relate to the cause of death?"

The interns and residents never really believed his version of cross-examination. They listened attentively, but they came prepared with an upper-middle-class understanding of the justice system. They would always be able to merely explain what was accurate and true and absolve any such problems.

"Here's a nurse's note: *Subjective: My tummy hurts. Objective: Pain in area of incision. Assessment: Postoperative pain, one day post-appendectomy. Plan: Demerol as ordered.* First of all, the nurse who invented this SOAP system should be sentenced to three years at hard jury duty. It's stupid, it's unnecessary. It clutters up the chart. But how would you like this in court? 'Did you see this nurse's note, Doctor? Did you do anything about it? When did you first diagnose the wound infection? Did that extra three days contribute to this child's pain and suffering? Was the wound infection present when the nurse noted the abdominal pain? I didn't ask your opinion, Doctor; was the infection present or was it not? That's a simple question. Well, if it was there and the nurse knew about it, why didn't you know about it? What did the nurse do about the pain from the infection? Was that based on your order? Are you in the habit of ordering Demerol for wound infection?'"

Browne always cited three or four more examples. This annual dissertation probably improved the brevity and accuracy of the charts to some extent. Steven Crane was one who never took these warnings very seriously. But Browne's admonition did come to mind as he picked up the chart marked "Washington, Susie."

The chart was in a three-ring binder with separators marking the various sections. The ICU charts were always in a state of disarray, with lab data and X-ray reports lagging two or three days behind the actual events. The reliable information was in the progress notes and the vital sign sheet at the bedside. Crane opened to the section tabbed

144

"History and Physical." The official "History and Physical" had been written by J. Mendelssohn, M4 (a fourth-year medical student) and countersigned by S. Schulman. The history began:

> *Chief complaint, Burns. Hx: 13-month-old black female burned with hot water in bathtub. Brought to ER by paramedics. PMH: normal growth and development, no accidents, no hospitalizations, no major illnesses, no allergies (per ER note).*

The description went on to describe the burns and facial injuries including a fairly accurate diagram. This is no help, thought Crane, turning to the first page in the progress notes. There he found the admitting resident's note, signed by Bill Redford.

> *Child admitted with scald burns, brought by paramedics. Child allegedly burned with hot water in bathtub, along with sister age 2. Distribution of burns plus multiple facial injuries suggests BCS (see ER note).*

Redford's record went on to describe the physical findings, but held no more background. He had obviously not talked to the family.

Crane dug into the back of the chart hoping that the emergency room record would be there. When a critically ill patient is admitted through the emergency room directly to intensive care, the notes are usually scanty and often get lost altogether. It was there, however–a flimsy yellow sheet which had been the third part of a multiple imprint ER packet. The carbon was difficult to read, but with effort he deciphered the following:

> *Time in: 9:32 PM Time out: 11:45 admit. Informant: Paramedics History: 13-month-old black girl burns and trauma. Allegedly burned by hot water while father giving bath 4 hours PTA. Facial abrasions and bruises (father states baby fell on edge of tub). Burn involves back, perineum, thighs and calves, heels. Back of knees, sacrum not burned. Remainder of exam neg. Impression: Battered Child Syndrome—BCS–with 30% second degree burn, facial contusions and abrasions. Disposition: 1. Admit Peds ICU 2. Report–Child Protection Team. D. Stone, M.D.*

Crane was beginning to understand why Walter Reed was uncertain about the history. He returned to the progress notes. The descriptions chronicled the course of intravenous fluids, antibiotics, infection, and systemic sepsis. There was a note from Suzanne stating that the child had been placed in protective custody. There were a few other notes from her describing the events of the abuse team meeting, and finally the fact that Susie's sister had been transferred to juvenile hall. There were several of his own notes describing the progress when Redford was on vacation, but no detailed account of the accident itself.

He turned through the fact chart to the nurses' notes. (On rounds that day, one of the interns had described a hospital in California where nurses, doctors, therapists, everyone wrote on one set of interdisciplinary notes. "God help us all" had been Edward Browne's response.) The nurses' notes contained the usual information about bowel movements, general appearance, and the subjective impressions of the nurses–all adjectives. There were a few notes about the family (father in, parents seem nervous, father hostile, father distant, no family visit this shift). In the midst of this non-information Steven came across handwriting he recognized as Beth Bonnell's. The note summarized the vital signs and laboratory data–all nouns. Then it said, *Father visited, seems concerned, warm and loving.* Crane paused, checked the stamped name to be sure he had the right chart, and read the note again. He resolved to follow up on it. He found two other notes by Beth Bonnell, equally concise, but with no mention of the family. Finally he turned to the consultations. There was a two-page, typed discussion from Dr. John McNamarra which began with the sentence, *One-year- old child with typical inflicted immersion burns* . Crane thumbed the entire chart again, but found nothing more. He got up from the rolling stool, racked the chart, and walked to the end of the room to look in on Susie Washington. The dirty eschar had been debrided away in the operating room. Susie looked much better; her eyes were bright and she was avidly sucking on a plastic bottle of milk.

"Looks better, doesn't she?" The voice came from behind him. Crane turned to see David Stone. Stone was dressed in surgical greens, stained with blood and some other undefined fluid.

"She sure does. Looks like you've been in a war."

"Only the local war," he said. He pointed to the child they had just wheeled into bed four. "Gunshot wound of the abdomen, nine years old. They said he got in the way of a family fight. Spleen, pancreas, kidney, and left colon. Nice case. Too bad for the kid, of course, but a nice case."

They watched awhile as the figures around the bedside scrambled and unscrambled drains and catheters and IV lines.

"Say, Dave, do you remember talking to the family of this little girl?"

"I talked to the mother a couple of times. I got her consent for the debridement that we did yesterday. I saw the father–or the boyfriend–around here a few times, but I've never talked to him."

"Then you didn't talk to him on admission?"

"Hell no; they weren't even there. I remember that night. I had a head crunch and a hot belly and these two burns came in on top of that. I was in the ER and the OR all night. Why?"

"The case is going to court and I might have to testify. I was just trying to find out who took the history from the father."
"Why is it going to court?"

"It's a custody hearing, actually, to determine the long-term disposition." Stone looked blank. "These kids are in protective custody–remember?" Steve explained.

"Oh, yeah, the child abuse thing." Stone had forgotten the exact circumstances of the initial injury. "Did anything pan out on the investigation?"

Now Crane looked incredulous. He had become so involved with the case that he assumed everyone else had the same intensity of interest. "What do you mean, how did the investigation pan out?" he asked. "You're the one who reported it in the first place."

"Damn right," said Stone. "It's the most classic case of immersion burns I've ever seen. In fact, it's the only one I've ever seen. You've gotta report those things. If you don't, you get a fine and they suspend your license. Well, hell, you know that."

"But you admitted them as battered child syndrome. There must have been something in the history or some other evidence–"

"Hey, Steve," he interrupted, "I'm a surgeon, not a lawyer. All I did was flag it as suspicious. There's some committee that was supposed to investigate those things."

"Yeah, I know, I'm on it," said Crane, wondering what he would tell Reed.

"Well, there you are, you solved your own problem. I'd better get back to the war," said Stone on his way to bed four.

"Somebody must have taken a history," muttered Crane to himself.

* * * *

Walter Reed had never actually met either Kevin or Sally. He had talked with Sally on the telephone twice and arranged for a conference just before the custody hearing.

His brief visit with Mavis Johnson was cordial. She supplied photocopies of important sections of the hospital record, Korinsky's report (including the text of Washington's sworn statement under interrogation), the hospital social service summary, and finally her own analysis representing the Department of Child Welfare. She brought his attention to the last paragraph of the last document, which said that although the mother exhibited "a flat affect and shallow personality" and "behaved under observation more like a big sister than a mother," she also showed "a juvenile but genuine affection" and "could probably be entrusted with the responsibilities of motherhood for these three children–if she manifested an awareness of her responsibilities by permanently terminating her relationship with Mr. Washington, the abuser of her children." Mavis pointed out that this was written two weeks before Sally had ousted the boyfriend. Based on that action, Mavis was sure that the mother would be awarded custody promptly—in six to twelve months. She was, if anything, too helpful, but Reed attributed this to her sense of fairness and empathy. After all, in a custody hearing, all the parties have the same motivation–successful reunion of a stable family unit. Mavis did not mention anything about the district attorney or the possible felony charges against Kevin.

Steven Crane had called back, only hours after his inquiry, with the report that there was no solid physician's history related to the accident. Reed had thanked him, and explained that it didn't really matter. There was a very thorough account signed by Washington in the detective's report, and that wasn't an important issue anyway, not for purposes of this hearing. Washington was largely out of the picture.

Reed decided that he did need a medical witness, however, since Child Welfare did not plan to call one. It would be important for the judge to know about the medical status of the little girls and any

148

special treatment that they might require over the next year or two. Reed invited Crane because he knew that he would be less pompous than the older staff physicians. Crane agreed.

The football game, played two days later in a cold drizzle, was an exhausting escape for both of them. They didn't discuss the upcoming hearing.

CHAPTER 15

In later years, Murray realized that if the Coran case had started on schedule, he never would have heard of Kevin Washington. The Coran case–scheduled for division five of juvenile court–involved the teenage son of a prominent local politician who was accused of manslaughter in a hit-and-run accident. The second week of the trial was to begin that Monday morning, but one of the jurors was stricken with abdominal pain in the middle of the night and hospitalized for what later proved to be an ectopic pregnancy. James Murray had been assigned to cover the case for the *Detroit News*. The *News* had entered into another of its perennially unsuccessful attempts to match the circulation of the *Free Press*. The thrust of the campaign was veiled sensationalism–crimes, disasters, and court cases presented as "You Are Government: The New Sociology." Murray left the empty court-room and considered whether to call for a new assignment, take the day off, or forage the social forest on his own. Since he hated the hard wooden benches in the hall even more than the smoke and stale rolls of the coffee shop, he took a seat in the back of division four to contemplate his options. The bailiff was just announcing the next case–a custody hearing regarding the children of Sally Flynn, aka Washington. Judge Thomas Nelson–proclaimed by the nameplate on the big desk–quickly perused the courtroom over his glasses and opened the folder that the court attendant had set before him. "Let's see if everybody's here. I know Miss Johnson," he said, nodding toward Mavis, "and I recognize Mr. . . . Mr. . . . ."

"Reed, your honor, Walter Reed from the public defender's office."

"Of course, of course. And are the parents here?" He looked at Sally because she was sitting next to Reed.

Reed spoke. "Yes, your honor, this is Mrs. Sally Flynn, the mother of the children. Our office is representing her in this hearing. Mr.

Kevin Washington is also here." Reed pointed at Kevin sitting behind Sally. "Mr. Washington is the father of the girls, and is also involved with the events which led to this hearing."

"Very well," said Nelson. He had reviewed the folder before leaving his office on Friday, and had a better knowledge of the circumstances than he showed. "Miss Johnson, would you summarize the case for us, please?" He leaned back and looked around the courtroom, trying to guess the identity of the other individuals in the room–Korinsky, Steven Crane, Suzanne, and Murray.

"Judge Nelson, this hearing is to determine the custody of three children–Sammy Flynn, age six, Rebecca Washington, age two and Susan Washington, age thirteen months. On October 20, these children were placed in protective custody by a court order which you signed, with guardianship assigned to the Department of Child Welfare. The current situation is–"

"Excuse me, Miss Johnson," interrupted the judge. "The reason for the protective custody order?"

"Suspected child abuse, your honor. The girls were burned with scalding water."

"Oh yes, I remember," muttered Judge Nelson, squinting slightly. "Carry on."

"At the present time the baby is still in the hospital, the older girl is in juvenile hall and the boy is in juvenile hall extension at Wayne County Hospital. Miss Hathaway, the clinical social worker at Presbyterian Hospital, and myself have both talked with the mother–in fact with both parents–on several occasions. I believe you have those reports." She pointed toward the folder.

"Yes, I do," mused the judge. He turned toward Sally. "Mrs. Flynn." He looked carefully for the first time, and perceived that she was younger than his own daughter. Her quivering lips and wide eyes told him that she was terrified–probably more with the procedure than its content. "Mrs. Flynn–" He looked into the folder. "May I call you Sally?" She nodded. "Sally, don't be nervous. Have you ever been in a courtroom before?"

"No sir," she said in a faint whisper.

"Sally, courtrooms make people nervous. They're all so serious. Now, this is not a trial, it's just a hearing. All these folks," he waved around the room, "are here for just one purpose: to do the best they can for your little children. And generally speaking, that means to get them home with their mommy. I think we'd be better off holding this kind of a meeting at some nice comfortable place like your living room. Would you like that?" Sally nodded affirmatively. "Well, so would I, Sally, but it would be sort of impractical, don't you know, to get all these folks together there. But let's pretend that that's where we are. Just you and I, sitting down in your living room to settle up this problem. Is that all right?"

"Yes sir." She smiled gratefully. The tremor was gone from her lip and her hands became quiet.

"That's good. Now Sally, I'm just a little confused by the fact that you and your children have two different names, Flynn and Washington. Could you explain that to me?" He took off his glasses and deliberately pushed aside the folder of papers as he spoke. Sally felt as if they were alone in the big room.

"Yes sir, that's easy. Me and my first husband–that's Sam Flynn–moved here from West Virginia about three years ago. Sammy–that's my little boy–was three years old. After a few months my husband just up and left us, so Sammy and me, we just got along as best we could. Then I met Kevin." She turned to smile at him. "He was wonderful to me and to Sammy. We've been–like married–for two years. We are . . . we were going to get really married just as soon as we can. There's some legal problem–about my first husband." She sighed as her attention wandered. "But we've been married," she began again, resolutely, "as far as God and the world knows, for over two years. And we had two sweet little girls and their name is Washington. It says so on the birth certificate. And they're our little girls and I love them." She suddenly realized that she was speaking too loudly and shaking her finger at the judge. She looked around as if to see if her disrespectful act had been noticed. "I'm sorry, your honor," she said quietly.

"That's quite all right," said Nelson kindly. "I can see you care about your children and you're worried about them. I certainly would be. Tell me, how did they come to be in the hospital?"

Jim Murray had sorted through the notes in his pockets and decided to call his editor for another assignment. He was peripherally aware of the activities in the courtroom, and the judge's discussion of a conversation in the living room attracted his interest briefly. Murray watched the judge as he brought Sally into his confidence. He was masterful, really, slipping from legalese into Sally's vernacular as easily as shifting gears. Was he as compassionate as he seemed, or just clever? Either way, he certainly was getting the information.

"Kevin called me at work–I'm a waitress–and said the girls turned on the hot water while he was giving them a bath. He said that Susie was all red and raw and part of her skin came off. When I got home we called the emergency number and the ambulance came and took the girls to the hospital. They got real sick in the hospital. Susie's still there."

"Now, Sally, Miss Johnson here started to explain about this protective custody business. Tell me what you think about that." The judge was still smiling and leaning across his big desk toward her.

"They said that Kevin burned the girls on purpose. They said he beat up Sammy. But I don't think he could do that. He couldn't do that." She turned around and reached out her hand toward Kevin who had frozen into his rocklike defensive posture. Reed nudged her firmly with his knee under the table, and spoke to the judge.

"Your honor, Sally understands the protective custody order. She's been very cooperative and she appreciates the fact that the state can intervene on behalf of her children. She still finds it hard to believe that her former companion, Mr. Washington, would–"

"Hold on, hold on a minute, Counselor, Sally was doing very well at telling us what she believes." His brusque rebuke to Reed mellowed abruptly as he turned to Sally. "Go ahead, Sally."

"Kevin loves our children," she said, more composed. "I don't think he would ever hurt them on purpose. Sometimes parents over-react or lose control. Sometimes they need professional guidance." The now-familiar phrases had infiltrated her vocabulary as well as her thought patterns. She didn't even realize what she was saying. Mavis Johnson smiled at Suzanne. Sally continued. "I suppose the protective custody was good. It helped us start to analyze our problem, but now I just want my children back." The judge seemed satisfied with her response.

"What steps have you taken to assure that this will not happen again?" Sally looked at Reed. This was the question that they had rehearsed during their brief meeting just before the hearing. He nodded encouragement.

"I'm going to counseling," she said cautiously, "and I'm going to join a group of other parents who've worked through these problems before. I have a good job and I'm . . . I'm a good mother."

"I'm sure you are, Sally," said the judge. "And how about Mr. Washington?"

He was still speaking to her, so she responded. "We've separated. He won't be around the children anymore." The impact of what she had said made her eyes burn and her throat hurt. She shook her head to dispel the feeling and sniffed loudly. The judge was still kindly, but unrelenting.

"But Sally, you told me a minute ago that Mr. Washington loves the children and you have a nice family. Now you tell me that the children won't have a father. Which is it?"

"Well, sir, we thought—I thought—the quickest way to get the kids back was for Kevin to go away. I mean, he's the one with . . . with the problem. We thought . . ." Her voice trailed away.

"Mr. Washington is out of the picture, your honor. Besides, that's not the issue here." Reed rose to his feet and silenced Sally with a hand on her shoulder. "The children are legally and functionally those of Mrs. Flynn and this hearing is to decide . . ."

"The children, Counselor, are functionally the children of these two people, but fortunately for them, they are custodial and legally wards of the county of Wayne." Judge Nelson was just a little testy with Reed. He was particularly offended when lawyers told him what was legal. "Now, the disposition of these children depends to a large extent on what kind of family life the parents can and will provide. That is what I'm trying to ascertain, if you will allow me to continue."

"Yes, sir," muttered Reed, resuming his seat.

"Now, Sally, how long have you and Kevin been separated?"

"Five days today," she said, still sniffing.

"And what do you and Kevin want to do?"

Sally started to respond, but Kevin stood up. He cleared his throat and spoke directly to the judge. "Your honor, we'll do whatever we have to do to get the children back for Sally. If we have to stay separated, then we'll stay separated." He said this firmly, but in his carefully affected flat monotone.

"Mr. Washington, do you mean to tell me that you have so little regard for your family that you intend to leave them in the midst of this difficult situation?"

"Just the opposite, your honor. I love my family so much that I would do whatever it takes to keep them together—including leaving if necessary." Kevin was standing and grasping the back of the bench in front of him.

"Mr. Washington, either there is something backward in your reasoning, or our goals of family service are not being well-served."

"I agree with you on that, Judge." he sat back, realizing that he was about to go out of control again. Sally pushed her knee against his, which was trembling. Judge Nelson turned back to Mavis Johnson.

"Miss Johnson, I'm afraid I interrupted your presentation with the hope of resolving this quickly. But it seems we need more information. Please continue." He leaned back in his chair and glanced at the clock. Mavis stood up again.

"I hesitate to say too much about the allegations against Mr. Washington himself, for fear it might prejudice the court. For purposes of custody, we think Sally's action to effect a separation shows understanding and maturity. If she continues to show this good judgment, we are prepared to recommend another review hearing and a trial of home placement in six months."

"Six months?" Sally was on her feet. "Six months—I want my children back right now. That's why we're doing this. You said that's why we're having this hearing." She pointed at Suzanne, crying and shouting uncontrollably. "You stole my children. You took my little boy right out of his bed. You told them lies about their father. You made us break up our home, and then you say six months. Six months! This isn't right. This isn't fair." She collapsed into her seat. Kevin moved forward to join her, giving up any pretense of estrangement. She clung to the lapels of his new suit and sobbed loudly.

This outburst gained the full concentration of Jim Murray. As an investigative reporter and an amateur sleuth he had become a student of reactions under stress. If Judge Nelson's thoughtful probing had been intended to lay bare the raw emotions and motivations of this couple, he had certainly done that. Child Welfare had given up on the father. That was unusual for them. Was it because of the unofficial marriage? Not likely. Was it because of the racial mix? Or something else in the father's background? Perhaps because of the injury itself. There must be some ominous facts in that thick folder. Bylines and

156

headlines began forming in his mind. "Child Abuser Seeks Custody of Children." "Mother Charges Court with Kidnapping." "Family Must Split to Regain Children." "Wife Torn Between Children and Child-Abuser Husband." "Court Saves Children from Torture and Death." He pulled the notepad from his pocket and settled back, filling in the names he could remember: Sally Flynn, Kevin Washington, Somebody Johnson.

Judge Nelson waited calmly for Sally to finish her tirade. Then he said, "Sally, let me tell you once again. Everyone here wants to do what's best for your children. Our goal is to keep families together. From what I've seen here this morning, it seems to me that the two of you want to stay together. Is that correct?"

"Yes, your honor," said Kevin. Sally was still crying but shook her head affirmatively. Judge Nelson paused, watching the terrified couple. They look so distraught, so vulnerable, he thought. He had a sudden insight that they might be right and the system might be wrong.

"Miss Johnson, here are two young people who care about each other and care about their children. You've recommended splitting them up and holding on to the children for a long time. You're going to have to find some very compelling reasons why I should follow that recommendation."

Walter Reed could not believe what he was hearing. He had been formulating a statement in his mind—a motion to cancel the hearing and reschedule at a later date. In his limited experience he had never seen a judge decide against the recommendation of Child Welfare. The separation was the whole basis for Sally's case. Welfare had even agreed to return the children if the separation held up. Now that plan was down the drain, but the judge seemed to read that as a plus for the family. Reed decided to remain silent and see what developed.

Mavis Johnson turned around to talk to Korinsky. They put their heads together and whispered, and then Korinsky stood and left the courtroom. Mavis addressed the judge. "As I said, your honor, we had hoped to avoid a lengthy discussion of the injuries because that is still under investigation, but it is the injuries which prompted us to come to this recommendation. I'd like to ask Miss Hathaway to discuss the medical opinions, and then have Lieutenant Korinsky describe the rest of his investigation."

"Very well," said Nelson, now skeptical of the charges. "Miss

Hathaway, would you come forward so we can hear you better, please?" Suzanne came through the low-swinging gate and stood at the small lectern on the table. "Would you tell us your exact position?" asked the judge.

"I am Suzanne Hathaway and I am the social worker in the Department of Pediatrics at Presbyterian Hospital." Murray wrote, "Suzanne Hathaway, hospital social worker" on his pad.

"I am also chairperson of the Child Protection Committee, and it was in that context that I became involved with the Washingtons. Dr. Stone, a surgeon on our staff, was the first physician to see the Washington girls when they were admitted. He immediately recognized the injuries as inflicted immersion burns and notified the Child Protection Committee. We in turn reported the cases to the Department of Child Welfare. In addition to the burns, the smaller child also had evidence of a severe beating around the head and neck. These are the pictures taken shortly after admission on October 19." She handed a set of eight-by-ten color prints to the judge. Judge Nelson's face became pallid as he looked at the first picture. He put the photographs down for a moment and looked away, swallowing as if he were nauseated. He took a deep breath and looked again, then went carefully through the stack.

Suzanne continued. "As you can see from the photographs, the burns on the older child begin just below the knees and are clearly demarcated. The burn gets deeper going down the legs and involves both feet. This is a typical immersion burn which occurs when the child is held in scalding water up to the level of the watermark that you can see there. The burns on the smaller child are also clearly demarcated; the water line is halfway between the back and front. The burns on the lower back, the backs of the legs, and the heels are typical inflicted injury. Dr. Stone and Dr. Browne, chief of pediatrics, and all the other doctors agree that intentional immersion in scalding water had to be the mechanism of injury."

"I don't understand the significance of the burns on the heels," said the judge, studying one photograph carefully.

"Even a small child would fight to get out of hot water," said Suzanne.. "A person who burns a child in this fashion has to hold the baby down in the water with both hands, one on the chest, and the other on the legs, flexing the hips and knees. This puts the back and

158

the bottom and the heels in the water but keeps the knees out."

"You're saying to get this kind of injury, a person would have to stand there and hold a baby in scalding water, is that right?"

"Yes, your honor, that's what our doctors say." Suzanne did not risk a look at Washington.

"My God," said Judge Nelson to himself, barely audible.

Suzanne continued. "Then the severe bruises on the face in the other photograph are—"

"Your honor, may I interrupt this for a minute?" asked Walter Reed. "We have not had the opportunity to examine these photographs. May I ask that we delay—"

"Well, you should see them, Mr. Reed, and so should the Washingtons." He flipped the stack upright on the desk so that Reed and everyone else could see them. "This is amazing, quite amazing," he said, leaving each photograph exposed for several seconds, then dropping it to expose the next one. He watched the Washingtons as he flipped them over. Sally hid her face in Kevin's chest. Kevin had resumed his no-response-to-anything pose. Jim Murray stopped writing and watched the horrible montage. After he had flipped through the stack, the judge handed the entire pile to Reed. He made no attempt to hide the look of disgust on his face. Reed sat down with the photographs.

Suzanne started again. "The bruises involve the forehead, cheek, jaw and neck, and shoulder on the left side. Dr. Stone said these were typical of battered child syndrome and that was his admitting diagnosis. In addition to the injuries themselves, both children had a flat affect and seemed inappropriately quiet. They were terrified by authority figures. They seemed to crave affection and emotional stimulation. The children were brought to the hospital by the paramedics in critical condition. The paramedics estimated that the injuries were six to twelve hours old when they were first called. The family did not appear until long after the children were in the hospital. They seemed more frightened about what might happen to them than to the children. In fact, when the officer served the protective custody order, Mr. Washington physically attacked him. The girls had a long and difficult hospital course. The baby is still dangerously ill. During the hospitalization, the nurses and medical staff noted that the father visited infrequently, and when he did he appeared hostile and sullen. His relationships with the hospital staff have been–" She looked directly at Kevin for the first time since he ran out of her apartment. His face was impassive, but his eyes had the fiery glare which still wakened her at night. "Uncooperative," she finished, looking back at the judge.

In the midst of Suzanne's discussion, Korinsky had returned to the courtroom, accompanied by a uniformed Detroit police officer. Mavis Johnson introduced him. "Your honor, Lieutenant Korinsky will present the results of the police department investigation. Gus." Korinsky came to the small lectern.

"There is more?" said Nelson, softly, shaking his head.

"Your honor, I'm Lieutenant Korinsky, juvenile division, Detroit Police Department. I served the protective custody order in this case. I interrogated Mr. Washington and conducted the remainder of the investigation. Also I investigated injuries to Sammy Flynn, the little boy in this family."

"What injuries?" asked the judge. "We haven't heard about any injuries to other children."

"When the little boy was picked up on the protective custody order he had evidence of beating about the head. I didn't bring photographs–"

"That's quite all right, I don't want to see any more photographs," said the judge, as the look of disgust returned to his face.

"The little boy's six years old and he's a smart little fella. The father and mother said that the injuries occurred when the boy fell down the stairs, but the boy said his father beat him because he spilled a glass of milk. Regarding the burn injury, in sworn testimony, Mr. Washington stated that the girls were in the bathtub and he left to answer the telephone. When he returned the water coming from the tap was very hot and spraying on the girls. The girls were standing in the hot water. He took them out and in the process dropped the little one such that she struck her head on the edge of the tub."

"Just a minute, Lieutenant," Judge Nelson turned toward Kevin. "Mr. Washington, is that an accurate summary of your statement?"

"No sir, one was standing, and one was on her hands and knees."

"Mr. Washington, I find that hard to believe. Why didn't they climb of the tub?"

"I don't know why, your honor. It wasn't very long–"

"Your honor, all of this material is very damaging to my client."

Reed suddenly found his voice and came to his feet, "I move to cancel this hearing and schedule it for a later date when we can prepare properly for these new allegations."

"That's a reasonable request, Mr. Reed, as long as Child Welfare agrees to that extension. Hold on for just a minute." He turned toward Mavis and Korinsky. "Could I talk with the two of you for a moment, please?" He indicated the door to his chambers. Mavis and Korinsky disappeared behind the judge.

Reed came back to Steven Crane. "Steve, if we're lucky, we'll get this extension. All that evidence is very damaging. I'm afraid if he made a decision now . . . anyway, thanks a lot for coming. I'm sorry I didn't get the chance to have you testify. But under the circumstances we'll be lucky just to get out of here with the status quo."

"I understand," said Steven. "I've learned a lot." He looked at Suzanne who was still sitting at the table in front of the courtroom.

Around the corner, Nelson turned to the representatives of society. "Jesus, that's awful. You should have warned me. Why haven't you filed charges–felony charges?"

"It's taken time to get all these facts together, your honor," said Korinsky. "We have talked to the district attorney's office. They suggested we file charges if the case still looked solid after this hearing."

"If you're going to do it, you'd better do it soon. I worry about letting that fellow out. Into the hall, let alone into society."

"Thank you, sir," said Mavis. They returned to the courtroom. Judge Nelson mounted the three stairs and settled into his swivel chair. He turned toward Sally and Kevin. "It is clear there are extenuating circumstances in this case, beyond the concern and affection that you seem to have for your children." He was speaking primarily to Sally. "I will grant Mr. Reed's motion for an extension and schedule a repeat hearing in two months." He looked at the bailiff as an instruction to schedule the hearing on the court calendar.

"But, your honor," Sally began, but Judge Nelson's manner convinced her that protestation was futile.

"In the meantime," the judge began again, but stopped when a court officer entered abruptly and approached the bench. The judge recognized Amos, the most senior bailiff, who coordinated schedules and important messages. Amos walked directly to the bench and handed the judge a folded piece of paper.

"I thought you'd need this right away, your honor. It concerns this case." He turned and looked around the room, briefly and professionally, then left.

The judge opened the paper and read the message. He studied it for almost a minute, looking up at various individuals and back down at the paper. Finally he said, "Lieutenant Korinsky." He held out the slip of paper which Korinsky came forward to take. The judge rubbed his face with both hands as if he were deep in thought. Korinsky read the note, handed it to Mavis, and walked to the back of the room where the police officer was sitting. Korinsky looked up at the judge. "Your honor, with the permission of the court—"

"Go ahead," said the judge, not looking up from his anguished, contemplative position.

Korinsky walked up to Kevin accompanied by the police officer. In a voice that was quiet but audible throughout the room, he said, "Kevin Washington, you are placed under arrest, charged with the crime of willful child abuse and murder. You have the right to counsel. You have the right to remain silent. Anything you say may be held against you." Kevin did not move, frozen to the chair.

"What's happening?" asked Sally. "What's happening, what did he say? I can't believe this, what did he say?" She was speaking to Judge Nelson who had uncovered his face and was leaning heavily on the big desk.

"Sally," he said softly, "Sally, that message was from the hospital. Your . . . there's no easy way to tell you this . . . your little girl . . . just . . . died."

CHAPTER 16

If it's a good day for the world, it's a bad day for newspapers, thought Rosenberg, surveying the mock-up front page. The headline read, "Prime Rate Increases to 16%" and was tied to a two-column article on the national economy. The minor headlines were worse: "School Board Refuses Pay Hike," "Price of Gold Drops," "First Snowfall Predicted." The best picture he could find for the front page was a seasonal photograph depicting a single corn stalk which stood in a farmer's field in Birmingham. The left-hand column headed by the small box "You Are Government: The New Sociology" was blank. He was trying to decide between a piece on the parole board and old filler on sewage treatment.

Can't sell newspapers with this stuff, he thought to himself, chewing on his unlit cigar. Sol Rosenberg had worked his way through the ranks at the *Detroit News*. He had been city editor (along with a dozen other jobs) for the last seven years. For a lifetime of effort he had been rewarded with a modest house in Ferndale, a Pulitzer Prize nomination for his coverage of the 1967 riots, a duodenal ulcer, and a two-pack-a-day smoking habit. After both of his brothers had coronaries, he had given up cigarette smoking in favor of cigar chewing. Cigar chewing rather than cigar smoking because Alice would never allow the latter. "So you stopped smoking, so you shouldn't get lung cancer. Big deal, so now you get lip cancer."

With a red pen he changed "Increases" to "Jumps" and "Drops" to "Plummets". He decided on the parole board article and tried to dress it up with a catchy headline. "Cons Con the Can Keepers." He scratched it out and tried again. "Dull," he said out loud.

Two desks away, Jim Murray pulled the last of three sheets from his typewriter, bounced the pages on his desk to align the edges, and then tossed the fresh manuscript on Rosenberg's desk. "Sol, why don't you ever light that cigar?" he challenged.

"Alice won't let me." Rosenberg spit tobacco fragments toward the wastebasket. "What's this, Jim? That hit-and-run case?"

"No, better than that, new stuff."

Rosenberg read the first two sentences out loud. *"In a tension packed courtroom today, police interrupted the proceedings to arrest Kevin Washington, 25, charged with torturing then murdering his own daughter. Social workers from Presbyterian Hospital and the Department of Child Welfare placed the three Washington children in protective custody as soon as the brutal injuries were discovered on October 20, but too late to save the life of 13-month-old Susan Washington. Arresting officer Lieutenant Korinsky stated . . ."*
Murray, you just made my day. This is terrific. Does the *Free Press* have this?"

"Nobody has it, Sol. It's a *bona fide* exclusive."

"How did you get it?" asked Rosenberg, quickly reading through the three-page report.

"I sort of stumbled on it. But it's accurate. Straight out of the courtroom at juvenile court."

"It looks okay to me as it is," said Rosenberg. Does it have all the right 'alleged' and 'charged with' and that sort of stuff?"

"I think so, So. I'll double check it."

"And these social workers you have in here, are they really heroes? I mean did they really jump in just in time and save lives?"

"It sure seemed that way to me. They were reluctant to be interviewed and I haven't talked to the police yet."

"That's okay, that'll be great follow-up. You'd better get on it as soon as you can. I'm gonna run this right up the middle." With his red pen he crossed out the bucolic photograph and created a larger box in the center of the front page. He wrote, "You Are Government: The New Sociology," at the top of this box, blanked out a large space for an editor's note and wrote, "Murray text" under that. He moved columns and stories to fit the rest of the page. Finally he crossed out the prime rate headline and wrote, "Father Suspect in Child Murder." He turned to his typewriter and dashed off an editor's note that was characteristically perfect, requiring no revisions.

* * * *

Pediatric grand rounds had been held at noon on Tuesday ever since anyone could remember. For the pediatric residents, there was something secure about knowing that every Tuesday, they could find cold sandwiches and warm milk outside of the door of Fisher Auditorium, and settle in for an hour of didactic academia, sweet sleep, and beeper silence until one o'clock. The sandwiches were always made the day before, wrapped in plastic wrap, and kept in the freezer until an hour before the conference. The cookies were always stale but plentiful. But it was free, and attendance was required.

The seating arrangement was unwritten, but never violated. Dr. Browne sat in the front row on the left side. Dr. Charles Foster and Dr. Muriel Myers, the most senior members of the staff, sat behind Browne. Other members of the attending staff in pediatrics were scattered around the next ten rows on the left side. Outside attendings—those members of the staff who practiced at other hospitals, but came for the weekly conference—sat on the right side, along with occasional visiting surgeons, pathologists, radiologists, and the staff members of other departments. The residents and students filled the rest of the room. A handful of nurses and therapists could usually be found in the back two rows. This seating arrangement was perpetuated by the presence of both a back and a front door, thus providing access for those who wished to be seen (who sat in the front) and those who did not (who sat in back).

On this particular Tuesday, the subject was cystic fibrosis. The guest speaker was William Oliver from the university, so the room was almost full. As a prelude to the dissertation, Chatterjee was presenting the case of Cindy Scott. Chatterjee was wearing a freshly starched white uniform. With the nervousness of a novice in the presence of the professor, he read the two-page history verbatim. "In 1972, she was admitted four times for pneumonitis. In 1973, she underwent bronchoscopy and lavage with transient improvement in symptoms. In 1974 . . ."

Finding that Suzanne was not in her office, Crane decided to look for her in grand rounds. He entered the auditorium through the back door and paused, adjusting to the dim light. Her ponytail was recognizable five rows down on the aisle. Chatterjee was concluding his presentation as Steven squeezed past Suzanne and sat next to her. She smiled a greeting, which he did not return. He quietly opened the folded newspaper which he had been carrying and laid it in front of her.

"Have you seen this?" he whispered.

"No." She absorbed the headline and began reading. "Oh my." He waited until she finished the segment on the first page and opened to the continuation on the third page.

"Did you say this?" he whispered loudly, indicating a paragraph quoting Suzanne.

"Not in so many words. At least they got my name right."

"Sue, this is awful. It's just dishonest. You've got to do something about this." His whisper was getting louder. Dr. Browne, in the process of introducing the guest speaker, frowned in Steven's direction.

"Steven, I don't see what you're so upset about. I'm surprised they made a big news item out of it, but it's fairly accurate reporting."

"It is not," he said. "Look at this." He pointed to the editor's note printed in italics at the head of the article.

> *"In this series, the News has aimed the bright light of investigation into the dark corners of government. We have been objective, even critical. But in this News exclusive, we see the New Sociology at its best. A team of social workers and police—the heart and muscle of our society—working together to save helpless children from a depraved attacker. It is a story you should be proud of, because you are government."*

"I know it's corny, Steven, but at least it presents a favorable image."

Dr. Oliver was discussing the management of Cindy Scott. Heads were beginning to turn toward the conversation in the back of the room. Steve recognized Beth Bonnell, who was sitting in front of them.

"Sue, this article has Washington already tried and convicted and it misrepresents the facts." He was talking quite loudly now. Dr. Oliver paused and peered to the back of the auditorium. Dr. Browne stood up to see what was interrupting the decorum of his conference.

"Steven, you are making a scene," said Suzanne, trying to smile at the curious audience.

"Well, I don't care, this is important."

"Let's get out of here," said Suzanne, leading the way to the side aisle. Crane followed, and Dr. Oliver continued with his speech.

"As I was saying, when acetyl cysteine became available, many thought it would be the answer to this problem. We did a series of studies . . ." As the door closed behind them, Oliver's droning delivery was abruptly stifled.

"Steven Crane, what is wrong with you?" Suzanne hated to be embarrassed. Her neck was blotchy, showing her emotional strain.

"Sue, this thing has gotten completely out of hand. Everyone's jumping to conclusions. This article is just plain libel. I can't see how they could print anything like this. And you're supporting it."

"And you are completely irrational. We're talking about the man who burned those little girls, remember? The man who attacked me in my apartment. Remember?" Crane held up his hands in exasperation.

"But Sue, that's not the point. Do you realize that no one ever took a history from Washington? No doctor ever even talked to him? Now he's in jail because of a picture that Dave Stone saw once in a journal. There's something about this that isn't right."

"Maybe there's something about you that isn't right, Steven Crane. You're too close to this problem. If you'd just take an objective look at it—"

"Yes, and you're one to talk about being objective. With all those little innuendos and half-truths and outright fabrications that you were presenting at the hearing. I couldn't believe some of the things you were saying."

"I don't know what you're talking about." Her earrings were vibrating. She looked away, uncomfortable under his direct gaze.

"No, I can see you don't," he said. "And that's the sad part."

"What do you mean?" she asked, still looking away.

"Are you going to call the *News* and straighten this out?" he demanded, shaking the paper in his hand.

"Of course not," she said, looking down.

"Well, then I will." He left her standing outside the auditorium.

* * * *

The walls of the visiting room at the Wayne County jail were covered with that insipid gray-green paint which is monopolized by veterans hospitals and penal institutions. The last painter had over-lapped the black molding in several places, and left thick cakes on the wired glass window where he had carelessly wandered off the pitted putty—passive indications of distaste for the job. The floor—a sickly green vinyl tile flecked with white and black—bore the pockmarks of a thousand cigarettes maliciously snuffed into the floor rather than the single ashtray provided on the low table. Sally was seated on one of the two brushed-aluminum chairs when Kevin was ushered in through the door with the small barred window. The rumpled green-gray prison suit matched the walls. Sally stood as he entered and they clung to each other for almost a minute. "How are the kids?" he said finally.

"They're pretty good," said Sally, clearing her throat. "Better than me. Better than you too, I guess," she added, noticing his bloodshot eyes and gaunt expression. She settled her cheek on his chest so she wouldn't have to watch his face. "They buried Susie this morning. Nobody—" Her throat went into spasm and the next word was lost in a gurgle. She coughed. "Nobody came except me." She felt him shake. Another minute elapsed.

"Any word on the bail?" he asked, still holding her tightly.

"I can't get it, Kevin. A hundred thousand dollars! The man you told me about was going to lend it to me until he read the story in the paper." More silence.
"How 'bout the lawyer?"

"I called Mr. Jennings. He wasn't . . . he wasn't very nice. I called the public defender's office. They're supposed to call me back." She paused. The silence was painful. "How's it going for you?" she asked, relaxing her hold so they could sit in the two chairs, knee to knee, holding hands. He shrugged.

"I got a cell by myself. Nobody talks to me. I guess it's better that way."

"What happened to your roommate?"

"That fellow from Highland Park, we . . . we had a fight." His pained expression told her the reason why. More silence followed, interrupted by an occasional shuddering sigh. He thumbed the shiny wedding band on her finger. "Any luck on finding my little brother Ritchie?" he said absently, knowing what the answer would be.

"Nothing. That telephone number in Denver was disconnected. Your mother hasn't heard from him either." Kevin looked up sharply.

"You called my mother? You didn't tell her—"

"No, I didn't tell her anything. I just asked where Ritchie was and

168

she said she didn't know. She asked about you . . . I didn't tell her about Susie yet. I just said she's still sick and in the hospital."

"That's good. We'll have to tell her sometime. I don't know. Did you bring any cigarettes?"

"Oh, yes," she said, remembering. She produced a fresh pack from her pocket and waited while he puffed the first inch into a turbid cloud. "Kevin, I've got to ask you this one more time. All those things they said in the courtroom–about Susie and how she got burned. Are you sure you remember it right? I mean, is there any way that they could be right? They seem so sure." The look on his face passed from grief to fury to blank despair in an instant.

"Oh baby," he said, gently wrapping his fingers into her soft blond hair. "They finally got to you, too." He dropped the cigarette and, standing, rubbed it out with his heavy boot, then walked out the back door without another word. Through the barred window she could see him disappearing down the hall.

"You didn't answer my question," she said softly.

* * * *

"Pete, you don't know how happy this makes me," said Edward Browne, bringing a mug of coffee from the outer office. "These Washington kids have been on my mind all week–well hell, ever since they've been in the hospital. And when the baby died I just couldn't stand the thought of them lying around juvenile hall." Peter Blake took the coffee mug. It was a heavy brown and white ceramic affair purchased by some long forgotten secretary. "Oh, they do a great job over there–as you very well know–but those kids need the warmth of a home and family. I'm pleased as punch." Browne settled into the leather couch.

"If you really want to know, Ed, it was that newspaper story that did it. When Val saw that, she said we didn't have any choice." Blake gestured with his coffee cup. "Cheers."

"That's another reason I'm glad you're taking the children," said Browne. "The reporters are badgering the hell out of the social workers and me and my residents, anyone they can get a hold of. There's a lot of interest in the story. I suppose it's good publicity for the hospital, but it sure is annoying."

"I hope you won't tell them where to call next." Blake smiled.

"Of course not," said Browne. "It's a little out of the ordinary to have you come over here, but I wanted to give you all the medical history on Becky and let you talk to our social worker, Miss Hathaway. It seemed to be the most convenient meeting place."

"No problem, Ed," said Blake. "I was in court this afternoon anyway. It was right on the way."

Suzanne knocked on the open door. "May I join you?," she asked brightly.

"Of course, of course, come in, Miss Hathaway. Miss Hathaway, I think you know Mr. Blake." She entered the room confidently, encouraged by Blake's friendly smile. She hadn't noticed before, but by comparison to Browne's rather middle-aged appearance, the lawyer was strikingly handsome. Blake rose to shake her hand.

"Miss Hathaway, it's so nice to see you again." He squeezed her hand just a second longer than was necessary.

"It's nice to see you, sir, and it's so nice of you to help us out with the Washington children. Dr. Browne said he would try to twist your arm." She winked at Browne and flashed a demure smile at Blake. Browne experienced the same self-conscious feeling he got when being introduced to his daughter's boyfriends.

"Well, sit down, sit down. I was just telling Mr. Blake a bit about the children's background."

"Miss Johnson from Child Welfare will have both of the children at juvenile hall tomorrow morning, if that's convenient," said Suzanne, speaking directly to Blake in a warm voice. "They'll probably arrange some sort of visiting schedule for the mother."

"That will be a new experience for us," said Blake. "Most of our other foster children have been orphans. Are there any special medical problems, Ed?"

"I'm told the little boy is fine. The two-year-old girl is recovering nicely from the burns. She wears a little elastic suit—sort of a leotard. She's taking some medication for itching. Other than that, there's nothing special. We'll have to see her every couple of weeks for the next few months."

Browne's secretary poked her head in the door. "Excuse me, Dr. Browne. The Tyler family is still waiting to see you."

"Oh yes." He turned to Blake. "Pete, would you excuse me? I have a family waiting up on the floor. I'm sure Miss Hathaway can answer any other questions."

"Go right ahead, Ed. Thanks a lot. I'll call you at home if there are any problems–if you won't charge for a house call."

"Call anytime you need to," said Browne, donning his long white coat. "We'll run a tab." He closed the office door as he left.

The feeling in the room remained professional but the atmosphere had changed. Although the conversation remained practical, Suzanne was thinking about his tie, his eyes, a vague recollection of his wife. Although he looked attentively concerned, Blake was remembering how she looked in the tight black dress at the concert. They discussed the Washington children, then the Thanksgiving holiday, then the Michigan-Ohio State game. In ten minutes the gray afternoon passed through dusk and into evening. In a twenty-second silence they stared at each other, wondering.

"Isn't that a Princeton tie?" she asked.

"As a matter of fact it is," he said, surprised. "Do you make a study of Ivy League ties?"

"My cousin went to Princeton," she admitted, smiling.

"You're very perceptive, Miss Hathaway. After all, it could have been Pittsburgh–or Birmingham High School."

"Not likely," she chuckled, "and please call me Sue."

He rose to leave. "Okay, Sue." He stood close to her. "Do you know that your eyes change color as the sun sets?"

"Why no, I . . ." She felt spellbound. Self-consciously, she touched the back of her neck to stop the tingling. Blake looked serious, then smiled.

"I have to be going. May I give you a ride home?"

"Why, yes, I'd like that. That's very thoughtful of you."

As they entered the elevator, she thought about her car in the hospital
parking lot, and decided to leave it there overnight.

CHAPTER 17

> We gather together to ask the Lord's blessing.
> He chastens and hastens His will to make known.

It was the bayberry candles that did it. The oak logs in the fireplace provided the baseline aroma. Pine has a resin smell; birch and poplar logs burn with a musty sweet smoke reminiscent of fires in vacant lots. Only oak provides the rich foundation upon which to present the permeating essence of roasting turkey. Yes, turkey basting in butter, pungent stuffing, and a hint of oak smoke; it enters the nose and goes straight to the soul. But to top it off with a hint of bayberry, that was the subtle difference between Thanksgiving at the Browne's home and anywhere else.

Edward Browne had learned it from his grandmother. In his boyhood, they made the bayberry candles during the rainy days in late August on Martha's Vineyard. Then she saved them away, to be brought out the night before Thanksgiving when their aroma would provide the first soft note in that olfactory symphony which would culminate in the most satisfying and most sentimental of all meals. This was Steven Crane's third Thanksgiving in the Browne home, and he still couldn't place the faintly spicy odor that always elicited such a flood of pleasant memories. The compulsory singing of Thanksgiving songs merely added to the unique warmth of the holiday.

> The wicked oppressing
> Now cease from distressing.

Dr. Browne himself always played the piano, always wore a gold suede vest, always told the same stories about shucking corn, crushing cranberries, and picking birdshot out of wild turkey on Thanksgiving at his grandmother's house. On their first Thanksgiving in Detroit, the

Brownes had invited a Philippino resident for dinner. The next year they invited all the foreign residents, and thereafter invited all the residents who would not be home with their own families on Thanksgiving Day. The Browne children grew up with delightful memories of Thanksgiving as a sort of international celebration which began with the Lions game and ended with cold turkey sandwiches and dill pickles after all the guests had left. This Thanksgiving Edward Browne II was visiting from Oregon with his young wife and little Edward Browne III.

> Sing praises to His name,
> He forgets not His own.

"All you singers must be getting thirsty," said Dot Browne, interrupting the last four-bar piano introduction to "Come Ye Thankful People, Come." She came from the kitchen, bringing a huge tray holding pewter mugs of hot cider, each with a stick of cinnamon and a dash of nutmeg floating on the top. This signaled the beginning of the feast and Steven recalled that it always accompanied the introduction to "Come Ye Thankful People, Come," so that the singing of that lusty hymn was always accented by the clinking of tankards and an inspired basso profundo from Dr. Browne himself. The day was very cold and the year's first snowfall had dusted the dark pines and barren lawns of Hunting Valley, noting the glinty promise of a heavy winter. There would be, of course, a heady vouvray and a hearty burgundy with the turkey, but for now, the hot spicy cider was perfect.

There were fifteen in all who sat down at the big table. Each person had something to serve so that all the plates circulated around the entire table eliciting a buzz of anticipation and appropriate commentary. After the steaming golden brown bird was brought to the table—amidst the oohs and aahs and bravos of those assembled—and before the trussed legs were freed and the carving began, Browne announced the giving of thanks. "Before we partake in these fruits of God's bounty and our own hard work, let us pause for a moment to render thanks to whatever deity each of us holds sacred." A ten second pause. "So be it."

Muhammad El-Azir was grinning continuously. This family knew how to keep a feast day! Chatterjee had struck up a conversation about

Chuck Mangione with sixteen-year-old Andrew Browne. Dot brought in the second heaping bowl of extra stuffing from the kitchen. Edward Browne II commented, to his young wife's embarrassment, that he had not had real squash (glazed with brown sugar and marshmallows) since his last Thanksgiving at home three years before.

After the seconds and the domestic conversation (hospital talk was forbidden), Crane leaned back in his chair. "A thoroughly consuming and delightful experience," he thought, downing the last rapturous bite of Grandma Browne's pumpkin pie.

After dinner they slumped, painfully but pleasantly distended, into the soft chairs of the living room to sip strong coffee from gilt-edged cups, and smoke fine cigars sent for the occasion by a former Cuban resident now practicing in Miami. They sampled a plum brandy sent by Akio Taramatsu, professor of pediatrics at the University of Tokyo, who had spent three Thanksgiving days at the Browne's home. Although they had successfully avoided it during dinner, the conversation slowly turned medical. It was Mrs. Browne who inadvertently brought up the Washington case.

"Have you seen those articles in the *News*? About the child abuse case? The third one came out yesterday. It was an interview with a detective from the police department. Have you seen those articles, Steve?"

Steve was the wrong one to ask. He had been up most of the night before, and had just consumed four glasses of wine, a plum brandy, and a Courvoisier, in addition to the sumptuous dinner.

"I've seen the articles," he said. "And I know all about the case. We'd better not discuss it."

She did not perceive the warning. "The second article had a nice interview with the social worker–Miss Hathaway, isn't it?"

"I didn't read it," lied Crane. "It could have been Sue Hathaway."

Other conversations began throughout the room. Dr. Browne turned to Steve. "Steve, didn't you bring Miss Hathaway to the department picnic last spring?"

Steve had not talked to Suzanne for more than a week. The more he thought about her attitude, the more bitter he became. "I can't remember; I might have." He tried to drop the subject, but Mrs. Browne was obviously very interested.

"Do you know the family–and the children?" He nodded. "How

could the father do such a terrible thing to his own daughter? I don't understand it."

"Well, there's . . . there's still a lot that is not clear. It's possible that he might not have done anything," said Steven. His statement seemed like an announcement to everyone in the room. "In fact, the evidence against the guy is all circumstantial and very flimsy at that." This statement, a little too loud because of the wine, came at a quiet moment and the others turned their attention to Steven.

"Really?" asked Dot Browne, astonished. "The newspaper accounts are awfully certain. And Ed says—"

"Don't tell me you two are on the Washington case," interrupted Edward Browne. "Every place I go someone's talking about the Washington case. It's that series in the *Detroit News*. I don't know how they got a hold of it." He gestured at the living room's large window. "You know, the children of that family are staying with the Blakes—right over that hill."

"Peter Blake, the lawyer Peter Blake?" asked Steven. He remembered their conversation at the symphony.

"Yes, that's the one," said Browne. "Didn't you know that?"

"No, I didn't," said Steven, trying to recall what it was that made him feel uneasy about that association.

"The Blakes have taken in several foster children—I think I've told you that—and they're helping us out with the Washington kids. I just couldn't stand the thought of that little girl rattling around in juvenile hall. My friend Blake agreed to take them in."

Steven observed that Browne at home among his family was a more relaxed, more compassionate, more ordinary man than Browne at the hospital. He felt a bond of friendship which prompted him to be unduly candid.

"I'm glad he's taken in the children," said Steve. "He's done a better job than we have. We haven't been very fair to that family, especially to the father." The room became quiet. Other conversations now stopped altogether. The logs crackled in the fireplace.

"Unfair? In what way, Crane?" Steven was too sedated by food and wine to detect the change in Browne's tone of voice.

"We never gave him a chance to tell his story. No one ever took a history. None of us ever heard his side of the story."

"Of course we did, Crane, we all did. Why, it's even in the newspaper." Browne's irritation was becoming noticeable.

"It may be in the newspaper, Dr. Browne, but it's not in the chart. I tell you, no one ever took a history from the fellow–or the wife. And that's the most important factor in a child abuse case. You've taught us that."

"That's right, Ed, you've told me that a dozen times," said Dot Browne. "Why didn't anyone take a history?" she inquired of Steven.

"Everyone took a history," interrupted Browne, quite annoyed now. "Stone, Redford, even old Dr. Mac took a history. If it's not in the chart, they just forgot to write it down. The guy's guilty as hell. His actions show that. One little girl's dead. Jesus, Crane, what do you want?"

"I'd like to see a little justice," Steven said heatedly. "I'd like to know what the man has to say, that's all. He hasn't had a fair shake. There he is in jail–his wife's home alone–his children are at the Blake's–all on the basis of our negligence and some social worker's enthusiasm. There's an abuse of power there somewhere."

"Crane, you're off on a wrong tack. You'd better check your facts." He narrowed his eyes and lowered his voice to an icy tone.

"So should you," muttered Steven under his breath.

"What's that?" snapped Browne.

"Yes, I will," said Crane in a louder voice, suddenly aware of the tension he had created. "I'm sorry we got into it. This brandy is fascinating. Where did you say it came from?"

"From Tokyo, from Dr. Taramatsu. He was with us around 1963 or '64, wasn't he, Ed?" said Dot Browne, quickly hurrying to get off the painful subject. "He was a delightful fellow. He could barely speak English when he arrived here and now he's the professor of pediatrics at the University of Tokyo."

"A delightful fellow," said Browne, repressing his anger and resuming the genial tone of the evening. Crane slumped back and dipped the tip of his genuine Havana cigar into the plum brandy.

* * * *

"And what does that mean to you?" asked Mrs. Starkweather. This question followed almost two minutes of silence, and Sally had forgotten the original statement.

177

"I'm sorry. What does what mean to me?"

"What does what you just said mean to you?" Mrs. Starkweather was leaning back on the springs of her desk chair, slowly swiveling from side to side, suspending a freshly sharpened pencil between her two index fingers. She waited for a response, eyeing Sally lazily, her fat lips hanging open as if it would be an effort to close them.

"I'm afraid I can't remember what I said," said Sally, with a fleeting embarrassed smile.

"Oh? What does that mean to you?"

"What does what mean to me?"

"The fact that you can't remember what you just said a few minutes ago?" Women who weigh 193 pounds should never wear slacks. Mrs. Starkweather was wearing lavender slacks made of a sleazy material that seemed like it would stretch forever. Great mounds of fat exuded from the short sleeves of her fuzzy pink sweater. It was like the sweater she wore in high school in 1956; in fact, it might have been the same one. The sweater and the slacks folded around three rolls of fat that hung like putty around her. Sally guessed that the upper roll contained her breasts.

"I guess it means I wasn't really concentrating," said Sally. She imagined the raw rash, doused with talcum powder, that must be smoldering under each of those pendulous rolls.

"And what are you concentrating on?" asked Mrs. Starkweather, digging under one fingernail with the pencil. Sally was thinking of the dispute over payments for foster care. She was furious when her salary was attached to pay for the care of her own children in another home. But she had lost MPR points arguing over the issue so she wasn't about to bring it up again.

Instead, she put on her best Goldie Hawn face and said, "Actually I was thinking about my children having Christmas in that big house in Hunting Valley. It will be nice for them; it's probably for the best." She was learning the system. She found that if she tried to imitate Goldie Hawn, social workers always smiled and said, "That's good."

"That's good," said Mrs. Starkweather. She had short little teeth that gave her a porcine appearance. "And what will you get for the children for Christmas?"

"I think I'll get Becky one of those new dolls that you can put in the bathtub." She couldn't resist the grim joke, but she was also testing

Mrs. Starkweather. Since she had taken over for Mavis Johnson two weeks ago, Sally had developed the impression that Mrs. Starkweather knew nothing about her case.

"That's good," said Mrs. Starkweather. "She'll probably like that. I would." She adjusted her amorphous bottom in the chair, pleased at the thought of such a practical toy.

"Do you have children, Mrs. Starkweather?" asked Sally.

"Why do you ask?" The chair springs groaned as she shifted from cheek
to cheek.

"Miss Johnson didn't have any children. She wasn't even married. Sometimes I thought she didn't understand me. But counseling with you is so . . . different. You seem to know just what to say."

"Why, thank you, dear! I like you too." She smiled wider and heaved her heavy arms onto the desk. Sally noted that she never answered the question. "I think our time is up for today."

"Mrs. Starkweather, can I bring my children home for Christmas?"

"Probably." She thought for a minute. "Probably; I'll ask Miss Johnson about it."

"Miss Johnson? Aren't you in charge now?"

"Well, yes, I'm in charge of counseling, sort of temporarily. I'll ask Miss Johnson." She smiled her grimy grin.

"But Christmas is next week." Sally could see the inevitable shuffle. She felt like the pea in a shell game.

"Yes, I know, I know. Well, you call back tomorrow and I'll let you know. Right now I have another appointment."

"I'll call tomorrow," said Sally, knowing that it would be impossible to get through the switchboard. Dejected, she left the office and the building. The doleful little man who rang the bell beside a red Salvation Army bucket had his collar pulled up and the flaps on his leather cap pulled down over his ears, but he was still frozen, judging by the way he pulled his elbows into his sides, dug his chin into his scarf, and bounced from foot to foot. Not surprising that he's cold, thought Sally. He had been standing in the same spot when she entered the building two hours before. It was mid-afternoon, still light, but a depressing day. The gray, overcast sky had come to stay for the winter. The sun would rarely be seen from now until spring. But the colored lights and the plastic wreaths and the clanging bell gave a feeling of cheer for now. The real gloom of sunless days would not set in until January.

As Sally trudged away, head down, she resigned herself to giving up on the idea of getting the children home for Christmas. But she resolved to visit the Blakes on Christmas. She had been there once before—at their invitation. They seemed pleasant enough. They certainly took good care of the children. Actually, it bothered her that the children seemed so happy. They seemed to belong in the mansion, although Sally felt as if she were in a museum.

The combination of high clouds and the cold atmosphere made the snowflakes big, dry, and lacy. The heat had gone out of the pavement and the snow was just starting to stick, creating a fresh fairyland appearance that would last until the snow in the gutters turned to brown slush. When the light changed, she crossed the street to the little parking lot levered in between the tall buildings. She found the yellow parking ticket in her purse and pushed it through the hole in the window to the young black man who was trying to stay warm in the small booth. He turned to the board behind him, scanned it with his finger, and came up with a set of keys.

"Uh-oh. You driving an old blue Volkswagen?"

"Yes."

"Well, there it is, right there." He pointed out the window. "But you see, some dude that was driving that black Chrysler pinned you in there and didn't leave his keys. I can't get you out of there until he comes back."

"But you have to. I have to be at work in an hour." Nothing seemed to go right for Sally anymore.

"I'm sorry about that, lady. That fellow in the Chevy in front of you has to go somewhere too. *Oowee*, he's mad." Nondescript Motown disco blared from the portable stereo behind him. "Hey, look, take your keys and warm it up. That fellow will probably be back by the time you're ready to go. Here you go." He passed the keys through the window. Sally edged between the sardine-packed cars. She could only open the door about a foot, but it was enough for her to squeeze in. She started the engine as the attendant had suggested, although she knew the VW would stay cold no matter how long she ran it. Sighing, she picked up the scraper-brush from the back seat and began brushing the accumulating snow off the windows. The fellow in the

Chevrolet in front of her was doing the same.

"Isn't this a bitch?" he muttered, more to himself than to her. "Stuck in a damn parking lot. Can you believe this?"

"I know. I'm going to be late for work." She looked up as she moved to the back window. The Chevy driver looked familiar. He was looking at her as if he thought the same thing. He shrugged and leaned across his hood, getting snow and grime on his coat. "Can you believe this?" he repeated. He looked at her again. "Hey, don't I know you from somewhere?"

"Yeah, I was just thinking the same thing. You look very familiar."

"Oh, I know, you're the lady with the missing husband and the burned kids. Susie, isn't it? Or Sally?"

"That's right. Why, you're Mr. Jennings." She recognized his voice more than his face, which was bundled up in a large scarf. "Aren't you Mr. Jennings, the lawyer?"

"Yes, that's right." He pulled the scarf down and smiled, exposing the gap between his front teeth. "Now, we're both in a tight spot. Can you believe this?" His voice was no longer bitter. "Well, good luck to you," he said, climbing back into his warm car. He fumbled through some papers for a while, swore a few times, and then looked into the rearview mirror. Sally had taken off her stocking cap and was combing her hair. She looked cold. He closed his briefcase, turned off his engine, walked back to her car, and knocked on the window. She waved and opened it a crack. "Have you had lunch?" he asked.

"No," she said, shivering.

"Well, there's no point in sitting here freezing. There's a little place around the corner. Come on."

"Sounds like a plan," she said, using one of Kevin's favorite phrases. They hurried along the sidewalk, too cold to talk, until he pointed out Angelo's Downtown Diner. A little bell above the door rang as they swept in along with a blast of cold air. Two men sitting at the counter turned to see who else had found refuge from the snow. One had on a uniform–a postman or perhaps a bus driver–and the other wore white coveralls that said "Hostess Bakery" across the back and "Fred" above the front pocket. They looked up, made an assessment, and returned to their plates without ever taking their forearms off the counter. Sustained by the lunch crowd from the city-county building and the post office, the diner had withstood the ravages of urban decay. It was growing old, along with Angelo Eraklis, who was sitting in the back booth reading the newspaper.

The only things that had changed in the diner in twenty-five years were the songs on the jukebox. Each of the six booths had its own jukebox selector, a blond-wood-grained Formica table, and seats of cracked green vinyl–the kind that got hard and crinkly in cold weather. The stools and the counter were made of the same materials. Dirty glass and chrome cabinets displayed individual pieces of cream and fruit pies, illuminated by a yellowish forty-watt bulb. The smell of cigar smoke and burned coffee hung heavy in the air. They settled into the first booth. The jukebox fascinated Sally. "What's this?" she asked, cautiously pushing the red plastic buttons. Jennings laughed.

"This is a jukebox. See, it's hooked up to the big one over there." He nodded to the corner where a vintage Wurlitzer loaded with records was stationed. "Look, here are all the songs." He pulled the selection cards forward using the metal knobs that stuck out of the windowed box.

"Oh I see. That looks like fun, let me do it." Sally flipped the cards around, reading the selections which ranged from Waylon Jennings to the Harmonicats. Freshly typed cards had been inserted in the last four slots. "How do you do it?" asked Sally. Jennings, still smiling, pulled a quarter from his pocket and put it into the slot. Lights went on in the Wurlitzer.

"Which one do you want? We get three."

"Oh, let's have these." She pointed to the recently added Christmas songs. Jennings pushed J7, J8, J9. The Wurlitzer hummed, clicked, and groaned, and soon Gene Autry was singing "You'd better watch out, you'd better not cry . . ."

Angelo emerged from the back smiling and wiping his hands on his already-greasy white apron, "That's nice; I'm glad you like my Christmas songs." He tossed down two menus. Jennings recognized the blue printing as originating from a genuine ditto machine. The single sheet menus were held in plastic carriers that had, at one time, been clear. "I put those Christmas songs in every year. Some people play them. I'm glad you like them," repeated Angelo. As an afterthought he added, "The meat loaf is very good today."

Jennings nestled comfortably into the corner of the booth. His fingers must have been colder than he had realized, because now they were getting hot. He placed his hands on the table gently and regarded Sally.

"Well, Sally, what's happened to you? I haven't seen you for months."

"You were right about one thing. You have to tell those people what they want to hear. I just came from a counseling session," she said. "I have a new social worker–Mrs. Starkweather?" Jennings did not recognize the name. "She doesn't know anything about my case. Maybe that's just as well. The last one said things about me that aren't true."

"How are your children?" asked Jennings, hoping to get off a subject that might lead to an unsolicited consultation.

Tears brimmed in Sally's eyes. She usually managed to push little Susie into the back of her mind as long as she stayed busy, but she still could not deal with a sudden reminder like the diapers she came across in the closet, or Jennings's direct question.

"She died. Susie, my little one-year-old, she died in the hospital." She sighed and wiped her cheeks. "Becky's fine. And Sammy. They're in a foster home. It's a nice place, really, in Hunting Valley." She smiled and wiped away more tears.

"Oh, I'm sorry, I really am." If he had read the articles in the *News*, he did not remember. Almost subconsciously he pulled two paper napkins from the bulging dispenser and handed them to her. She had regained her composure when Angelo appeared with lunch–a meatloaf special and a BLT.

Jennings hunched over his plate–pre-World-War-II heavy crockery, white with a blue line, near the edge–and drained the lake of gravy onto the meatloaf.

"Hey," he said, surprised. "It's real mashed potatoes."

"What dija expect," said Angelo, offended. "We wouldn't serve that powdered stuff. It tastes like paste." Although they hadn't asked for coffee, he plunked down two heavy white ceramic mugs and filled them with steaming black liquid from the glass pitcher on the Corey coffee maker.

"What's happened to that fellow you were living with? Is he still there?" asked Jennings, pausing to slather butter on a cold roll.

"He's in jail," said Sally, not wishing to go further.

"In jail? What for?"

"They charged him with child abuse and . . . murder."

Jennings paused with a mouthful of mashed potato and gravy. "Murder? You mean, because the little girl died?" She nodded.

"Wow, that's heavy stuff." He inhaled two bites of meatloaf, thinking. "Yeah, that's heavy. Of course, he can plea bargain it down to manslaughter. Shouldn't be too bad." He was thinking out loud to himself, and then suddenly realized that he might seem to be offering his services. "That's out of my line, out of my line, of course, but a good trial lawyer could probably help him out. Does he have a lawyer?"

"Mr. Reed from the public defender's office."

"Don't know him."

"He's very nice. He knows what he's talking about." Sally was speaking softly, hoping the men at the counter would not hear.

Jennings nodded. "How are you getting along, you and him?" he asked cautiously.

"Oh, I'm doing all right. To tell you the truth, I really don't know who to believe now. Mostly, I just want my children back. I'm going to try to get them home for Christmas," she finished resolutely.

"Sure, that sounds good," said Jennings, buttering the second roll. Rudolph clicked off and the robot in the Wurlitzer cranked J8 out of the upright turntable and brought in J9. Sally was too young to have heard Nat Cole, and too country to know about Mel Torme.

She associated "The Christmas Song" with an Andy Williams TV special. But she liked the version that played now very much nonetheless, and began to hum along, eager for a dreamy diversion. Jennings watched her for almost a minute. She seemed too young and naive to be forced into such weighty problems. He began to think of her as pathetic, vulnerable, and unwittingly sexy–like Daisy Mae, he thought. "How long's your old man been in jail?" he asked.

"Six weeks." She continued humming.

"God, you must be horny."

"Why, Mr. Jennings!" She blushed violently. He wasn't laughing. "What a thing to say!"

"Well, I didn't mean to be so blunt." He smiled at last. "But a good looking woman like you, on these cold nights . . ." He smiled again, letting the sentence hang.

"What a thing to say!" She sipped at her coffee. She leaned across the table. "You're right, I'm going crazy," she said, seductively, her tongue pausing on her upper lip, "but what a thing to say, right over lunch!" She blushed redder than ever, watching him grin and squirm in his seat.

He paid the bill and the bell on the door tinkled as they went to see if the Chrysler driver had returned.

CHAPTER 18

Few children had ever enjoyed Christmas as much as Chris Fischer. On December 23, 1951, when he was eight years old, full of excitement and anticipation, Chris rode his bike down to the corner of Fox and Grand River to await the appearance of his father's car. It was dusk. He hit a patch of ice and skidded out onto the highway. The driver of the lumber truck didn't even feel the impact. They took him to Presbyterian Hospital where he died on the evening of December 24 of skull fractures, cerebral contusions, and a variety of other injuries. On Christmas morning, 1951, Mr. and Mrs. Martin Fischer arose from a sleepless night and surveyed their little living room, overflowing with presents intended for their only child. Without speaking they loaded the presents into the car and within an hour were distributing them to the children on the pediatric floor at Presbyterian Hospital. Each year thereafter, the Fischers appeared at Presbyterian on Christmas morning, and, with gentle smiles and trembling hands, touched each child and distributed a carefully selected array of brightly wrapped presents. This year was no exception.

Steven Crane, it seemed, was always on duty on Christmas Day. He remembered the Fischers from the year before, and guided them from room to room, introducing them to each little patient. Crane didn't know their story, nor did they volunteer it. He thought of them as a nice couple, getting on in years, who brought presents at Christmastime. When they came to the bedside of David Cooper, a skinny, freckle-faced eight-year-old with his head shaved for a shunt revision, Mrs. Fischer had to leave the room.

When the Fischers had departed, Crane prepared a second cup of coffee and resumed reading his newspaper at the nursing station. A traditional but professional rendition of "Good King Wenceslas" by the Robert Shaw Chorale was playing through the paging speakers. Feet on the desk, Crane pulled loose his tie and settled into the sports section. A page for the neurosurgery resident to come to the emergency room interrupted the chorale. The page made him feel cozy and secure. It reminded him why he liked pediatrics. Christmas season in the adult hospital was a depressing time. The emergency room was filled with suicides, overdoses, burns, and drunks. The decreasing elective surgery schedule was more than compensated for by the street trauma, variceal bleeders, frostbite, and fractures. Residents who would rather be with their families found themselves working harder than ever, covering two or three services for their friends in order that they might get a few days off themselves.

But the pediatric service was different than the rest of the hospital at Christmas. Christmas Eve is difficult, to be sure, as the combination of darkness, twinkling lights, and pathetic little faces fans memories from emotional embers. But by Christmas Day the pediatric ward is like a happy family. There are toys to play with and cookies to eat. Santa will come (for the tenth time), as well as parents, at least two groups of caroling choraliers, and a few people–like the Fischers–who warm the soul. The residents can finish off whatever is left of the cheese balls, cans of nuts and candy, and peppermint candy canes that grateful families have left at the nursing station. With a little luck, Schulman would appear at noon, giving Steve the rest of the day for sipping brandy by the fire. The latter thought brought Crane out of his pleasant reverie. For the last two years, he had shared Christmas evening with Suzanne, but, aside from passing in the hall, they had not been together since the hearing. He resolved to call her that night.

"Dr. Crane, stat NICU, Dr. Steven Crane, stat, neonatal, Dr. Crane" came from the speakers–in the same bored voice that would announce a car with the lights on. Crane dropped the newspaper and ran down the hall. His beeper went off when he was halfway there. As he burst through the door, it was not difficult to identify where the problem was. Three nurses and a respiratory therapist were gathered around one isolette in the back corner of the room, hovering over a little humanoid form, trying to appear calm, but looking frantically toward the door every few seconds. Crane didn't stop for the usual washing and gowning.

"What's the problem?" he asked.

"This little guy's gone brady on us and we can't get him going again," said the charge nurse, who had her arms through the access holes of the isolette and was spanking the baby's feet. A glance at the monitor and the interval between the beeps told Crane that the heart rate was about forty. The baby, a little boy who looked to be about a thousand grams, was blue and flaccid. The respiratory therapist was trying in vain to coordinate the small bag and mask with the baby's face inside the isolette.

"Well, let's get him out of there and get him intubated," said Crane, dropping down the side door and pulling out the tray containing the baby.

"Wait a minute; don't break my arm and don't let him get cold," said the charge nurse, now standing with her arms inside the empty plastic box.

"Come on, Betty. We've done this before," chided Crane. "Where's the stuff?"

"Here it is." Crane recognized the confident voice behind him as that of Beth Bonnell. He turned to find the apparatus prepared. She handed him a miniature laryngoscope and smiled, as if to say "welcome." She had already tested the batteries and locked open the blade, turning on the light. "Do you like it straight or curved?" she asked, referring to the laryngoscope blade but grinning ever so slightly.

"I wouldn't touch that with a ten-foot pole, Miss Bonnell," said Crane, adjusting the baby's head and inserting the laryngoscope which he held between the thumb and two fingers of his left hand. The beeping stopped.

"He's arrested! He's arrested!" said Betty frantically, flipping through the leads on the monitor as if that would somehow restore the electrical activity of the heart.

"We can all see that, Betty, just cool it for a minute," said Crane, in a soft voice. Without taking his eyes from the miniature larynx he held out his hand. Beth put a small plastic endotracheal tube in it. "Too big," said Crane rolling it between his thumb and forefinger without moving his eyes. She replaced it with a smaller tube which he slipped into the trachea without difficulty. He withdrew the laryngo-scope and transferred the tube to his left hand, holding it firmly against the upper gums while the bag was attached. With a small stethoscope Beth listened to two breaths on each side of the chest.

"It's okay. Do you want to listen?" she said, holding out the earpieces toward Crane.

"No thanks, I'm sure you're right." He smiled. Over the last few months he had become accustomed to her unusual efficiency. She fixed the tube in place with one long piece of clear plastic tape. The whole process took no more than thirty seconds. Crane stood up and stretched his back, looking at the monitor. Still no heartbeat. He encircled the baby's chest with one hand, pressing rhythmically on the rubbery sternum with his thumb. "Let's start an IV." Beth was already examining one little arm for that purpose. "What's the story on this baby?" asked Steven.

"He's about three weeks old," said Beth. "He was on a ventilator for RDS for a few days, but he's been doing fine recently. He started on feedings last week. He's up to full strength breast milk now. He's had a few apneic spells but nothing major. A few hours ago he just got the dwindles." While reciting the history she placed a small tourniquet, miraculously found a patent vein near the elbow, and inserted a number twenty-five scalp vein. Dark blood flowed briskly into the tubing, and she attached the IV while Crane continued his cardiac massage. In the past he had noticed her long slender fingers, and the lack of wasted motion. As she bent over the IV, he looked into the waves of dark hair and allowed his mind to wander briefly. He waited to see what she would do next.

She picked up a syringe of sodium bicarbonate, stuck the needle into the rubber connector near the scalp vein and pushed in three cc. The black blood in the tubing turned bright red in the alkaline fluid. She looked up and smiled.
"All right?"

"Of course. It's a big dose but . . ."

" . . . but he needs the volume anyway because he's probably septic," she said confidently. Crane was the only doctor she had met who actually enjoyed her independence.

"Undoubtedly septic," agreed Crane. Crane's thumb was triggering the monitor at a rate of 120. Although he was bothered by the fact that the heart did not resuscitate with a few minutes of good ventilation, his mind registered that he and Beth were essentially having a private conversation. The charge nurse had left to go wherever it is that charge nurses go during an arrest, and the respiratory therapist was occupied bagging with one hand and preparing the ventilator with the other.

When the bicarbonate bolus reached the coronary circulation, a spontaneous rate came up from under Steve's massage, reaching 160, then 180. He stopped compressing. The carotid pulse was bounding. "Better check some gases," he said, noting that Beth had already wrapped a foot and prepared a heparinized tube.

Crane held the knee while she held the ankle, drawing the dark capillary blood from the puncture site with her other hand. The baby was flaccid; he wouldn't move his knee. But Crane held him anyway in order to place his little finger against hers to see how it would feel, to satisfy his growing impulse to establish the slightest bit of physical contact.

"Blood sure looks dark," she said, showing no sign of acknowledgment.

In two minutes the ruddy-faced bearded respiratory therapist returned with a slip of paper. "Fifty-two, forty-nine, and six-point-nine," said Steve. He and Beth looked at each other, silently affirming what they knew the next few hours would bring. Beth drew up some more bicarbonate as Steve called across the room. "Betty, who's this baby's doctor?"

"Horowitz is covering for the group today."

"Get a hold of him, would you please? Ask him if he wants to call the family, or have me do it. Tell him that the pH . . . oh nevermind, just get a hold of him and let me talk to him."

For the next two hours they plied the baby with bicarbonate, Tham, epinephrine, atropine, and dopamine. The portable X-ray machine came and went, verifying the unmistakable evidence of gas bubbles in the wall of the intestine. An annoyed Horowitz, a blasé surgical resident, and a young, tear-stained family came and went. Five times the heart stopped and four times it started again. Fifteen minutes into the fifth arrest Crane felt the bulging fontanelle with his index finger, lifted a gossamer eyelid with his thumb to expose a vacant black pupil, and said, "Ready to quit?"

"I'm ready," Beth said quietly, blowing a wisp of hair out of her field of vision. He looked at the clock.

"Let's call it 12:35." He flipped off the monitor and crossed the unit to slump on the rolling chair and write in the chart. There was a hospital policy for unexpected deaths which required leaving the tubes, monitors, and wires in place until the coroner released the case.

When he looked up he noticed that Beth had removed the endotracheal tube and IV, and wrapped the IV site with tape to prevent oozing. She wrapped the little body in a blue blanket and put it in a clean bassinet by the window. She detected his concern. "The family," she said simply, and he nodded agreement.

Throwing a sheet over the isolette to put the rubble and carnage temporarily out of mind, she ushered in the Jacksons, and put James Jackson II in his mother's arms. Mrs. Jackson had never been allowed to hold her tiny son during his brief three weeks of life. Crane finished his note and telephone calls. He waited until the parents reached the door and spoke to them in the hallway. In simple sentences, he reiterated what had happened, explained again that they did all there was to do, and solemnly agreed that it was God's will. He got the post-permission and guided the family to the elevator. At that point, Schulman arrived and they made quick rounds, exchanging the intern's stack of three-by-five scut cards which they had inherited for the day.

They finished rounds in the neonatal ICU, which now looked as if nothing had happened. Grabbing his coat from the residents' room, Steve descended the elevator, just beginning to experience the aching exhaustion that follows a long spurt of nervous energy.

As he crossed the lobby, Beth Bonnell arose from one of the bright blue couches. Crane was surprised but neither spoke as they walked to the parking garage. The nonspecific disappointment which he felt in the elevator was dissipated by her presence. When they reached a red MG, she located her keys in her pocket and said, "Thank you, Dr. Crane; Merry Christmas." She leaned over and kissed him softly, briefly, on the cheek.

"Thank you, Nurse Bonnell. I'll drive." He took the keys from her hand.

* * * *

It was definitely true. Every time Valerie Blake came near, Becky looked terrified and started to cry. The first two times, Sally thought it was just coincidence, but now even Valerie commented on it. "Becky, Becky, what am I going to do with you?"

"No, no, no, where's Susie? I want Susie! Mommy, where's Susie?" Becky reached back and clutched at Sally's dress.

"I'm afraid she still associates me with the loss of her sister," explained Valerie. "Maybe I look like someone in the hospital. Come on, Becky." She leaned over to pick up the little girl, but desisted when Becky screeched and tightened her grip on Sally.

"Maybe that's it," said Sally, smoothing the little girl's forehead. Sally was very uneasy at the Blakes', despite their efforts to make her feel welcome. Although she'd only been there for a half an hour, she was looking for an excuse to leave. Since it was Christmas, she had been allowed an extra hour of visiting time with Kevin, but he seemed to become more sullen and withdrawn each day. They had shared only a dozen sentences, separated by long periods of silence during which he smoked continuously and looked at her rarely. She had hoped that the empty feeling left by that experience would be filled at the Blakes', but it was a vain hope.

There were two Christmas trees. In the living room was a small Scotch pine sprayed with white flocking and decorated only with large silver balls and blue lights. It matched the white and chrome decor of the living room and served as the focal point for the official family festivities. The main tree, however, stood twelve-feet high in the central hallway. It was a lovely Engelmann spruce–special ordered from the Hunting Valley Nursery–and it was decorated with twenty years worth of homemade ornaments and garlands. It was lit by spotlights from the second floor balcony and it seemed the perfect manifestation of a warm and richly resonant Christmas spirit. Even little Sammy proudly showed his mother the paper chain that he had made which stretched over three of the lower boughs.

But to Sally the tree meant something else. It was just another sign of the kidnapping and brainwashing of her children. She knew that the Blakes were merely trying to help, but she could not repress her feelings of hostility.

Peter Blake picked up the last wrapped present from under the tree and handed it carefully to Sammy. "Sammy, I think this last present's for your mother, from Santa Claus. Yes, that's what the card says, 'To Sally, from Santa.' Would you like to give it to her?" Sammy took the box, shook it, and trotted it over to Sally's lap.

"Oh Mr. Blake, you shouldn't have. I mean I didn't bring any presents for you."

"Now, Sally, we didn't do a thing; it's from Santa," said Blake, smiling. "He hopes you like it."

She peeled off the silvery commercial wrapping, exposing a white box which was faintly embossed: Hunting Valley Pharmacy. The box contained a bottle of popular cologne. The price tag–which had been left by mistake–said $11.95. It was, ironically, twelve dollars that Sally was required to pay each week for foster care.

"I think Mrs. Claus picked that out," Blake said lightly. "I hope you like it."

"Oh yes, it's wonderful. One of my favorites," said Sally, smiling and nodding as she had learned to do, but inwardly disgusted. "Thank you very much. And thank you for having me over today. It means a lot to me. To Kevin and me."

"Well, we're glad to have you, dear," said Valerie. "And the children are especially delighted, isn't that right, Becky?" When Valerie reached out to pat her knee, Becky trembled and pulled closer to Sally.

* * * *

"Hello, Walter? Are you there?" Brenda Reed stopped picking up wrappings and leaned over his face.

Walter Reed left his thoughts of the Kevin Washington defense in midair and focused on his wife. "What?"

"Your son is asking you a question."

He smiled at Brenda apologetically, acknowledging that he had been detected on a mental foray away from their Christmas afternoon.

Now he turned to his son, all attention. "What is it, Stuff?"

"Daddy, when can we put this thing on?" asked Walter Reed, Jr., holding up a small STP decal. "Stuff" was an abbreviation for Short Stuff, a nickname that derived from the need to differentiate Walter I from Walter II.

"Well, Stuff, we can't put that on until we're all through. That's the last thing. Now this is getting to look like something good." He pushed the nearly completed model dragster across the kitchen table. Stuff's eyes glowed. "Let's see now, what's next," said Walter, comparing the residual plastic parts–still attached to one another–to the printed instructions. He found a gray plastic roll bar and handed it to his five-year-old son.

"Here you go. This is a roll bar. It goes right in here. Give it a try

. . . Hey, that's good! Yes, it really looks like something now." He marveled at the growth process of his son, watching as little Walter's pudgy fingers guided the roll bar into position. His deliberate efforts were assisted by some vigorous chewing on his extended tongue.

"That kid's a born engineer," said Walt to Brenda, swelling with fatherly pride at the minor accomplishment.

"Just like you, Big Stuff." She smiled with him at the efforts of their little boy. Best Christmas ever, she thought to herself, rising to give them both a kiss and to finish cleaning up the happy rubble of wrapping paper, boxes, bows, and ribbons. "Who sent you this shirt, Stuffy?"

"Grandma."

"I know that. Which grandma?"

"Grandma Grace. She always sends me a shirt." He resumed chewing his tongue, reinserting the roll bar which had now been anointed with two drops of Testor's glue.

"Don't lose any instructions," cautioned Walter. "And try to find the guarantee on that tape recorder."

Later, with their son safely tucked away, Walter Sr. and Brenda sprawled on the shag carpet watching the embers glow in the fireplace. She snuggled into his warm chest. Sighs, murmurs, and glowing silence. After a while she asked, "What's on your mind today? Is it that drug case?"

Reed chuckled. "It's not the drug case. That's not worth thinking about. But playing with the Stuff today reminded me of a fellow named Washington."

"Washington's a five-year-old kid?"

He chuckled again. "No, he's the suspect in a child abuse/murder case. Remember the wild custody hearing I told you about a couple months ago?"

"You mean the mixed marriage and the guy that burned the little girls? How could I forget? Walter, they're not gonna make you defend that guy!" Concern caused her to sit up and turn away from the fire so she could look directly down into his face.

"It won't ever come to trial. The guy burned the little girl and she died. That's open and shut; it's just a matter of bargaining down the charge. He did ask me to represent him, though. I talked to him last week. That's what kept coming back to me today."

"How to bargain down the charge?"

Reed paused, analyzing his feelings. "No, not really. I was thinking about the way that guy looked when he talked about his children and how we feel about little Walt, you know? I started getting the feeling that the guy might actually be innocent."

"Every suspect is innocent until proven guilty by a jury of his peers," pontificated Brenda in a low voice, mimicking the axiom he quoted so often. She rapped an imaginary gavel on his chest. He rolled over and laughed aloud, then became pensive again.

"You know, that's true for everything except rape and child abuse. No matter how you pick the jury, they're going to assume guilt and you have to prove innocence. That's why we never let them go to trial. For Washington, the whole system works that way. The guy's been guilty since those girls arrived in the hospital. Hell, he probably is. But I just keep getting the feeling that the guy might have told the truth all along. Maybe the whole thing was an accident. I don't know."

"I remember that case now. There was a story in the newspaper about it. Something about saving the lives of the other children."

"Yeah, that's right. Protective custody. But what if the guy's telling the truth? And how 'bout the mother? I mean, could you imagine what you would do if someone came to our house now, tonight, and picked up Walter and put him in a foster home? Could you imagine what that would be like?"

"They can't do that, Walt, there has to be a reason and a court order. God, you know that."

"Sure I know that, but that's what happened to the Washingtons. They took all their kids. They're still in a foster home."

"But Walter, that's different; the man burned his own children."

"See, now you did it." He grinned and sat up beside her, pointing a finger in her face.

"I did what?" she said defensively.

"You said he was guilty. You just assumed he was guilty."

She had no response.

* * * *

"Stan Kenton is a genius, a genius. He should get the Nobel Prize for music." Steve Crane could become hyperbolic when discussing orchestral jazz as an art form.

"There is no Nobel Prize in music." There was something about the mischievous light in her dark eyes and her soft tone of voice that convinced Crane that her sarcastic rebuffs were well-intended. Whether in the hospital or not, Beth always seemed to be one step ahead of him, but strangely, he didn't mind.

"I know that. But if there were, Kenton should get it. When you consider the influence that that one man had on modern music, hell, the guy is amazing."

"Was amazing," said Beth. "He died last year." Crane could not tell if she was fooling or not.

"Come on, really? He was just here on tour."

"Yes, really. Did you ever hear Kenton's 'Christmas Carols'?"

"No," laughed Crane. He was sure now that she was putting him on.

She got up from the couch and riffled through the shelf of record albums. Through his amusement, he observed that her apartment was exactly what he would have expected. The long non-windowed wall was taken up by floor to ceiling shelves fashioned from red bricks and one-by-six foot planks. The shelves were filled with books representing a diversity of interests: modern American literature, mythology, architecture, classic literature, Central America, medical text books, three books on Picasso, four books on Mayan art, a stack of paperbacks on the Kennedy assassination, and all the works of Ayn Rand (Crane knew all six books and, sure enough, they were all there). The walls were covered with prints depicting illuminated sailboats, churches, and clouds, obviously all painted by the same individual. Crane did not recognize the artist, but derived a satisfying sense of confidence from the strangely angular paintings. Although the furnishings were definitely spartan, the feeling in the room was warm and scholarly, made so by the soft yellow lighting, the polished walnut draftsman's table which served as a desk near the window, and the brown, gray, and white Navajo rug on the floor.

He was struck by the contrast with Suzanne's stylish riverfront apartment. The decor was different, to be sure, but it was the little things he noticed most. Suzanne had a fancy Italian version of Mr. Coffee; Beth had a teakettle and a box of big filter paper. Suzanne had balls of scented colored soap in a glass bowl in the bathroom; Beth had a big red candle mounted in a homemade pinecone base. Suzanne's coffee table held *Cosmopolitan, Vogue, Time, and Holiday,* carefully arranged in order of decreasing size. Beth had something that looked like an old seaman's trunk, upon which were irregularly strewn the *New England Journal of Medicine, National Geographic,* and some remnants of last Sunday's *New York Times.* Despite the lack of fashion magazines, makeup, and pierced ears, Crane imagined that Beth would be equally elegant in jeans and a sweatshirt (as she was now) or a backless gown. Suzanne was always the latter, but never the former.

Beth found the record for which she was searching, delivered it from its jacket and placed it deftly on the turntable. "A celebration of Christmastide by Stanley Newcombe Kenton, et al.," she announced. Crane laughed again, expecting to hear the Philadelphia Brass Ensemble or the Mormon Tabernacle Choir. To his amazement, a crisp, racing, unmistakably Kenton version of "Angels We Have Heard on High" filled the room.

"Wow," said Crane. "Fantastic. Where did you get that? Let me see." She tossed him the record jacket with a satisfied chuckle.

"It is terrific, isn't it? This record is out of print. Would you like some more brandy?" He nodded affirmatively, his attention distracted by the fat Kenton sound, perfectly presented through the Infinity Q4s. When he recovered from his musical ecstasy, she was sitting next to him, smiling at his response.

"Is there anything you don't know about?" asked Crane, swirling the second glass of brandy.

"I know we like the same things. You're the only person I've ever met who prefers turkey sandwiches for Christmas dinner."

Crane felt himself slipping from the witty banter which had characterized their conversation throughout the afternoon, but he didn't care. "Hey Beth, let me ask you something. Do you ever use curlers?"

"No."

"Shower cap?"

"No."

"Did you ever wear a girdle?"

"No." She was laughing now.

"Satin bedroom slippers? Face cream? Slinky nightgowns?"

"Oh, God, no."

"Christ, you're incredible."

"Not incredible. Just like you. Do you ever smoke cigars?"

"Only good ones."

"Go to baseball games?"

"Bore me to tears."

"Play golf? Bridge? Go dancing?"

"Only under threat of death or social ostracism." Now he was laughing.

"What do you think of ties?"

"Can't stand 'em."

"How about a big black velvet tie and a matching vest under a black tuxedo with velvet lapels at the opening of the San Francisco Opera?"

"How did you know about that?"

"Just a guess."

They both laughed. "Incredible," he repeated.

Later in the evening he remembered that he had not called Suzanne.

CHAPTER 19

The winter was mild and spring came early to the Midwest. In the second week of March there was an unseasonable burst of clear weather with crisp starry nights and hot sunny days. The crocuses and the apple blossoms were almost fooled into believing that this long languorous preview was actually spring itself. The boys in Walter Reed's neighborhood left their down-filled vests hanging in the hall, and rummaged through the sprinklers, tire pumps, and car wax until they found the balls and gloves and bats.

Reed's court case had finished unexpectedly on Tuesday afternoon, and he had every intention of taking Wednesday off. While Brenda prepared Walter, Jr., for school, he dozed and stretched, savoring the option to ignore the clockradio and drift in and out of consciousness. While he was shaving, he was sure he heard the song of a robin mixed in with that of the chickadees. He came to breakfast wearing old clothes and flipped open the newspaper. At that point his plan for the day made an abrupt change.

On the front page of the *News,* under the heading "The New Sociology," was an article titled, "Who Pays for Courtroom Inefficiency?" It was written by
James Murray.

> *Each morning when you get up to go to work, Kevin Washington sleeps in. While you fight freeway traffic, put in your eight hours, and fight the freeway again, Kevin Washington ambles from room to room, reading, watching TV, and eating meals that he neither prepares nor pays for. Each day a big chunk of your salary goes to the County of Wayne instead of into your pocket. And each day the County of Wayne shells out $27.50 of your hard-earned cash to provide the accommodations of Kevin Washington. You*

wouldn't want to trade places with him. He's an inmate of the Wayne County Jail, accused of child abuse and murder, awaiting trial. In fact, his case may not even come to trial, but each and every day for the last three months, while the judge, the district attorney, and Washington's lawyers spend their time on other pursuits, the cash register rings. You, Mr. Taxpayer, have already spent thousands of dollars to keep Mr. Washington comfortable, and there's no end in sight. Multiply the case of Kevin Washington by 5000 or so, and you begin to get an idea of the staggering expense and inefficiency of our judicial system.

The article went on to discuss the average waiting time, the overcrowded jails, and the apparently lackadaisical civil service attitude of judges and district attorneys who come to work at nine and leave at three with two hours for lunch. Washington's case was just a teaser to get into the substance of the article, but Reed knew it would precipitate activity at the DA's office. The flowerbeds would have to wait. Today he would visit Washington.

On the freeway he made a mental review of the case. He had talked to Washington twice. Once in the courtroom immediately after he was arrested, and once at the arraignment in December. The first meeting had consisted of a promise to be available. At the second, Reed suggested pleading guilty to a lesser charge. Washington became furious. Reed was used to that reaction, and he was glad to let a little time go by. Washington would be ready for plea-bargaining now.

When Washington came into the interview room, he was carrying a newspaper and laughing. "Hey, man. I figured I'd see you today." He grinned and held up the front page of the *News*.

"Actually I'd . . . I had planned to get down here for sometime now . . ."

"Yeah, I know, I know. Whatever the reason, I'm glad you're here, man. This will speed it up, won't it? I mean, speed up the trial? I gotta get out of here."

"It will speed up the trial, if there is a trial," said Reed, "but that's not good. You need time between you and the trial. Time to let the jury forget all that stuff in the papers."

"Man, I don't have time. I have things to do. I can't stand it in here anymore. The sooner the better, I say."

"Well, the quickest way is what we discussed last time. I'm sure I could get you five years for manslaughter and you could be paroled after two, maybe sooner."

"No man, I can't do that." But Washington was not hostile this time. He seemed to realize that Reed was giving him the best advice. "I thought a lot about it after the last time you were here. It probably would be the quickest way, but it's just not right, y'know? I can't plead guilty to something I didn't do. Do you understand?"

Reed looked at Washington carefully. There was unmistakable confidence in his frank gaze. To Reed that denoted honesty. The two men stood facing each other as the clock behind loudly announced the passage of each second. Reed's mind was racing–he hadn't expected this. When at last he spoke, though, it was with genuine calm and resolve. And there was a feeling inside he recognized as something like relief. "All right. Then let's go to work on your defense."

"All *right*," said Washington, grinning. He was more relaxed and optimistic than he had been in months. "What do you need? I can tell you anything, anything." He seemed eager to help.

"Okay, let's start from the beginning again. Tell me everything you can think of. Don't leave anything out." Reed settled back in an uncomfortable chair. From his briefcase he took a folder which seemed to hold only a notepad but also contained a transcript of Washington's statement to the police. He followed along as Washington recounted the story. The narrative, which seemed boringly familiar to Washington, had been told in its entirety only a few times before. Reed listened carefully, interrupting from time to time to go back over details until he understood them clearly. He tried to imagine himself as a juror, a judge, a prosecutor, a police interrogator. He automatically pictured Washington on the witness stand. Now, as Washington described in detail that afternoon, tears came to his eyes whenever he discussed the girls under the torrent of hot water. Reed's conviction that this man was telling the truth grew stronger. Of course it was possible that he was just a remarkably good actor, but in either case, he would make a good witness.

"Now Kevin, why didn't Becky get out of the hot water? She was old enough to walk."

"I don't know. How do I know? All I know is there they were, like frozen, with the hot water pouring on them."

"The same every time," thought Reed to himself, checking off a line in the police transcript. "And how long were they there under the hot water?"

"Just a little while. Just a few seconds."

"Show me," said Reed. He pointed toward the opposite corner of the interview room. "Go stand over there like the telephone was there. How far was it to the bathroom?"

"Oh, probably from this side to that side, with a partition in between."

"Okay, let's see how long it takes," said Reed. He crouched in the corner of the room diagonally opposite from Washington, simulating the girls in the tub. "Now you're on the phone—who were you talking to?" Reed was testing him again.

"My brother, my little brother Ritchie. He called from San Francisco. I told you that."

"Oh, that's right. Okay, you're talking to Ritchie on the phone. Then what happened?"

"Screams. I heard screams from the bathroom and I ran right in."

"Did you hang up the phone, did you say anything?"

Washington thought for a minute. "No, I just dropped it, I'm sure I just dropped it when I ran for the bathroom."

"Let's try it. You talk on the phone." He waggled his finger as if to start the action. Washington complied. "Now when I scream, you run down that wall to the other corner, then over to here, okay?" Washington nodded. "Turn around now so you can't see and start talking on the phone."

He waited about ten seconds—until the second hand of his watch hit twelve. Then he screamed loudly. Washington was completely startled. He had anticipated a simple command. It was just what Reed wanted. Washington froze in place for almost two seconds, his eyes wide as the sound jarred his memory. Then he ran, heavy-footed, along one wall, turned the corner, and ran to the crouching Reed. "Six seconds," said Reed. He looked up to find Washington trembling as if he had relived a terrifying dream. "Let's try it again." Washington gained composure with a deep breath, then walked back to the opposite corner.

"Four seconds," said Reed, when they repeated the exercise. They did it four more times, each measured at four seconds.

Washington was panting slightly as they sat back down on the chairs on opposite sides of the desk with the green linoleum top.

"Where's your brother now?" asked Reed.

"I don't know. He's on the move. He hasn't called back since that night."

"We have to find him," said Reed. "If we can find him and he can verify your story that will be very helpful, very helpful."

"He usually calls my mama. She knows we're looking for him. She'll tell him to call."

"I'd better follow up on that. Where was he last?"

"He said he was in San Francisco." Reed wrote on the note pad.

"Now when you got to the tub, did you turn the water off?"

"No, I just reached in and picked out the girls."

"Why didn't you turn the water off?"

"I don't know. I guess I didn't think it was all that hot. I thought they were just scared, y'know?"

"You didn't know they were burned?"

"No, I didn't think nothing of it until I picked up Susie and her skin came off that way, that's when I knew something was wrong."

"Now tell me about that." Reed did not know if the skin came off or not following a scalding injury, but if it did, he figured Washington would only know it from experience. A good point to make to the jury. "You mean it just peeled
right off?"

"It came loose while I was holding her. Not all of it, just the top layer, like a big blister–like a snake skin."

"And that's when she fell?"

"That's right, she fell out of my hands right on the edge of the tub." Washington had to stop because his voice choked and his eyes filled with tears. Reed made another entry in his notebook. He was beginning to think he had a good case. Now he needed some confirmation.

"Who did you tell this to–this whole story about the accident?"

"Everybody."

"I know that, I mean who did you tell all the details like you told me?"

"Well, I told Sally." He thought for a moment. "And I told the

205

police. That big detective. He asked all those questions." He thought again. "I guess that's all."

"That's all? How about the doctors in the hospital?"

"They never asked me."

"How about the paramedics? The nurses in the emergency room?"

"I told them they got burned in the tub–that's all. What does it matter?"

"It matters to establish your credibility. To convince the jury that you didn't just make up this story to tell the police. Was there anyone else you told? Your boss, a nurse?"

Washington rubbed his head and leaned on the desk. "No, I don't think so, every time I started to tell someone, they used it against me. Pretty soon I learned to shut up."

"What about the doctor in charge? Dr. Browne. Didn't he ask you about the accident?"

"Oh no, I only saw him once. It was at a committee meeting. He didn't ask anything. He just talked. That's the only time I saw him."

"Man, I can't believe that. Your baby's doctor and you only talked to him once?"

"That's it." A sad, resigned look came over Washington's face. "He's supposed to be a good doctor, too, the best there is. One man, some rich dude, told me Dr. Browne was his doctor too. He said he was the best pediatrician in the city."

"Who told you that?," asked Reed, absently reviewing the next part of the police interview.

"Some dude I talked to that first day in the hospital. In the cafeteria. I was telling him . . . hey, I told him all that stuff . . ."

"What stuff?" Reed brought his attention back to Kevin.

"That stuff about the accident and my brother on the phone and the girls in the hot water and all that stuff I just told you. I told him that."

"Who, who? Hey, man, this is important."

"I don't know his name; his kid was in the hospital. He had a broken arm or something. I talked to him in the cafeteria. He had a vest and tie and a briefcase just like you."

"Can you think of his name, his kid's name, anything else about him?"

"Nope, that's all I know, just what I told you."

They sat in silence for almost a minute while Reed made notes. When he finished he sat tapping his pencil on the yellow pad, frowning. After a time, Washington said softly, "Hey man. You believe me, don't you?" He sounded surprised at his own observation. "You're going to help me fight it, aren't you?"

Reed studied the look on his face. It was a relieved, nervously gleeful expression that follows sudden resolution of panic–the look of a person saved from near drowning. "Yeah man," he said. "We'll fight it."

* * * *

Three days after the publication of Murray's article on courtroom inefficiency, four copies appeared on Norma Baldridge's desk in the prosecutor's office. They had been selected by Joel VerPlank, the district attorney, from a total of ninety-four that he had received in the mail. One said, "Dear Joe, with my compliments, Sol Rosenberg." Another said, "Joe–who the hell is Murray?" scribbled on a memo pad headed "From the desk of Superior Court Judge David Marshall." The third was from the American Civil Liberties Union with a promise to investigate the case of Kevin Washington. The fourth and only important one was from the mayor with the cryptic note, "VerPlank–get this done now." The articles and memos were stapled together under a yellow interoffice form bearing the note, "Norma–in the words of our noble mayor–get this done now, Joe." On the back of her office door was a dartboard which she used as a bulletin board for the most disliked project. She removed the Ted Kennedy campaign poster and put the stack of memos in its place, impaled on one large metal dart. She looked at it for several minutes, sighing occasionally and squinting alternately at the dartboard and the rain outside. Finally, she buzzed her secretary and asked for the file on Kevin Washington.

Leafing through the file, the details of the case came back to her. Unwittingly, Murray had made a good point. Although Washington pled not guilty to a murder charge at the arraignment, the case should have been bargained down and settled months ago. She was sure that VerPlank would settle for manslaughter, or even felony abuse without the murder charge. Mavis Johnson's summary of the custody hearing–with important sections identified with a yellow marker–indi-cated that the evidence was even more solid than she had thought. Mavis concluded by recommending a light sentence, early parole, and enrollment in the abuse counseling group sponsored by Child Welfare.

There was a new report from Korinsky. Attached to his brief letter was a transcript of an army hearing dated July 1969. The hearing concerned the death of a little Vietnamese girl who was killed in a hit-and-run accident near the airfield in Da Nang. She was hit by an American jeep and the driver was Kevin Washington. The transcript was over one hundred pages long. Baldridge skipped to the summary and recommendations. Washington admitted hitting the child and claimed that the captain for whom he was driving was on an impor-tant military mission and had commanded that Washington continue driving.

Testimony corroborated this explanation. The hearing board dismissed the case against Washington and delivered a mild reprimand to the captain. There was nothing helpful in that report except, perhaps, some shock value. She decided not to use it, but kept it in the folder.

* * * *

"God made Good Friday so lawyers could get caught up on their business," said Norma Baldridge to Mavis Johnson.

"And for social workers to get a long weekend," countered Mavis, sipping her Almaden Grenache Rosé. (The house wines at Gallagher's were Almaden. They wrote it in the menu with an accent over the "e," and half the patrons thought it was French.)

"Walt Reed was in court this morning, so I know he'll be here. He promised to make it by half past twelve." She looked at her watch–a big man-sized wristwatch with a leather band. It was twelve twenty.

Reed came through the big oak door a few minutes later and surveyed the room. Gallagher's was a big barn-type restaurant with hardwood floors, no decor aside from blown up photographs of old Detroit buildings turned brown with age, male waiters in tuxedos, and very good food. "Here he comes now," said Norma Baldridge. "Jeez, he's a good looking man."

"Hmm," agreed Mavis. "Damn good for a colored boy." Norma

did not know her well enough to know if she was kidding or not.

Reed hung his coat on the hook by the table and pulled up a chair. "Hi Norma, Miss Johnson. Nice to see you again."

"Mavis, please," she said cordially. He nodded acknowledgment.

"Thanks so much for coming over, Walt. Mavis and I thought we could get the Washington case settled and have lunch with a handsome man all at the same time." Baldridge smiled. Her attempt at flirtation came out sounding menopausal.

Reed mentally summed the situation up and could see only an hour and a half of dull conversation for five minutes of information. "I'm all for settling the Washington case, but I'll have to take a rain check on the lunch. I'm going to church with my family; it's Good Friday, you know." He kept a straight face.

"Oh yes, of course. Well maybe you'll just have a glass of wine with us," said Baldridge, disappointed.

"Yes, thank you." As she poured from the carafe, he asked her, "How about Washington?"

"I am sure I can get VerPlank to go for a light sentence on a second-degree murder or even a manslaughter."

"I told him that," said Reed. "There isn't any reasonable defense. I advised him to accept the lowest charge we could get and go for early parole with counseling." Mavis and Baldridge smiled at each other.

"VerPlank will be delighted with that," said Baldridge. "That article in the *News* really rattled the cage down at city hall. I know that Judge Marshall will hear it Tuesday. We can have him in Jackson by Friday and get the *News* to run a Sunday special on the efficient legal system."

"My boss will like that too," said Mavis. "I must have had twelve calls about that case yesterday."

Norma Baldridge held up her wine glass to salute their success. Mavis and Reed did the same, clinking them together in the center of the table. As the women sipped, Reed said, "My boss would be happy with that too. In fact, the only person who wouldn't is Washington. Unfortunately, he's not going to cop a plea." Baldridge almost choked.

"What did you say?" she said between coughs.

"He won't plead guilty to anything. He has an old-fashioned sense of justice that's honorable, but impractical. He insists on pleading innocent." Now Reed sipped his wine slowly, watching their expres-

sions change from incredulous
to vengeful.

Mavis spoke. "Why would he do that? The guy must be some kind of a nut. Well, we know he's a nut, but I thought he was smarter than that."

"He'll get life—maybe worse," said Baldridge. "Marshall is already mad. You know what the sentences are like in an abuse case, let alone a murder case. You have to convince him to bargain, Walt."

"I've tried, Lord, I've tried. He's a stubborn fellow."

"Well, maybe he'll get what he deserves," said Mavis, bitterly. "Hell, even his lawyer knows he's guilty."

"I didn't say that," said Walt, settling his glass on the checkered tablecloth. "I said I advised him that the best thing to do would be to plead on a lesser charge. Personally, I think he's innocent." The women were stunned.

"No. Walter, you don't mean that," said Baldridge.

"Yes, I do," said Reed. "I've talked to him a lot in the past few weeks. Have you ever talked to him?" Both women shook their heads no. "Well, his story's always the same and he believes in what he says. I think he's telling the truth and he just got caught up in the system."

"Then you must be the only one who thinks that, Walter." Baldridge was getting a little huffy.

"Not really," said Reed. He reached down and opened his briefcase, shuffled through the papers and pulled out a letter on Presbyterian Hospital letterhead. He placed it on the table so that both of them could read it. "There's a doctor at Presbyterian—the chief resident in pediatrics—who thinks the medical folks dropped the ball. No one ever took a history from Washington. That is the most important part of a child abuse investigation, and none of the doctors ever did it. The whole case is based on what some intern said about the burns. The fellow who wrote this thinks Washington might be telling the truth." He waited for their reaction while they read through the letter.

"Look, this is from Dr. Crane," Mavis said with obvious disdain.

"Do you know him?" asked Baldridge.

"Sure, he's the one who was so uncooperative during our investigation; I remember him. Wouldn't tell us a thing. He acted like he had something to hide. This doesn't surprise me coming from Crane. How did you get him to write this, Walt?"

"He's a friend of a neighbor of mine," said Reed, candidly. "I asked him to look over the medical records and he came up with this. It came as a surprise to me too."

Baldridge lit a cigarette and spoke to Mavis. "Well, this doesn't hurt the case at all. It doesn't address the beating of the little girl, the little boy, and the fact that he lied to the police. This won't hold any water at all." She blew angry smoke across the table.

"It does make Crane look suspicious. I can check on that," said Mavis.

"I can't understand why he would come out on Washington's side," said Baldridge. "Well, it's only a letter. Will he testify, Walt?"

"Yes." Reed paused. "I've got an expert too, a Doctor David Lower, from the Children's Hospital. Perhaps you've heard of him?"

"David Lower? No!" Mavis was astonished. "He's a zealot on child abuse. We've used him several times, haven't we, Norma?"

"Walt, now I know you're kidding," said Baldridge.

"No kidding, Norma. I talked to him for an hour yesterday. He went through the hospital records with a fine-tooth comb. He was really upset. He said the care was shitty, to use his expression. 'Grounds for malpractice,' he said. 'Typical pediatrician screw ups,' he said. He said the social workers 'don't know what the f– ' excuse me, Miss Johnson. He said, 'social workers were . . . disoriented.' He said that Washington's no more guilty of murder than any grandmother who ever put a kid in a bathtub." He paused for effect.

"Egotistical bastard!" seethed Baldridge. "That's just an interhospital feud, not an expert witness. Those doctors have balls, I'll tell you. Egotistical bastards." She snuffed out her cigarette with contempt. Reed was surprised by her reaction. She and Mavis were obviously shaken by the thought of Lower as an opposing witness. Maybe he had stumbled onto something worthwhile. He showed no expression except to mirror her own.

"Yeah, you're right," he said. "Just a bunch of egotistical money-grubbing bastards. His friend from Boston will probably really cost me." He shook his head in disgust.

"What's that?" asked Baldridge.

"Oh, it's nothing. Some child abuse expert friend of his who is going to testify for us. I can't remember his name. It'll probably cost me two months budget right there." He shook his head again, looking

211

at them cautiously. Of course there was no expert from Boston, but he wanted to see how deep her concern went. She shrugged and showed no expression.

"Well, as you said, Walt, it's an indefensible case. I don't envy you. Is there anything else we can do to help you? Any other information that might speed the thing up?" She was back to businesslike cordiality.

"No, I think you've got everything. I'll send you a copy of this letter from Crane. If you want to talk with him or Lower, it's fine with me." He looked at his watch. "I'm sorry, I must be going. My family's waiting." He smiled and nodded at Mavis, then Norma Baldridge. "Thanks for the wine." He turned and left.

When he was gone, Mavis turned back to Norma. "Is it always like this . . . sharing information back and forth?"

"Like what?" asked Baldridge, still unsettled by the news about Lower.

"This exchange of information, I mean the defense and the prosecution sharing evidence back and forth. I'm a little surprised."

Baldridge chuckled in her low voice. "Only with the public defender's office. Hell, we're all just trying to get the cases through as quickly as we can. We have to work with each other all the time, you know. It doesn't pay to keep secrets or make enemies. Damn this'll be messy. Headlines and egotistical doctors. The guy must be a nut. He should have bargained down. He's just a nut." She drained her wine glass to end the conversation. She had planned to bring up Korinsky's report about the hit-and-run accident. Now she was glad she had not.

Instead of heading home, Walter turned toward the county jail. He had to tell Washington that he had found the man he talked to in the hospital cafeteria. It was Peter Blake, the same man who now had Washington's children as foster children. An ironic stroke of luck, thought Reed. Also a fact which he had carefully withheld from Baldridge.

* * * *

In the dream he always had the energy of youth and the wisdom of age. He strolled the grounds of an Irish castle, adored by his subjects. Across the moat a cloud of misty fog materialized into a

212

beautiful girl with the darkest of hair and the whitest of skin. But as he reached out to her, the drawbridge pulled up, stretching him apart, and he would wake up but remain hopelessly paralyzed for long minutes, his skin soaked with sweat.

That was how Peter Blake found himself now, awake and looking at the ceiling of Suzanne's bedroom. The taste in his mouth told him that he had been asleep for over half an hour. He was awakened by a pleasant pressure in the arch of his left foot combined with a stretching of each toe to the point of pain in his calf. With his right foot he pushed back the sheet, exposing Suzanne stretched across the foot of the bed, massaging his foot. "Welcome back," she said, looking up and smiling. The massage worked up his leg until she was kneading the spaces between the tendons at the back of his knee. "You were having a dream. It was time for you to wake up," she said, straddling his foot and skimming her fingernails across his upper thigh. He wiggled his left toes and she shivered, causing her breasts to shake even more. He returned to the almost painful state of arousal which seemed to be his normal condition during the months that they had been seeing each other. Laughing, she slowly stretched out on his leg, digging her fingers into iliac crevices he didn't know he had. Reaching down with both hands, he found her gold earrings through her tousled hair, then deliberately massaged each millimeter of her ears. Very slowly, he followed each convolution of her pinna, exactly matching one side to the other. Finally he pushed his fingertips into the hollows in front of her mastoids causing her to moan and grind her pelvis on his ankle.

Half an hour later she was waking him up again, more sedately this time, by stroking his eyelids. "What time is it, Sue?" he mumbled.

"Ten thirty," she said. "You'd better get going."

"Jesus, I'll say," he said, swinging up to a sitting position and scanning the room to find his clothing. Suzanne stretched out to full length on the bed.

"Peter, how long have we been in love?"

"I don't know, five months, maybe six," he responded, retrieving a sock from the inside of a pant leg.

"Are you going to tell your wife about us now, or wait until you start the divorce?"

He buttoned his shirt, looking the other way, as if he had not heard her question.

"Peter?"

"I don't know, Sue. It depends on my kids mostly. I have to wait at least until summer, like I told you last week." She knew he became annoyed and abrupt at this kind of questioning. She softened the subject.

"I know you're right. And you have the foster children too. That's my fault. I didn't do us any favors there." She saw his expression relax as he bent over to find his shoes. He stood up smiling.

"Speaking of the kids, did I tell you that I got a call from the public defender's office?"

"No. Is there another custody hearing coming up?"

"No, it was about Washington. He's coming to trial in a couple of weeks on the murder charge. The lawyer wants me at the trial."

"To help with the defense? I know you're a good lawyer, Peter, but why would he ask you?"

"Not as a lawyer, as a witness. Apparently I'm the only one that Washington told about the accident. It was right there in the cafeteria, when Petey had his broken arm. Anyway, he needs me to corroborate his statement to the police."

"You never told me about that."

"Actually I'd forgotten all about it until this fellow Reed reminded me. He has your old boyfriend Crane and a few other witnesses to testify for Washington. But he needs me most of all."

"Why bother? I mean, the evidence is so overwhelming." She sat up and wrapped the sheet around her, feeling that she somehow needed better coverage to discuss serious business.

"I don't think he has a chance. He doesn't, really, but he's going to give it
a try."

Suzanne thought for a while. "What effect would that have on the children, Peter? And on us?"

He put on his shoes and sighed, deep in thought. "If he's convicted, then the children will probably remain in foster care a long time. That's the most likely. If he's acquitted, then the children could go back to the family in a hurry."

"And that would mean one less thing for you to worry about at home," she said enthusiastically.

"That's true, I suppose. Although I have grown quite attached to those Washington children." He was talking softly, almost to himself. He had finished dressing and looked at his watch. "God, Sue, I have to get going." He bent over to kiss her on the cheek. "I'll call you tomorrow, will you be at work?"

"Sure," she said, still thinking about the implications of his testimony at the Washington trial. "Be careful going home."

He was already at the door. "I will. Good night." And he was gone.

CHAPTER 20

The dishwasher was churning, the beds long since made, and the dog fed. The first year that all the children were in school, she had felt just a little lonely during the day. But now she enjoyed the efficiency of the morning solitude. Pouring her second cup of decaffeinated coffee, she sat down at the kitchen table to sort the morning mail. She stacked the magazines in three piles–*Boys' Life* and *Ranger Rick* in one pile; *Fortune* and *Sports Illustrated* in another; *Smithsonian*, the U of M Alumni magazine, and *Better Homes & Gardens* in the third. She threw away three advertisements ("Open this! You have already won!"), put the bills on top of the *Better Homes*, and shuffled the remaining personal letters. There was a note from her husband John's mother, two birthday cards for little John, an announcement-type letter from Camp Seagull, and an official looking window letter from the clerk of courts, Wayne County, addressed to Constance Bosworth.

One of her friends had said that Connie Bosworth should be the subject of a hairspray commercial. Her days always began at six. The house was immaculate by eleven. She always had one, sometimes two luncheon meetings of this or that league, society, auxiliary, or cultural group. Three days a week she did volunteer work at Henry Ford or Crittenden Home. On the other days she wrote her column for the *Birmingham Eccentric*. Dinner was always ready exactly at six for her loving husband and three semi-perfect children. Then three or four nights a week they were off to a fancy dress ball, a special showing at the art gallery, a neighborhood political party, or a recital in Ann Arbor. Always with a cheerful smile, a casual confident air, and every hair precisely in place.

She scanned the letter from Mother-in-law and, realizing that she might be late for the Committee on Race Relations in Detroit (CORD), she put the letters from Camp Seagull and the County in her purse, let the dog out, and backed the Ford station wagon out of the driveway.

The CORD luncheon was held in a meeting room near the top of the RenCen. (Mrs. Ford was a board member.) Connie Bosworth sat between representative Gloria Berkowitz–who thought the sauce on the chicken crepes was too heavy–and the Reverend Jesse Price–who wondered why they always served rolled up pancakes at the CORD luncheons. The speaker for the day was Clarence Campbell, director of Welfare Services for greater Detroit. Campbell was a graying, crusty, former marine who was appointed to the department during the conservative backlash in the sixties. He was a good administrator, but a hard-nosed realist who believed that his job was to get people off welfare and back into production. Subsequent mayors publicly disavowed his policies and methods, but they kept him in the job because he (and the chief of police) kept the conservative vote for the incumbent, while providing a position which made any mayoral state-ment sound liberal. He was clearly out of step with the enlightened sociology of the seventies, however, and had to be replaced. At least that was the conclusion of the director of the new Human Services Agency, which had been created to include the welfare program. The director of that agency so advised the mayor, who solicited the opinion of CORD, CORE, HUD, and a host of other acronymic liberal groups.

Connie Bosworth had been a member of the Committee on Race Relations in Detroit for the past two years. She thought she had been appointed because she had worked on the campaign committee which resulted in the election of Representative Berkowitz. In reality she was appointed because she was the only member of the Birmingham School Board who favored suburban integration busing–a position which had gotten her off the school board in a hurry. She listened attentively to Clarence Campbell's opening remarks. He was pointing out that 73 percent of welfare recipients in Detroit were black, and that should concern any committee on race relations, since race rela-tions in Detroit were basically black-white relations. Therefore his department and the committee shared the responsibility for the black ethnic group. "We don't need to use big words. Let's just call a spade a spade." He continued talking, and it was not clear whether he meant this to be an attempt at a joke or not. No one laughed.

218

"This relationship between the black population and the welfare program might seem obvious to you," continued Campbell. "Black people are poor, poor people need help, therefore there will be lots of black people in the welfare program. But if you assumed that syllogism to be obvious it should scare you. You're a bigot." He paused, letting this sink in. "There's no inherent truth there. Black doesn't equal poor. Help doesn't equal money. Welfare money isn't for poor people, it's for needy people. Old folks without families and big medical bills. The welfare program is not a giveaway program. It's not an altruistic exercise. It's a return on investment. The working members of our little society set aside money to be used for the time when a member of that society cannot contribute. The money is invested in that individual with the expectation that he will return to the work force and thus pay back the investment with interest. I'm just the steward of your investment fund. I don't levy the taxes. I don't write the laws that determine the conditions of making the investment. I just watch the store."

There was a gathering cloud of hostility in the room. This was definitely not what the CORD members wanted to hear. As he spoke, committee members looked at each other as if to say, "Do something. Don't let him carry on
like that."

"Mr. Campbell, just a minute." Reverend Price finally broke in. "You're giving us one old-fashioned idea about welfare, but a lot of us don't see it that way. Black folks are poor folks, now that's a fact. They have a right to the bounties of our society. Now that's another fact. A constitutional fact. They're entitled to it."

"Why?" Campbell's question left him flabbergasted.

"Because . . . because they are. Poor men, black men, make the cars that hold this city together. But they are the first ones laid off and the last ones hired. And then they're hired at the jobs that keeps 'em poor folks. No sir, you owe 'em. You owe 'em good and now's the time to pay 'em." The Reverend was sweating profusely, and switched into a singsong mode of speaking, as he did whenever he became evangelistic on any subject. He stopped to mop his brow.

"Do you mean to tell me, Reverend Price, that the Welfare Department should give taxpayers' money to people just because they're poor, or just because they're black?" Campbell's low voice became gravelly. Only his bulging neck veins indicated the intensity of his feeling.

"I do indeed. That is exactly what I mean to tell you. Hallelujah."

"Then you, sir, are a racist bent on destroying your own kind. You do not understand the first principle of social welfare."

The room was hushed, stunned. Reverend Price was exasperated beyond words.

"And that principle . . . in your expert sociologist's opinion–?" The sarcastic question came from the president of the committee, Sheila Pelston. Dr. Pelston was an associate professor of sociology at Wayne State University.

"The way to destroy a segment of society is to subsidize it. You pay a man for not contributing, then his children, then his children's children, as if they've somehow earned something by living at the short end of the stick. Look at the Indians. For God's sake, look at the Eskimos. The poor man–the black man–has the right to work. If we pay him–or anyone else–to give up that right, then we ruin him."

The discussion became an argument, with the fiery problems raised by Clarence Campbell soon lost in emotional smoke. Connie Bosworth had heard all these arguments before. Never quite in the blunt terms expressed by Mr. Campbell, but she had long since decided that his ideas–while interesting–were not practical for the new Detroit. While the discussion ebbed and flowed, she opened her purse to examine her hair and lipstick in the mirror. In so doing, she noticed the letters she had placed there that morning. Quietly she opened the letter from the clerk of courts and examined its contents. It was a notice to appear for jury duty May first.

* * * *

Throughout his chief resident year, whenever Steven was summoned to Dr. Browne's office, they sat in the overstuffed chairs by the coffee table–a sign of acceptance and cordial camaraderie. Today Browne remained seated behind his desk. His flinty glare was anything but cordial.

"Sit down, Crane." He indicated the stiff chair across the desk. He handed a letter across the desk to Crane. "Just what the hell is this all about?"

The letter was on familiar Wayne County letterhead with the subtitle "Human
Services Agency, Estelle Oswald, Ph.D., Director. The letter was nearly two pages long and attached to it was a photocopy of Crane's letter to the public defender. The letter was addressed to Edward Browne, chief of pediatrics, Presbyterian Hospital (with copies to the hospital administrator, executive committee, and board of trustees). The letter began:

> It has been brought to my attention that Dr. Steven Crane of your staff has consistently interfered with the investigation of child abuse cases in your hospital, and has represented the hospital's efforts in child abuse control as inadequate (see attached). This is a shocking position for a physician to take, particularly coming from the prestigious Presbyterian Hospital.
> I am sure you are aware of the state laws which require full reporting, disclosure, and investigation of child abuse cases.

Crane felt a surge of adrenalin powerful enough to make his back hurt. He flushed and trembled. After reading the first paragraph, he looked up at Browne.

"This is the sloppiest piece of—"

"Just read it," directed Browne, coldly. Crane returned to the letter. It went on to detail the Washington case as reported by Suzanne Hathaway, MSW, and Mavis Johnson, MSW. It described how Crane had been uncooperative throughout the investigation. It went into detail about the "charges against the justice system" and "misrepresentation of the hospital records," all of which were contained in his "inflammatory and obstructionist letter." The final paragraphs presumed that Browne could provide a reasonable explanation for Crane's actions, and hinted that the HSA would bring charges against Crane unless the matter was promptly resolved. It closed, "Awaiting your reply, I am, Estelle Oswald, MS, Ph.D."

Steven's first reaction was to tear the letter into pieces, but he suppressed that impulse and laughed weakly instead. "Can you believe this?" He was emotional almost to the point of tears. "Excuse me sir, but this is pure bullshit. I can't believe this."

"What I can't believe, Crane, is that you would write such a devious letter. I warned you about this very case, and then you send a letter like this behind my back, to the defense attorney no less, on hospital letterhead, saying that we don't know what the hell we're doing. Here I am, in charge of every goddamned committee in this town that deals with child abuse and you send a letter saying that we don't know how to recognize it. How about it, Crane?"

Crane was surprised at Browne's reaction. Browne always backed his residents. He must have missed the point. Steven relaxed, even smiled. Surely the chief would accept his factual explanation. "First of all, my letter was written at the request of the public defender's office. They wanted an explanation of the medical records from the chief resident. That's what my letter is. There's nothing secret about it. There's a copy of it in the charts."

"What? What charts?"

"In the charts of the Washington girls. Medical correspondence typed it up for me," said Crane, as if that fact should have been obvious.

"Oh my God, Crane, what are you trying to do to us?"

Steven progressed from surprise to annoyed disbelief. "I'm not trying to do anything, Dr. Browne. I was just supplying information for the public defender. The fact is, there is no medical history, or social history, anywhere in the record. The second thing is, this letter from Oswald–whoever that is–is just tripe. There's some bureaucrat dealing with third-hand information who doesn't know the first thing about this case, who's never seen the children or talked to the family, and this jerk is accusing me of obstructing an investigation. And finally, this letter I sent to the public defender was confidential. What's it doing in the Child Welfare Department? And more important than that, why are they taking sides? They're supposed to be social workers, not prosecutors." Steven had lapsed into talking to himself, flipping back and forth between the copy of his letter and the letter from Oswald.

"Dr. Crane, either you have been taken in by this . . . murderer–what's his name–Washington, or you are incredibly naive. I prefer to believe the latter. I will try to salvage whatever is left of our shattered reputation, and I expect you to straighten this matter out as quickly as possible."

Steven had the feeling he had entered into a game without rules, but he was still trying to make the point which seemed crystal clear to him. "I can set it straight all right, sir. It's straight as can be right in my letter. Those are the facts. At least you gave me a chance to respond. I'll just call this Oswald person–"

"God no, Crane, you've done enough. You deal directly through me. I have already responded to Ms. Oswald . . ." he tossed a carbon copy of a short letter across the desk. "And I will forward your written explanation, which I expect by tomorrow morning."

Crane read the carbon copy with mounting horror.

> *Thank you very much for bringing this matter directly to my attention. Dr. Crane's letter is an embarrassing misrepresentation and does not reflect the opinions nor the reputation of Presbyterian Hospital nor the Department of Pediatrics. As you point out these are very serious charges. I will bring them to the Professional Conduct Committee and direct them to conduct a full investigation. In the meantime I will discuss the matter with Dr. Crane, and render a response to you immediately. Sincerely, Dr. Edward Browne*

Crane was shaking, rattling the onionskin paper. "You sent this letter?" He could barely talk.

"Indeed I have. And I will send another in the morning with your retraction and explanation."

"Christ, you could have called me. You get a crackpot letter and send off this kind of a response. It seems to me that common courtesy–"

"It seems to me that you're a fine one to talk about courtesy, Dr. Crane. After all I've done to try to teach you something and all the years I've tried to build the reputation of this hospital . . ."

Crane was seething. He rose to his feet with fists clenched, tears in his eyes. He knew that he had to get out of the office or he would jump across the desk and attack his mentor. With all the willpower he could muster he closed his mouth and walked to the door.

"In the morning, Dr. Crane. Have it on this desk, first thing in the morning."

He slammed the door so hard that three of Doctor Browne's thirty-one diplomas went askew. Ignoring the elevator, he ran down the four flights of stairs and out into the rain.

* * * *

223

Connie Bosworth had been called for jury duty once before, so she knew enough to bring ample reading material to fill the otherwise wasted days in the jury assembly room. By May 3, she had not been called, and she was beginning to hope that the mandatory week would elapse before her services would be required. She had spent the time well. Using Toffler's "Future Shock" to explain and rebut DeLorean's scathing denouncement of the automobile industry, she had prepared two columns for the *Eccentric* discussing the social responsibility of labor unions and big business. She had just started into a John Updike novel when her name was called.

Judge Marshall explained the case briefly to the prospective jurors. The defendant was accused of murdering his own daughter by inflicting burns. He claimed that the injury occurred by accident in the family bathtub while he was bathing her. The prosecutor was a woman and the defense lawyer was a handsome young black man. Connie liked that, feeling that equal rights and opportunity had found their way into the legal profession. That was as it should be. It would set a healthy example for the rest of the city.

The two lawyers seemed to be mutually respectful, even friendly, as they shared whispered remarks between interviews. The first four jurors were picked without much discussion. The bailiff called Mrs. Connie Bosworth. She sat on the broad wooden chair and smiled approvingly at the questioners. Norma Baldridge asked a few questions about her husband's occupation, her family, the ages of her children and where she lived. She nodded approval to the judge.

Walter Reed remained seated, smiled, and asked, "Mrs. Bosworth, when your children were small, did you bathe them in a bassinet or in the bathtub?"

"Both," she said simply. "When they were old enough I put them in the bathtub. I usually put them all in together. That was always a happy time in our house." She smiled.

"How old were they when you put them in the bathtub?" asked Reed.

"Oh." She thought for a minute. "When they were cruising—you know, holding on to things and moving around. Little John—that's my middle boy—was walking at ten months," she added with maternal pride. Reed seemed satisfied.

"Mrs. Bosworth, suppose I told you that the defendant in this case, the father of the girls—was a Negro—a black man," he said.

"That wouldn't mean anything special to me," she said. "We all need to bathe our children." They all smiled.

"Suppose I told you that the mother of the girls was a white woman?" There was a minor stir among some of the other prospective jurors. Connie shrugged.

"Some of my very good friends are in mixed marriages," she said, in the tone she had used to describe the accomplishments of her ten-month-old. "I'm certainly not against it. In fact, I think . . . I think it's probably a good thing for our society." She looked quickly to see the reaction of Norma Baldridge. By now she was quite interested in the case and actually wanted to sit on the jury. Baldridge showed no response.

Reed nodded and continued. "Knowing what you do now about this case and with the brief information about the people involved, do you have an opinion as to whether the defendant is innocent or guilty?"

"Absolutely not." She was surprised that he would ask the question. "I have a completely open mind. I will have to hear the evidence on both sides and make an unbiased judgment."

Reed drew a line on the pad before him. "Thank you, Mrs. Bosworth, you're excused." He smiled. Connie was disappointed.

"Wait. I don't understand . . ."

"Either counselor has the option to refuse a juror, Mrs. Bosworth," said Judge Marshall. "Thank you very much for coming. You may return to the assembly room."

"But I'm, I'm impartial and honest . . ."

The judge turned to Reed. "You don't have to make any explanation, Mr. Reed, but if you would like to explain . . ."

"Mrs. Bosworth is a prejudiced juror, your honor," said Reed. "It would not be in the best interest of my client—"

"Just a minute." Connie was not accustomed to being rejected, and was insulted at being called prejudiced. "I just told you that I don't care what color the man is. Didn't I say that?"

Reed looked at her calmly. "It has nothing to do with his color, Mrs. Bosworth. You said you have an open mind regarding guilt or innocence. You said you have no preconceived notions."

"That's right."

"That's prejudice, Mrs. Bosworth. On the basis of the information you have, you should believe that my client is innocent. All the jurors must believe that." He turned to the other prospective jurors in the room. "Mr. Washington is innocent as far as you know, and he must remain so, in your minds, unless Mrs. Baldridge here can absolutely convince you otherwise. That's the law."

"Thank you again, Mrs. Bosworth," said Judge Marshall. "You're excused."

CHAPTER 21

Jim Murray arrived in court early on the day the Washington trial was to start. He joked with the bailiff and the court reporter while they waited for everyone to arrive. He even introduced himself to Norma Baldridge, with apologies for his articles and an explanation of how tough it was to sell newspapers these days. She understood. They all had their jobs to do.

He took a seat in the third row of benches. There were only two other spectators–Sally Washington and an assistant from the DA's office. The bailiff called the court to order as David Marshall took the bench.

Norma Baldridge was very low key in her opening statement. She spoke in a soft voice, leaning on the lectern and smiling at the jury members individually. She referred to Kevin as "the defendant," never by name. She described "the victim" as an unsuspecting happy one-year-old, whom she referred to thereafter as "little Susie." "It will be hard for you, ladies and gentlemen, in the course of this trial, to imagine how a man could hold his own baby daughter, screaming and writhing, in a vat of scalding water. It's hard for me to imagine. It's hard for me to think about." She shuddered and sighed effectively. "But . . . forgive me, I'm sorry for this . . . I'm going to make you think about that gruesome scene over and over and over until you are convinced that is what the defendant did to his own daughter, little Susie." An older woman in the jury looked nauseated. One man openly glared at Washington.

Reed fumbled with his notes, then walked slowly in front of the jury, waiting for the effect of the prosecutor's scenario to subside. Finally, he began. "What Mrs. Baldridge just described to you would be an unspeakable crime–if it ever happened. You will learn that Kevin Washington, here, is a thoughtful, loving father who would be incapable of such an act. Now let me describe for you a different kind of torture. All of you have children, or grandchildren." He smiled and nodded at the white-haired lady in the front row. "Suppose when you go home tonight, you give your children a bath, just like you do every night." He nodded affirmatively and got three or four of the jurors nodding with him. "They're splashing and playing and giggling while you're down on your knees trying to find the soap and the rubber duck, right?" Many jurors were grinning now nodding with him. "Now you have to go out to get a towel or answer the phone or turn off the stove, you know? And while you're out there, you hear your children cry. You run into the bathroom and they've turned on the hot water. You take them out, wipe them off." He pantomimed the action. "It looks like they are hurt so you take them to the hospital. You sit there on a hard bench while doctors and nurses and X-ray machines come and go. Just when you are so worried you can't stand it anymore, a policeman comes up and charges you with burning your own children. You try to explain, but no one believes you. The next day the police come in the middle of the night and pull your other children from their beds and take them away in order to 'protect' them. You can't get a lawyer; you're fired from your job. Meanwhile, your child in the hospital gets sicker and sicker but no one will tell you anything about her. Then she dies, but instead of letting you hold her little body close to your heart one last time, you're arrested for murder and slapped in jail where you spend every lonely night grieving and every day trying to get someone to believe you."

The impact of this rapid transition from security to concern to fear to grief was obvious on the faces of the jurors. One woman was sniffing loudly and searching for a tissue. To break the intensity and soften the effectiveness of Reed's argument, Norma Baldridge coughed and said sarcastically, "Your honor, I object to this piece of dramatic fiction. Mr. Reed is leading the jury on a wild fantasy."

Judge Marshall held up his hand, both to acknowledge and silence her. "Carry on, Mr. Reed."

"Ladies and gentlemen, that's what has happened to Kevin Washington. The state's case is based on circumstantial evidence and conjecture. An intricate imaginary house of cards just like the story that Mrs. Baldridge just told you. We will, of course, present the witnesses and evidence which will convince you to end Mr. Washington's nightmare. But as we go through this trial, I think you will see that the same terrible experience could happen to any of you."

"I'll be damned," thought Murray to himself. "The guy's going to make a case out of it. It'll never fly." He reached into his pocket and turned off the small tape recorder. He was glad now that he had brought it. The opening arguments alone gave him enough for two columns.

The first prosecution witness was Dr. David Stone. Baldridge knew it would be better to put Korinsky first, with his matter-of-fact narrative of the case, but she needed Stone to get the photographs into evidence, and she wanted to do that at the beginning. Stone was nervous. He had never testified before. Baldridge led him gently through the preliminaries, then asked him to describe the events of the night of October 19. He was a surprisingly good witness, thought Baldridge, as he described the paramedics' concern, the painful, frightened attitude of the little girls and the appearance of the burns.

Reed objected to the photographs on the grounds that they were unnecessarily inflammatory, but he was overruled and Baldridge produced the eight-by-ten glossy color prints. Stone described each one as it was marked and numbered. Baldridge passed them one by one through the jury, then tacked them in a row across the top of a large bulletin board at the front of the courtroom. As the trial progressed, she added new photographs, taken over a sequence of dates, so that by the end of the trial, the bulletin board was filled with hideous evidence.

On cross-examination, Reed established that Stone was a resident of limited experience, that he had never seen nor reported a case of child abuse before, that he had never talked to the parents, and that he did not know the temperature of water which would produce a scalding injury. The jury was only half-listening. They were focused on the photographs.

Baldridge had only one question in redirect. "Dr. Stone, from your examination of the patient, did you come to a conclusion as to how the burns occurred?"

"The burn had to be caused by intentional immersion. Nothing else could explain the pattern of the burns." He stepped down and the judge declared a short recess.

* * * *

The next witness was Gus Korinsky. His unpolished, big brotherly approach was very attractive to the jury. With only a few leading questions from Baldridge, he recounted the results of the police department interrogation, his encounters with Washington in the hospital and the house on Calvert, and the facts regarding Washington's marital status. (He referred to the arrangement as "shacking up." Reed objected and the jury was directed to ignore the remark.)

With gentle, almost fatherly concern he described the injuries to little Sammy. Photographs of his battered face were passed among the jury and tacked to the board.

"Did the little boy tell you how he got this injury?" asked Baldridge.

"He said Mr. Washington hit him for spilling his milk." Korinsky looked with disgust at Kevin.

"I'm not sure I understood you Lieutenant. Did you say that the defendant beat him up like that just for spilling his milk?"

"That's what the little boy told me. He said, 'Kevin hit me because I spilled my milk'." Reed rose to his feet.

"Objection, your honor; how often do we have to go over this hearsay evidence from a six-year-old?"

"Overruled."

"Did the defendant explain how this injury occurred?" asked Baldridge.

"Mr. Washington told the officers who placed the boy in protective custody that he fell down the stairs. Mrs. Washington supported that story."

"Now, just to be sure I've understood your testimony, Lieutenant," said Baldridge. "Mr. Washington physically attacked you personally twice, even knowing that you are a police officer."

"That's correct."

"And his son—really Mrs. Flynn's son—told you that he sustained that black eye when the defendant hit him for spilling milk? Is that correct?"

"That's correct."

Baldridge shuffled her notes. "Was the tap water at the Calvert house hot enough to cause burns, Lieutenant?"

"No."

"Did you find anything at the house that might have been used to produce the burns?"

"I found a large metal trash can on the porch."

"Is this it, Lieutenant?" With some effort she placed a large galvanized steel tub on the table; "929" was written on it in yellow paint. "What was this used for in the Washington house, Lieutenant?"

"Mr. Washington said it was for cleaning car parts."

"And how did he do that?"

"By putting them in boiling water."

She paused, letting the jury look at the large tub. "No further questions at this time, your honor," said Baldridge, making notes. Reed wanted to get Korinsky off the stand as rapidly as possible, but he was surprised that they had not gone into the temperature of the water. He stepped up to the lectern.

"Just a few questions, Lieutenant. You said you went to the Washington home to measure the temperature of the water. What was the temperature?"

"142 degrees."

"Is that hot enough to cause third-degree burns in a small child, Lieutenant?"

"I don't think so; I'm not an expert in that area. But I could hold my hand in it."

"Now, let's see, Lieutenant, when did you measure the temperature of the water? The day after the accident?"

"No sir, it was . . . " He scanned his notes. "It was October 28."

Oh, so that's it, thought Reed. "October 28? Ten days after the accident? What are we supposed to make of that?" He did his best to sound astonished.

Korinsky shifted his big frame and cleared his throat. "All I know is the temperature was 142 degrees when I measured it."

"What was the water temperature on October 19th, Lieutenant?"

"I don't know," Korinsky said softly.

"What? What did you say, again?" asked Reed.

"I don't know," said Korinsky, louder this time.

"What was the weather like on October 28 when you made this measurement?"

"It was raining, almost hailing, I remember, because I had to run through it to get to the house."

"Was it cold?"

"Yes sir, damn cold."

"What was the weather like on October 19, on the day of the accident?"

"I don't know."

"Well, it was hot, Lieutenant, very hot. Indian summer. We had it for a week, remember?" He paused. "Have you ever had the hot water run out while you were taking a shower in your house, Lieutenant?" The jurors smiled. Korinsky smiled. Everyone had experienced that unpleasant phenomenon.

"Sure." He grinned self-consciously.

"Did it ever occur to you that when you measured the temperature at 142 degrees on that cold morning, right after Mrs. Washington did the breakfast dishes and washed the clothes, that the temperature of that water would be a lot colder than it was on October 19 in the evening, after a hot day when no one used the hot water?"

"Objection, your honor, this is purely speculation."

"Sustained."

Reed began again. "Suppose the thermostat of a hot water heater is set at 190 degrees. You turn on a hot water faucet. What's the hottest temperature the water could be?"

"190 degrees, if the thermostat's working right."

"That's right. What's the coldest the water could be?"

"Same as the cold water, I guess, if you'd used up all the hot."

"Now Lieutenant, if the thermostat was set to 190 degrees and it was the evening of a hot day and no one had used any hot water all day long, what do you think the temperature of the hot water would be when you first turned it on?"

"Probably 190 degrees."

"What's that, Lieutenant? I didn't hear you."

"190 degrees."

"190 degrees, almost boiling. How long could you hold your hand in boiling water, Lieutenant?"

"Objection, your honor. How did we get to boiling water?"

"Sustained," said Marshall.

Reed looked at the jury. He had made some points. They were interested. "Now just one more question, Lieutenant. When you first started investigating this case, did you think it was a case of child abuse?"

"Yes, of course."

"Why?"

"Because it came from Child Welfare. That's my job, to investigate child abuse cases."

"And who said it was a case of child abuse?"

"Child Welfare." Korinsky thought this was an inane discussion.

"Specifically, who in Child Welfare?"

"Oh, I see. Mavis Johnson, Miss Mavis Johnson."

"And why did she think it was a case of child abuse?"

"I don't know. Because the doctors reported it, I guess. You'll have to ask her."

"Thank you, Lieutenant, I intend to. No further questions."

* * * *

On the second day of the trial, the prosecution began with Mavis Johnson. She defined the social factors which set the stage for battered child syndrome: parents of different races, drugs and alcohol, violent temper in an otherwise introverted parent, childhood neglect of one of the parents, and so on. Reed objected repeatedly during the recital of this litany, but he was consistently overruled. Baldridge asked which if any of those factors Mavis had discovered in her analysis of the Washington home. Washington's temper, the interracial situation, and the fact that he was, in essence, the live-in boyfriend were identified. After more discussion of the behavior of the children in institutions and a foster home, Baldridge sat down.

In cross-examination, Mavis admitted that there was no problem with alcohol or drugs, that both parents were solid citizens, who, between them, earned twenty-eight thousand dollars a year. Reluctantly, she categorized that as a middle-class income. Finally, she admitted that she had never seen the burned children. In fact, she had never seen anyone with a serious burn injury. She didn't know the difference between a second- and third-degree burn.

At lunch in the jury room, the bearded young man who sat in the back corner commented on this to the little old lady. "That social worker didn't really know anything about the little girl in question, did you notice that?"

"Yes, I did. She seemed very nice. Her teeth were nice and white and straight and she seemed so intelligent."

Suzanne Hathaway was scheduled next, but Reed had handled Mavis Johnson so effectively that Baldridge was having second thoughts. She wanted to get Washington's attack on Suzanne into evidence, but there would be other opportunities for that. She decided not to call Suzanne, and proceeded to her final medical witnesses instead. Of all the nurses who worked in the pediatric ICU, Baldridge chose Delvina Lockhart to testify. She normally worked the PM shift, so she'd had as much contact with the family as anyone. She had several notes in the chart, so her opinion was well-documented. She was articulate in a simple soft-spoken way, and she was fortyish, plump, and black. She could have been Kevin Washington's mother.

Mrs. Lockhart was very believable. She described the girls and their injuries in simple terms that the jury could understand. She described Sally as loving and concerned. She thought Kevin was scared, defensive, and hostile.

"Did you ask Becky how the injury occurred?" asked Baldridge.

"Yes, I did. She said, 'Daddy burned me in the tub.' Reed had no cross- examination.

Kindly old Dr. McNamarra was an equally impressive witness. He described the medical care in some detail, saying it was the best available anywhere. He testified that the injury was unquestionably the result of forced immersion in a hot liquid and showed a picture of an almost identical injury published in a paper about child abuse by Dr. David Lower.

Under Reed's questioning he admitted that he had never seen a similar case, nor did he remember the last case of child abuse he had treated. Finally, he agreed that he had never met either parent, explaining that the residents had done that. He could not find a record of any discussion with the parents in the chart. Reed excused him.

* * * *

James Murray left halfway through Edward Browne's cross-examination to call in his story. Browne's credentials, both as a pediatrician and as an expert in child abuse were perfect. Smoothly, he had defined the characteristics which made this a classic case of child abuse. Murray's article began, "One witness after another heaped facts upon the pile of evidence presented against accused child abuser murderer Kevin Washington. Prosecutor Norma Baldridge skillfully . . ."

Murray had left during Reed's cross-examination. He did not hear Browne admit that no one from the hospital had ever taken a formal history from the family. It wouldn't have mattered anyway.

* * * *

On the third day of the trial, Reed called the defense witnesses. There were only five: Steven Crane, David Lower, Peter Blake, Sally, and Washington himself. Steven had never been in a courtroom before. His concept of courtroom procedure was based on portrayals by Henry Fonda and Raymond Burr. Therefore, he was surprised by the lackadaisical attitude of the bailiff and clerk bantering with the court reporter, and the total disregard of efficient use of time. At twenty minutes after nine, he took the stand.

Reed had explained the questions he would ask and instructed him to speak to the jury, looking at each member individually. Steven started to do this but was repeatedly interrupted by the court reporter, who asked him to go slower and spell various words. By the time Reed asked his third question, he was responding directly to the court reporter in front of him. After establishing his credentials, Reed prompted him by saying, "Now, Dr. Crane, please tell the jury if you are familiar with the case of Susie Washington who was admitted to Presbyterian Hospital on October l9."

"I am very familiar with that case," said Steven, with a formality worthy of Mr. Fonda himself.

"Did you care for that patient?" asked Reed.

"I did."

"Do you have an opinion as to the cause of the injury? Specifically, is the injury characteristic of child abuse?"

"Initially, I thought the burns were child abuse, but now I am not at all sure."

"Could you explain that to us?"

"The admitting diagnosis of battered child syndrome–child abuse–was based on the appearance of the injury, and there was cause for suspicion and investigation. But no one ever talked to the family, and that's the most important part of any child abuse investigation.

When I finally talked to Mr. Washington—which I am embarrassed to say was only a few weeks ago—I was convinced that the whole thing was just an accident. And that we had all made a terrible mistake."

Members of the jury shifted in their seats and looked at one another. There was some murmuring in the audience which now included most of the prosecution witnesses. Edward Browne stared fiercely at Crane.

"What gives you that impression, Dr. Crane?" asked Reed. "I thought that the appearance of the injury was the most important factor."

"The appearance is the clue to suspicion," said Crane. "It should lead to reporting and investigation. But the most important factor in deciding what actually happened is the history from the family. Dr. Browne always emphasizes
that point."

"Dr. Browne?"

"Dr. Edward Browne, chief of pediatrics at Presbyterian Hospital. He's sitting right over there." Steve pointed toward Dr. Browne. It suddenly occurred to him that this method of question-and-answer testimony was time consuming and stupid. Why didn't Dr. Browne stand up and engage in a dialogue? They could settle that particular point right now. Why didn't members of the jury have the option to ask questions? Someone should ask Washington about the history right then, when Browne and Suzanne and Mavis Johnson and his other accusers were sitting there. The jury would learn the most if they could all talk it out. "Why don't you just ask him what he thinks, and ask Washington if anyone talked to him?" said Crane, in a burst of naiveté that caused both lawyers to smile, several jurors to nod their heads, and the judge to become irritated.

"Dr. Crane, we don't tell you how to take care of babies, please don't tell us how to conduct a trial," said Judge Marshall. "Just confine your answers to the questions. Carry on, Mr. Reed."

"Dr. Crane, other witnesses have already explained this to us, but I would just like to be sure I understand you. Did any member of the medical staff or social service staff of the hospital ever talk to the defendant, Kevin Washington, about the mechanism of injury?" Reed had decided to get Crane off the stand as rapidly as possible. He showed signs of launching into an indictment of the justice system.

Reed had seen a young doctor do this once before, and it negated his testimony.

"As far as I can determine, no one ever took a history on this patient,"
said Steve.

"Thank you, Dr. Crane." Reed sat down and nodded toward Baldridge. Baldridge referred to her notes as she stood behind the podium.

"Dr. Crane, do you consider Dr. Browne–whom you identified a minute ago–an expert in child abuse?"

"Yes."

"And an expert in pediatrics?"

"Very definitely."

"And are you familiar with Dr. John McNamarra?"

"Of course."

"And is he an expert in plastic surgery and burns?"

"Yes. He's the best."

"How many years ago did you graduate from medical school?"

"Almost three years ago."

"And you are currently an intern in pediatrics?"

"No, a resident."

"Oh yes. Thank you." "Dr. Crane, are you an expert in pediatrics? I don't mean a competent practitioner. I mean an expert of the type that Dr. Browne is, for example."

"No, but I–"

"And are you an expert in child abuse?"

"No."

"Are you an expert in burns and plastic surgery?"

"No, but–"

"How many burn cases have you personally treated? Major burns, now. Do you know what a major burn is, Dr. Crane?"

"Objection, your honor," said Reed, trying to interrupt the obvious chain of questioning. "The prosecutor has asked two questions."

"Sustained."

"I'm sorry, Dr. Crane, if that's confusing. What is the definition of a major burn?"

"I'm . . . I'm not quite sure; a large burn, one with a significant risk attached to it, I would say."

"How large, 5 percent, 10 percent, 30 percent?"

"I'm not sure. Over 20 percent I'd say."

"All right, Dr. Crane. How many burn patients have you personally cared for with burns greater than 20 percent?"

"Not very many. Three or four maybe."

"And on the basis of that extensive experience, you claim to know the cause of the injury in this complex case, is that correct?"

The paraphrase was not entirely accurate. Steve tried to explain. "I didn't claim to know the cause of the injury. I merely said that Mr. Washington's explanation was reasonable."

"Based on your experience with three or four other cases, and contrary to the opinion of your teachers, whom you identified as experts?"

"Based on my experience and common sense," said Crane, getting angry.

"Common sense? Oh come now, Dr. Crane, you mean any of us could walk in off the street and decide that this horrible injury," she was at the bulletin board defining the precise edges of the burn in the photographs, "was a simple accident? Common sense, Dr. Crane?"

"Common sense combined with expert medical opinion," said Crane.

"Oh, we have plenty of expert opinion, Dr. Crane, and it does not include yourself, as you've just told us. No further questions."

"Look," said Crane, "you make it sound like I have to prove the burns were an accident. Mr. Washington's explanation is perfectly reasonable. It's up to you to prove otherwise, not to me. What is this, a kangaroo court?"

"Dr. Crane, you are entirely out of order," snapped Marshall. "I will instruct the jury to disregard those remarks and insist that you respond only to the questions that are asked." Steven slumped back in his chair. "Mr. Reed?" said the judge.

"No further questions, your honor," said Reed.

"Please step down," said the bailiff, who had come to the front of the
courtroom.

Norma Baldridge had planned to ask Crane about the encounter with Washington in Suzanne's apartment. As his testimony proceeded, however, she could tell that he was about to self-destruct and thought it wiser to continue in that direction. Her reading of the jury told her that she wouldn't need the extra evidence against Washington, and Marshall would probably not allow it anyway. Besides, she had seen Dr. David Lower enter the back of the courtroom, and she wanted to get Crane off the stand quickly, anticipating that Marshall would call a recess which would give her the chance to talk to him. Marshall did.

She waited until Lower was engaged in conversation by Mavis Johnson, then walked by, appearing to be going to the door.

"Hi, David, what a surprise. What brings you here today?"

"Hello, Norma, it's good to see you again. I didn't know you were prosecuting this case."

"If I'd known you were available, I would have got you to testify for me." She smiled.

"I don't testify *for* anyone, Norma, you know that. I'm just an impartial lover of justice. I'm glad I don't have to make a living at this expert witness business."

"I wish I could," said Baldridge. They all laughed.

"This fellow Reed is unusual for the public defender's office. The guy came to see me twice. He's really done his homework."

"Yes, he's a good man. We're trying to recruit him for the DA's office."

"Good luck." He looked across the room to see Steven shaking his head and talking to Reed. "Excuse me, would you please, Norma?" He walked away without waiting for her response.

"Dr. Crane?" Steven looked up, embarrassed. "I'm David Lower. I enjoyed your testimony. You made a good point. You'll get used to this courtroom bullshit after a while." He smiled and shook Steven's hand. Lower was friendlier than Steven had expected. He was a very young looking fifty; blond and deeply tanned from a recent lecture cruise in the Caribbean. He was impeccably dressed in a beige leisure suit that had a slightly military quality to it. His dark blue, wide-collared silk shirt was open at the neck, exposing two gold chains. The suit had a sort of vest—more of a weskit, actually—that Crane had seen only in a *Playboy* fashion review. There was a dark blue silk handker-chief protruding from his pocket, and a heavy gold chain on each wrist. Dark brown boots, by Gucci.

On the witness stand, Lower was the picture of poise and confidence. As he sat down, he shook hands with Judge Marshall, saying, "Hi, Dave, good to see you again." Just loud enough for the jury to hear.

Reed said, "Dr. Lower, please state your name and describe your background," as Lower had instructed him to do. He launched into a three-minute speech, pausing to spell Lower, Cornell and reconstructive. Reed's next instruction was to ask, "What is your expert opinion regarding the mechanism of injury in this case?" The jury listened intently.

"I'm glad you asked that, Mr. Reed, because this case is a great example of what can happen when well-intentioned individuals go off on a tangent without having all the information." He embarked on a long and erudite discussion of inflicted burns in childhood. He repeatedly emphasized that it was impossible to determine the precise mechanism of injury from looking at the burn surface itself. Scald burns, flame burns, and chemical burns had particular characteristics, but beyond that, the suspicion of inflicted injury depended on the history, the behavior of the family, and the extent to which the explanation matched the examination. He rambled, giving several examples of apparently accidental burns which turned out to be inflicted and vice versa.

Ordinarily, Baldridge would have interrupted this recitation and insisted he stick to the case, but, knowing Lower, she decided against it. Finishing his discussion, he said, "So, in this case, like any other burn case, we come to the question, does the injury match the history? The answer here is clearly yes. We see cases like this all the time in the Children's Hospital Burn Center. The mistake here was that people jumped to conclusions based on incomplete information. No one on the medical team talked to the family. They just pushed the button that activated the system. The system cranks through, just like it always does, resulting in a long, expensive process which is quite unfair to Mr. Washington and his family."

In response to more questions from Reed, Lower dismissed the opinions of Stone, Browne, and McNamarra, pointing out that, according to the records, they had never talked to the family. He went over the photographs in detail, explaining how Washington's explanation matched the injury exactly. He carefully refused to comment on the medical care, simply saying that he would have done it very differently. When asked who was responsible for the death of the child, he responded, "Let me put it this way. We treat about two hundred children with major burns each year and we haven't had a death from a scald burn for seven years."

Reed asked the clerk to hand Dr. Lower prosecutor's exhibit number thirty-four, Lower's own paper on child abuse to which Dr. McNamarra had referred. "Dr. McNamarra showed us this photograph from your paper which is a picture of an immersion burn. It looks quite similar to little Susie's injuries, don't you think?" asked Reed.

"Yes, it's almost identical; burns on the back, perineum, heels, skip areas, bruises, almost exactly the same," said Lower, reviewing the reprint.

"Dr. McNamarra said that this proved that Susie's burn was an immersion injury. What do you say to that?"

"That just demonstrates the point I've been trying to make for the last hour," said Lower, earnestly looking at each juror's face. "You can't tell much from looking at the burn. The child in this photograph was brought to the hospital the day after the injury by the grandparents. The mother lost her temper and burned the child. She admitted it. That's how we knew the mechanism—not from looking at the burn. We got her to appropriate help; actually they're now a very happy family. That has nothing at all to do with Susie Washington. Look, this article was published four years ago. It says, 'A common mistake made by inexperienced physicians is to construe the mechanism of injury from looking at the surface. It simply cannot be done.'"

"Thank you, Dr. Lower. Your witness."

Baldridge knew better than to joust with Lower, but she had to try to discount his testimony—somehow—to introduce just a hint of doubt in the minds of the jurors. "Dr. Lower, suppose that you just saw these photographs, but you didn't know anything else about the case." She indicated the pictures on the bulletin board. "What would you say about the mechanism of injury, just from examining these photographs?"

Lower smiled and adjusted his gold bracelet. "Norma, I just told you that. You can't say anything by looking at the surface of the burn, particularly when all you have is a few pictures. It looks like a scald burn, that's all you can say." He smiled again. She smiled back, realizing that he had detected her intent and blocked it before it started.

"Dr. Lower, did you ever see this child? Did you ever examine the burns that we've been discussing?"

"No. Ed Browne asked me to see the child when they were in trouble . . . that is, when they were having a difficult time in management, but . . . ah . . . it never worked out." This was news to Baldridge. She chanced a look at Ed Browne, who nodded. If Lower had refused to render care, that would effectively cancel his testimony. She decided to try it.

"Why didn't it work out?"

"Well . . . Dr. Browne decided he didn't need me after all." He smiled at Browne, who was sitting stiffly in the third row of seats.

"Would you elaborate on that, please?"

"You really want me to?"

"Yes," said Baldridge, who had committed herself to the question but already knew she would regret the answer.

"I told Dr. Browne I'd be delighted to see the patient, talk to the family, take care of her, and get her well, but only at the burn center. You see, burn care is such a highly specialized team effort that it just isn't fair to the patient to try to kluge it up in some community hospital. We would have been glad to treat little Susie; I wish we had. Dr. Browne just decided not to get us involved. Isn't that right, Ed?" He smiled at the audience. Browne nodded affirmatively, responding to the conceited but charismatic nature of Lower's personality.

"No further questions," said Baldridge.

CHAPTER 22

Peter Blake had been in the courtroom sitting next to Ed Browne for most of Lower's testimony. Reed was ready to have him called, but Marshall decided to break for lunch. Blake invited Browne and Suzanne to lunch at Gallagher's across the street. His favorite booth was waiting as usual. Blake and Suzanne rubbed knees and enjoyed their special relationship right under the nose of Dr. Browne, who was still seething from Lower's testimony.

"Pete, are you really going to testify for the defense?" asked Browne, between bites of knockwurst and sauerkraut.

"I have to, Ed. I'm under subpoena. That's an unusual situation for me."

"That testimony from Lower is the only thing going for Washington–depending on what you say, of course." He looked at his friend cautiously. "One of our residents–Steve Crane–testified for him, but the prosecutor took him apart." Blake and Suzanne exchanged amused glances at the mention of
Crane's name.

"What do you think, from what you've heard so far?"

"Lower's a good witness. Sometimes juries don't like that approach, though. He came across just a little too slick. I don't know. It depends on the rest of
the testimony."

"What do they want from you, Pete? Is it about the foster children and the parents' care? Is that what it is?"

"No, Ed. Remember when my Petey was in the hospital, with the broken arm?" Browne nodded. "Well, I ran into Washington in the cafeteria. It was the day after the accident. And he told me the whole story. The defense lawyer wants me to corroborate it. It seems that . . . ah . . . no one wrote it down in the hospital record." He smiled at Browne, realizing that it was a sensitive point. Browne was aghast.

"Really? Jesus, Pete, that would hurt us if you corroborate his story. I mean, the guy's guilty as hell–you've seen that–Christ, he even forced his way into Sue's apartment, isn't that right, Sue?" Sue flushed.

"Yes. I . . . I think Mr. Blake knows about that." He had heard her version, briefly.

"The guy's a maniac, Pete, but that public defender lawyer is pretty clever. You'd better not give him much to go on or that nut will be out on the streets again. Hell, they might even give the kids back to him. You'd better be careful." He laughed at his own forwardness. "Listen to me, telling Detroit's best lawyer to be careful on the stand."

Mention of the children obviously had an affect on Blake. His eyes became somber and he leaned away from the table, squeezing his paper napkin into a small, hard ball. "Oh yes. The children," he said, shuddering at the thought of returning them to Washington. He looked up suddenly, as if discovered in a private daydream, and said, "Don't worry, Ed, far be it from me to contradict Detroit's finest pediatrician."

Suzanne changed the subject to her upcoming vacation in Hawaii.

* * * *

When the trial resumed, Steven was sitting in the back of the courtroom with Gus Korinsky. After responding to what came to be known as "the Oswald letter," Steven had met with Korinsky. His intentions were simple. He wanted to know about Washington's statement to the police, to see if there really were any discrepancies. And he was still concerned about the propriety of sharing a confidential letter between the defense attorney and the prosecutor. Reed had assured him that it was standard practice, but Steven still felt that it should be investigated. It was Reed who suggested that he talk with Korinsky. Korinsky was rough, almost crude, but Steven was attracted by his inherent honesty. Korinsky was surprised, even amazed, that the young doctor would be so concerned about the facts as to come to his office and read through the reports. The two developed a Mutt-and-Jeff-type friendship which led to their second meeting. Korinsky was in Presbyterian Hospital at noon and searched out Steven on the wards. They had egg salad sandwiches in the cafeteria. ("Tangy egg salad and crisp lettuce," it said on the menu board.)

Crane could not understand Blake's testimony. Reed had said that he would corroborate Washington's story, but his answers were vague and evasive. Reed was obviously having trouble understanding too.

"Mr. Blake, you're a very experienced lawyer. I'm trying to get a simple answer to a simple question. When you talked with Mr. Washington in the hospital, what did he tell you about the accident the day before?"

"Well, you know, the more I've thought about that conversation—in preparation for this testimony—the less certain I am of some of the details. I remember that Mr. Washington was very nervous. He seemed frightened. He was shaking so hard he had trouble lighting a cigarette. I remember that. He said that his daughters had been burned. Somehow the hot water got turned on in the bathtub; the paramedics brought them to the hospital, and when I talked to him, they were in the intensive care unit. I remember discussing the intensive care unit." To the jury, Blake seemed to be deep in thought, rubbing his temple and trying to recall the conversation. Baldridge relaxed. Reed had misjudged his witness. Blake wasn't going to provide any help.

"Did Mr. Washington say why he left the room with the girls in the tub?"

"I can't remember."

"Didn't he tell you that he was going to answer the telephone? That his brother was on the telephone?"

"Objection, your honor," said Baldridge. "Counsel is leading the witness."

"Sustained."

"Did Mr. Washington tell you why he left the girls in the bathtub?"

"He might have. He probably did, I just can't remember precisely."

"And did he say anything about other injuries? Did he say he dropped one of
the girls?"

"Quite possibly, I just can't be sure. It was such a brief conversation."

"Do you recall him saying anything about the little girl's skin?"

"Yes, now that you mention that, I do recall. He said her skin came off in his hands. It was very graphic. I remember that. He did say that."

Reed continued questioning Blake for a few minutes, and then concluded on the most positive note he could find. Baldridge had no cross-examination. Blake joined the small audience again. Reed called Sally to the stand.

Dressed in frilly cotton, Sally made a good appearance. She described Kevin as loving, warm, a wonderful father, and a concerned provider. She described her encounters with the police, social service, and hospital personnel. She tried to explain how Sammy got the black eye, and why they invented an alternate explanation that frightening night. Baldridge did not have any questions.

* * * *

Kevin wore the suit that he had bought for the custody hearing. His hair was cut short. He smiled frequently, as Reed had instructed him, but it was an unnatural action and appeared so on the witness stand. Frequently, the court reporter had to interrupt him to ask him to speak louder.

Carefully, Reed took him through the history of the accident. Kevin described for the jury the relationship between himself and Sally, describing her and the children in loving terms. He spoke of the little girls and the early events of that evening. He recounted that the day had been very hot, and the fact that the hot water had not been used until the evening bath. He described the high bathtub and the new faucet that had been installed by the landlord. Then Reed led him into the accident itself. In the intensity of recounting the events, Kevin forgot that the jury was hearing him for the first and only time. He blocked out the rest of the room to the point where it seemed to him that he was having an isolated conversation with Reed–the lawyer's dream for cross-examination, but not for this type of exposition.

"How long was it between the time you heard the screams and the time you took the girls out of the hot water?"

"Six seconds."

"And who was it that called you on the telephone?"

"My brother Ritchie. Come on man, I told you that a hundred times." Reed perceived, a bit too late, what had happened. He noted the surprise on the faces of some of the jurors. He tried to recoup the situation.

"Of course you have, Kevin," he said, smiling uneasily. "I just want you to tell the jury here and Judge Marshall. Forget all the times you've explained this before and tell them what happened next. Tell it like you were telling it for the first time, what actually happened."

Washington sighed deeply and rubbed his head. The first time he told the story was to Peter Blake and Blake had just denied most of it. He began again, with the bitterness of this most recent betrayal in his throat. He turned to the jury. "I saw the girls with the hot water pouring on them from the faucet. I reached in and took them out. Becky first, then Susie." He sounded like he was reading from a script. Reed tried to signal him to slow down, soften up, with a pacifying gesture of his hand, but to no avail. "When I picked up Susie, she slipped. She fell out of my hand onto the edge of the tub. She hit her face pretty bad." Tears came to his eyes, to be sure, but combined with the hard edge of his voice and the tightly clenched fists it was difficult to tell whether the tears arose from compassion or zeal. "I dried them off and they looked burned. That's when I called my wife." He looked over at Sally, who had a look of shock and suffering on her face—not from the recount of the accident, but from the realization that the case was lost.

Reed was granted a short recess. He conferred earnestly with Kevin and Sally, explaining again that the jury was hearing him for the first time—that he needed to show gentleness and concern. This was not the time to express his anger at the system. Kevin understood, and did a little better when they returned to testimony. Reed asked him to describe the girls in the hospital, to explain his reactions, his feelings. He responded softly until Reed asked about the night that the police took Sammy from his bed. Now was the time for Washington to become openly bitter, and he did. His description of the banging on the door, the flashing light, the police officer who twisted his arm while the other pushed his wife aside and tore his son from the bed was graphic and moving to the jury. One man in the second row shuddered when Kevin described the policeman carrying Sammy down the sidewalk while he called for his mother. Reed was pleased, and now encouraged Kevin's biting answers. He asked him about meetings with the doctors ("None, never saw 'em, they never talked to me."), and the police interrogation. He asked him about meetings with the Child

Abuse Committee and Social Workers. He asked him about his employer and his attempt to get a lawyer and the treatment he received from other prisoners ("They treat me like shit; well, excuse me, sir, but that's what they do.").

Reed watched the clock, trying to string out his questions to fill the entire afternoon. He had to get Kevin off the stand and calmed down before Baldridge had a chance at him. At half past four Marshall was yawning and Reed decided it was safe. He asked his final question.

"Mr. Washington, you have described to us the terrible, frightening things that have happened to you and your family since the accident. It has obviously been a cruel form of mental torture for you and your wife. Has anyone suggested to you how to end this harassment?"

"Sure," said Washington. "Everyone told me, the social workers, the counselor, the police. Even you. Even my wife."

"Told you what?"

"Told me to confess. Told me to say I burned the girls on purpose. Then they said I could get out of jail, get the kids back, go to counseling. They said it would be cool."

"Now Kevin, if you could end all of this as simply as that . . . why haven't you done it?"

Washington was furious. "Because I didn't do it. I told you that over and over. You don't believe me. Nobody believes me." He covered his face with his hands and sobbed. Reed remained standing, looking at each jury member. They, in turn, looked at him, then at Washington on the stand. The effect was exactly what he had hoped for. He had raised a doubt in their minds.

"No further questions, your honor."

Marshall glanced at the clock, and then chanced to notice Jim Murray sitting in the front row of the gallery. He was writing notes, quickly looking directly at Marshall and at the clock. He fingered the handle of his briefcase and sat on the edge of the bench, as if he was ready to bolt to the telephone at the first opportunity. His article two days ago had described Marshall as a gentlemanly individual who enjoyed long recesses and early adjournments. Marshall knew that Murray would have to call in his story very soon to make the next edition. He postponed his desire for a cigarette and his nightly martini and addressed Norma Baldridge.

"Your witness counselor."

Reed was stunned. He rose to his feet. "May I suggest, your honor, that we adjourn for the day, Mr. Washington has been through a difficult emotional experience . . ."

"It's a reasonable request, Counselor, but it's only four thirty. We have plenty of time left today. We wouldn't want the newspapers to accuse us of squandering away the taxpayers' money, now would we?" He directed a sneering smile at Murray who saluted with his pen. "Do you think you can continue, Mr. Washington?" Marshall asked.

"Yes, let's go on," said Kevin, wiping his sleeve across his face. "Let's get this over with."

"I object, your honor," said Reed. "Mr. Washington is not in any condition to—"

"Carry on, Counselor," Judge Marshall said to Baldridge, ignoring the
sputtering Reed.

Baldridge was surprised by the turn of events. She had made several notes but had not planned to have the opportunity of cross-examination today. It was a rare opportunity. She tried not to appear too eager.

"Just a few questions, Mr. Washington. I know this has been difficult for you. You said that when you went to answer the telephone, the little girls were running around in the tub. Is that what you said?"

"That's right."

"Were they healthy little girls?"

"Oh yes, very healthy."

"If healthy children are exposed to something very hot, do you think they would try to get away from it?"

"I suppose so," he mumbled.

"What's that, Mr. Washington? I didn't hear you. Speak a little louder, please. Would healthy children try to get away from something hot? Yes or no?"

"Yes." His voice was husky. He was gripping the edge of the seat now.

"Then why didn't the little girls try to get out of the hot water, Mr. Washington, if everything happened as you said? Why would that be?"

"I don't know."

"But Mr. Washington, you just said that children would normally try to avoid something very hot and that your girls were capable and

249

healthy and running around in the tub. Do you expect us to believe that they just stayed there in the hot water?"

"That's what they did."

"Now, Mr. Washington, do you really expect us to believe that?"

"That's what happened!" exclaimed Washington, rising up out of the chair on the witness stand.

"Objection, your honor," exclaimed Reed. "Counselor is harassing the witness."

"Sustained."

"Mr. Washington, you testified that you got advice from the social workers. Do you know this lady?" She pointed to the front row. "Miss Suzanne Hathaway, social worker at Presbyterian Hospital?" Kevin looked suddenly frightened.

"Yes."

"You have met with her at the hospital on several occasions, isn't that correct?"

"Yes."

"Have you ever been to her home?"

"Objection, your honor," said Reed, who knew what was coming. "This line of questioning is not relevant to the case in question."

"Judge Marshall, Miss Hathaway is the social worker who was responsible for reporting the injuries to Child Welfare and ultimately responsible for disposition of the girls. I intend to show that Mr. Washington transferred his violent aggressions from the children to Miss Hathaway."

"Proceed."

"Well, Mr. Washington, were you ever in Miss Hathaway's home?" Kevin looked from side to side, as if searching for a direction to bolt and run. "Mr. Washington, please answer the question."

"Yes."

"Is it true that you forced your way into her apartment?"

"No, not really, that is—"

"Did she let you in voluntarily?"

"No, she didn't have any—"

"She didn't have any what?"

"She didn't have any . . . clothes on." A middle-aged man in the jury who had been dozing suddenly sat upright. The blue-haired lady in the front row gasped audibly.

"Mr. Washington, you said Miss Hathaway did not let you in voluntarily, you said she was not dressed, yet you came in through the door. Is that correct?"

"Yes."

"Then I will ask you again. Did you force your way into Miss Hathaway's apartment?"

"Well, not exactly . . ."

"Nevermind, Mr. Washington, I think we have the picture. Do you know Dr. Crane who testified here earlier?"

"Yes."

"Did Dr. Crane enter Miss Hathaway's apartment later that same evening while you were still there?"

"Well, yes, but–"

"And what were you doing when Dr. Crane entered?"

Washington sat silent, his nostrils flaring, his mouth pasty dry. The blue-haired woman put her hand over her mouth in response to a mental image of some lurid act.

"Mr. Washington, what were you doing when Dr. Crane let himself into the apartment?" It was a subtle difference in statement that reached only the subconscious understanding of the jurors. "Mr. Washington, you must answer the question."

"I was–I was holding on to Miss Hathaway, but she was–"

"Holding on to Miss Hathaway? In what way were you holding on to Miss Hathaway?"

"By her hair." It was almost inaudible.

"What's that again? Speak up please, the jury can't hear you."

"By her hair."

"And where were you when Dr. Crane broke in?"

"In the bedroom," said Washington, in a mean, growly voice meant to direct hostility at Baldridge, but sounding generally rapacious.

"And what did you have in mind? If Dr. Crane had not come in at that very instant, what were you going to do to Miss Hathaway?"

"I object, your honor, that question is completely conjectural and this entire line of questioning is prejudicial and irrelevant."

"Sustained," said Marshall.

That was fine with Baldridge. She had exposed the jury to just enough of the scene to let their imagination do the rest. Later, in the redirect examination, Washington clarified the episode as best he could, but the jury never believed that conservative, intelligent, lovely Miss Hathaway would ever let Washington into her apartment, let alone try to seduce him.

"It's getting late, your honor, I have only one more question for Mr. Washington," said Baldridge. Marshall nodded. "Nurse Lockhart testified that she asked little Becky how she got burned and Becky responded, 'Daddy burned me in the tub.' Did you hear that testimony, Mr. Washington?"

"Yes, but she meant that I put her in the bathtub and that's where she got burned. That's what she meant."

"How do you know that's what she meant?"

"Because that's what happened. I told you that. I put the girls in the bathtub and that's where she got burned."

Baldridge had the bailiff put the shallow trash bucket on the table. The metal handles clattered against the sides. "Mr. Washington–do you recognize this?"
she asked.

"It looks like . . . it looks like the trash can from my house," said Washington, carefully.

"It is the trash can from your house, Mr. Washington, 929 in yellow paint, isn't that your address? 929 Calvert?"

"Yes, that's it."

"What would you call this in your house, Mr. Washington?"

"Beg pardon?" Washington stalled, hoping that he would sink into the floor.

"What would you call this? What do your children call this?" She rattled it on the table as if to jar him awake.

"A tub."

"What? What's that Mr. Washington?"

"A tub," he said ferociously. "We call it the tub."

"Your honor, I object to this display." Reed was on his feet. "Counselor continues to harass the witness by producing a metal trash can that has no relevance in this case."

"It seems relevant to me, Mr. Reed," said Marshall, his cold gaze, along with that of most of the jurors, fixed on the large metal tub.

"What do you do with this tub in your house, Mr. Washington?"

"We put trash in it, that's why we call it the trash tub. That's why it has the numbers painted on the side."

Washington sounded progressively meaner in his responses.

"What else do you do with it, Mr. Washington?"

He shrugged. "Sometimes I use it to clean greasy things, like my carburetor, or an oil filter."

"I see. And how do you use the tub to clean your carburetor? Tell us about that, Mr. Washington."

"I put the parts in the tub and fill it up with boiling water. That floats the grease off the carburetor parts."

"How do you do that, Mr. Washington? Describe that to us a little more."

The jury continued to stare at the steel tub.

"I boil water on the stove in a big pot, then I pour it on the carburetor parts. Then I reach in with a big rubber glove and take 'em out one by one and put them back together." Washington was becoming more sullen and subdued, resigned to what he knew the ensuing questions would be. He glowered at Sally, sitting in the first row of the gallery. The information could have only come from her. She was shaking, with tears rolling down the sides of her cheeks.

"Why do you use the rubber glove, Mr. Washington, why not just reach in and take out the carburetor parts?"

"Because the water's too hot, you'd burn your hand." He was giving up now.

"When you pour in the boiling water, Mr. Washington, how far does it fill up the tub? How much water is in the tub?"

"I don't know, three or four inches, something like that. I don't know." His voice trailed off. His eyes became vacant.

"Did you use the tub on October 19, Mr. Washington?" Her voice suddenly went very soft so the jury had to strain to hear. "Did you fill this tub with boiling water that evening?" She lifted it six inches off the table.

"No, I didn't."

"Did you get mad at little Susie that night? Did she spill her milk? Was she crying?" She raised it a foot off the table.

"No!" Washington was shouting now. "Don't say that, don't say that!"

"Did you put your own little girls into boiling water in this tub?"

She dropped it on the table with a reverberating clang that caused everyone to jump. It drowned out his anguished answer.

* * * *

The next morning Washington had returned to his carefully contrived composure. Baldridge had achieved all the emotional imagery and innuendo that she wanted. She was now anxious to get the trial over with. Reed carried out a skillful redirect questioning. Washington outlined in a few sentences what actually happened in Suzanne's apartment. As it became progressively more confusing, the jury was obviously not convinced and Reed dropped the subject. He asked Kevin calmly if he had ever put his children in hot water in the steel tub and Kevin replied calmly that he had not. Reed asked a few more questions about police and prison harassment to leave that impression with the jury, then excused Washington. Reed had no more witnesses, and Marshall declared an early morning recess to prepare for arguments.

Baldridge had requested that Mavis Johnson bring the Washington children to court that day. One look at their happy little faces would undoubtedly win over any juror with lingering doubts. She had planned to simply bring them in to the front row of the gallery during her dissertation, but now, sensing an easy victory and concerned over an appeal, she decided to consult Marshall.

The three of them sat in his chambers, drinking coffee and congratulating one another on the fact that the trial had taken only a week. "That damn reporter's been here every day," said Reed. "I hope he puts all this in the newspaper." They all smiled.

As Baldridge argued the case for bringing the children into the courtroom, Reed listened attentively. His initial reaction was against it. Presenting the children would be devastating to his case. But as she talked, a new plan for a closing argument began to evolve. He had not thought of bringing the children into the courtroom, but it was just the touch he needed. When Marshall asked him if he objected, he said no.

"Are you sure?" asked Marshall, thinking that Reed did not understand the implications of his answer.

"Yes, sir. That's fine with me," he responded. Baldridge thought he had given up.

Jim Murray recorded the prosecution's closure as perfunctory, solid, each fact hammered in followed by another like nails in a coffin. Not a bad metaphor, thought Murray, sketching headlines for the next article. There had been no rebuttal–save Washington's denial–to any of the prosecution's case. The star witness–Lower–canceled his own testimony by saying that history from the family was the most important factor, then explaining that he had not taken a history from the family. Blake had contributed nothing except evidence of a vague conversation with Washington, so it boiled down to a list of uncontested facts against Washington's denial. They had even produced the instrument of torture. Baldridge clanged the metal tub on the table again as she discussed it, causing Becky Washington to begin to cry. The jury looked alternately at the pictures on the bulletin board, the children in the front row, and Washington, who stared at Baldridge with increasing anger.

* * * *

Reed began his closing argument after lunch. He was glad for the break, because the jury's attitude toward Washington by the end of the morning had been obviously hostile. Reed walked slowly in front of the jury, studying each face.

"Ladies and gentlemen, before this trial started, both Judge Marshall and I reminded you to begin with the assumption that Mr. Washington is innocent. What has the prosecution produced to change your mind? This steel tub? Most of the houses in Michigan have a steel tub like this. Just courtroom theatrics. These photographs? Just pictures of a scald burn, according to the only burn expert to testify here. Horrible? Hideous? Of course, but just courtroom theatrics. The police investigation? Absolutely nothing to contradict Mr. Washington's statement. And they tried hard enough, even that ridiculous business about the water temperature.

"You've heard every witness for the prosecution state the only reason this entire procedure got started was because a doctor at Presbyterian Hospital said that this was a case of child abuse. There is the root of the problem, because child abuse is an emotional issue. One that makes you angry. One that is so inflammatory that it's almost impossible to stay objective, especially when doctors have said this is clearly a case of child abuse. Yet we have brought out in testimony that the doctors who made that judgment were either totally inexperienced and incapable of making such a judgment–like Dr. Stone–or witch-hunting zealots that find child abuse around every corner–like Dr. Browne. Dr. Browne, who never even bothered to talk to this young family about their little girls, not to mention determining whether the injury fit the history. Finally, we heard from Dr. Lower, the only real expert to review the case, that our basic assumption–that Mr. Washington is telling the truth–is correct, there's no reason to think otherwise. So the prosecution has not presented a single bit of solid evidence to change your mind from your basic assumption of innocence. Moreover; the defense, although we didn't have to, has provided expert and incontrovertible testimony that your basic assumption is correct. Therefore, you must find Mr. Washington innocent.

"Now, aside from all that, the prosecution presented a lot of testimony about the relationship of these young people: their home, their family, their jobs, and their race. You heard a policeman discuss their marital status. You heard a nurse discuss their emotional reactions and mental health. You heard an unmarried social worker discuss their qualifications as parents. You heard a white, grandmotherly, holier-than-thou prosecutor needle and harangue and tease this young man about the death of his own daughter until he couldn't stand it anymore. I objected to all this irrelevant testimony as it went along, but Judge Marshall allowed it. And now I'm glad he did, because it points out a much larger and, in fact, a much more important issue than the innocence of Mr. Washington, which we've already established. It gets to the heart of the issue which is on trial here–the right of a society to force its collective value judgment on a member of that society.

"We all have our own hopes and goals and dreams and problems, and people we love, and people we hate, and parents and children who care about us and for us to care about. The most personal and most special treasure of all is our children. And we go about the business of living as best we can, trying to make life acceptable for us, but better–always better–for our children.

"We decide that all the children in our society should be educated, and we provide, as a society, the schools and teachers and wherewithal to do that. We agree that society should take care of children who lose their families until they're old enough to get along. We even agree to give some of our society's money to families who don't have enough to provide for their children. And since we've decided to do all this, of course we need a group of people to do those things for us. These are the social workers.

"By undertaking social service we, the society, intentionally take the subtle step into making value judgments. In our legal system, we make the laws, then decide if the law has been broken or not. Guilty or innocent. Yes or no. But the social worker must decide between good and bad, better and worse, adequate and inadequate. Good compared to what? Worse than whom? Worse than the other people in the society? Which other people? How would you like society to send a representative into your home for a while to see if you're doing an adequate job of raising your children? To see if you're providing enough parental love and financial support. Someone who might decide that the society can do a better job than you can. How would you like to have that happen to you? Or how would

"Since the job involves value judgments, the social worker, and the court, and the society, all of us, must compare to something. We have placed ourselves in the difficult position of hiring representatives who must define the standards of our society, and furthermore determine the extent to which an individual member of our society must meet those standards. Usually, in the case of Child Welfare, that's an easy job—even a pleasant job. A member of the society comes to the social worker asking for help in raising a child. Financial, educational, psychological, disciplinary—whatever. The social worker has access to all of the resources that we have set aside to offer to that family. The society has provided what it has set out to provide.

"But in this case, the individual case of this young family, our carefully designed system has gone awry. A social worker, acting on what she thought at the time to be correct information, set into action a combination of legal and social procedures which have destroyed the lives of five members of our society—this family. The family was not asking for the help, but yes, we determined that it needed help, and it was going to get it. The representatives of society—legally and with good intentions—kidnapped the children of that family and held them hostage. The ransom to be paid was to meet the value judgments. Take advantage of the help offered, pay for it, be grateful for it. Strive to improve. Meet the standard.

"And what happens if the parents deny the accusation? You've seen the results. Children torn from their beds. Torn from their mother's arms. Social ostracism and legal ostracism. Suspicion. Fear. One parent pitted against another. Children pitted against the parents. Accusations. Imprisonment. Prosecution. Until a close and loving family is irreversibly torn apart as you can see here right in front of you. Young children—you see them before you—held by society, by us, dangled in front of the poor parents. The mother, distrustful, not knowing whom to believe and the father so convinced of his innocence that he is unwilling to barter away his soul and pride, even for the freedom of his children.

"You have heard that the principals in this case are Kevin and Susie Washington. But I submit to you, ladies and gentlemen, that there are three principles. This young, frightened, isolated couple, these unsuspecting children, and us, the society. Assume—as you must—that Mr. Washington is innocent. Look at us sitting here. Look at what we have done. And I ask you, who is the abused and who is the abuser?"

* * * *

The jury was out for only two hours. Guilt was not an issue, only the extent of premeditation. They compromised on second-degree murder. The burly man from the back row and the young bearded man left together. The burly man was taking his son to the Tigers game and was glad to be out on time.

"Well, I'm glad that's over. I'm sure we did the right thing," he said.

"God help us all if we're wrong," said the young man.

CHAPTER 23

Steven wasn't exactly fired, just suspended until the committee completed its investigation. Browne wouldn't even talk to him. He just sent a note telling him to leave the hospital and think things over and come back on July 1 when he was scheduled to start his fellowship.

If he thought about the trial, he got so angry at himself and at the system that he could neither concentrate nor eat. So he avoided thinking about it by doing something else–anything else. He polished his car. He reviewed charts for a paper on aspirin poisoning. He tried (again) to read Kant. After a week, he decided to go north.

Beth Bonnell absorbed Steven's misery with characteristic equanimity. After his testimony, when he was sure he had personally upset the judge and lost the case, she agreed with his frustration at the legal system. By the end of the evening, she had convinced him that the jurors felt the same way and he had actually helped Washington. When he described Norma Baldridge and her imperious attitude, she told him a joke about a male chauvinist and a castrating female. He chuckled for an hour. She seemed so interested in his description of Reed's closing argument that he had to stop halfway through, because he was distracted by the glowing excitement in her eyes. Whenever he was with her he felt wise, important, and secure. He never understood exactly why. In fact, after enjoying that pleasant sensation for almost six months, he was still surprised each time it happened. When he arrived unannounced at noon on Sunday and declared they were going north, she smiled and asked simply, "Rough or fancy?"

"Rough," he responded. She stuffed a dozen articles into a small duffel bag, including three paper-backed books. She poured the remains of the pot of coffee into a thermos, called the hospital, and in ten minutes they were headed north on I-75. For two hours they hardly talked, occasionally looking at each other and smiling impishly, as if they had succeeded at some mischievous plan. The city and its people and its cares fell behind as they crossed the Saginaw River. When they passed the West Branch turn-off the smell of pines and sweet fern was heavy in the air.

"Where are we going?" she asked, stretching back with her palms on the roof of the Porsche.

"Bois Blanc Island," he said, using the French pronunciation.

"Any particular place on Bois Blanc Island?" She yawned.

"You'll see," he said, giving way to the urge to reach under her sweatshirt and squeeze her belly, made tight and vulnerable by her stretching.

The ferries were through for the day, but the captain of the old mail boat was making one more trip and he was glad to take them along. They stood aft, watching the late afternoon sun settle into the huge sweep of the big bridge, as the old lapstrake Lyman churned through the swells. Disembarking at the little wharf, they found a young man with a pickup truck who agreed to take them to the deserted Coast Guard station on the southeast end of the island.

"Don't know why you'd want to go there," he commented. "The place is all run down. No one's been there for years." That was, of course, exactly Steven's plan. He had seen the boarded-up white buildings from a sailboat while crewing in the Mackinaw race. He thought at the time it would be a perfect wilderness escape. He was right. They explored the solid old buildings for an hour, climbing over weathered boards lashed by raspberry bushes and peering through cracks into military-clean vacant rooms. Frustrated hunters had peppered the inland side with buckshot and twenty-two slugs. But in the early-evening glow, the small encampment had a hoary sense of permanence, like a stone fence in New England. With the sunset came cooler, stiller air, and unending squadrons of mosquitoes and black flies, as if a signal had been given in every swamp in the adjacent cedar bog. They retreated to the water's edge a few hundred yards away, carrying duffel bags and the boxes of provisions they had purchased in Cheboygan.

The shore was covered with the white one-inch pebbles that made up the beach on northern Lake Huron. There was abundant driftwood in the large cove, and a dilapidated Coast Guard boathouse. The large sliding door to the lake had long since been knocked free, forming a cavernous but airy shelter with a commanding view of the full length of the silver lake. A few lights were coming on in Mackinaw City across the straits, eight miles away. Two big freighters plied the channel and a third long, trailing wisp of smoke could be seen fifteen miles to the south. There was a stiff westerly breeze on the shore—strong enough to push the mosquitoes back into the woods, but warm enough to mollify the chill of the gathering twilight.

Finding a piece of sheet metal and some large rocks, Steven fashioned a fireplace on the dock just outside the mouth of the boathouse. They broiled the steaks (not at all bad for the A&P in Cheboygan) on green stick skewers, accompanied by stone-baked bread and Beck's beer, cooled to perfection in the crystal water of their private slip. Beth discovered that their two sleeping bags would zip into one large one. She spread it over a bed of fresh white cedar boughs that they had collected and piled on the dock, inside the boathouse but close to the fire.

Comfortable and tired, they slid between the Dacron liners, alternately sipping Courvoisier and strong A&P coffee from their two large enameled metal cups. The breeze fanned one final flame, then the birch logs mellowed into embers and the night grew dark and the stars became brighter than the lights across the water.

They awoke with the sun high in the sky, a brazen seagull shouting a salutation from the stone fireplace. They dipped briefly in the exhilarating fifty-degree water. There was no need for bathing suits; the southern end of the island was deserted. After a breakfast of eggs and Canadian bacon, they set out down the shore to explore the island. It was two days before they mentioned the trial, and three days before they puzzled over why Blake had lied.

* * * *

The three veteran window air conditioners chattered and buzzed, but could not keep up with the rapidly accumulating BTUs in the Child Welfare section of the city-county building. August would be unbearable, but this was still June—really the first hot day of the year—and no one minded. No one, that is, except Mrs. Starkweather, who shifted from one massive cheek to the other on the vinyl chair with a sound like wet sheets drying in the breeze. "Cub in, cub in," she mumbled in response to a knock on the frosted glass door. She was having the first of a series of summer colds, and her edematous adenoids not only distorted her speech, but made her mouth hang open more than usual.

Sally entered cautiously, surprised not to hear Mavis Johnson's familiar voice. Sally had finally found a soft spot in Mavis's heart, and had gained the promise of the return of her children as soon as the trial was over. She had been working with Mavis for months, and was now dismayed to recognize the corpulent Mrs. Starkweather.

"Where's Mavis?" Sally's startled look had no affect on Mrs. Starkweather, who was pawing through the desk, looking as if her nose was about to drip.

"She dubn't work here anymore (sniff, snort). Transferred (blatt)." The tissue failed under the force of her blast, and she wiped her hands on her lavender slacks. "Don't I know you from somewhere?"

"I'm Sally Washington. We worked together in counseling several months ago. You were filling in for Mavis."

"Oh yes, I remember now. The lady with the burned children."

"Yes, that's right." She had become resigned to accept this designation. "It's been two weeks since the trial. We were supposed to start on the papers that would get my children back home today." Starkweather was thumbing through the pile. There were two volumes now.

"It says here that your husband was convicted. Got twenty years." She looked up, surprised. "Twenty years for child abuse and murder. Murder?" She looked at Sally for an explanation.

"One of the girls—my littlest girl—died." She could talk about it now without crying.

"Oh yes, I remember (snort). One girl died of the burns." She shook her head, expecting confirmation from Sally, and Sally obliged. Starkweather closed the folder and tapped it with her pencil.

"Well, I don't see how we can let your children return home," she said after a few moments. "I mean, to a home where the father's convicted of child abuse? And murder? I hardly think we could get the judge to go for that."

"But I wasn't there when it happened. I wasn't even home!" Sally could see six months worth of bowing and scraping going for naught. "Where's Miss Johnson? I must see Miss Johnson."

"I told you, she dubn't work here anymore." Starkweather found an economy-size bottle of Dristan in her desk drawer and rooted in a teaspoonful. "Besides, Miss Johnson and the judge would never allow it. Can you imagine that? Sending children back to the home of a murderer?"

"But Kevin–Mr. Washington–is in jail. He's in jail for twenty years." Sally's voice began to rise both in pitch and volume. "Don't you see that? We went through the whole horrible trial and lost. He's not coming back. Now I want my children. Miss Johnson said . . ." Sally sat forward in her chair, leaning on the desk toward the heavily breathing leviathan. "Mrs. Starkweather," she said in an urgent undertone, "Mrs. Starkweather, I don't think my children are safe in that foster home. Strange things have been going on. My children are scared to stay there."

"Oh cub now, Sally. You are imagining things."

"My Becky cries every time I see her. She never used to cry."

"Cries?"

"Yes, she cries, whenever I go to see her."

"See her?"

"Don't start that damn silly psychology again. I have to talk to someone who knows what's going on."

"Going on?"

"Oh, Christ, I can't believe this." Sally stood, scudding the chair away from the desk. "What the hell is going on here?"

"Going on here? What do you think is going on here?"

Sally left without answering. Starkweather went back to the tissue.

∗ ∗ ∗ ∗

Turning the last corner, Browne aimed the riding mower straight down the last remaining strip of high grass, proceeded directly onto the driveway and around the back to the tool shed. He pushed the stop button and the noisy engine coughed and died. After becoming accommodated to its penetrating whine, the stillness was almost oppressive. He seemed to feel the vibration for minutes after he climbed off the metal seat, and his legs felt slightly unsteady as he unhooked the loaded grass catcher. Although he complained about it, Browne enjoyed mowing the huge front lawn. He was away from the telephone, at home but away from the family, and free to let his mind wander for two hours every weekend. It was, at once, the most relaxing and the most creative time that he spent. There was something inherently satisfying to his compulsive personality about mowing long, precise rows. The combination of semi-surgical precision and the earthy sensuality of growing and reaping satisfied all his instincts. Without realizing it consciously, he was invigorated by the sweet and heavy aroma which came from the grass catcher as he carried it into the woods behind his house. Trillium bloomed along the footpath through the oaks and maples. He crossed the bridle trail and dumped the contents of the grass catcher into the ravine. Returning, he heard footsteps on the trail.

Peter Blake ran three and a half miles, five days a week. Five days because that was all the time he could afford, and three and a half miles because that was the length of the circular bridle path as it wound through the woods behind the homes of Hunting Valley. He had almost completed his circuit as he saw Ed Browne coming out of the woods with his empty grass catcher. He slowed to a walk and then stopped.

"Hello, Ed. Don't you get tired of mowing that big lawn?"

"It beats running around in the horse shit as a form of exercise. Hi, Pete, you're looking good." Blake's breathing was returning to its normal pace, but he was still sweating profusely, shaking one leg after the other to forestall any cramps. He rubbed some manure from his shoe on the grass at the side of the path.

"What a great day!" said Blake. "I'm ready for summer."

"So am I," said Brown. "Have you put your boat in yet?"

"No, I'm going to wait another couple of weeks." A bumblebee came out of the woods and circled each of them, then disappeared down the trail.

"I heard that Washington got twenty years," said Browne, watching the bee disappear.

"That's right," said Blake. "I guess we'll have the children for quite awhile."

"I want to thank you for helping out at the trial," said Browne.

Blake shrugged. "I just told what I could remember."

"Of course, I mean, I'm glad you couldn't remember any more

than you did." They both grinned. "That defense lawyer was a sharp fellow."

"Yes, he was good. Too good to stay in the public defender's office very long."

"Well, I'm glad you didn't help him. Say, we're having a little get-together next week. Why don't you and Valerie come over? It's Wednesday night. Just cocktails and dinner for a few friends."

"Thanks, Ed. We'd like that very much, but I'll be out of town next week. Maybe Val would come."

"I'll get Dot to ask her. Where are you going?"

"San Francisco. I'm going to the American Trial Lawyers Association. I'll be back on Sunday."

"Have a good time. It's a good time of year to be in San Francisco." He left the bridle trail for the footpath, dragging the grass catcher behind him.

Blake stretched back and forth. "Good time of year to be anywhere. Good to see you, Ed. Take it easy." He broke into a jog, heading down the bridle trail.

* * * *

Reed got off the elevator and walked down the long corridor to the interview room. He was not looking forward to this meeting with Washington. He had avoided seeing Washington since the trial, but now he would have to discuss the sentence, appeals, and possible options—of which none were optimistic. The sentence was unusually heavy, and Reed's arguing merely resulted in a slightly earlier parole review. But tomorrow Washington was being transferred to the state penitentiary in Jackson, so Reed had to make the visit, no matter how unpleasant.

When Washington came in, he was in irons. He looked like his spirit was gone. Reed asked the guard about the heavy manacles. That had never been done before. The guard explained that he was a convicted murderer and about to be transferred. The county didn't want to take any chances. Reed suspected it was a disciplinary, or, more accurately, a vindictive action.

They shared greetings and discussed general things at first. Washington was quiet and sullen, as he had been when Reed first met him. Finally Reed said, "It doesn't look good for an appeal, Kevin. I raised a few points with the judge–that business about Suzanne Hathaway–but he didn't think there were any grounds for a retrial. I'll still send in a formal appeal, but I don't know if it'll do any good."

"Try it anyway," said Washington, with a vacant expression.

"I got the parole moved up. You'll be eligible in eight years." Reed tried to look encouraging.

"I'll be dead by then," said Washington, without emotion.

"Nonsense."

"No, I will. These guys in here–they don't understand. The other dudes, the guards, they make it real tough."

"That'll wear off. Don't let it get to you, man."

"Yeah, thanks. Is that all?"

"Yeah, I guess so. Where are you going?" Washington had risen from the chair and turned toward the door.

"Nothing more to talk about, man." He clanged and rattled over to the door, then turned and looked at Reed. "Hey, bro. Thanks for trying. You did the best you could. Try to help Sally get the kids back. Would you do that for me, please?"

"Why sure bro. I'll see you again soon."

"Good-bye." He disappeared through the heavy door.

* * * *

Gus Korinsky had been touched by Reed's discussion at the trial. More than anyone else, he brooded over the thought of Kevin Washington, incarcerated on the basis of his testimony. What if Reed was correct? It gave him a recurring nightmare.

There was the matter of Steven Crane. He had come to like Steven. He knew that Steven was in trouble at the hospital, just for supporting what he thought was right. Korinsky could see that happening to him as well. The young doctor had been so thorough, going over the police records, comparing them to the hospital records. He probably knew more about the case of Susie Washington than anyone else who testified. Yet it was obvious that the jury paid little attention to him. Korinsky worried about that, and about the fact that there was no answer every time he called Steven's phone number. Korinsky hoped he was on vacation with the pretty nurse with the

266

dark eyes.

Several weeks after the trial, Korinsky got a call from Mavis Johnson, who had been promoted to a supervisory job at Child Welfare.

"Gus, how are you? I crave an egg salad sandwich. I'm having withdrawal symptoms." It was obvious to Korinsky that she needed to have something done. He waited for the inevitable request.

"Egg salad season is almost over, Mavis. What would you say to a pastrami sub?"

"Sounds good to me, Gus. I'd just like to see your smiling face again. Everyone else around here's too serious."

"Well, I expect you'll see it when I come over to pick up that new assignment you have for me."

"Why Gus, how did you know? As a matter of fact, I do have an interesting case for you."

"Then I'll bring you a nice pastrami sub. Could it be a case of child abuse?"

"You guessed it again, Gus. This one is awful. A couple in Flat Rock were keeping their son tied to the bed. It's been going on for years. The poor kid is sixteen years old. A neighbor turned them in."

"That sounds strange," said Korinsky. "How could they keep a sixteen-year-old kid tied up?"

"He's retarded. The story is they are afraid to let him out or he'd wander away."

"Maybe that's right. Don't you think that could be right?"

"Aw, come on, Gus, tying a kid to a bed. Really!"

"Maybe there was a reason. I mean, it has to be checked out." There was silence on the other end of the phone for a while.

"Whatever you say, Gus, but someone should get over there this afternoon. Can you come by soon?"

"Half an hour. Pastrami or sausage?"

"Whatever you think. Thanks."

* * * *

With Peter gone on a trip, Valerie Blake slept in a little longer than usual. Since school was out for the children, she had allowed herself the luxury of an extra half hour each morning. Today she was awak-

267

ened by the sounds of young children, friends of Sammy, playing intergalactic cops and robbers on the spiral staircase. Although her bedroom was well away from the central atrium, the heavy oak steps shook as the children ran to the top, fired imaginary laser weapons, and sailed and tumbled down the banister, to the noisy delight of the others. When she could stand it no longer, she pulled on the robe she had been given at Christmas–a maroon color cotton suede with a high white collar–and stamped out of her room.

"Will you *please* stop that screaming and running. Go outside or go somewhere else. How many times have I told you not to run up these stairs? Sammy!" She grabbed him by his T-shirt as he ran up the stairs, totally disregarding her warning. He was surprised at her reaction. "Sammy, you stop it, do you hear? You stop it." She shook him firmly and gave him a swat on the behind. "Now, go outside, all of you. Everybody outside." Frustrated, she returned to the bedroom.

The older children had helped distribute the Cheerios so that, aside from half-empty bowls and a dusting of sugar on the tabletop, the kitchen was relatively intact. She picked up the paper from the front door, walked to the back of the house, and put a cup of yesterday's coffee into the microwave. Consuming the coffee and a stale roll, she perused the newspaper. There, on the third page, was a picture of Kevin Washington being escorted from the transport van to the dark interior of Jackson's prison. He had the same fierce expression that she remembered from their single encounter. She was glad she had picked up the paper before the children saw it. She folded over the page to cover the picture and read the article by Jim Murray.

It described Washington's efficient trial and rapid sentencing, and gave credit to Judge David Marshall and Norma Baldridge. "David will like that," she thought smiling to herself. "He's very concerned about his public image." Reading further into the article she found a brief discussion of Peter's testimony. It was short but accurate–at least it concurred with the account he had given. She would save it for his return from San Francisco. There was a brief discussion of Washington's assault on Miss Hathaway, along with an admiring if not provocative description of the young social worker. Valerie remembered her as Crane's date at the symphony. Murray's article commented that "Miss Hathaway, currently vacationing in the west, could not be reached for comment." That gave Valerie a sense of discontent, although she could not identify exactly why.

As she read the other articles, a small fist smashed through the paper. Petey was not getting enough attention.

"What was the meaning of that, young man?"

"Where's Daddy?" asked Petey, ignoring the question.

"Petey, you do not come up and hit . . . Look, look here what you've done."

"Where's Daddy? Why isn't Daddy home?" Sizing up a large photograph, he punched at it again, tearing the entire front page in half. She grabbed his wrist and bent it back. "Peter, what did I just say to you? Can't you hear? You do not hit the newspaper. Daddy is at a meeting in San Francisco." As he twisted to get free of her grasp, he put his other elbow in a half spent bowl of Cheerios and milk, sending it and another bowl crashing to the floor.

"That does it, young man. That simply does it."

CHAPTER 24

She eased the pain in her hip by tilting her pelvis askew, exposing a different portion of her femoral head to her ragged acetabulum. To maintain the more comfortable position and still stand upright, she bent the other way at the spine, giving the appearance of kyphos scoliosis. Her hip joint–damaged by a childhood infection almost sixty years ago–would have to be replaced one of these days. She would ignore it, for now, because she was essential to the functioning of the hospital in June and July.

Mabel Povlitz had worked in the Presbyterian Hospital laundry since anyone could remember. She had seen them all come and go–doctors, nurses, administrators, orderlies, and aides–and she remembered every name. She could tell stories for hours about the famous and near-famous doctors of Detroit, almost all of whom had come to know her–directly or indirectly–over the years. The stories were always happy stories. Pleasant anecdotes to show how this or that professor or world-renowned surgeon was, at one time, just a boy. Each story she told with new excitement, as if for the first time. Her blue eyes sparkled behind the old wire-framed glasses, and she rocked back and forth on her high stool, clapping both palms on her knees each time her lilting laugh interrupted the narrative. The hair which framed her merry face was absolutely white. All the doctors who remembered her as beautifully blond had long since died or retired. The new interns started tomorrow, June 23, and all forty-six of them would visit her today to collect their new uniforms. Mabel enjoyed this day more than any other. She greeted each one with a laugh, a smile, and "So nice to have you here at Presbyterian, Doctor."

She loved to watch their faces when she said that, because she knew it was the first time that they had been officially recognized as such. "Each year there are more young girl doctors," she said to herself, as she surveyed the forty-six stacks of white coats and white trousers or skirts.

$$* * * *$$

After the orientation lecture and the hospital-provided lunch (turkey or roast beef sandwiches in plastic wrap), Michael Rubelle, M.D. left the auditorium, checklist in hand. The Rs were scheduled for physical exams at four-thirty, so he decided to spend the next few hours finding his locker and mailbox, and talking to the graduating intern he was replacing. For the tenth time, he looked through the thick packet of information and fingered the plastic nametag which identified him as a bona fide doctor. Rubelle made up in intensity and competitive spirit anything he lacked in size. That personality had led him to apply for internship in surgery. He had been sure that he would get his first choice, which was Barnes Hospital, or at least his second choice, which was Ohio State. He figured he had a better chance at the top programs if he came from the bottom half of the class at University of Chicago than the top half of the class somewhere else. That had been a mistake.

Detroit Presbyterian was his sixth choice–a fallback hospital that he listed just to be insured against not matching. He was extremely disappointed when the assignments came through in March, but he had had three months to rationalize it, and, seeing the eyebrows go up among his new colleagues when he mentioned the University of Chicago, he had now decided it was not so bad after all.

New interns are all insecure, but they express it in different ways. Some are uncontrollably nervous. Some are quietly conscientious. Others, like Rubelle, attempt to hide their lack of confidence in arrogance. He copied the brusque mannerisms and condescending phrases used by a third-year surgical resident he had met at the university hospital. The personality had seemed to fit that resident, who was chronically unhappy anyway. Adopted by Rubelle, it resembled a small boy wearing a man's hat.

He was annoyed by the twists and wrong turns he took trying to find the laundry. When he finally found it, he had to wait behind three other interns. By the time he reached the front of the line, his face registered impatience.

"Oh, you must be Dr. Rubelle. We're proud to have you here at

Presbyterian." The lively little lady took him by surprise. "From the University of Chicago! My, so impressive." She rolled her eyes, laughed gaily, and patted her lap. "You must know Dr. DeMeester."

"Why, yes . . ."

"Tom was here for a short time, just after he left Hopkins. My, what a nice boy. I always had trouble finding coats that were long enough for him. Did you know Dr. Dragsted?" A surprised look from Rubelle. "Oh, of course not, he was long before your time." She limped over to the shelves behind the counter and pulled down a stack of uniforms. "Now these match the measurements you sent us last month. You'll probably lose weight, so when the pants get baggy, just come back and I'll fix them."

"Here, let me help you," said Rubelle, moving around behind the counter.

"Well, thank you, Doctor, thank you so much." He took a bundle under each arm. "What's your first rotation?" she asked.

"Emergency room."

"Oh, you must be very good. They always put the best ones in the emergency room first," she said confidentially. "Come back to see me if you have any problems. And come back just to tell me how it's going."

Rubelle retraced his steps through the catacombs lined with steam pipes and chipped cement blocks. What a wonderful hospital, he thought to himself.

* * * *

Jan Hansen looked at the crowd in the emergency room waiting area with concern. "Is there anyone here to have sutures removed, dressings changed, or casts checked?" she shouted. A handful of hands went up. "Would you come to the desk, please?" She turned to the secretary. "Send these folks to surgery clinic tomorrow," and she returned to the bustling ER.

Emergency room nurses get the brunt of the June-July changeover. Just when they have a whole class of neophyte physicians trained in ER efficiency, they have to start all over again. Suddenly it takes an hour to put on a cast, two hours to suture a laceration, six hours to work up a fever or a belly. It was Thursday night. "There shouldn't be any horrendos," she thought. "Tomorrow will be a disaster." She decided to take Friday off.

Jan approved of Rubelle. He was catching on much faster than his counterparts. After they had established the ground rules on the first day ("Look, Rubelle. We're all in this together; don't get on your high horse down here. Just ask and we'll help you. Understand?"), Rubelle was tolerable, even pleasant, to work with.

"Hey Mike, you getting hungry?" she asked. It was nine o'clock at night.

"Boy, I'll say."

"Here's a quickie," she said, tossing him a chart. "There's a fresh pizza in the back. Do this one and come join us."

Rubelle entered the small cubicle to find an attractive woman and a small boy whose right hand was resting on a surgical glove filled with ice—the standard ER temporizing measure for bone and joint injuries. "Hello, I'm Dr. Rubelle, what's the problem?"

"My little boy caught his fingers in the car door. Our doctor said to come here for X-rays . . . Dr. Browne?" Rubelle guessed the woman was about forty. She seemed nervous.

Dr. Browne meant nothing to him, so he said, "Well, let's have a look." He examined the little hand. "My, that looks bad. Must hurt, eh? What's your name?"

"Petey." The little boy withdrew his hand from Rubelle's amateurish grasp, then winced in pain. All of his fingers were black and blue and swollen. The nail was hanging loose from the little finger. Rubelle pulled it back for closer scrutiny.
"How did this happen again?"

"He smashed his fingers in the car door. Are they okay?"

Petey responded, "I didn't do it. You did. Mommy did it." Rubelle watched the mother clench her fist, then gain control.

"Petey. I told you to get your hand out of the way. I tell you every time we get in the car." She flashed a quick, nervous smile at Rubelle. "Do you think we should get an X-ray?"

"Oh yes, of course, an X-ray." He looked at Petey's hand more carefully. The little finger was particularly tender. His thumbnail was black also. He wrote a brief description on the ER sheet, filled out the X-ray request, and joined Jan Hansen, two other nurses, and two of Detroit's finest from Division Twenty-Five for pizza. He was beginning to feel like an old pro, and this was only his second night on duty.

After eating, he saw two more patients, and then walked over to X-ray to see the last half hour's worth of films. He reviewed a sprained ankle and a chest film, and then came to the films on Petey Blake. The swelling was obvious, but he couldn't make anything out of the bones. He took the films around the corner to the little reading room where Rob Cole was sitting. Cole was just finishing a second-year residency in radiology. He was droning into a tape recorder, flipping racks of barium enema films before his eyes by manipulating the pedals on the floor.

" . . . mucosal pattern, the appendix fills and appears normal period in the midsigmoid colon there is a lesion approximately eight centimeters long which involves the entire circumference comma has well defined edges comma and has the apple core appearance strongly suggestive of carcinoma period thickening and indentation of the bowel wall proximal to the tumor suggest transmural extension period." As Cole talked, he leaned forward deliberately, as if it were a great effort, and drew black circles on the film with a large felt-tip pen. "Lesion is also identified on post evacuation film period diagnosis constricting lesion of the midsigmoid colon strongly suggestive of carcinoma period." With a touch of the pedal, the rack of X-rays disappeared and another took its place.

Rubelle was still new enough to be impressed by the businesslike irony of his profession. He guessed that the patient was a woman in her fifties, with children and grandchildren and dreams and hopes and plans for the ripening of life. Now, with a two-minute glimpse of the shadows of her entrails, a man about the age of her son had suddenly given her life an identifiable end-point. Two, maybe three years. And in so doing, he changed the lives of all who knew her. Click, clunk. Next case. "Hi, what can I do for you?"

Rubelle handed him the small X-rays. "This kid got his hand caught in a car door. He's two or three years old. I don't know what's supposed to be ossified and what's not at that age. This just looks like a bag of bones to me." Cole took the films and held them over the bright light at his side.

"The way to tell is to compare it to the other hand. I hope they took it. Oh yes, here it is." He shifted two films back and forth over the bright light several times. "Car door injuries in little kids hardly ever cause fractures. They're so elastic, you know, and there's a fair amount of clearance the way they build cars these days." He was talking absent-mindedly. "Look here, there's a crack in this fifth metacarpal. It's hard to see. It's only partly ossified but look at this." He pointed at the right-hand X-ray with a corner of the other X-ray. Rubelle bent over, peering through the dark celluloid.

"Yeah, I see what you mean," said Rubelle, not completely convinced. "This is a strange place to have a fracture for that kind of injury. Are you sure this was a car door injury?" asked Cole.

"That's what the mother said."

"Hmm, what are these other films? It's a pretty thick jacket for a three-year-old."

"What other films?"

"Here, look. The kid has a jacket of old films, they pulled it for you." Rubelle had not noticed the difference between a new and an old X-ray jacket. Cole looked at the notes on the jacket cover. "Normal skull series at age one. Fractured humerus at thirty months." He pulled the films from the jacket and put them up on the big board, examined each for a few seconds, then put them back in the folder. Cole wrote "FXR 5th metacarpal" on the wet reading slip and handed the folder and X-rays back to Rubelle.

"This kid's had a lot of trauma for three years old. Might be a BCS. You better check it out." He turned back toward the barium enemas.

"BCS?"

"Battered child syndrome, you know, intentional trauma."

"Oh, I don't think so," said Rubelle. "This is a nice looking, middle-class lady and a cute little kid."

"Yeah, that's just the type. We see it all the time. Just let the abuse team know, they'll check it out for you."

"Thanks a lot."

Rubelle paged the orthopedic resident. While he was waiting for a response, he read the two pages in his house staff manual which covered child abuse.

Multiple episodes of trauma. Injury doesn't fit the history.

Delay in coming to the hospital. Signs of other injuries.

Some match, some don't, he thought.

Rubelle returned to the cubicle. "The X-rays show a fracture of one of the bones in his hand." He watched the mother for her reaction. "Peter sure has had his share of injuries. How did he break his arm?"

"Oh that? He . . . ah . . . I guess he fell out of a tree," said Valerie Blake, who was concerned only with the present problem.

"Out of a tree? He climbed trees at age two?"

"Well, maybe it was off the porch. I can't remember."

"Why did he have those skull X-rays when he was a baby?" Rubelle was becoming more suspicious.

"Did he have skull X-rays? I had forgotten. He must have fallen out of bed or something. Yes, that's right, he fell out of bed. How about his hand, doctor? What should be done? Should we call Dr. Browne now? Or Dr. Henry? He's the orthopedist who took care of his broken arm."

The names meant nothing to Rubelle.

"Well, I've just called Dr. Pollock. He's the orthopedist in the hospital tonight. Let's see what he thinks, then we can go on from there." He had given Petey a cursory examination while he spoke.

"What's this big bruise on his knee?" He pressed on it, to which Petey responded with a shout.

"I don't know," said Valerie. "I hadn't seen that there."

Rubelle took a deep breath. Valerie looked tense, uncomfortable.

"Well, let's wait for Dr. Pollock. I do think he'll have to be admitted, so we'll have to make plans for that. I'll start the paperwork."

"Shouldn't we call Dr. Browne?"

"Oh yes. I'll take care of that." He left the cubicle and returned with a clipboard and a stack of history-physical forms. "Now let's see," he sighed. "Was he the product of a normal labor and delivery? . . ."

* * * *

Dorothy Dow had been asleep for only twenty minutes when she was clattered back into consciousness by the ringing telephone. Her husband answered it. Being a clinical psychologist, he was the one who usually got middle-of-the-night calls. But it was Presbyterian Hospital calling, looking for the social worker on call. Dorothy had been on the staff for almost a year and had never been called at night.

The caller identified himself as Dr. Rubelle from the surgery service. He wanted to report a case of possible child abuse. Dorothy knew there was a procedure to follow, but she did not know what it was. "Dr. Rubelle, why don't you call Suzanne Hathaway? She's the pediatric social worker and she always handles these things. I'm sure she wouldn't mind if—"

"I tried that," said Rubelle. "She's on vacation. The operator said that you are covering for her."

"Oh that's right. Okay. What time is it?"

"It's eleven thirty," said Rubelle, who assumed that everyone on call for the hospital would be wide awake all night awaiting important calls.

"Did you say the child is going to be admitted?"

"Yes, he already is admitted."

"Okay, then I'll review the procedure first thing in the morning and notify whoever needs to be notified." She slumped back onto the pillow, eyes closed, lazily holding the receiver against her ear.

"Are you sure that's all right?" asked Rubelle. "I mean, in the house staff manual it talks about protective custody and things like that."

"Well, are the parents going to sign him out AMA, or anything like that?"

"No."

"Then I'm sure I can handle it in the morning."

"Okay, I've done my job. Have a good night." He returned to his attempts to catheterize a guerellous nursing home transfer with a huge prostate and urinary retention, forgetting about his promise to call Dr. Browne.

* * * *

Suzanne was well-organized. There was one entire loose-leaf notebook entitled Child Abuse Procedures. Dorothy was surprised at its bulk. The book was divided into sections by tabs marked "psychological," "abandonment," "rape," "city law," "state law," and so on. She opened to the section marked "reporting procedure." She found a neatly typed step-by-step protocol. "This is going to be easier than I thought," she said to herself. Following the directions, she found the reporting forms and abstracted the information out of the chart. The next step was to call the attending physician–listed as Dr. Edward Browne. Browne's secretary explained that he was out of town and patched her through to Ben Greenfield, who was covering. Dorothy started to explain the situation to Dr. Greenfield, who was in the midst of a busy Friday morning.

"The child has had two fractures in a year and a history of head injury in infancy. He has a bruise on his leg. The hand injury is not typical for being caught in a car door–"

"Why are you telling me all this?" said Greenfield. "I thought the orthobones were looking after that kid."

"Well, sir, I'm just filling in for Sue Hathaway who usually does this sort of thing. The protocol says to get the okay of the attending physician."

"Okay for what?"

"For reporting the case to Child Welfare."

"Oh my God, is that all? Sure, go ahead, go ahead. What did you say the name was?"

"Petey Blake."

The name meant nothing to Greenfield. "Thanks for calling. Is that it?"

"Yes." He was already off the phone.

The name of the father on the admitting sheet was Frederick P. Blake, so that was the name she used in reporting the case to the Division of Child Welfare. Consequently, neither the social worker nor the judge who processed the protective custody order recognized the name. Korinsky thought the Hunting Valley address was unusual for such a case, but his job was not to question the order, merely to serve it.

The next item on the protocol was to convene a meeting of the Child Abuse Committee. That presented the biggest problem. She had already learned that Dr. Browne was out of town. She had found that Dr. Crane could not be reached and Dr. Redford was leaving the resident staff. The new chief residents would not arrive until Monday. After checking with Browne's secretary, she typed up notices announcing a meeting at noon on the following Monday and distributed them to the appropriate mailboxes. The thought of a mother crushing her own child's hand was appalling to Dorothy Dow. She was glad that she did not routinely deal with child abuse cases.

Korinsky knocked on the door of Suzanne Hathaway's office. He was glad to get this assignment. He had been getting mostly juvenile crime cases and missed visiting the hospital, especially Miss Hathaway. He knocked again. A pert young brunette stuck her head out from the next office. "Miss Hathaway's on vacation. Can I help you?"

"Maybe. I'm Lieutenant Korinsky, juvenile division. I'm here to deliver a protective custody order and start an investigation. Usually Miss Hathaway—"

"Yes, I know, I'm the one who sent in the report. I'm sort of filling in for her while she's on vacation. Come on in." She popped back into her little office.

Not Miss Hathaway, but not bad, he thought to himself.

"I'm Dorothy Dow, Lieutenant. This child abuse business is all new to me. I just followed our protocol. What do I do now?"

"You've done what you have to do. I'll take up the investigation from here. Let me just check my information." He read down the list of particulars–basically the same facts that she had reported to Child Welfare. He double-checked Rubelle's name and asked how to locate him. He left the custody order on her desk, explaining that she merely had to notify the nurses not to release the child. Welfare had not drafted any charges against the family as yet. The Washington case had prompted a slightly less aggressive policy.

"Are there other children in the family?" asked Korinsky.

"Yes, there are four, one in college and two others at home. They have two foster children. Two of their children died in infancy. I've already asked the record room to see if they were patients here."

"Oh, that's good, that'll be helpful. Say, is this family related to the lawyer Blake, the one who takes in foster children?"

"I don't know," she said. "I have no idea."

"Did you have photographs taken?" he asked.

"Yes, that was on Miss Hathaway's list." She smiled at the efficiency of the entire procedure. Korinsky put another piece of gum into his mouth and slam dunked the wrapper into her wastebasket as he stood to leave.

* * * *

On her first day back from the island–sunburned, chigger-bitten, and deliciously sore–Beth drew a Saturday morning assignment on six-east. She left Steven asleep in her bed and joined the sparse weekend traffic.

When Valerie came to take Petey home, she immediately noticed the change in the attitude of the nurses. They were unnecessarily polite, but rarely smiled. They seemed to try to avoid any contact, even a greeting. Petey was his usual playful self. His right hand was encased in plaster from his fingertips to his elbow. The nurse in the room was pleasant enough. She was a tall, dark-eyed nurse who looked vaguely familiar. Ignoring her premonition of trouble, Valerie sat by the bedside waiting for Dr. Henry.

The early-morning sun cast the shadows of the crib bars on the pale yellow wall which, combined with Petey's mobile form, gave the impression of a silhouette zoo. Cartoons blared from the television set.

When Dr. Pollock, the orthopedic resident, came in, he was accompanied by two younger residents and stately Dr. Henry.

Valerie stood when they entered. "Good morning, Dr. Henry, you're right on time."

"Hello Mrs. Blake. How are you . . . how are you doing this morning?"

"I'm fine. It looks like Petey's ready to go. Pete–my Pete–will be just shocked. He's out of town and I haven't been able to reach him." They nodded acknowledgment and stood around as if there were more to say, but no one volunteered anything.

Aware of the tension, but unsure why, she paused, then asked, "Well, what are the things I should know to take care of this little guy?" She patted his hair. Beth stopped what she was doing and listened.

Dr. Henry finally spoke. "Mrs. Blake, hasn't anyone spoken to you about . . . about keeping Petey here in the hospital a little longer?"

"Why no, is there a problem?" A chill began in her back.

"No, no. Petey's just fine. It's probably just a technicality. There's probably a perfectly good explanation."

"Explanation for what?" She was starting to shake.

"Petey," Henry was having a hard time getting it out, "Petey is in . . . ah . . . protective custody. Rather than send him to juvenile hall, I thought it would be better to keep him here until this matter is settled. I'm sure there is a simple explanation. You see–" he smiled and shrugged nervously. "With his recent fractures and all–" He paused uncomfortably. They found out the social service had to report him as a possible child abuse. It's just a technicality. You understand."

Her face had gone pale and her eyes showed terror. They found out, was her only thought.

CHAPTER 25

Fighting to retain composure, she threw back her head and tried to look insulted. "That's ridiculous," she said. "Little boys are active, they have accidents. Look, Dr. Henry, I feel badly enough about Petey's hand. I don't need more aggravation."

They all stood, watching her reaction. She felt like a small animal in some psychological experiment, with the observers peering in to see what move she would make next. They watched with a cold, clinical attitude that suggested suspicion, even disbelief. She decided that a good offense is the best defense.

"Have you talked with Dr. Browne, Dr. Edward Browne? He's been our family pediatrician for almost twenty years. He can straighten this out in a minute." She now appeared close to tears.

"I'm sure he can, Mrs. Blake." Henry put a kindly hand on her shoulder. He was beginning to think that their system had overreacted. "Ed–Dr. Browne will be back tomorrow. Little Petey here needs an extra day or two in the hospital. The swelling under the cast is pretty bad." The residents passed around a cynical look. "And besides, we probably can't do anything about this legal stuff on the weekend. Don't worry about it. It's just a technicality. Okay?" He smiled and gave her shoulder a gentle squeeze. She appeared to relax somewhat.

"I'd better call my husband," she said.

"Fine," said Henry. "We'll see you tomorrow." He pressed his lips together in a firm grin and nodded, his standard gesture indicating the end of a conversation. As they turned to leave the room, he squinted quizzically at the residents to indicate a sense of skepticism. His back was turned to Valerie but Beth Bonnell could see it clearly.

* * * *

When Peter Blake awoke, Suzanne was already in the shower. It took him a few seconds to get oriented–the bland trappings of an expensive hotel room, his clothes draped carelessly over a chair, an unfamiliar light blue suitcase on the rack by the desk. San Francisco. Suzanne's room at the Hilton. Details of the preceding night began to come to his mind; the more he remembered, the more sensually luxurious it seemed. He stretched and padded into the bathroom.

He found her toothbrush, loaded it with paste, popped it into his mouth, and joined her in the shower. Blake had a habit of brushing his teeth in the shower, gargling from the showerhead, and spitting at random. Suzanne thought it was vulgar, but she ignored it as she pushed him under the pulsing spray. She scrubbed him to a lather from head to toe, then soaped herself by sliding her slippery body over his. She managed to cover almost every square inch.

They dressed casually and an hour later they navigated their way through the nearly deserted Saturday morning streets of San Francisco. They crossed the Golden Gate Bridge at nine thirty. They dallied lazily over breakfast on the outside porch of the Alta Mira. The food was superb–eggs Benedict made with real Virginia ham and shrimp crepes. But the clientele (mostly blue-haired ladies with their companions in brown and white wing tipped shoes and assorted tourists) detracted from the ambiance that Blake remembered from twenty years before. They wandered through the shops and galleries of Sausalito and quietly consumed the splendor of Muir Woods. By the time they came back over the big bridge, the sun was illuminating the heavy fog over the Pacific into a rosy glow.

The red light on the telephone was blinking as Blake entered his room at Stanford Court. Tossing his jacket on the bed, he dialed the number for messages. "Please call Mrs. Blake," said the hotel operator, "Area code three-one-three–"

"I know, I know. Thank you very much. What time did this call come in?"

"Oh there have been several, sir, starting at ten to seven this morning."

"Thanks again." He pushed the button down on the phone, then dialed his home in Hunting Valley. "Damn," he said to himself.

"Peter, where have you been? I've been frantic trying to find you!" Her voice was shaking.

"I went jogging this morning, then I've been at meetings. What's the trouble?"

"Oh Peter. This is awful. Can you come home?"

"Right now? I have to go to the banquet tonight, Val. What's the problem?"

She sighed into the phone. Blake imagined that she was forcibly exhaling
cigarette smoke.

"Remember I told you about Petey's hand getting caught in the car door?"

"Yes."

"I went to the hospital this morning to bring him home and they wouldn't let me take him. They said he's in protective custody."

Blake's mouth went dry. "What? That's preposterous. What the hell's going on?"

"I don't know," she answered. "No one will give me a straight answer. Dr. Henry said he needed Petey in the hospital a few more days anyway, but I don't think that's right. They said something about having to report multiple injuries–remember his broken arm? Apparently it's some sort of routine . . ."

"Well, what's the matter with Ed Browne? Just get Browne to settle it." Blake was pacing back and forth, looking out of the window at a spiny skyscraper and the turbulent bay beyond.

"That's the trouble, Pete, Ed's out of town until tomorrow. He doesn't know anything about this. I'm sure he could settle it in no time. Please come home tonight."

"How about Tom Nelson? Have you called him?"

"I haven't called anybody. Every time I talk to someone they look at me like I'm Jack the Ripper."

"Val, you're overreacting. This is just some technical detail. I'll be home tomorrow afternoon and we'll straighten it all out."

"Pete, you don't understand. A detective called this afternoon. They are investigating me for child abuse."

He stopped pacing. "I'll be home as soon as I can get a flight," he said.

* * * *

When Beth got home, Steven was sitting on the lawn in a bathing

285

suit, taking in the sun, and finishing the carving he had started on the island. She shouted a greeting through the bedroom window as she changed into a pair of shorts. She joined him on the lawn, bringing the last of the Beck's beer.

"It's looking great," she said, referring to the abstract form taking shape from the heavy piece of cedar. "What is it going to be?"

"It's an impressionistic fetus, or a symbol for infinity, or an Indian club. I haven't decided yet."

"Well, I'm sure it'll be the best of whatever it is," she said, threading her long legs around his knees. The now-familiar feeling welled up in his chest. They had grown so close during the week on the island that they communicated well, even without speaking. Minutes later she remembered what she had to tell him.

"Oh, Steve!" Her sudden exclamation startled him, sending an extra-large chip flying from the war club. "I forgot to tell you. Remember the Blakes–the lawyer that took in the Washington kids? Their little boy is in the hospital with a broken hand–I took care of him this morning–and some new intern reported it as battered child syndrome."

Crane started to laugh, choking on a mouthful of beer. "You're kidding!"

"No, really. The kid's in protective custody. The mother was in this morning. She actually looked scared."

"Hah!" roared Crane, rolling over on the grass. "Fantastic. How about Browne? How did he let that happen?"

"He's out of town. He doesn't know anything about it. So is Mr. Blake, the lawyer." She grinned at his amusement.

"Oh, that's terrific." He laughed heartily, rolling back to a sitting position. "So the chicken's come home to roost. Can you imagine Browne when he gets back and finds his next-door neighbor is accused of child beating? Oh, that's hilarious."

She became more serious. "Well, it is ironic, Steve, but it's not all that funny. I mean, the kid's hand is smashed up, fractures and all. Maybe she really did it."

"No way," said Crane, still laughing. "That's a good solid family. But it serves them right–"

"How do you know she didn't do it? There you are, jumping to conclusions without knowing the history."

"No way, Beth." He was still laughing, then became contemplative. "I hope someone took a careful history from the family. Did they?" He squinted at her as the afternoon sun came into his line of vision.

"I'll say. New interns, remember? There's a four-page history in there that goes through every injury every child in that family ever had. There are a lot of them. This little boy had a broken arm last fall. You took care of him. You remember that?"

"Sure, I remember. Cute little kid."

"Well, he was also admitted for head injuries as an infant, did you know that?" Crane became more serious now.

"No, I didn't know that."

"And one foster child had a subdural hematoma—died in infancy. I can't remember the other details, but the intern really got a history."

"What happened this time, how did he break his hand?"

"The mother said she slammed the car door on it by mistake."

"Hell, I've seen dozens of those car door injuries, but I've never seen a fracture."

"That's what the orthopod said. He has a big hematoma under his thumbnail too. Did you ever see a car door injury involving the thumb?"

"No, I never did," he said softly. "Jesus, Beth, do you think . . . do you suppose Mrs. Blake's really a child abuser? Could you imagine that?"

"I don't know. It's possible."

"Maybe that's why Blake lied at Washington's trial." He rolled over, stimulated into action by the gravity of his thought. "Is he protecting her some way? Does that make sense?"

"I don't know, I just don't know, Steve."

He shrugged it off. "Probably nothing to it. Hell, they're a great couple. But I sure would like to see Browne's face when he hears about this. Hah!" He returned to laughter.

* * * *

Edward Browne's face evolved from amusement, through embarrassment, horror, and concern, and finally settled into the narrow eyes, bulging jaw, and distended forehead veins which signified barely controlled anger. They sat in the library of the Blakes' home while

Beethoven played softly through the big speakers. The scotch was poured but untouched. Browne had driven directly to the Blakes' from the airport. The message from his wife, Dot, was "See Peter Blake immediately. Urgent." Peter Blake had described the events of the last few days with an affected casualness that suggested deep-seated concern.

"Pete, I'm so sorry. What an awful experience. I'll take care of it right away." Browne was genuinely embarrassed. The Blakes relaxed noticeably.

"Oh, Ed," said Valerie, "that makes me so relieved. You don't know what a nightmare this has been."

"I'm sure you're right," said Browne. "And after all you've done for the hospital." He shook his head. "Pete, may I use your phone?"

"Of course." Blake opened a small chest that looked like a walnut cigar box and produced a push button telephone. "Who started this whole thing?" asked Browne, as he was pushing the buttons.

"A young doctor from surgery. I think it was Dr. Rubelle," said Valerie, breathing more easily as each minute passed.

"Must be a new intern," observed Browne, waiting for the hospital operator to answer.

"He looked like a new intern," said Valerie, smiling for the first time in two days.

"Six-east," said Browne. "This is Dr. Edward Browne, who is this, please? Hello, Sandy. Listen, there's a child named Peter Blake on your floor. Yes. Has he been cleared for discharge by the orthopedic staff?" He paused for several seconds. "Yes, I understand that, but is his hand okay? All right, then he can be released. Yes, that's right. Cancel the protective custody order. I'll take care of all the details. Yes. The family will be there to pick him up in"—he looked at the Blakes, they nodded—"an hour. Yes. Don't worry about it. I'll take the responsibility. Thank you, Sandy. Good-bye."

* * * *

Steven found it difficult to get up on Monday morning–a symptom of anxiety over returning to the hospital rather than lack of sleep. But once he was back in the high, drafty lobby, walking along the corridors with paint chipped at gurney level, through the controlled confusion of the six-east nursing station, he was secure and at home. Dr. Browne was back to his friendly best. They sat on the armchairs, chattered amiably, and never mentioned the Washington case. Steven was starting the one-year fellowship in general pediatrics–an invention of Dr. Browne who detested and resisted progressive specialization in pediatric allergy, pediatric lung disease, pediatric cardiology, and the like. It was only a glorified chief residency–scoffed at by the specialists across town and discussed with bemused detachment over cocktails by academic pediatricians around the country. It led to no further board certification or recognition. However, each year it attracted a pediatrician like Steven who wanted more than the perfunctory two years of specialty training in a hospital which was not already full of specialty trainees.

On top of the large stack of mail that had accumulated over Steven's two-week absence was notification of the Child Abuse Committee meeting at noon. He stuffed it in his pocket, working his way through the rest of the mail. Making rounds on the service, he learned that Petey Blake had been released the night before and that Dr. Browne had removed the custody order himself. Steven smiled to himself.

Shortly after noon, the paging operator reminded him of the meeting. Hoping that lunch would be served, Steve worked his way toward the residents' conference room. As he entered, he noticed that the diagrams on the blackboard–describing cardiac output in relationship to filling pressure–were the ones he had drawn there two months before.

He recognized Miss Whitely, Mr. Heisal, and Sam Schulman, the new chief resident. Expecting Suzanne, he was surprised to find a different social worker, who introduced herself as Dorothy Dow. He learned that the intense young man with curly dark hair was Michael Rubelle, an intern in surgery.

"I think almost everyone is here," said Dorothy Dow. "Dr. Browne is on his way. Let's get started. First of all, Miss Hathaway is on vacation, so I'm just following her protocol. This committee is supposed to meet as soon as possible when a case is reported. Dr. Rubelle identified a case in the emergency room last Thursday night. That's the first of three "I's" of child abuse–Identify, Investigate, and Intervene." Steven tried to keep a straight face. He found the juvenile homilies of social work more amusing than informative. "Dr. Rubelle, would you like to summarize the case please?"

"This little boy is three years old. He was brought to the emergency room by his mother with an injury to the hand. She said the child got his hand caught in the car door. The injury seemed to be much more serious than the history suggested. There was a fracture of the metacarpal," he held up his right hand and pointed to the area of injury with his left index finger, "and there was a hematoma on the tip of the thumb. They came in at night, but the injury had occurred that morning. Then I found that the child had been hospitalized twice before for major trauma."

"Wait a minute," interrupted Steven. "Is this the Blake child? Peter Blake?"

"Yes, Petey Blake," said Rubelle.

"Then we're wasting our time. This whole case has been dropped."

"No it hasn't," said Dorothy Dow, somewhat irritated at this interruption. "The child is in protective custody. We're just starting the investigation–the
second 'I'."

"Dr. Browne canceled the protective custody and the investigation," said Crane. "The child went home last night. Browne's been their pediatrician for years. This whole thing never would have come up if he had been in town in the first place."

Heisal, Miss Whitely, and Schulman considered the matter ended and prepared to leave. But Dow and Rubelle, who did not know Edward Browne, were confused. "Protective custody is a court order," said Dorothy. "Nobody can just cancel it, I don't care who he is."

"Who's this Dr. Browne?" asked Rubelle. "He never even saw the kid, and if he's been their pediatrician for years, why hasn't he reported this woman before? The children in that family have had more injuries than the Chicago Bears."

Heisal was shocked by Rubelle's disrespectful indignation. "Dr. Browne is the chief of pediatrics in this hospital, and has been for twenty years. He's been chief of staff three times. Why, he's been the staff advisor to this committee for ten years or more. I don't think it's appropriate to question his judgment, Doctor."

"Excuse me, who are you?" asked Rubelle.

"Mr. Heisal, assistant administrator of this hospital."

"Well, Mr. Heisal, you must be aware that both the hospital and the physician must report all suspicious cases of child abuse. Isn't that right?" He asked his question to Dorothy Dow.

"Yes, that's the law. In fact, it's a felony not to report child abuse in this state." The door opened and a well-groomed gentleman entered. Rubelle did not recognize him.

"Right," said Rubelle. "I don't care if this guy Browne's pediatrician to the Queen of England, he'd better straighten this out or his ass will be in a sling."

"I beg your pardon?" The icy question came from the man who had just entered.

"Oh there's a guy named Browne who thinks he knows more than me, the social workers, and the juvenile court."

"Perhaps he does, young man," said Browne with a contemptuous glare.

"Excuse me, who are you?" asked Rubelle.

"I am Dr. Edward Browne. Who are you?"

"Dr. Michael Rubelle." He showed no sign of intimidation. "We were just discussing the Blake case, and I was pointing out that a physician cannot cancel a protective custody order. Perhaps there has been some misunderstanding."

Steven could have interrupted Rubelle and avoided the encounter, but he was rather enjoying it. He liked Rubelle, despite his aggressiveness.

"There has indeed been a misunderstanding, Rubelle, but not by me," said Browne, biting off the words. "I am, if anything, over-committed to the identification and investigation of child abuse, as Dr. Crane here will attest. And the Blakes are not only a model family, but also strong and reliable supporters of this hospital and the foster parents program of the Division of Child Welfare. You should have done your homework more carefully, Rubelle. You are way off base. You are the one whose ass is in the sling." He turned from Rubelle to Dorothy Dow. "Is there anything else to be discussed at this meeting?"

"Well, no but—"

"Then the meeting is adjourned." He stood and delivered another menacing glance at Rubelle. Rubelle started to speak, but Crane kicked his shin and signaled him to stay silent. Schulman, Heisal, and Miss

291

Whitely dutifully followed Browne out of the conference room, leaving the door open. Rubelle was furious.

"He can't do that, what the hell is this?"

"You're right," agreed Steven. "Technically, you're absolutely right, but realistically, he can do anything he wants. Take my advice and cool it. You've done your job. You'll just get into worse trouble if you try to fight Browne. Believe me I know."

"I suppose you're right," Rubelle sighed. He realized they had not met. He extended his hand. "I'm Mike Rubelle. I'm a new intern in surgery."

"I know. I'm Steve Crane from pediatrics."

"Are you on the staff?" asked Rubelle.

"Sort of," said Crane. "I just finished the chief residency. I'm taking a fellowship this year."

"I see," said Rubelle, reaching a calmer emotional state. "I guess I'd better find out who the players are before I shoot my mouth off around here."

"No, you're absolutely right and I loved the way you stood up to Dr. Browne," said Dorothy Dow. "The hospital could be in real legal trouble for releasing that child. Those Blake children have had a lot of injuries–deaths too." She pointed at the stack of charts on the table.

"Browne's right about one thing," said Steven. "The family is above suspicion. The father is one of the best lawyers in Detroit." But Steven was uneasy even as he said this, realizing that Peter Blake had, for whatever reason, given evasive testimony in the Washington case.

"I don't care if he's Oliver Wendell Holmes, "said Rubelle, who had a knack for making grandiose comparisons. "These cases need to be reported. Besides, it's not the father, it's the mother. She's the one in question."

"Lieutenant Korinsky will be very upset," said Dorothy, gathering the charts into an orderly pile.

"Korinsky? Does he know about this?" asked Crane.

"Yes. Why, do you know him?"

"Yes, I do," said Steven. He thought for a moment as the facts jostled for an interlocking position in his brain. "Look, you've done what you're required to do. I'm sure it will all work out all right. Would you like me to take these charts back to the record room?"

"Why yes, thanks," said Dorothy, handing him the stack. They started toward the door.

"Rubelle," said Steve, feeling fatherly, "you're going to make a terrific surgeon."

"Thanks," said Rubelle, surprised and not quite sure whether the comment was derogatory or complimentary, coming from a pediatrician.

CHAPTER 26

It might have been the humidity on that muggy last day of June, the lack of a letter from his girlfriend, or the black guard that kicked him in the shin. Whatever the cause, Billy Joe Scoggins was developing an overwhelming urge to smash something. He jostled his way through the cafeteria line, reviling the con who was serving the soup with a barrage of vulgar obscenities. He pushed the man ahead of him so hard that coffee spilled all over his metal tray. But no one complained. Billy Joe was six-feet-seven. It was still rumored around Tulsa that he could carry a calf under each arm. He had been in these moods before; the other inmates in Jackson learned to stay out of his way. He had come to Michigan to find work in the auto industry but wound up stealing cars, not making them. This was his second trip to Jackson–the result of an attack on his parole officer which had sent the man to two weeks in intensive care. Jesus Martinez, a little banty rooster of a man who was as tough as he was small, was the only companion Scoggins would tolerate during his fits of violence. They looked over the huge dining hall until Jesus spied one of the new black cons, eating by himself. They moved to sit opposite him.

"I hear we got a new black dude who lives with a white girl," Martinez said loudly. Kevin looked at his soup and did not respond.

"Sheet," drawled Billy Joe. "Some white whore, you mean. Some rotten crotch whore who sleeps with any mother f— nigger she can find." No response from Kevin.

"I heard they had a kid. Some black and white little bimbo kid."

"Sheet. Probably turn out to be a mother f— cock sucker just like her mama."

"Well, she won't do that," said Martinez. "This black dude got mad and boiled her little ass good. Just like them good ole crayfish."

"Sheet. That ole sucker just got hungry for a little ole black baby meat."

Washington leaped across the table, arms flailing, pushing the tray, full of hot soup and coffee, into Scoggin's lap. Martinez shrieked with delight. The other men continued eating but turned their heads to watch the diversion. Kevin landed two or three blows, which seemed to bounce off without effect, before Scoggins grabbed the front of his shirt in one giant hand and slammed him to the floor. All the frustration of the hot June day came out as he slapped Washington around like a doll. Billy Joe loved the feeling of ribs breaking under his fist.

None of the black enforcers moved to assist Washington. They had just gotten out of lockups from a free-for-all in April. Besides, Washington was ostracized as a child abuser. When the guards finally stepped in, Kevin had a gash across his eyebrow and a searing pain in his chest.

* * * *

The six charts were spread out on Beth's kitchen table. Taking records out of the hospital was strictly against the rules, but Steven wanted to study them more carefully than the constant interruptions at the hospital would permit.

He arranged them chronologically according to the first admission: 1960, Margaret Blake; 1965, Monica Stevens; 1967, Linda Cibarelli; 1971, Mary Blake; 1973, Eric Blake; 1976, Peter Blake. Two of the charts contained only autopsy reports. These were both crib deaths—sudden infant death syndrome. Crane pushed these charts out of the line for later consideration along with the last one, Petey Blake's chart. Eric Blake was hospitalized in 1973 at age eight for appendicitis. The recorded signs and symptoms were classic. The path report showed typical appendicitis. Nothing out of the ordinary was described in the operative note. There were no subsequent hospitalizations. Crane put this chart aside.

"Why are only four of these kids named Blake?" asked Beth, looking over
his shoulder.

"These two are foster children," explained Crane. "The record room called up all the charts with the Blakes listed as parents or guardians. If they had done it any other way we would have missed these."

"What does it look like so far?" asked Beth, pulling a chrome and rattan chair around the corner of the table to sit beside him.

"Don't know yet," said Steve. "This kid had straightforward appendicitis." He handed one chart to her and picked up another. "Beth," said Steve, reading the yellow discharge sheet, "look at this. Chronic subdural hematoma, postoperative; acute vitreous hemorrhage; greenstick fracture right femur. Mary Blake was admitted in '71 at four months old for vomiting and failure to thrive. Turned out to have a chronic subdural that required operation."

"That's not unusual, is it?" asked Beth.

"No." He perused the back of the chart. "No skull fractures. It took them quite a while to make the diagnosis. It looks like they focused on the GI tract for quite awhile. Then, she was admitted again, about a year later. 'Fell down the stairs' it says here." He read from the history:

> *Informant: Mother. Fifteen-month-old girl allegedly fell down one flight of stairs. Mother heard noise and crying, came to find child at bottom of stairs. Baby is learning to walk. Possible ataxia related to subdural hematoma treated one year ago. Injury occurred yesterday. Mother states she noticed no problems aside from black eye until today. Child now refuses to walk. Has pain and swelling in right leg. Other children in family allegedly healthy (one SIDS 5 years ago) This child adopted as a newborn.*

The chart went on to describe the physical findings, X-ray findings, and hospital course of the fractured femur. The last note was "Discharged to the care of Dr. Browne."

"What do you make of all those 'alleged' phrases?" asked Beth. "Sounds like someone was suspicious don't you think?"

"Either that or just careful," said Crane. "Let's see who the admitting resident was." He flipped through the chart. "Ben Greenfield. That's interesting; I'll bet he doesn't remember anything about it. What's that one?"

Beth continued thumbing through the thick chart of Monica Stevens. "This is a sad case, but probably nothing out of the ordinary," said Beth. "This is a two-year-old who died in 1965 after open heart surgery."

"What did she have?"

"AV canal, it says here. Arterio-venous canal?"

"Atrial-ventricular," explained Crane. "Here, let me see it." Crane encapsulated the discharge summary. "Heart failure as a newborn. Admission for catheterization at six months. Admission for heart failure. Disposition problems, foster care started at age one. Operated on age two and died on the third post-op day." He briefly perused the history and physical and laboratory data. As he put the chart down with the appendicitis case, a word noticed only by his subconscious suddenly registered. He picked up the chart again and looked for the green sheet bearing the word "fracture." He found it in a radiology report—a chest X-ray taken during the final admission. Stuck in the middle of a lengthy description of the heart and lungs was the sentence, "Rib fractures and previously reported healed fracture left humerus again noted." Interested, he turned to the green radiology reports on the previous admission. In the report of the chest X-ray, the healed fracture of the humerus was recorded, but there was no mention of rib fractures. In fact, the report read, "old fracture of left humerus is again noted. No other evidence of bony abnormality." Steven showed his finding to Beth.

"Look at the admission before that, Steve," she urged.

"Okay, okay." The child had several chest X-rays during each admission. The green sheets were easy to find. The X-ray at nine months said, "no bony abnormality." The X-ray at fifteen months, showed a fracture of the left humerus "relatively recent with callous formation and minimal angulation." Steve and Beth reviewed the discharge summaries and progress notes, but could find no reference to a broken arm or chest injuries.

"What do you make of it?" asked Beth.

Crane shrugged. "Fractures at different ages, humerus and ribs. No other bone films."

"Why wouldn't they say something about it in the progress notes?"

"Her docs were looking at her heart. These X-ray reports probably didn't get in the chart until after she went home. We're probably the first people that ever looked at them."

"Did she have an autopsy? Wouldn't they find those fractures at the autopsy?"

"No, they never look at the extremities. Let's take a look." The autopsy was done by the medical examiner's office, because it was a post-operative death. The report was a terse description of the gross findings. Chronic retroperitoneal hematoma, fractured ribs, and pale swollen kidneys were all described in addition to the expected findings in the heart and lungs. The medical examiner attributed all of this to the recent heart operation.

"No way," said Beth. "I don't know about this other stuff, but kids don't get rib fractures after open heart surgery. They do all that through a sternotomy incision. Look at the op note." Sure enough, a midline sternotomy was described. Steve put the chart on top of the subdural hematoma chart.

"Two possible, one negative, and Petey Blake uncertain. Not much to go on. Probably just coincidence," said Steve, getting up to search for something munchable.

Steve consumed two chocolate chip cookies, poured a large mug of coffee, and sagged onto the couch. Beth was reading Petey Blake's chart. "Hey, Sherlock! she exclaimed. "Some guy named Crane did the workup on the Petey Blake kid last year. Doesn't say a word about battered child syndrome."

"Of course not. That fellow's a well-known protector of child abusers."

"Oh yes, the infamous forensic pediatrician." He threw a pillow from the couch, missing her and scattering the charts. She picked up two that fell on the floor. "What are these, Steve?"

"Those thin ones? Those are the two crib death babies. They're just autopsy reports."

She opened the first one. "Margaret Blake, died December 25, 1960. Sudden infant death of unknown etiology. Changes secondary to resuscitation," she read from the autopsy summary. "There's an ER sheet in this one, Steve."

"What's it say?"

"Informant: Ambulance driver. Three-month-old, previously healthy baby found dead in bed. Father called ambulance. DOA. Cold, mottled, rash over upper body. Impression, crib death. Then here on the path report—"

"Wait a minute," said Steve. "Read the summary again. The second part."

"Infant death of unknown etiology; changes secondary to resuscitation. Ecchymosis over chest and mediastinum. Petechial hemorrhage in the skin, sclera, mucous membranes of the mouth and throughout the brain," read Beth.

"Let me see that," said Steven, rolling off the couch and walking back into the kitchen.

She showed him the sheet photocopied on slick paper that predated the Xerox machine. As he carefully read the full autopsy report, he eased into the chair, letting out a low whistle.

"Beth, this is incredible. Look at this stuff. Hematoma in the thymus, base of the neck, petechiae in the brain stem."

"Couldn't that all be caused by resuscitation, I mean pushing on the chest and holding the head for breathing? I've seen that on plenty of babies."

"Sure, but this was 1960. Were they doing CPR then?"

"Before my time." She smiled.

"Well, an ambulance driver wouldn't do it, that's for sure. And they didn't do it in the emergency room. See, the baby's listed as DOA."

"So what?"

"So all this hemorrhage and brain stem bleeding had to come from something else. It's like . . . like drowning . . ." He turned to the description of the lungs. "Left lung, 100 grams, right lung, 120 grams."

"What's that mean?" asked Beth.

"Looks normal to me. I'd have to look it up."

"What else could cause that besides drowning?" asked Beth.

"I don't know, anything that caused a strong Valsalva. Straining, suffocation . . ." They looked at each other with a sudden awful realization. Deliberately, Beth handed him the other crib death chart.

"1967," she said. "You read it."

Steve opened the chart labeled Linda Cibarelli and read for almost a minute, pushing the chart forward on the table so she could read too. He held her hand as if sharing support for an emotional crisis. Her fingers were cold.

"It's the same," he said softly. "Nothing on the skin, but look here." He pointed to the description of the brain. "Petechial hemorrhage throughout the cortex, mid-brain, and brain stem."

"And look here," said Beth. "Hemorrhage in the mediastinum, base of the neck, pharynx, and eyelids." Crane turned to the last page and found the section marked "epicrisis."

"What does epicrisis mean?" asked Beth.

"It's an old pathologist's term for summary," said Crane. "Let's see."

> *This six-month-old infant was found dead in bed by parents on the evening of September 4, 1967. The family summoned Dr. Edward Browne, who notified the medical examiner's office and requested that the autopsy be done at Presbyterian Hospital. According to Dr. Browne, the child had been in excellent health. This was a foster child and the remaining family history is not available. The history is typical for crib death syndrome. The mother put the child to bed in routine fashion. Approximately one hour later when the father checked the nursery before retiring, the baby was cold and pulseless. As is usually the case in this syndrome, there were no unusual findings at postmortem examination, specifically the heart, great vessels, epiglottis, large and small airways were all normal. Petechial hemorrhage found in the brain, thymus, thyroid, and pharynx is probably simply an agonal event. It is possible that these could represent a manifestation of viral illness, as this distribution of petechiae can be found in various viral and Rickettsial infections as well as barotrauma, drowning, and . . .*

"And what, Steve?" asked Beth, who had been listening rather than reading.

"And suffocation."

* * * *

Sally was still wearing her brief waitress uniform, although she had been home for almost an hour. She was simply too hot to move. She reached into her brassiere and pulled out the sock that she used to push her breasts together in the middle. It was an uncomfortable practice and seemed stupid to her because her breasts were large anyway, but it almost doubled her tips. It was Monday night; Jennings would be arriving soon. Sally decided to make him take her to an air conditioned movie before going to bed. It was too hot this early in the evening, and he had been taking her for granted of late anyway.

She was sitting on the porch, trying to catch the slight breeze that moved the hot air from one side of the yard to the other, when the doorbell rang. "Let yourself in, Brian," she shouted toward the front door, thinking it strange that Jennings should ring the doorbell. Eventually the doorbell rang again.

"Christ," she muttered, getting up. "The dummy must have forgotten his key. I'm coming, I'm coming!" she shouted as the door-bell rang again. She released the lock and pulled the door open.

"Dammit, Brian, why don't you–" It was not Jennings, but a young black man who stood in the doorway.

"Uh . . . Sally Washington?"

"Yes," she said cautiously, instinctively pushing the door closed until only a small crack remained.

"Hey baby, you're even better than I heard. *Oowee*," he murmured approvingly, looking her up and down, one hand holding the door open.

"I beg your pardon?" She pushed on the door, feeling resistance.

"I'm looking for Kevin. Is he here?" He leered again.

"Kevin. Kevin Washington?"

"Yeah, Kevin, my brother Kevin."

"Kevin . . . Kevin's not here now. Are you–"

"Ritchie, I'm Ritchie Washington. I'm lookin' for my big brother. He said he lived here, 929 Calvert." He examined a dog-eared paper which he pulled from his pocket, looking around to re-identify the house number.

"Ritchie? You're Ritchie, Kevin's brother?"

"Why sure, baby, you got it. Ain't this the place?" He looked around again. She opened the door wider to see him fully. He stepped in, but she kept the door open, gently putting a finger on his chest to hold him back so she could get a full look. She studied his face.

"Ritchie, when was the last time you talked to Kevin?"

"Jesus, a long time ago. Last fall, probably. I called him on the phone from San Francisco. We talked for a while and he said something about screaming and hung up on me. Just hung up."

"Oh Ritchie, really?"

"Yeah, the dude. I asked him for some money, you know, and I figured he got mad at me. Well, hell, since then I've been to Mexico, South America, Costa Rica, and Texas. Man, I got a bundle of money now. Hey, where is my man Kevin now?"

"Oh Ritchie." She shook her head and squeezed his arm, with an excitement bordering on tears which he did not understand. "Oh Ritchie, come in. Am I glad to see you!"

* * * *

"Walt, this is Beth Bonnell," said Steve Crane, as they entered Reed's stuffy little office.

"Hi Beth. Walt Reed. Please have a seat."

"Beth is a nurse at Presbyterian," explained Steve. "She's been in on the Washington case in one way or another ever since the beginning."

"Yes, I know," said Reed. "She's the only nurse who wrote anything good about Washington in the chart."

"You have a good memory," said Beth.

Reed was struck by the soft, self-assured tone of her voice, even though she had said only a few words.

"Not really, Miss Bonnell. I considered calling you as a witness. Now I wish I had." She accepted the compliment with a graceful smile. "You know, it's strange that you called today. You know who just walked out of here? Sally Washington."

"Why was she here?" asked Crane.

"Ritchie Washington showed up yesterday. You know–Kevin's brother?"

"The one who made the phone call?" asked Crane.

"Yes, that's the one," said Reed." And he backed up Kevin's story one hundred percent"

"So he was telling the truth," said Beth.

"To hear Ritchie tell it, he was. It might be enough to ask for an appeal. I don't know, though. It's only his word. It could be a put-up. I'd need something stronger." He had been muttering, mostly to himself. Now he looked up. "What could possibly be important enough to move you from an air conditioned hospital to this miserable little office on a Tuesday afternoon?"

"Maybe just what you're looking for," said Steve. He described Petey Blake's injury, and the series of events which led to his review of the records. He recounted the cases in chronological order, tossing each chart on the desk before Reed as he described it. As Steve talked, Reed forgot about the fly buzzing around the light fixture, the sweat dripping down his back, and the cold beer he had waiting at home. As the credibility of Steve's thesis grew stronger with each supporting fact, the implication loomed larger. Could it be that Valerie Blake had pursued this malicious derangement for twenty years? Did her husband know? Why did he lie in the Washington trial? To protect her? To keep the Washington children? Some other motive? His mind raced ahead. Washington was right all along. He could certainly appeal with this extra evidence, but how about Browne? He must have suspected. How many others in the system were implicated? Reed's fantasy outraced his realism.

"Hold on, Steve. Let's back up for a moment. This is very heavy stuff. Is there any other documentation? Any support?"

Beth spoke up. "We spent the morning with Sidney Vawter, the pathologist at Children's Hospital. He said that those babies would never be signed out as crib deaths today."

"The characteristic of sudden infant death syndrome is the lack of findings at autopsy," explained Crane. "Vawter wasn't sure of the cause of death, but the hemorrhage and petechiae are typical of strangulation or suffocation."

"What are petechiae?" asked Reed. "That word is all through these autopsy reports but I don't know what it means."

"Oh, I'm sorry," said Crane. "Petechiae are microscopic areas of hemorrhage–signs of ruptured capillaries. They occur in bleeding disorders, or when the pressure in the capillaries gets very high." Reed sat back in his chair, holding up the list which Steve had prepared.

"1960, '65, '67, '71, '73–"

"That's the boy with appendicitis," said Crane. "Nothing suspicious about that one." Reed nodded and continued.

"Seventy-six. Do you think this is all of them? Could there be more?"

"That's all there were at Presbyterian Hospital," said Crane. "There could be some at other hospitals."

"Or some who never made it to the hospital," added Beth. "Apparently they've taken in a lot of foster children over the years."

"How many of these are foster children?" asked Reed, indicating the stack of six charts.

"The first one was their own daughter," said Crane, pointing to the names on the list. "The others were all foster children or children they adopted."

"How many children do they have now?"

"According to the intern's admitting history on Petey Blake, they have four. There's a twenty-year-old daughter in college, a eleven-year-old boy—he's the one who had appendicitis. An six-year-old girl—the one with the head injury and fractured femur—and Petey."

"And the two Washington children. Sammy and Becky," added Beth.

"What do you think, Walt?" asked Steve. Reed ran a hand through his bushy hair and sighed.

"I don't know, Steve. I'm a defense lawyer, not a policeman, but it sure sounds solid to me. I'd be worried about that little Washington girl. How old is she—two?" Crane nodded. "The ones that died were all little girls."

"That's right," said Beth. "And the one with head injuries—Mary—is a little girl."

"Have you shown this to Dr. Browne?" asked Reed.

"No," said Steve. "To tell the truth, I'm afraid to. He and I—we aren't getting along too well. And he got really indignant when Petey Blake got reported. He's taken care of these children for twenty years. He knows about these cases. I'd . . . I'd rather not discuss it with him just now."

"You mean you think he's involved somehow?" asked Reed. "That would be hard to believe."

"I don't know what to believe now, Walt. Maybe this is all just coincidence."

"But, Steve, you can't deny those autopsy reports," said Beth.

"Well, look," said Reed, "I can't do anything about it myself. I think you should report it to the police—let them investigate it. You're just going to get into trouble again."

"That's what I thought," said Steve. "But I don't want it to get lost. How about Korinsky?"

"Korinsky? That big detective from juvenile division?"

"That's the one. I got to know him during the Washington case. He's a pretty good guy, actually."

"Let me call him for you," said Reed. He reached over to the telephone.

CHAPTER 27

D inner is ready whenever you are, Mr. Frog," said the little girl, repeating what she had heard the caterer say at her parents' dinner parties. She put a sow bug on the flat pebble she had designated as the dinner table. Mr. Frog was not a frog, but actually a common toad. At six years of age, Mary Blake did not differentiate between amphibians, nor did it matter. "Come on, Mr. Frog, eat your dinner." She picked up the sow bug, which had waddled off the pebble and was burrowing into the dirt. She returned it to the pebble, lying it on its back, its many legs frantically seeking traction, but finding none in the evening air. The toad, trapped in a roofless house made from the four sides of a cardboard box, eyed the sow bug with the disdain of a satiated gourmet at a taco stand. He had found enough flies, mosquitoes, and larvae to make his bulbous abdomen drag on the pine needle carpet. She nudged him from behind with a pudgy finger, causing him to leap from one side of the house to the other, still ignoring the proposed entrée.

Mary's brother Eric came back from his exploration into the woods and stood beside her, kicking the box just enough to irritate her.

"Don't, Eric. You'll scare Mr. Frog. He's going to have his dinner." Eric was fourteen, a gangly, freckled-face boy with a bowl-shaped haystack haircut.

"It's not a frog, it's a toad," said Eric, squatting down beside her and peering into the animal's apartment. The evening shadows were growing long and the mosquitoes gathered on his bare legs. "Besides, toads won't eat sow bugs and they never eat while you're watching." She pondered this dogmatic appraisal for
a moment.

"It is a frog. It's Mr. Frog and he likes sow bugs, and besides, what do you know?" She centered the sow bug on the pebble again.

"It's a toad. Look, I'll show you." He picked up the sprawling, scratching, warty animal and turned him belly up to demonstrate some anatomic variation. The toad released a puddle of clear liquid onto his hand. "Oh yuck!" he exclaimed, throwing the squirming toad high into the branches of the oak tree and wiping his hand on his T-shirt. The toad flew so far they couldn't hear where he landed.

"Eric, you're mean! Damn you!" Mary wailed, breaking into tears and kicking at his shins. He laughed the malevolent fourteen-year-old laugh.

"Eeeeeric, Maaaary!" Sammy's high-pitched call came filtering through the woods from the big house. "Eeeeeric, Maaaary. We're going for pizza, hurry up!" They forgot their bickering and ran through the woods. Breaking into the backyard, they saw Sammy standing at the screen door that led to the kitchen. "Hurry up, your mom says she'll take us for pizza if we hurry." Sammy still referred to Mrs. Blake as "your mom" when addressing the other children. While the older children ran inside, slamming the door, Sammy waited in the backyard, fascinated by the lightning bugs that hovered over the azaleas near the woodpile. He could hear his little sister crying loudly through the open window of the third-floor bedroom. As he ran back and forth trying to catch the lightning bugs, her crying became louder, then stopped abruptly. It did not begin again. The light in the third-floor window went out.

Peter Blake sat in his baronial study, arms outstretched over the back of the leather couch, watching the twilight settle into the valley. The dark dissonance of Schoenberg's *Transfigured Night* filled the room. A section of the newspaper lay on his lap, undisturbed. He sipped his scotch and stared into the valley, lost in thought.

The door opened, abruptly casting a bright light from the hallway directly across his face. Irritated at the intrusion, he shielded his eyes. "What the hell is it?" He looked up, seeing Valerie in the doorway. "Oh, I'm sorry Val. You surprised me."

"Pete, I'm taking the children out for pizza." Her face was drawn; she seemed tense and harassed.

"Come on, Mom, hurry up," came Eric's voice down the hallway.

"Would you like to join us or shall I bring some home for you?"

"Oh, just bring it home, Val."

"Okay, suit yourself." She paused, as if there were more to say, but uncertain whether to continue. Finally she said, "Pete."

"Yes?" He was already lost in the music again.

"Becky was crying . . . I put her to bed. I think she'll be all right."

"Okay, see you later," he replied, only half aware of what she had told him. She closed the door. Soon he heard the sound of the station wagon pulling out of the driveway. A summer storm was developing and lightning flashed down the valley. The music seemed to get louder as the evening grew darker.

* * * *

"This had better be worth it," said Korinsky, lowering his bulky frame onto the old swivel chair behind his desk. "I drove all the way back from Livonia in a goddamn rain storm—excuse me, miss—just to talk to you." Steve, Beth, and Walter Reed had been waiting in the hallway for Korinsky to open his office. He arrived at eight thirty, half an hour late, his brown suit soaked in the front—the result of a run from the parking lot to the back door of the DPD headquarters.

"Thanks for coming out at night, Lieutenant," said Reed.

"Gus," corrected Korinsky." Most people call me Gus."

"Well, thanks anyway, Gus," said Reed. "I think you know Dr. Crane . . . and this is Miss Bonnell, a nurse at Presbyterian Hospital."

"Yes, hello." He smiled his toothy grin, slicking his short hair with his palm in a self-conscious attempt to look more attractive. He had not anticipated the presence of such a good-looking lady. Korinsky waved at Crane and awkwardly extended his hair-oiled hand to Beth, who shook it without flinching. "I assume this is about the Washington case," said Korinsky.

"It has some bearing on the Washington case," said Reed. "More specifically, it concerns a woman named Valerie Blake. Dr. Crane has turned up a series of very worrisome facts concerning injuries to her children. Steve, tell him the story."

"It all started, Gus, when Mrs. Blake brought her little boy Petey Blake to the emergency room at Presbyterian Hospital last week."

"Wait a minute," interrupted Korinsky. "Is this the kid whose hand was smashed in the car door?"

"Yes," said Steve, confused.

"I know about that kid. I served a protective custody order on him last week. One of these days I have to start looking into it." He shuffled through the disheveled stacks of papers on his desk as if there was something to find related to the case.

"You served the order?" Korinsky nodded.

"Well then you know about the other injuries to Petey Blake."

"Yes."

"And the other children"

"I heard something about the other children. I haven't really checked into it yet."

"Well, I checked into all of them," said Steve. "These are the hospital charts." He held them up. "There are six children from the Blake family that have been hospitalized over the last twenty years."

"Did you know that Valerie Blake is the wife of Peter Blake, the attorney who testified at Washington's trial?" asked Reed.

"No," said Korinsky. "I thought about it, I saw the address in Hunting Valley, but the first name was different."

"It's the same family," said Reed. "And it's also the same family that has the Washington children as foster kids." A look of understanding gradually came over Korinsky's face. He leaned forward with interest.

"Tell me what you found," he said. Steven Crane handed Korinsky the list, summarizing the hospitalizations of the Blake children. He explained the clinical course of each one, beginning with Petey and working backward. Korinsky interrupted from time to time with questions and the need for definitions. As he leaned forward to review the names on the list with Korinsky, Crane handed the stack of charts to Beth, who began absently reading through them again.

When Crane had finished, Reed said, "What do you think? Sounds to me like Steve's on to something."

"I'll say," said Korinsky. "We've convicted a lot of child abusers with less evidence than this. Well, hell, you know that," he said to Reed, with an embarrassed grin. Korinsky continued. "She seems to specialize in little girls," he said, running up and down the list with his finger. "Except for the last one, little Petey here. Are there any little girls in the family now?"

"No," said Steve.

"Well, there's little Becky Washington," said Beth. "She's there as a foster child."

"That's right," said Korinsky, furrowing his continuous bushy eyebrow. "I wonder if we should . . ." He looked at his watch and picked up the telephone, then put it down. "I forgot, we don't need a protective custody order. Little Petey's already on a hold in the hospital. I suppose we could just extend it, or at least call an investigation."

"You mean tonight, right?" said Reed, surprised. "Don't you think we ought to—"

"Oh, we ought to move right away," said Korinsky. "Once we decided to wait on a custody order until we had more evidence. The next week the kid had his head smashed in. That was at Presbyterian Hospital. Maybe you remember that, Steve."

"I think I've heard about it," said Crane, who well remembered Suzanne's recitation of that particular case. "But Petey isn't in the hospital. Browne canceled the protective custody order."

"Bullshit. He can't do that. That's a court order. He can't cancel that." Korinsky was incredulous.

"Well, he did and Petey Blake went home on Sunday evening, day before
yesterday."

"It's just possible that Browne is in on this business—at least protecting the family," said Reed.

"Oh no, Walt, I just couldn't imagine—" interrupted Steve.

"It's possible," said Reed. "That's why we came straight to you, Gus."

"That does it," said Korinsky. "We'd better take care of this tonight. At least we can get those kids under a safe roof until we have time to check it out." He stuffed some papers from his drawer into his coat pocket and checked a small pistol in a shoulder holster. He started to rise.

"You mean, you're going there right now?" asked Steve.

"You bet," said Korinsky, who then paused, thinking, looking at Reed. "Or do you think I should wait until tomorrow so as not to pull the kids out of their beds at night, Gestapo-style."

"You made your point," said Reed. "Is there anything we can do to help?"

"No. I'll call the Hunting Valley Police from my car." He patted his pockets, being sure everything was in place, then paused again. He sat back in his seat, pulling out the suburban phone book. "You know, I think I'll call out there first. I'd hate to drive all the way to Hunting Valley in the storm and find out they're off sailing or something." He found the number he was looking for and dialed it. After waiting through four rings, he said, "Hah, see! Damn near drove off on a wild goose chase. Maybe we should wait until–" Someone answered the phone.

"Hello, Mr. Blake?" Pause. "This is Lieutenant Korinsky, Detroit Police Department." Pause. "I'm fine, sir, thank you. How are you?" Pause. "That's good, sir. Is your wife at home, sir?" Pause. A slightly concerned look came over his face. "I see. With all the children?" Pause. "Except which one, sir?" His expression became deeply concerned, then agitated as he listened. He leaned forward on to the desk, feeling his pockets again as if preparing to leave abruptly. "Mr. Blake, this is important," he said carefully. "How long ago did your wife put Becky to bed?" Pause. "And have you heard any crying since?" Pause. "Yes sir, I'm very sorry, I know these questions sound ridiculous." Pause. "Well, I, I could explain, sir . . ." He looked nervously from Reed to Crane to Beth and back to Reed. "I'm coming out your way, sir. Perhaps I could just stop by this evening and–" Pause. "I'm sorry, sir, I can't hear you, the music is so loud that–" Pause. "No, sir, this is not harassment. It's an important matter of police business. Mr. Blake, if you'll let me explain, sir." Pause. "Well, sir, it concerns your wife. We'd like to talk to your wife about a series of injuries involving children in your family." Pause. He looked again at the people in his office. Sir, I'd suggest you go check on that little girl." Pause. "Yes, sir. Thank you for your understanding." He hung up.

Korinsky took a pack of chewing gum from his coat pocket and offered it around the room. When all refused, he extracted one stick, freed it from its wrappings, and popped it into his mouth. "Thanks for telling me about this. I'll let you know how it comes out." He wadded the gum wrapper into a ball and, holding it in the palm of one huge fist slammed it into the wastebasket. "Two," he said to himself, rising to go.

"Hey, wait a minute," said Beth, looking up from the chart she had been reading. "Listen to this: 'Only the father was at home at the time. The mother was on an extended vacation in Europe.'"

"Which chart is that?" asked Steve.

"It's Margaret Blake, the first one, the 1960 crib death," she said slowly. The impact of the finding slowly came over the group.

"Where did you find that? Let me see that," said Steven, taking the chart.

"It's in the epicrisis from the autopsy. We must have read it five times but I didn't remember that particular statement."

"Christ," said Reed, "that means it couldn't be the mother. That means it must be . . . Blake . . . himself."

"And I just told him to go check on the baby," said Korinsky. He moved quickly now. "Jesus, I'd better move. I'll call you later." He was out the door and down the hall.

"No way," said Crane. "We're coming with you." They left the lights burning and the door open.

* * * *

F. Peter Blake returned the telephone to its walnut case and pushed it deliberately across the table, lining it up precisely square with the tips of his thumbs. With a long sigh, he leaned heavily back on the leather couch, rubbing his eyes and twisting his neck from side to side as if trying to rid himself of a persistent headache. He drained all of the remaining whiskey into his throat. As he put the glass down, he was startled by a brilliant flash of lightning just outside the high window, which shook at the sonic boom of thunder that followed almost immediately. The music had finished, and he heard only rain riveting against the window. Then, from far off in the great house, he heard the baby start to cry. It seemed infinitely far away at first, like chimes in a belfry far above the floor of a medieval cathedral. Deep in thought, he tried to drink again from the glass, but it was empty. He stood slowly and walked to the bar. Pouring from the bottle of Bushmill's, he heard the crying again, following another clap of thunder. It seemed to be twice as loud.

He flipped the selector to FM with the hope of drowning out the crying child so he could think. Suddenly he was plunged into the haunting second movement of Saint-Saëns's Third Symphony. It was the piece of music he had shared so long ago with Kathleen. The almost inconceivable beauty of the delicate melody elicited a torrent of memories–her dark hair, her long white neck, her incredible eyes—memories he had carefully and consciously repressed for twenty years. Valerie had left for Europe when she found out about the affair. "Decide," she had said. But the choice was not between Kathleen and Valerie, it was between Kathleen and his family. Valerie and his infant daughter Margaret. The frustration had been more than he could bear. Even now, sixteen years later, he could not remember exactly how or why he did what he did. He tried to make himself turn the music off, but he could not.

The death of their daughter had brought Valerie home and their common grief braced the crack in their lives. Kathleen disappeared—he never knew where. Every few years he thought he found her again. In the darkness, a slender body, a cascade of hair on his chest, a warm and tender mouth could become her, bringing the same divergence, the same emotional struggle—on occasion, the same distorted solution to his torment. As the second movement settled into its final phrases, he thought of Suzanne.

The surging third movement of the Saint-Saëns combined in his mind with the incessant crying. Blake's finger hold on reality gradually gave way, creating a macabre concerto grosso, the tortured semblance of a melody passing between the frenzied orchestra and the wailing infant. He drank the smoky liquor and turned up the gain. The volume of the crying increased proportionately, amplified in his mind until a neuronal short circuit deep in his thalamus tripped open. The insoluble conflict cauterized its way from the dark cellar of his brain to the cortex, stimulating him to turn and walk toward the door. Passing his desk, he picked up a brochure from a pile of junk mail. Without looking at it, with contained ferocity, he wadded it into a tight ball. He walked the carpeted hallway toward the stairs.

Reaching the second floor by the huge spiral staircase, he was startled by another flash of white light which threw his own shadow on the wall, startling him briefly back to reality. He shook his head as if awakening, opened his eyes widely, and looked at the crumbled brochure in his hand. He threw it over the railing like a child playing hot potato and hurried back down the stairs. When the crying started again, he froze, grasped the spokes of the banister, and sank heavily onto the stairs, burying his head in his folded elbow. The crying and the music became louder again. He put his hands over his ears and shook his head, to no avail. He stood quickly, turned, and ran up the remaining stairs, down the hall, and threw open the door of the nursery just as the pedal tones of the organ joined the orchestra in the

314

profound announcement of Saint-Saëns's fourth movement.

Becky Washington was standing in the crib, holding onto the bars, silhouetted against the achromatic light that flashed in irregular patterns through the window.

He stood in the doorway for what seemed to be an eternally long time, palms pressed against the doorjamb in a posture which resembled that of the terrified infant across the room. Carefully inhibited memories crawled out of his association tracts and sparked to consciousness. Looking at Becky, he thought he saw his daughter Margaret, saw Valerie at the funeral, saw an elusive apparition with beautiful eyes, Suzanne. Was it? Perhaps Kathleen. Perhaps Margaret. His hands pulled away from the doorjambs a millimeter at a time, pulled away by a balance of massive opposing forces, delicately teetering between reason and the irrational, slowly favoring the latter.

As he approached the crib, the crying became louder. She let go of the bars and reached out with her hands, the harping, gnawing cry of a child scared in the night. Her eyes flooded with tears, she assumed with the innocence of childhood that the figure would shelter her, calm her, deliver her from the insecurity of the storm. She thought this until the figure was directly in front of her. Then a flash of lightning ignited the face. The awful horror of the face. The child was struck silent, falling back against the bars of the crib, frozen for an instant, as she had been in the boiling water from the faucet of her bathtub. Then her terror found voice in a shrill, piercing scream that seared into Blake like a moth evaporating in a flame. Swiftly he dropped the crib bars, grabbed her ankle, and flipped her onto the mattress. Pressing her throat with one hand, he reached about the bed, and, finding the pillow, pressed it over her face, smothering the sound. Her arms and legs jerked frantically, erratically, then rhythmically, then not at all. Sweat dripped from his face onto the pillow, mixed with blood where he had chewed his lip. Finally there was silence.

Suddenly the room was filled with light and noise. The giant paw of Gus Korinsky clasped his chin and flung him sprawling to the floor in a single motion. Crane threw off the pillow and placed his trembling fingers above the bruises on the neck.

"There's a good pulse," he said. Her next agonal breath was successful, then the next, then she coughed, sputtered, and began to cry.

CHAPTER 28

When Valerie nosed the station wagon around the bend in the driveway, she knew that twenty years of anguish had come to an end. Through the driving rain she could see three police cars and Edward Browne's Cadillac. It could have been anything, of course—an accident, a heart attack, a prowler. But somehow she knew it was what she had dreaded most. The terrifying truth that she had kept controlled and hidden. Tears clouded her eyes as she felt relief and remorse simultaneously. Then she thought of Becky.

"Hey Mom," said Eric, "Look at all the police cars. What do you think it is?" Sammy and Mary dropped the hot gooey pizza on the backseat and leaned forward to get a look.

Valerie sniffed, coughed, and wiped her eyes. "I don't know, Eric. I hope it's nothing serious."

She stopped the station wagon near the front door, following the signals of an officer in a yellow slicker. He approached the driver's door. "Mrs. Blake?"

"Yes, officer. What is it? Is it my daughter?"

"I'm afraid, so ma'am. Would you come inside with me, please?" He bent lower to look at the children in the backseat. "Come on inside, kids. Everything's okay." He opened the door and guided her gently by the arm as they trotted through the downpour. Dot Browne was standing in the hallway. She and Valerie exchanged nervous glances as the young officer escorted her down the hall to the library.

"Dot, is Becky . . . ?" Her eyes showed terror. She glanced around, unable
to finish.

"Becky's okay. Now. Everyone's in the library," said Mrs. Browne. The children sensed disaster through the tense interchange of the adults, but had no hint of its exact nature. Dot Browne changed her tone to address the kids. "Hello Eric, hello little Mary, hi Sammy. Come on in the kitchen. We're all having something to eat."

"We're having pizza," exclaimed Sammy, who had managed to bring a stringy piece in each hand, dropping bits of sausage on the floor as they moved toward the kitchen. Eric looked back toward the library as he was being pushed in the opposite direction. "What's happened, Mrs. Browne? Where is Dad? Is he sick
or something?"

"He's all right," said Dot Browne, without conviction, as they entered the kitchen. More adults he did not recognize were sitting at the small table. They shuffled the chairs until there was room for everyone.

"Children, this is Dr. Crane and Mr. Reed and Miss . . ."

"Bonnell," said Beth. "Hi kids, come on over here."

* * * *

When Valerie entered the library she saw Peter first. He was sitting across the room, head in his hands, handcuffs on his wrists. He did not look up. Valerie guessed what happened. Edward Browne was leaning on the railing. Valerie walked directly to him.

"Ed . . ." she began.

Gently he took her face in both of his hands, tenderly wiping tears from her cheeks, and softly putting his thumb over her lips. "Val . . . " His eyes moved from side to side. "The officers here told me some . . . some pretty shocking things. They caught Peter while he was . . . I don't think you should say anything until–"

"Ed, is Becky all right?" she interrupted.

"Yes, I'm sure she'll be all right." He studied her face. "She has some bruises . . ."

"Oh, Ed." Shaking and sobbing, she held the railing so she would not fall.

Browne stepped closer, putting his arm around her shoulders. "Dr. Crane reminded me about the crib deaths. It just never occurred to me that they could have been . . . intentional injuries. All these years, and Pete's been such a friend. I never suspected . . ."

"I know, Ed. You never knew and I blocked it out. I thought it was over." She dried her cheek on his shoulder, unable to look at her

318

husband.

"Val?" He whispered now so no one could hear.. "Val, do you think that Pete might have done this before? Those crib deaths?"

"I never knew for sure, but I suspected. And there were other times too, that you don't know about. But I thought it was over . . ."

After what seemed to Korinsky to be a discreet interval, he came forward and touched her on the shoulder. "Mrs. Blake, I am Lieutenant Korinsky from the juvenile division of the Detroit Police Department. We've arrested your husband on the charges of murder, attempted murder, and child abuse. You are charged with being an accessory to the same crimes. You have the right to remain silent. You have the right to–"

"I told you, Lieutenant," shouted Blake, looking up for the first time since she had entered. "She had nothing to do with it. She wasn't even here when I did it. That was the goddamn trouble. Didn't I just tell you all that?"

Korinsky ignored him. "To remain silent. You have the right to an attorney." He paused only a second. "Mrs. Blake, did you know what your husband did to your children?" She rubbed her face on Browne's shirt, sniffed loudly. He handed her a handkerchief.

"I suspected it for many years after Margaret died. I was afraid to talk to Peter about it. When Linda . . . when Linda died, I asked him, but he denied it and I wanted to believe him. There was only one time after that. Mary's skull fracture." She directed the last sentence to Edward Browne, assuming that he would remember. "I thought he was over it. I thought . . ." She sobbed again. They waited. "I knew you would find out. In my heart, I knew it."

"Mrs. Blake, do you remember Monica Stevens?" asked Korinsky.

"Of course I remember Monica," she said. "She died after open heart surgery a long time ago. You remember, Ed?" He nodded.

"Did you know that Monica Stevens had evidence of a broken arm and several broken ribs?" She was obviously shocked. "Oh Peter," she gasped. "Little Monica . . ."

"For Christ's sake, Officer," mumbled Blake, behind his cupped hands. "Do we have to do this here and now?"

"Fair enough, Mr. Blake," said Korinsky. "We have lots of time to talk. Just one more question. Did anyone else know about these . . . murders?" It was the second time the ominous word was stated aloud.

The word had a fatal ring to it. It sounded like cancer coming from a doctor.

"No," Valerie said quickly.

"Dr. Browne attended all these children. Did he ever know the real cause of these injuries?" Browne's face was impassive—the carefully trained unemotional look of the physician which is designed to mask the extremes of emotion. One vein on his forehead distended slightly.

"No. Ed knew nothing about it," said Blake. "We've always been such good friends. He never even suspected." Valerie shifted her gaze to meet Peter's, looking directly at him for the first time in a long time.

"That's right," she murmured.

* * * *

Sammy talked incessantly during the ride to the old Wayne County Hospital. His acquaintance with Korinsky gave him a privileged status among the children. Even Eric was impressed as he jabbered into the microphone and pulled the shotgun barrel out of its clamp. "Hey, take it easy, little guy," said Gus. "Never take out a gun unless you plan to use it. Now there's a rule to remember." He turned off Telegraph onto Ford Road.

"Where are we going, Lieutenant?" asked Eric, who was much more frightened than the other children but trying not to show it.

"Call me Gus," said Korinsky, over his shoulder. "We're going to a place called the campus. Just a sort of temporary place where kids can stay. Sammy can tell you about it." And Sammy did, for the next six miles.

* * * *

In response to an unusual combined request from Norma Baldridge and the public defender's office, Judge Marshall agreed to a special hearing on the Washington case immediately following Blake's arraignment. He could feel no empathy, only disgust, toward his friend and colleague. He referred to him as Mr. Blake throughout the brief proceedings and returned Blake's attempts at friendly smiles with tolerant contempt. Both the Blakes pled guilty. Marshall scheduled sentencing for September, hoping to be over his initial anger by that time. He released Valerie until the sentencing to care for the children.

"Thank you, David, thank you so much," she said. He smiled back at her, sharing, to a small extent, her pain.

"Now let's proceed with the Washington hearing," said Marshall. "I know this is a little irregular, but it seems possible that we've made a terrible mistake and I'd like to set it straight as soon as possible. Now Blake, I want straight answers from you this time, do you understand?"

"Yes, sir," said Blake, very softly.

"Mr. Reed?" said Marshall.

"Counselor Baldridge will present our request, your honor," said Reed.

Baldridge walked to the lectern. "Your honor, there is a large amount of new evidence which has appeared in favor of Mr. Washington." She put on her glasses, and began to read from her long yellow pad. She described her meeting with Ritchie Washington in some detail. She explained that Dr. Edward Browne, the primary witness for the prosecution, had voluntarily rescinded his testimony on the basis of new information. She hastened to read into the record that this was not construed as perjury, but merely enlightened honesty of a well-meaning, upstanding citizen. She explained that Blake had lied about his conversation with Washington, and in fact, had corroborated Washington's claims exactly.

"And is all that true, Blake?" asked Marshall.

"Yes, that's exactly what he told me."

"But Pete," Marshall said, returning to the familiarization out of habit, "why did you perjure yourself? I don't understand . . ."

"I . . . I decided to keep the Washington children in my home for Valerie and for . . . personal reasons. And as a favor to Dr. Browne." There was no point in bringing Suzanne into the discussion, he decided. Marshall assumed that "personal reasons" related to his demented attack. Revulsion registered on his face.

"Finally, your honor," continued Baldridge, "Mr. Washington has consistently stuck to his story and claimed innocence, despite the 'harassment,' to use Mr. Reed's word, in this courtroom, despite his conviction, and despite extreme physical and mental abuse from other convicts. Mr. Reed has asked for an appeal or a retrial on the basis of all of this new evidence. However, the state is willing to drop its case completely and make restitution to Mr. Washington. The most expeditious way to do that is through a formal pardon. We make that recommendation."

Marshall was not surprised, but only because he had discussed the recommendations the week before. "Thank you, Counselor. I will review the information you have submitted and give you both a response within a week. Thank you."

Reed kissed Baldridge on the cheek, hugged Sally, and ran for the telephone to call Steven Crane.

* * * *

David Marshall did his best thinking at night. He folded his bathrobe, arranged his leather slippers for easy access in the morning, and settled into his bed, smoothing his monogrammed pajamas and folding the sheet precisely four inches over the blanket. He glanced at his broad-beamed wife snoring in the other bed, and then dispatched her from his sight and mind by switching off the light. Then he settled into the Washington case.

Recommending a pardon was too big a step. There was enough new evidence to justify an appeal, though, and the appeal would be successful. A retrial would surely bring the pushy reporter from the *News*. He would probably bring the Blakes into public scrutiny—not good for the bar. With more experience, Reed and Crane and Washington would be more convincing—and Browne was unpredictable. Washington would never win before a judge—reversing a felony sentence makes big headlines. But he might win before a jury. He might win. A pardon would get the bench and the social service off the hook. It could look good for the governor if properly worded. It certainly was the quickest way. Not bad, not bad. The pardon was not a bad idea.

He slept well.

CHAPTER 29

On the day the pardon came through, Sally was waiting in the warden's office. Kevin saw her through the glass in the door, and couldn't stop smiling through the warden's terse remarks. In fact, he had been smiling for the entire two weeks while the papers were in preparation. As they shook hands briefly, Kevin grinned and fingered the edges of the suit which Sally had brought for him. When the door opened, he kissed her quickly but never stopped moving toward the outer door. Holding her hand, he walked briskly, then jogged, then ran down the long corridor out into the July sunlight.

"Kevin, wait. The car's in the parking lot." Laughing aloud, he kept running, pulling her behind him. They crossed the two lane blacktop without looking in either direction, ran down a farmer's driveway, past the barn, past the silo, and far out into the flat reaches of the cornfield.

"Kevin!" She was gasping. "I can't run anymore." He stopped and picked her up under the arms, swirling her around in the knee-high stalks, laughing and giggling and whooping until they fell, dizzy and exhausted, onto the lush flat leaves. He landed on top of her and she held on, gasping for air. Promptly he rolled over and lay on his back.

"I gotta look at the sky, baby. Look at that sky, look at that space. Oh God, you feel good." Still holding her close, he struggled to his knees and shouted toward the huge prison, "You never got me, you bastards. I won. Do you hear me, you bastards? I won!" He whistled and laughed, jubilant with the heady victory over the ponderous system.

Sally watched him cavorting and dancing in the cornfield, waiting until he collapsed, completely spent. Then she walked over and sat on his chest. Still smiling, he tore off a corn tassel and gently caressed her cheek. "Hey baby, I love you."

"I love you too," she said softly.

Sally drove because Kevin was too excited. He laughed and giggled like a pubescent boy, nuzzling her ear and mauling her unashamedly.

"Careful Kevin, we'll have an accident." She giggled, squirming but not objecting.

"First I'm gonna make love to you for six hours," he announced. "Then we're gonna have a bucket of ribs and a bucket of fried chicken. And tomorrow morning we're going right to that big white building and get our kids back."

"Sounds like a plan," she agreed.

* * * *

In the morning he felt like he had a bowling ball between his legs, but it was a glorious ache. She made a real breakfast–ham and eggs and pancakes and milk and coffee–but they hurried through it, both incited by anticipation. Driving to the city-county building, Kevin rehearsed his speech for Miss Johnson. He would be constrained, courteous, he would listen graciously and accept her apologies, then the door would open and Sammy and Becky would run into his arms. He would leave without another word. "Yes, that's it." He'd turn and leave without another word. He liked that.

Hand in hand they ran up the forty steps to the revolving doors, took the elevator to the fifth floor, and swung open the doors to the Department of Child Welfare with a grandiose gesture that made up for all the times they had sheepishly pushed their way into the reception area.

"Miss Johnson, please," he announced loudly, beaming at the heavy-lidded girl behind the counter.

"Do y'all have an appointment?" drawled the clerk.

"I do indeed, and I'm here to pick up my children."

"Who's calling, please?" she asked.

"Mr. and Mrs. Washington," announced Sally, still holding his hand.

"Have a seat, please," directed the clerk, indicating the painfully familiar plastic chairs. Strangely, the dingy waiting room seemed more cheerful than it had before. Kevin turned the pages of a two-month-old *Newsweek* without reading any of it. Sally watched the clock. The clocks in the building were attached to a master system that advanced them all one minute at a time. The clock clicked forward seventeen times. Finally the clerk said, "Y'all can go in now, the office is–"

"Oh we know, we know," said Sally. They almost ran down the grimy corridor. They paused outside the door which said "Mavis Johnson, MSW," looked at each other, sighed, smiled, and walked in.

"Well Miss Johnson, we all make mistakes. Some are worse than others. I know that you were just trying to do your–" He interrupted his prepared speech in mid-sentence. The chair behind the desk, which had been facing away from them toward the window as they entered, turned slowly. It was not Miss Johnson.

"I beg your pardon, what can I do for you?" The nameplate on the small desk said "Nell Simpkins, MSW." Miss Simpkins had a thin face, black-framed glasses, short graying hair, and a series of vertical wrinkles around her mouth that gave the impression that she never smiled.

"I'm sorry," said Kevin. "We must be in the wrong office. We're looking for Miss Johnson." He turned to go, frightened by the familiar, foreboding figure of the omnipotent social worker.

"Miss Johnson is no longer with the department. I've taken over her position. My name is Miss Simpkins." She did not offer to shake hands, nor did she offer a chair. "I'm sure if you have a question, one of our other workers will be able to answer it. If it needs my attention, I will review it in due time. And now–"

"Wait a minute, wait a minute," said Kevin, putting both hands on the desk and leaning toward Miss Simpkin's pasty face. "I'm Kevin Washington. This here's my wife, Sally. We're here to pick up our children."

"Mr. Washington? I don't recall a Washington."

"Kevin and Sally Washington. We're supposed to pick up our children here. Mr. Reed contacted Miss Johnson." He started pushing through the stacks of folders on her desk.

"Please, Mr. Washington." She covered the piles with her hands. "Control yourself." She sounded like a second-grade teacher. Slowly Kevin withdrew. She glared at him down her pinched nose, then slowly moved the files from one pile to the other. "Here it is. Washington. Kevin and Sally Washington? Kevin and Sally Washington, did you say?"

"Yes."

"This file says Kevin Washington and Sally Flynn." She tilted her head backward and forward to look between the sections of her new bifocals, giving her the appearance of a chicken in a barnyard.

"That's us," said Sally. "My divorce isn't complete yet, but we're going to be married soon. We're here for our children," she said resolutely, squeezing Kevin's hand and bouncing slightly on her seat.

"Uh-huh," murmured Miss Simpkins. "Uh huh, uh huh," she repeated at intervals, flipping pages and reading random paragraphs in the thick folder.

"I see you've been delinquent in your foster care payments. That doesn't show me MPR. You're on the negative scale for MPR all through this folder."

"MPR?"

One eyebrow arched in the center while the opposite corner of her thin mouth twisted down, indicating surprise and disgust that Kevin had to ask. "MPR–manifestations of parenting responsibility–honestly! Now what are we going to do about the payments?"

"For Christ's sake," exploded Kevin. "I've been in prison."

"And besides, why should we pay, when you stole our children and put them in foster care they didn't need? They have a home–our home." Sally stood at his side.

"My, my, such an ungrateful, reactionary outburst. Your children are fortunate to be the beneficiaries of society's care. If you fail in your custodial role, the state intervenes on your children's behalf. We didn't ask to get involved, you know. You're the people with the problem not us. Honestly! Now sit down." They did. "The last entry I have here indicates that you were pardoned on the basis of evidence that came up after your trial, is that correct?"

"That's correct. A full pardon," said Kevin. Now they were finally starting to get somewhere. He would play the game this one last time.

"And apparently everyone agreed that the girls were burned by accident while you were giving them a bath, is that correct, Mr. Washington?"

"Yes, ma'am, that's correct. Now I'm here to–"

"Do the two of you plan to continue living together?"

"That's what I just said," said Sally. "We're going to be married soon."

"It seems to me that you both need help with the ongoing parenting experience. Leaving young children unguarded in the bathtub, Mr. Washington, that's terribly neglectful, don't you think?" She didn't wait for a response. "And there's something in here about beating a six-year-old. Apparently that was never resolved."

"Now, don't you start to pull that stuff again," said Kevin, in a threatening tone. "Mr. Reed from the public defender's office and Judge Marshall from superior court—"

"Oh, I'm afraid they don't cut any ice over here, Mr. Washington, not at all. You may be clean as a whistle in superior court, that's a good step, a very good step. It signifies a high compliance index with the dynamics of the ongoing social process. But we have a lot of work to do on parent-child and family-social interaction, don't we? A lot of work to do."

Stomach churning and knees shaking, Kevin left the Child Welfare office, pulling Sally with him.

"Just a minute, young man. You don't just walk out of my office. Now just
a minute . . ."

Kevin didn't speak in the elevator. Sally followed him to the center of the first floor lobby. "Kevin, what can we do? We're right back where we started. What can we do?"

"I don't know," said Kevin, "but this time we're going to have some help. This time we have a few people who believe in us." At the information desk, they asked for the public defender's office. Given directions to the second floor, they walked up the stairs and followed the arrows. They asked the secretary for Walter Reed, and she pushed buttons on her phone, made an announcement, and soon Walter Reed was at the door.

"Hey bro. Hello Sally. Is this the happy day? I'm glad you stopped by."

"It's not good, Walt. They assigned us to a new worker at Child Welfare. She's going to make us start all over again."

"I don't know if we'll ever get the kids back," said Sally, finally breaking down in tears.

Reed was as enraged as they were. "Look, let me handle this. You go home and wait there until I call. It won't take long. You just wait there." He was on the telephone before they were even out the door.

The drive home in the light mid-day traffic was silent. Kevin was not hungry, but he ate the last piece of cold bacon out of habit. Sally turned the television on, clicked the dial, then turned it off again. They sat at the kitchen table, afraid to talk, afraid to hold hands, sighing frequently. In time, rage was displaced by now-familiar despair, then despair by apathetic gloom.

When the telephone rang hours later, they were sitting in the same spot. Wide-eyed with anticipation, they allowed themselves to smile. Kevin answered.

"Hello? Yes, this is Kevin Washington." He listened for a minute. His face dropped and his shoulders hunched forward. He nodded negatively to Sally.

"Yes, I'm the one who worked at Metro Buick. I don't work there no more. What's the problem?" Pause. "Mr. VanPelt?" He stood a little straighter. "Yes sir I know you own Metro Buick." He expected the worst. "Now what is it?"

He listened for several seconds, his eyes widening. "Would you say that again?" A gleeful smile. "Yes sir. Yes sir, I can be there tomorrow if you want. Well, Monday then. Thank you very much . . . Wait, Mr. VanPelt. Wait." He held up his hand as if to stay his boss from hanging up the telephone. "Can you tell me why you did this? I mean, you didn't just decide out of the blue to give me my job back." Pause I see. Well, whatever the reason, I 'preciate it. I'll be there on Monday. Yes sir. Good-bye."

He picked up Sally and swung her around the room. "That was Mr. VanPelt himself. He wants me back on the job. With two months back pay."

"Kevin, that's wonderful." For an instant, the grief over the lost children was set aside. One small reason to be optimistic. "What made him do it? Did he read about your pardon in the paper?"

"No, that's the best part." A sly, satisfied smile spread over his face. "Dr. Browne told him to do it."

"Dr. Browne? That terrible doctor from the hospital who was in charge of the girls?"

"That's the one. It seems he buys a new Cadillac every year and knows Mr. VanPelt. He must be feeling a little guilty, 'cuz he told VanPelt that I was a good man and that I should have my job back.

Ain't that something?"

"Yes Kevin, that's wonderful."

With their moods softened by the good news, they managed some useful activity. Sally did the dishes and Kevin put some music on. They even talked a bit about the children, planning a visit to the juvenile home extension rather than the homecoming they had anticipated. In the late afternoon, Sally ironed her waitress uniform, preparing to go to work.

The doorbell rang just before five o'clock. Kevin went to the door, and through the window, he saw Mavis Johnson. "Uh-oh. Looks like more trouble." Cautiously, he opened the door.

"Mr. Washington. May I come in?"

"Sure." She entered and exchanged greetings with Sally, standing in the center of the living room. Kevin suspected another elusive lecture. Mavis Johnson stood uneasily, looking more vulnerable and more human than she had on her last authoritarian visit.

"First of all, I don't know if you'll believe this coming from me, but I am sorry. I was mistaken—our whole system was mistaken. I know that can't make up for the pain you've suffered, but I want you to know that we're sorry." She seemed sincere enough, but Kevin waited. He had been drawn into confidence, then rejected enough times to lose all trust in public servants. "We're only trying to do our jobs," she continued, "and I guess we're . . . human." She made a little gesture with her hands and tried to smile. Kevin remained impassive. "I'd also like to apologize for Miss Simpkins—the worker you met this morning?" She pressed her hands together and shifted her weight to her other foot, unaccustomed to being humbled. "She wasn't up to date on all the details of your case and I can understand how you might have been upset."

"That's nothing new," said Kevin. "Those people never know nothing."

"Worse yet, they think they know everything. You too, Miss Johnson." Sally moved to stand next to Kevin. "Your apology comes too late and too little."

"You don't know how hard it is for me to come here. You don't know how terrible we all feel, having contributed to this series of mistakes."

"Tell me about it," sneered Kevin. "Now unless you have anything more important to say, get the hell out of our house. There's only one thing you could do to make up for all this bullshit and you ain't doin' it." He opened the door. Mavis started to stammer a response, when a police car turned the corner onto Calvert, stopping in front of their house, lights blinking and siren blaring. Instinctively Kevin pulled back. Mavis smiled, looking relieved. Sally went out onto the porch.

"Kevin look," she exclaimed, running down the sidewalk. The door of the police car opened. Sammy and Becky Washington ran up the sidewalk. Sammy reached his mother first and she scooped him into her arms, bending over and waiting for Becky to catch up. Neighbors attracted by the siren came out onto their front yards. Kevin ran down the steps and joined the embrace.

Gus Korinsky turned off the siren and lights, moved his big frame out of the car, and came around to close the passenger door, leaned on the fender and beamed at the family reunion. Neighbors who had shunned the couple for months began applauding. Other six-year-olds who had not seen their friends since last fall shouted greetings.

Mavis Johnson looked relieved, even absolved. "I was trying to tell you that Miss Simpkins didn't have all the papers," she said. "When Walt Reed called this morning, we realized what had happened. We're terribly embarrassed. This is one time when our system got something done in a day." Kevin lifted his head from where he had been holding it on Sally's shoulder. He was crying openly, and acknowledged her comment with a smile, unable to speak. "Some day I hope you can forgive us for all of this. You are certainly a man of principle."

Kevin smiled again, more at the irony of her comment than at the joy of
the moment.

Korinsky came closer to speak to Kevin softly. "Washington, I do my job the best way I can and I don't apologize for it, but I'm glad for you. I hope you can understand that."

"I think so."

"Sammy and I, we got to be sort of friendly. My boys are about his age. Maybe we could all go to a Tigers game or something. Later . . . you know."

"Oh yeah, Daddy, can we go to a game with Gus? Can we, Daddy?" Kevin looked at Sally who was crying and laughing at the same time, holding Becky so tightly she squirmed. He looked at

330

Sammy hanging on his shirt with both hands, oblivious to the year of torture, forgetting the terror with the simple anticipation of a baseball game. Kevin stood straight and looked at Korinsky, trying to imagine him with his own sons, trying to imagine him as a person.

"Can we, Daddy?" he asked, tugging at his shirtsleeve.

Kevin Washington took a long breath of warm summer evening air. Sally held Becky with one arm and he lifted Sammy with the other. They turned to go into their little house. Another sigh–each one seemed to blow away more cloudy hostility. He smiled at Korinsky. "Sounds like a plan."

EPILOGUE

The characters and the narrative in this book are fabrications which exist only in the mind of the author and the reader. The story could be set in any American city. I chose Detroit because the social history of that city provides a background of examples and analogies which underscores the problems of societal value systems. Although specific places, agencies, policies, hospitals, and people are named in the story, they are, again, fabrications. With a few obvious exceptions (there is, for example, a Ford Auditorium and a Wayne County Hospital), the people and places are imaginary. Or to be more accurate, the people are imaginary and the public agencies and their policies, hospitals, and judicial system may or may not exist in fact. I have intentionally learned nothing about the names or functions of these elements of the social structure in Detroit, as any reader from Detroit will, no doubt, attest.

The problem of child abuse, and the broader problem of the value system of one individual compared to the collective values of a society, do indeed exist. This book is based on a series of events which actually occurred in the hospitals, jails, and courts of another state. The doctors, families, and children involved in those cases learned that making an incorrect designation of child abuse can be more damaging and disrupting to a family than missing the diagnosis altogether. That concept is, however, often eschewed by many of the people who render value judgments on behalf of the society. Doctors and nurses who report suspected child abuse must be suspicious beyond a reasonable doubt, because they can set into motion a relentless system reminiscent of the witch trials of Salem. We see what we look for; we look for what we expect to see.

Robert H. Bartlett

Robert H. Bartlett, MD is Professor of Surgery at the University of Michigan Medical School. In addition to running a busy surgical practice, his academic focus is on critical care and life support systems. His research has been recognized with awards from the American College of Surgeon, the American Surgical Association and the American Society of Artificial Organs. Dr. Bartlett has published hundreds of scientific articles and twelve scientific books. This is his first novel.

From 1970 to 1980 Dr. Bartlett was director of a large burn unit where he frequently dealt with the problem of suspected child abuse. *The Salem Syndrome* is a fictional account based on actual cases from his experience.